The Thomas Sisters

Kathryn Spurgeon

Memory House Press
Edmond, Oklahoma

Published by Memory House Publishing
Edmond, Oklahoma 73034
www.memoryhousepublishing.net

Certain names have been changed in this book
to protect the privacy of individuals involved.

Printed in the United States of America

ISBN 978-1946887207(Paperback) Christian historical fiction

Book cover design by Jenny Zemanek, Seedlings, LLC
Interior design and layout by Kathryn Spurgeon

Back: Sam, Ann, Till, Susie, Elmer, Jennie, Bob
Front: Mary Molly Shields, Unknown child,
James Tolbert Thomas

Dedication

Dedicated to my dear grandmother.
Anna Lee Thomas Akin, a sweet lady
and a god-fearing woman.
Her and her sisters exemplify how
family support each other through
good and not-so-good times.

Books

by Kathryn Spurgeon

The Thomas Sister
Mary Bobbie: Thomas Sister #1
Sally Matilda: Thomas Sister #2
Susie May: Thomas Sister #3
Jennie Rue: Thomas Sister #4
Annie Crump: Thomas Sister #5

The Promise Series
A Promise to Break
A Promise Child
Fremont's Promise
A Promise of Home

Jesus, One on One

Table of Contents

Mary Bobbie

Thomas Sister #1

Oma Jean & Robert Layne

Mary Bobbie

Born April 9, 1886

Chapter 1

December 1929

"You brought that cake along?" teased my husband Shannon Layne as we loaded into the Model T Ford. "I can smell it fermenting. It's probably older than your sisters."

From the open door, I shook my finger at him and grinned, showing off my dimples. "I'll wager you'll be the first one to sneak a bite," I placed the wrapped, ripened fruitcake on the floorboard of our motor car, tucking it between two tea towels.

"If there's anything left after you nibble on it." A twinkle filled his eyes as he climbed into the driver's seat. I loaded the last package into the Tin Lizzie and gathered the bottom of my long, faded travel dress. Putting my foot on the running board, I climbed into the front seat, straddling the fruitcake.

Grins passed between Shannon and I like shared candy. Our common interests were food and laughter, not bad staples for married life, on condition my conscience didn't surface and reveal a pile of guilt marinating at the bottom. Guilt I couldn't let anyone see.

Shannon started the motor and the old buggy sputtered like a dying locomotive chugging over the Old Galveston Trail. Highway 6, a pothole-stricken dirt road that got worse as we traveled north to Oklahoma. I loved the open plains where a body could see for hundreds of miles in any direction. The wide-open sky never ended, even if a person whirled around a dozen times. I got dizzy thinking of it.

As I stared at the bare landscape, we passed a dilapidated, crumbling farmhouse stashed in the middle of nowhere. A forlorn little tot sat on the front porch steps—scruffy, thin, and barefoot, her round eyes gaping at our speeding death trap.

"Stop the car!" I yelled.

Shannon's sudden response almost threw me out the front window. "What's wrong? Are you sick?" He looked back at Robert, our thirteen-year-old, round-faced boy, scrunched between carpet bags, wrapped gifts, and a box tucked under his feet. Knobby knees reached to his chin. "Are you all right back there?"

"Scrunched like this, I can hardly move."

Shannon gave his adorable grin and turned back to me and raised his eyebrows.

I pointed toward the run-down looking building. "That little girl. She reminds me of…" I couldn't finish the sentence. My thoughts felt heavy, remembering a child with blond curly hair, and sweet dimples. A tot that had snuck into my life and stole my heart. A darling lost because of me. I sucked back tears as gloomy feelings swept through my body. "Look how thin she is. She needs this cake more than we do."

I opened the car door and jumped to the ground, holding the fruitcake out to her. "Here. You can have this." I wanted to protect this little waif. Save her, like I hadn't been able to save my toddler.

The girl leapt up and disappeared around the side of the shack. "Wait!" I yelled. "I'm not going to hurt you." I stopped and bawled, right there in the middle of nowhere. Holding that stinky cake.

Shannon snuck up behind me and put his arm around me. "Honey, are you all right?"

I swiped away the tears before Shannon could see the sad side of me and gave a snicker. "Guess that was a foolish thing to do." I determined to try harder to cover my nerves. With a deep breath, I shoved the sadness down and put on a sunny smile, "I'm fine. Just fine."

We continued the drive, the flatlands an endless hodgepodge of mesquite bushes, baked arid plains, and longhorn cattle strung together, fascinating only to locals and western cowboy artists. Covered with brush, but underneath, empty and barren, just like me.

When our speed crept up over forty miles an hour, Shannon caught my eye, and I could see his excitement. My ample body bounced around like muscadine jelly over biscuits. The wind blew strands of hair into my face, and I brushed wayward wisps under my grandma's old bonnet.

"Slow down!" Gripping the door frame and holding onto that fruitcake, the weight of an infant, I yelled over the engine noise. "Don't be in such a hurry!"

We crossed the Red River in the beat-up jalopy, rushing to get to our hometown before nightfall. "I glanced into the backseat at Robert. "Do you have enough room?" I yelled over the noise.

He laughed and stuck up his legs, pretending he had plenty of room to spare. "Don't expect me to run laps when we get to Aunt Jennie's."

"Aren't you excited to get to Hollis for the holidays?"

He nodded, but within minutes, he slumped against the packages, a busboy cap pulled over his eyes. Dozing.

Lordy, how he managed to sleep, I'd never know.

***

Soon after Shannon and I married, he got a steady job as a policeman down in Burkburnett, Texas. A booming town, a few miles from Wichita

Falls where we felt right at home. We got to know the dry goods store owner and made friends at the First Baptist Church. Shannon's job kept him running as fast as the wells popped up and spewed oil.

My deepest desire was to have a family. A home full of dozens of children. Well, maybe not dozens, lands sakes, but at least a handful. Shannon and I both came from large families and shared a desire for a houseful of kiddos. He loved children, and they loved him. He was definitely father material. We looked forward to siblings chasing each other around a grassy yard, racing through meadows, and sharing our love for sourdough bread.

Soon after we moved into an old two-bedroom bungalow, I became pregnant and started sewing up a storm for the baby girl I thought I'd have.

Then I lost the baby.

Even though the pregnancy lasted only a few months, it broke off a corner of my heart. I wept for days, broken inside.

When the doctor told me I might never birth a child, I didn't believe him. We started over—tried to have another baby. I stayed busy with church activities, rocking infants in the nursery, and attending baby showers. Even a busybody like me could have anxiety roosting in her heart. Months went by, and I wished hard and begged the Lord until I thought he tired of hearing from me.

My smile just about fled, and an ache nestled deep inside me.

"Don't worry," Shannon had said. "I'm happy with just you and your cute little dimples."

But I wanted to be a mother so badly, my chest tightened to think about it. Every woman I knew had babies, including my four younger sisters. I tried to act like it didn't bother me, that I was happy for them, and honest I was, but an emptiness had settled in me that only a baby girl could fill. Truth be told, every one of us girls hankered for that baby girl, cheering hard during each pregnancy. So far, no baby girls had lived to wipe their hands on a mama's apron.

Our departed Mama would say, "Girl babies are like gold in your pocket, precious and valuable." Made us crave a baby girl. She also said daughters never ran off like sons. Like our brother ran off.

***

Reaching Highway 62, we turned west and drove until we could see the cotton mill towering in the distance. The buildings in Hollis stood out against the evening's wide russet and golden streaked sunset. I admit, Oklahoma had the most gorgeous sunsets the Lord could produce, stretching from Canada all the way down south to Mexico.

We drove farther before we spied two more sky-reaching buildings. I recognized the rooftops as we got closer. The Motley Hotel and the First Baptist Church—or was it the Harmon County Courthouse? Massive, but not as tall as the buildings in Dallas where the downtown towers stood lofty enough to shake hands with the man in the moon.

"Let's drive down Broadway," I said.

"I don't know. Can that rancid cake survive another mile bouncing around?" Shannon's voice held a hint of clowning, but he acquiesced and slowed as we reached the edge of town. We drove down the main thoroughfare.

"Robert, wake up! We're here! Look at all the Christmas decorations."

The boy roused from the backseat, pushed his cap back, and gawked along with us. I smiled at our adopted son. I loved that boy more than cotton candy.

"Look, Shannon! A new building. The town's changed so much since we moved away. Course, it's been over twenty years since we lived here."

“Hollis is certainly booming with energy.”

“Look, Ma!” Robert practically leaned out the window. “There’s a Santa Claus.”

The glow from J. C. Penney’s department store revealed a Santa flamboyantly displayed in the window. “There’s even an evergreen wreath hanging out front the Piggly-Wiggly grocery,” I exclaimed. “Something Mr. Jackson swore he’d never do.”

“Electric streetlights on the street corners. Never expected that,” said Shannon. Christmas ornaments, garlands, and stringed bells decorated the avenue. More horseless carriages than buggies rattled down the road.

“I’m looking forward to the week. It’ll be good to see my sisters.” I ached for sameness and wished for life to stop its rollercoaster ride.

Of course, that would never happen.

Life could never recover the exuberance of the last decade. The twenties fluffed up after the great war, pretending life would always be rosy. However, the war also taught that peace could be dashed at any moment which meant the thirties could be ushering in life down in the valley.

I hoped my family could survive the downside of this rollercoaster. I hoped I could.

Chapter 2

Jennie, my next-to-youngest sister, had a large, wood-frame home, one of the largest in town. As we pulled up alongside, my heart warmed to see the welcoming porch hadn't changed. Christmas lights glowed in the window and the wooden nativity scene sat out front. Our daddy built the faux stable and figures when we were a swarm of little girls.

When I stepped from the flivver, I breathed in the brisk Oklahoma air and released it slowly. I stretched my arms to loosen the tenseness from hours of gripping the door with one hand and clutching my bonnet with the other.

The family stampeded out the front door to meet us. "Mary Bobbie's here! Mary Bobbie's here!"

I never liked that name. Sounded like I was a Southern lady dressed up swanky. Even if I was living down in Texas, I was certainly no fancy belle of the ball. I preferred to be called Bob. Even Bobbie would do.

Robert unfolded his lanky adolescent body. Growing quickly into a young man, he needed the family's acceptance—mostly from the gang of male cousins who buzzed around us. We hadn't been to Hollis since last summer, and I worried my boy would feel unwanted, especially since the cousins were growing up together. I noticed that they kept their distance from him, looking like a pack of wolves scoping their prey.

After a round of hugs, we unpacked. "Here, Jennie, take care of this world-famous fruitcake." I deposited the cheesecloth-wrapped dessert into her hands, turned around, and bumped into my youngest sister, Annie.

"Bobbie!" She greeted me with hugs and mirth, as if I'd just arrived from the boonies. With high heels, she was a foot taller than me even when I stood on tiptoe.

"Darling! You're a sight for an old woman."

"Oh, pooh. In this old dress? You must be blind." Annie stood straighter and touched the scalloped collar of her starched, printed shirtdress. The best dressed of the bunch, she underestimated herself.

My sister Matilda wrapped her arms around me. "Sure glad you're here." She, her husband, and four boys lived in a ramshackle shack on the outskirts of Hollis.

I hugged her back.

As the oldest of five sisters who gathered every year for holidays, I felt responsible for their well-being. Our family had grown, multiplying like jack rabbits, each dear one adding to my task. Even Jennie's large home could barely contain us all now.

The only one missing was our middle sister, Susie. Her family was on their way from up north. I was not sure where they lived since they'd moved again. I'd have to get her new address.

***

Susie and her family snuck in on Christmas Eve morning. All the sisters gathered in Jennie's bright-colored kitchen to begin our cooking spree. Jennie, a take-charge kind of girl, rushed us to get us started.

We washed up, tied on worn aprons, and begin making desserts for the celebration. We talked and chuckled. I was sure, to the rest of the family, we sounded like a bunch of hens cackling.

"Here. Roll this pie crust for me."

"In a minute! I'm decorating cookies." Jennie pushed against Annie in the small kitchen, who bumped into Susie.

"Hey there! Where did you find peaches for fried pies?" Susie had always loved peaches.

"Is this meringue stiff enough? My arm's about to drop off." As always, Matilda complained.

"Umm, that chocolate pie looks delicious. Who made it?"

The chatter went on.

"Where's that box of brown sugar?"

"Hand me that thingamabob."

"You mean that doodad or this doohickey?"

We bustled about like a dozen elves making last-minute Christmas creations, funning around, and crowing at anything. The house breathed with delight. Whiffs of mouthwatering deserts smelled like paradise had dropped down for a visit.

I had a hand in all the delicacies, from the blackberry cobbler to the lemon pie, admiring our work as we moved the finished goods to the sunroom table. I couldn't resist swiping the meringue from pie I carried. Sweet Moses, it was good.

Shannon walked in on me. "Smells delicious in here." He eyed me suspiciously.

I smiled at his perfect timing and patted his chest as he wiped white meringue off my chin. "Honey pot, run over to the parking lot and round up the boys for lunch." I pointed a spatula toward the Methodist Church. "They went to play kickball. If they're using a sand rock, they've probably broken a few windows by now."

My Shannon glanced out the window, but the boys were behind the building. He recruited Jennie's husband, Tom Newberry, to help.

I chuckled as I returned to the kitchen. "Slap my head and call me silly. Shannon and Tom just went to corral our gang of animated boys. It'll take hours."

The room erupted in good-for-the-soul laughter.

***

While we prepped for the accompanying evening supper, we recalled past holidays with our parents and shared our children's shenanigans. None of us had any girls, a peculiar fact given we had ten boys running around outside, plus Annie's youngest asleep in Jennie's old baby bed. She'd hoped to give birth to a girl earlier in the year, but Jimmy, the eleventh boy, had come along.

Five middle-aged sisters and no young girls to help us cook.

Family problems crowded out the desire for a girl. From the weekly letters I received, unresolved issues and pallor surrounded my sisters. Over the years, my sweet siblings had needed advice about their prickly personal issues, and since mama died, I tried to help them. We often ended up discussing the baby girl we all desired to have.

With girls in the mix, the day could have been different. A lump in my throat replaced my giggles. Why, oh why, had I acted against every principle my policeman husband believed in?

Guilt weighed as heavy as a ton of coal in my womb, and I wished it'd hitch a ride to Dodge City. The secret I carried would change the dynamics of our family—and not for the better. If my sisters knew the disastrous truth about my second child, our closeness might crumble.

Disharmony was the last thing I wanted.

After years of struggling for a child, God's understanding fell on me like sunshine. I let the Lord have his way, allowing him to take charge of my heart's desire. Although often depressed, I tried to root out any sign of anger or bitterness. My Holy Bible almost lost its cover from the way

I searched for verses about enduring. The more I prayed about having my own daughter to hold, the more I learned to trust God to do what he thought best.

A smile returned to my face and light to my soul. God brought me a precious little boy, but a sweet young girl sitting in the kitchen with me would have brought a touch of glory. I choked, thinking about it.

I spun to the cabinet where the glasses were kept, and shoved the negative thoughts aside, heaviness not in my nature. Determined to keep the family smiling during the holiday, I contemplated on ways to bring back the lighthearted fun we had as children. To offer a positive note and live with joy again.

Dog gone it, I *would* set aside my feelings and be the good-natured prankster I'd always been, even if that meant burying my guilt and pretending to be happy.

Since I'd been the size of a toadstool, I promised myself to never carry a sad look.

Cheerful—that would be me.

Chapter 3

After Christmas Eve supper, the family gathered around the decorated tree. The kids lit the candles, which sat precariously on tree clips. I relaxed and gazed at the glow. The angelic faces of everyone I held dear reflected the soft candlelight.

An electric train ran around the foot of the evergreen as Tom read the Christmas story from his big Bible. Afterward, we sang “God Rest Ye Merry Gentlemen” and my favorite, “Joy to the World.” Shannon’s booming bass voice rang the loudest of all.

After drinking a gallon of hot chocolate and blowing out the candles, we corralled the children for bed. Rounding up that many boys was like shooing baby chicks into the chicken coop at night.

“We have to hang stockings first,” one of my nephew’s announced. The others echoed him.

The rascals rushed to hang up their clean socks.

“Mine’s bigger than yours!” another nephew yelled. “I’ll get twice as much candy.”

“That’s cause you have elephant feet!” Another adolescent voice cracked from the hallway.

“Yours smells like cow dung.”

“Do not.”

Annie's little boy ran to the front door. "I'll hang mine on the doorknob so Santa can find it first."

"There's no such thing as Santa," Susie's boy, Jack, exclaimed.

My stomach tightened.

"Is too! He brought me a toy tractor last year," Jerry stated in a determined manner for his tender years. "You're just being a baby," Jack pushed the little boy.

Up in arms at his young cousin being browbeat, one of Matilda's boys shoved Jack and soon a scuffle erupted right in the middle of the living room floor.

Tommy, Annie's husband, pulled the boys apart and lined them up in front of the sofa, threatening a licking to the first one who moved. Not that he would have done it. After a short lecture, he made them apologize. Grudgingly, they obeyed, eyes glued to the floor.

The cousins might tangle like balls of yarn, but they enjoyed being together. Tillie's four begged to stay the night with the other kids. What trouble were a few more children in a house full of rambunctious lads?

"Billy and Frank Junior. You two can stay." Tillie pointed to the younger two. "Christmas only comes once a year. I'll bring you clean clothes in the morning."

"Ah, Ma," Her eldest, Howard, folded his arms. "Why can't we stay?"

"You have chores at home." She held her son's gaze until he defeatedly headed for the door.

She kissed Jennie on the cheek. "See you tomorrow." Something in her voice held an unexpected tightness.

I followed Matilda out to her horse-drawn wagon. "Sugar, do you need to talk?"

Pain hung like a dishrag on Tillie's face. I assumed it had to do with her stressful marriage. Her husband, Frank, hadn't come to the family gathering. And she'd already apologized that he might not make it tomorrow for Christmas. I'd overheard grumbles among our husbands' that he'd been arrested for public intoxication again.

"I'm fine." She looked over at Howard and Thomas, both dependable, handsome boys. Obviously, she didn't want to talk in front of them. "Nothing can be done about it, anyway."

"The Lord can fix anything." I believed God could help Frank—if Frank wanted to be helped.

Matilda gathered up her long skirt and climbed into the wagon. "We'll be back tomorrow, bright and early."

When I returned to the house, Jennie was shooing the boys upstairs. She glanced at me, also worried. Leaning closing, she whispered, "Frank's probably on a drinking binge."

I wrapped my arm around her. "If anyone of us has the gumption to survive that marriage, it's Sally Matilda." I followed her upstairs, then scrambled up the narrow attic steps. A musty smell hit me, although I was sure someone had recently swept the place.

The large attic was tall enough to stand in. Trunks were pushed against one side along with Grandma's old dresser, covered with a sheet. A quilting frame sat in the corner where Jennie liked to gather with friends to work.

We put the eight boys to bed in the large room while the baby stayed with Annie and her husband. The boys bunked down on the floor on pallets of quilts, blankets, and pillows.

I gazed at the sleepy-eyed young-uns. Jack glared, reminding me of Count Dracula on a good day. Nonetheless, I loved to spoil him as much as my other nephews. Robert, my gangly boy, had the same pale skin and tousled brown hair as the rest. He resembled the lot, looking as if he fit in even although he wasn't blood kin. Jack, Thomas, and my Robert, who was half a head shorter, were the same age. The three mimicked Charlie

Chaplin, tickling me to no end. They all quieted and finally settled down on their floor pallets.

I'd hidden my sadness at not being able to birth a child, but I still got jolts of pain if I allowed myself to think about it. Adoption had brought joy and sadness, and I hoped my boy would feel welcomed by his cousins.

I went over and tucked the covers tightly around Robert.

"Mom, I have a question—but you might not like it."

I ruffled his thick hair, thinking I'd send him to Tommy's barber shop before we went back to Texas. "You can ask anything you want." I expected a query about being adopted, or Christmas secrets, like sharing what he expected to find under the tree in the morning.

"What happened to my sister?"

Shocked, all the muscles in my body tensed. I drew a deep breath, calming myself, and leaned closer. "Why do you ask?"

"Thomas told me only boys stay alive in our family. He lost a sister, but he doesn't remember much about her, except his mama cried a lot. I had a sister once, didn't I?"

I took another deep breath. "Yes," I spoke slowly. "But this isn't the time to talk about it."

He looked at me curiously. I turned away from his searching eyes, not wanting him to see how much the topic upset me.

"We'll talk later." I patted him on the head. "We don't want to spoil our Christmas with sad thoughts, now do we?"

Robert shrugged and turned over to sleep.

I'd kept silent for so long, and now I wasn't sure how to talk to Robert about his sister. First, I'd have to speak with Shannon. My husband needed to know the truth about what happened years ago. We'd never spoken about our baby's death. Never.

As I crept down the stairs, I felt a prick in my heart, a prick that stabbed all five of the sisters.

We wanted a real, living baby daughter among us. A girl who would laugh and play and wash dishes with the women. One to share our faith and calm down the menfolk. One to teach. One to carry on our faith. We wanted it so badly it permeated our daily thoughts—at least my daily thoughts.

As if the Lord was playing a trick on us, we had only sons. Maybe our family wasn't good enough to keep their girls. I wished I could explain the reason to Robert, but I could only shake my head.

Why not a living girl among the five sisters? Was God playing a joke?

Chapter 4

"We're going for stocking stuffers," my hubby whispered to me when I went downstairs. Shannon Layne was tall and husky, whereas I tended toward round and pleasant. He insisted he liked me that way, a little-bitty plump woman overflowing with chuckles and laughter. I married Shannon with a smile on my face, a light in my eyes, and my brown hair curled to perfection.

He and Tom grabbed their hats and snuck out the back door.

I caught the screen before it slammed shut and followed them. "Wait, fellows! You can't have all the fun." Running through the yard and the next two blocks, I caught up with them halfway to the mercantile store Tom owned. Even in the brisk cold night, T.A. Newberry Dry Goods and Clothing Store stood proudly along the main thoroughfare. The wealthiest of us, Tom was generous, especially to his wife's large and growing extended family.

The dry goods store smelled enticing. I paused, breathing in the scent of brand-spanking-new bolts of cotton, barrels of beans and cornmeal, jars of spices and oils. Hanging on a wall were sewing supplies and ready-made clothing. I could have spent days snooping around. Me and my curiosity.

I turned and bumped into a stack of little girl clothes on the counter—toddler dresses. Adorable handmade pinafores with lace down the front. My body stiffened, the reminder stabbing my belly like a knife.

Shannon laid his hands on my shoulders. I bathed in his big, warm presence. "Are you all right, honey?" He worried more than a mother hen, pressing to know what disturbed me.

I couldn't recount the number of times he'd asked me that. "I'm fine," I said. Fine, considering the hard pit in my stomach I attempted to push down to China. Little girls' dresses did that to me.

If only I could talk to Shannon about it.

"Grab a bag and fill it with fruit," Tom yelled from the storage room. "An apple and orange for each boy."

I snatched a gunny sack and held it open while Shannon loaded fruit from a tall, round barrel. He tossed two oranges in the air and tried to juggle them. I snickered as one fumbled back into the bin. Juggling was not his talent. But it eased the tension in my body.

As the sack grew heavier with fruit, I recalled the picnic at Hollis Baptist Church back in our early days. In 1906, dressed in Sunday clothes, which included my best dress and gloves, we sat under a shade tree outside of town surrounded by wide-open fields. More chaperones attended than teenagers, but that's how it was in the old days, especially after Shannon joined our group. A natural-born entertainer, he told jokes and threw his head back, laughing like he didn't have a care in the world.

Not long after, he came calling on me. Of course, he had to meet my family first—not that he hadn't already met them around town, but formally—as if they minded if he courted me.

I'm proud to say they were pleased as sugar punch, even if Shannon had only finished the seventh grade. He was an honest man from an upstanding church-going family and clear about right and wrong. We kind of matched. Both of us loved to joke around and enjoyed food as much as a pack of stray dogs.

Those were the simple pleasures I wanted to have with my own children.

Setting the gunny sack aside. I helped Tom add pecans and candy canes to a second one, while Shannon disappeared to the back. A few minutes later, he poked his head around the corner.

He held up a used 12-gauge shotgun. "How about this gift for Robert?" He grinned, revealing pride in his choice. "You know how he loves to hunt with me."

"Are you sure?" Guns were a normal gift for a boy growing up in Texas or Oklahoma, but I hesitated. Surely, it was not time to buy him one yet. However, the new shirt I'd sewn him probably wouldn't excite the boy much.

"How much is the gun?" Shannon asked Tom.

"Consider it my gift for him."

My brother-in-law's generosity made my heart tender, but we had plenty of funds, considering Knox City had given Shannon a Christmas bonus of ten dollars for being such a good undersheriff.

"No, siree. I'm paying for my son's Christmas present," said Shannon. "We aim to go rabbit hunting together before the winter's over."

The transaction done, we carried the sacks to Jennie's. Inside, my sisters were already stuffing the stockings with trinkets they'd brought their own kids. We joined them, acting like vaudeville players and underground Santas, rearranging the stocking to different locations.

Shannon stood on a chair and hung one stocking from a hanging light bulb. The chair wobbled, and he ungracefully jumped off it before it clattered to the floor.

I gasped, and he had the audacity to grin.

I poked his belly with a candy cane. "Santa's going to get caught if he keeps making so much noise."

Jennie snorted. "Not by my boys. They could sleep through a freight train horn."

The others chuckled as they took the filled stockings and scattered them around the house.

Ease settled like the wood in the fireplace. I carried the responsibility for our family's happiness since I was a tiny tot. Sometimes that required pretending. It wasn't very hard to put on a smile, because nothing bothered me.

Well, almost nothing.

***

The boys, ranging from toddlers to high schoolers, were awake and eager for presents at the crack of dawn that Christmas morning. The early risers must have alerted the others. Soon bright-eyed boys encouraged us adults to pry open our exhausted eyelids and come downstairs. Overnight, the weather had turned nippy. I pulled my worn housecoat around me and shivered. Tom built a fire in the fireplace.

The children didn't seem to mind the cold. They ran around the house looking for their knee-high stockings. Some socks were tied around bedposts, others to doorknobs, or hid behind the Christmas tree. My ears just about exploded from the noise that many boys created in the wood-framed house, especially when Tillie arrived with her boys.

Robert slid in front of me, his face frantic. "Mother, I can't find my sock!"

I pointed to the ceiling.

The grownups chuckled as Robert drew up the same chair and jumped to fetch his stocking from the hanging light fixture.

Successful, he plopped down with his cousins and stuffed a peppermint candy into his mouth. The fragrance of citrus wafted from the orange peels scattered around. The boys unwrapped their gifts, whooping like wildcats.

"Look, fellows! A football!"

"Boy, oh boy! I got a slingshot!"

"A train!"

"A toy car!"

I hoped Truman wouldn't drop the heavy cast iron replica. I shouldn't have worried though. For six years old, he was small but confident enough to hold his own.

Annie's boy got a red wagon. Seventeen-year-old Marvin got a crochet kit.

I turned questioning eyes toward Susie, and she shrugged and pushed up her wire-rimmed glasses. "That's what he asked for."

Naturally, Robert's shotgun was a hit, and Shannon put it in our automobile until an adult could take the boys out of town to practice and give them a what-if lesson.

Laughter lingered throughout the morning, setting a happy mood for the day.

My thoughts looked ahead as I dressed the wild turkey and put it in the oven. I hoped to find time to ask Susie about rumors concerning her husband and their moves, to cuddle Annie's sweet little boys, and to tell Jennie what a good job she did keeping the family going. But mostly, I felt compelled to approach Matilda about her deteriorating marriage and the bruises Jennie had seen on her face a few weeks ago.

I wasn't sure how I could help Tillie without sharing my own internal conflicts. Discussing heart matters meant being open to others' scrutiny, and in some ways, I was ready for that, and in other ways, I balked.

I liked my sisters looking up to me. That might change if they knew the heartache I'd caused. The horrible deed I'd done.

Before I talked to Robert about his sister, I'd have to admit my failure as a mother. I scrunched my lips together. No, not yet. My sisters' problems came first. I'd hold my hurt inside a little longer and maybe the anguish would simply disappear.

Chapter 5

"Bobbie, this turkey's going to dry up and run away if you don't take it out of the oven!" Jennie turned and wiped her hands on her apron.

I chuckled. "Guess I'll be chasing it down the road then. Can't you see this chubby little lady raising her skirts and hightailing it down Broadway?"

She rolled her eyes and returned to her bread dough. We spent the morning cooking as if everyone in Harmon County was coming to dinner. The smell of homemade bread settled like drops from paradise, invading every corner of the large, comfortable house on Jones Street. My mouth watered in anticipation.

Jennie may have learned to cook from Mama, but she'd elevated bread-making to an art form. Why I declare, she made the best sourdough bread in the whole state of Oklahoma.

The smell of roasted turkey blended with yeasty rolls rising in tin pans. I grabbed two loomed potholders and opened the door of the cast-iron stove. Steam spewed out and I stepped back.

"What did I tell you? We cooked it too long." Jennie's tiny mouth pouted. With her apron smeared with mashed potatoes, her hands on her hips, and her spectacles sliding down her nose, she resembled our deceased Grandma Shields enough to bring warm memories.

I almost laughed, but instead I examined the dark, golden-brown bird. It looked perfect. "We had to make sure the cornbread stuffing inside got done, dearie. Make room on the counter." I lifted and set the roasting pan on a trivet.

Setting my hands on my wide hips, I pushed my shoulders back and admired the luscious, golden bird.

Jennie shook her head and returned to making giblet gravy. She dropped the cut-up turkey innards and diced boiled eggs into the smooth broth, as if making food for her beloved family were her only care in the world.

Did all families do that? Go on with life—making gravy, laughing and joking, surrounding troubles with a bubble of love?

Matilda and Susie did their share of cooking to prepare for the holiday feast. Til buttered and mashed the sweet potatoes. Susie made deviled eggs and placed a beautiful gelatin mold covered with a cheesecloth in the icebox. Our baby sister, Ann, had a habit of burning food, so we relegated her to setting the table and making sweet, iced tea.

Stepping out of the kitchen, I found the house oddly quiet. I stuck my head out the front door and a cold rush of winter air burned my cheeks. I looked for the men but found only the older boys sitting outside. The row of tow-headed urchins sat on the porch or leaned against the wall, not catering to being cooped up inside. With all the cooking we'd done, the house had warmed up the area, making it cozy.

The boys peppered me with complaints.

"Is dinner ready yet?"

"I can't wait much longer."

"The delicious smell is torture."

"We're gonna starve to death."

I arched my eyebrow at the famished young boys who hadn't eaten in a couple of hours. Even my Robert could cram food in his mouth like a hobo who'd been riding the rail for months, subsisting on canned beans.

"It won't be long. Why don't you find the others and wash up?"

Still looking for Shannon, I glanced into the living room. The couches and a hardback chair were empty. The rocking chair swayed back and forth by itself as if someone had just left it. Our menfolk gathered around the big wooden box radio in the corner.

Tom turned the dial.

A news report blasted out like another person sat in the room. Radio was a phenomenal creation. Only Tom could afford one. The rest of us relied on newspapers and telephone gossip. However, even the wireless broadcast brought its own form of disagreements.

While Tom finagled the radio knobs, the other men argued about the recent stock market crash and the billions of dollars lost in a single day. Heavens to Betsy, I was tired of hearing about that.

Another voice came from the box for a few seconds before Tom turned the dials again. "Wait! I can't miss the farmer's news." Annie's husband, who bought and sold horses, liked to discuss current market prices, crop conditions, and weather forecasts. A farmer's wife might be interested in poultry raising and egg production, but most women preferred listening to the evening soap operas. Tales that carried us far away and left us hanging until the next week.

Music blared. Elmer, Susie's husband, sat up. "Oh. This is a great song. You guys might like it." A band director, he always wanted to listen to the newfound station, WKY more than her.

"No way." Shannon would never give up his football.

"Not going to happen today, buddy."

"That ball game should be on here somewhere."

The men's voices rose. I tapped my foot when none of them noticed me. Right after a news report about Saxony freeing 179 political prisoners as a Christmas gift, their conversation lulled.

I called out, "Shannon Layne, come on in here! We need you to carve the turkey."

Carving the bird was a man's job, after hunting it and bringing it home. Recently, slicing had become my husband's duty, since he was the most experienced, now that our brother Sam had moved away.

A little older than us sisters, Sam Thomas had married Miss Charlsie and moved to New Mexico several years ago. Before he left, I asked him why so far, joking I couldn't imagine anyone wanting to live miles from civilization with no friends but the lizards.

He'd hugged me. "Sis, I got me a good-paying job, and I'd like to try it out."

I chuckled at the notion of my large brother trying to find shade under a saguaro cactus plant. Truth was, we had hardly heard from him since he left Hollis. A few sporadic letters expressed he hated the heat but liked his job. We all missed him something terrible.

Shannon bustled into the small kitchen and eyed the wild bird on the table. A huge hunting knife lay beside the platter. Shannon was such a big fellow, we all stepped aside to let him work.

My husband sliced that tom turkey into nice, thin slivers of juicy meat. My, oh my. I didn't know what I was prouder of, my big, strong, handsome husband, or that perfectly cooked fowl.

Chapter 6

I loved to cook, and Shannon loved my cooking. Lands 'o living. At home in Munday, fried chicken and pan-fried okra were our favorite foods. Mashed potatoes were served once a week with loads of butter and smothered with brown gravy. It's no wonder we'd put on a little weight over the years.

When Shannon finished carving the turkey, Jennie took command of the kitchen. "Bobbie, slip those hot rolls into the oven." She perched in front of the gravy, shaking the wooden spoon in her hand.

I balanced the pan of raised rolls over my head. "Move over a little, Jennie, so I can get close enough."

"Yes, ma'am."

We danced around each other, giggling like schoolgirls before I could open the oven door and slide the two pans onto the rack.

Tillie popped open another jar of homemade creamed corn from Jennie's fall stash. I turned up the burner under the corn and poked my head into the dining room to see how the decorating fared.

Annie and Susie rustled around the table. The girls must've found every fork and plate in the house to make sure no person was left out. A wax candle glowed from the centerpiece and even the sidebar had doilies covering it.

I beamed at them. "Girls, you've set the table up nice and fancy. This is going to be the best Christmas meal of the decade, and it isn't even the new year yet!"

Suddenly, a high-pitched scream came from the front yard and a loud commotion followed.

All five of us rushed toward the door, pushing and shoving like the house was ablaze. We couldn't tell exactly which boy was hurt, but one of our next generation was surely dying.

We dashed toward the road.

Can't stop a mama when her young'uns a screaming.

***

The boys swarmed in such a tight circle we couldn't see the center. Mamas started pulling the rascals apart one by one. Robert, my boy, lay at the center of the pile. Sprawled in the dry, flaky dirt, his face was covered in blood.

My nerves buzzed, and my heart pounded. A bloody nose? Or worse?

I knelt beside him and wiped his face with a tea towel I gripped. Taking his face in my hands, I looked at it this way and that, checking his arms and legs. He didn't look too worse for wear.

Helping him to his feet, I glanced at the other boys. "What happened?"

Pale, contrite faces, ranging from little Jerry to Marvin, the oldest, avoided my gaze. Their resemblance astonished me. A stranger would have thought they were all brothers. Honey, what a mess of boys!

No one spoke. My four sisters took charge, grabbing the arms of their lads and giving them stern looks. The boys couldn't get away from mothers who were determined to make honest men out of them.

"It was Jack." Billy, Matilda's third boy, was too young to feel disloyal.

The others nodded, but nobody met Jack's eyes. He was Susie's youngest, the troubled one.

"Jack said I was an orphan and didn't belong here." Robert spit out the words. "He's a liar, and I told him so."

Jack jerked away from Susie's grasp. "Robert called me names, so I punched him."

"That's when the rest of us piled on," said another boy.

I scanned Jack up and down, noticing his shaggy hair and torn overalls. I wasn't sure why Susie's angry teen was unhappy, but I had an idea. His daddy, Elmer, couldn't claim to be the best male role model around. Nevertheless, as much as I'd like to, I couldn't butt into their domestic problems.

Susie ignored Jack's temper. She couldn't control the boy. Instead, she turned away when most mamas would have offered stern warnings and a good wallop to the backside. My poor sister was distracted by her own survival.

Robert, my noble outcast, was no match for his cousin, Jack. Thank the Lord, some of his cousins had defended him. Nevertheless, I couldn't overlook my son's bad behavior, no matter his age and size. I took him by the ear and led him behind the house.

Good thing his father wasn't around. Now that's a whopper if I ever told one. Shannon didn't have a disciplinary bone in his body. He might have lectured Robert, but he'd never laid a hand on the boy. Shannon's muscular body epitomized power and his raised voice could soothe any out-of-control situation. Being in law enforcement probably encouraged that.

I felt sorry for Robert and knew he'd only been defending himself. But did he fit in with the others or feel a part of the family? He'd been a tough little kid, ever since we adopted him at four years old. He loved to play army, and I could bet he'd join up as soon as he was old enough. Of course, I wasn't a betting woman. Not since I lost my silver hair clip to Matilda when I was fifteen.

Crisis over, I gave Robert a proper scolding, Then I skedaddled back to the kitchen to tend to the Christmas dinner.

Chapter 7

"Stir the gravy for me." Jennie took a slab of fresh butter out of the icebox. While her back was turned, I snatched a tasty bite of turkey from the platter on the countertop.

"Bless your stinky heart, Bobbie Lu, I saw that," said Jennie.

"Saw what?" I clasped my hands behind my back and gave her the most innocent look I could muster while drool dripped from my mouth. I was so hungry I could've eaten the north end of a polecat.

We hustled around, filled the serving bowls, and carried platters to the extended dining room table. The men and boys joined us, their hands and faces freshly washed, their male voices filling the dining room with loud talk and laughter.

I noticed Matilda was absent from our banter, and I returned to the kitchen to check on her. "You coming?"

She'd started cleaning up. "I'll wait and eat with Frank when he shows up."

I removed my apron. Her husband was probably sleeping off a night of booze somewhere. Stomp my negative thoughts!

I took Tillie's arm to guide her into the dining room, invoking my authority as eldest sister. "You can't sit around starving while dinner's served. Besides, Tom won't say grace until the family gets rounded up."

Matilda shook my hand off and turned toward the back door. "I'm going home. Go ahead and eat without me. And make sure my boys mind their manners."

I turned Matilda around to face me. "Look at me." The last time her husband came around, the brothers-in-law had to restrain him. "If you're worried about Frank showing up drunk again, we'll handle it. But we won't handle having you absent from the table you helped prepare."

Peace was essential during the holidays, and my job since mother died was to keep the family unit connected and intact. My sisters needed this togetherness. Our boys needed it. And if I was being honest with myself, I needed all my sisters present.

Tillie's shoulders fell. She removed her apron, and we joined the crowded dining room together. Folks gathered around the table, chairs scooting against the wooden floor as the adults found seats. The boys stood around waiting for a turn at filling their plates.

A Christmas feast! Buttered corn, mashed potatoes, and giblet gravy. Cornbread dressing seasoned with celery and sage. And of course, that big platter of sliced, juicy wild turkey. Homemade pickles and beets filled Jennie's best crystal dish, and two baskets of hot rolls kept warm under tea towels. My mouth watered.

Good goobers! I never saw such a spread. I licked my lips 'til they shined.

Everyone bowed their heads, and Tom said the blessing. "Thank you, Lord, for getting us through another year. Bless our families, especially these boys, and thank you for this wonderful food and those who prepared it. In Jesus' name, Amen."

"Thank you, Jesus. Amen," Jerry's happy little voice yelled.

"Amen," everyone echoed joyfully.

Chaos reigned as the hungry group filled their plates. Dishes banged, silverware clacked, and drinks were filled. Without talking, Matilda helped the young ones fill their plates before she sat down at the table. Relieved, I surveyed the food.

Conversation rattled around the table. The sound filled the house with happiness. Tom had fixed up a makeshift table for the boys in the back sunroom. "Now don't touch the desserts," he said. "Those are for later."

I wasn't sure of the wisdom in the desserts being on the sidebar closest to them.

My taste buds sparkled with about the best meal I'd ever eaten. I might've attempted to curb my appetite at times, but not now. As far as eating went, Shannon sped ahead of me, already delving into his mile-high plateful of goodies. Sitting to my right, he looked at me and winked. I loved that shared look, a connection like no one else existed in the room.

He ate several huge slices of turkey, three servings of dressing and gravy topped with a heap of cranberry sauce, and six hot rolls. Not to mention the pickled okra he could put down faster than a hot knife through butter.

Lordy, could my man eat.

***

Food was my way of helping people, but it didn't always bring joy. Ten years ago, when we lived in oil booming Burkburnett, Texas, Shannon met an oil field worker whose wife had died. The fellow was raising his two children alone.

The worker drank heavily. My husband arrested him and carried him to the slammer a time or two. The man lost his job and fell on hard times. To help his family, I'd send over a slab of bacon or a bag of dried peas along with baked goods.

Shannon tried to help him too, honorable man that he was. He reminded the fellow that his kids needed him, but it was no use.

Depression got the best of the once upstanding citizen, even a churchgoer.

One night on patrol, Shannon found the man unconscious in a ditch. The fellow didn't live to see the sunrise. When my husband came home that night, I met him on the porch.

"Look what I brought home, sweet cakes," he said.

Two youngsters sat huddled in the back seat of his patrol car.

My mouth fell open. The older was about four years old, with cute little dimples and a turned-up nose, just like mine. The younger was a little waif of a girl if I ever saw one. She looked at me with huge, sad eyes. Joy and sadness came together unexpectedly, and my heart leaped like jumping beans in a coffee can. I fell in love at first sight.

"Do you think you can take care of them 'til I find their family?"

"I'd be delighted to take these two dumplings into our home. What are their names?"

"Robert and Oma Jean."

Neither child said a word but stared at us. Oma Jean clung to me as I picked her up out of the backseat. Shannon hefted Robert, and we made our way up the steps and through the front door.

"These sugar pies probably haven't had a decent meal in a coon's age." We set the children on the sofa and covered them with blankets. "I'll whip up a pan of fried taters."

As they ate like starved urchins, I noticed their dirty faces and tattered clothes. I heated water for a bath, and after they were clean, I wrapped them in towels before rummaging around for soft, worn shirts.

The next week, church women gifted us hand-me-down blankets, rag dolls, hair ribbons, and britches for Robert. I found bedding and bought extra food at the mercantile. The little girl needed something fluffy and frilly, so I stitched Oma Jean a wardrobe of petticoats and ruffles.

Shame to say, their family was never found.

Shannon and I were overjoyed when the adoption went through easily. Celebrating with homemade ice cream and butterscotch fudge, we couldn't keep the grins off our faces or the light out of our eyes. After being childless for years, we finally had a loving family.

Ecstatic, I boasted about my two adorable children, as any proud mother would. I certainly loved them as my own.

My faith strengthened. God did the right thing by letting us adopt and giving the children a home. On the other hand, if he hadn't, Oma Jean might still be alive.

Chapter 8

After the grownups chewed the fat around the Christmas dinner table, the fellows slunk out to sit on chairs under the big oak tree, lighting cigarettes or spitting tobacco. One of them would probably pull out a deck of cards.

In the warm, mid-afternoon sun, they pulled their hats over their eyes and their collars up around their necks, pretending to watch the boys play football in the empty lot next to Jennie's house. But really, they slept off the scrumptious meal, an invariable men's holiday ritual every time we got together.

I stood to clean the table, and the ladies followed.

We five sisters had a method for cleaning up, the same since we were children. Unfortunately, we hadn't added any young girls to help, so the system stayed consistent. Annie and Susie cleared off the table while Matilda washed dishes and I dried them. Jennie put the dishes away. We chatted like magpies as if we were young girls again ourselves.

Tilli never mentioned leaving again, and washed the dishes much quicker than I could dry them, slinging water everywhere. Some splashed into my face, and I shook my curls and chuckled.

Unwilling to let her get away with that, even if it was an accident, I cupped some water into my hand and threw it at her. She shrieked.

Water dripped down my back and I squealed.

Jennie spoke from behind us. “Bless me, child, y’all are having too much fun.”

Annie popped my backside with a tea towel. “Take that, old lady.”

“Nine years older than you doesn’t make me an old lady!” I popped her back. “I’ll get you.”

“Who’s getting old, you say?” said Susie.

“Not me.” I shifted to keep an eye on both of them. “I may be in my forties, but I don’t plan on slowing down anytime soon.”

“You do have the most gray hairs.” Annie squinted like she considered it a disgrace. It wasn’t, of course.

“Gray hairs of wisdom, given by the good Lord.” I patted my wavy locks.

My joke broke the competitive air. We enjoyed a good chuckle.

I heaved a large sigh and cleaned up the water from the edge of the sink. “This reminds me of when we were small. Five girls crowded together, like peas in a pod, baking cookies in that itty-bitty kitchen. Do you remember?”

The girls grinned, which set us on a reminiscing trip. Time had brought heartaches and happiness. I wished I could hold on to my sisters like I’d held onto the side of the motor car on our way to Hollis, clinging on for dear life.

I enjoyed my role as the oldest daughter of our big family, but it sometimes wore me out. Even as a child, I took my responsibility seriously. Truthfully, those days about dilled my pickle. Especially the cooking and cleaning and taking care of them. Mostly, I felt responsible for their happiness. And with the lives we’d lived through, I wasn’t sure I’d been successful at lightening their load.

Mama never acted the same after Daddy died. Being a strong Church of Christ member all her life had taught her how to bring joy to our home.

But it hadn't taught her to cope with being alone. She took to her bed and died in 1921, still grieving for our daddy.

I felt like an orphan when she left us to fend for ourselves, even if I was grown. Guess I *was* an orphan. Sort of like my boy Robert before we adopted him.

Jennie put away the last of the clean dishes. When Shannon and I moved away to Texas, she took charge of caring for the others. It saddened me to think she'd bore the weight of being caretaker in my absence, although she seemed to take to it right well. It suited her—nursing, worrying, and bustling around, making sure every family member knew they were thought of and loved.

Clean up finished, we vacated the hot kitchen and sauntered into the sunroom where pastries lined the sideboard raised on blocks in the screened-in room. We admired the large assortment of Christmas desserts we'd produced in our marathon baking session. Sweets that would last through the next few weeks.

Chocolate cake and ginger cookies were my favorites. Well, that wasn't completely true. I also loved pecan pie and fruitcake and taffy and anything with a tad bit of sugar in it. I popped one of Jennie's fudge bites into my mouth. As smooth as molasses, it melted over my tongue. I could have died right there, a happy woman.

Stomach sated after a few choice nibbles, exhaustion hit. I joined my sisters in the living room with eggnog and pie, relieved and thankful the holiday meal had gone so well.

***

After all was quiet, my sisters and I began to exchange Christmas gifts wrapped in brown paper and tied with bows. Out of tradition, we opened the presents from the youngest sister to the oldest. We opened

Annie's gifts first—a pair of knitted mittens in an assortment of colors for each of us. Predictable, but nice.

Instead of a homemade gift, Jennie gave everyone ready-made shawls likely purchased through her husband's store. Mine was sky blue and felt as smooth as silk stockings.

Susie had crocheted white lace doilies with astonishing detail. Of course, we had to ooh and ahh over their intricacies.

Next, Matilda gave aprons, each slightly different. She'd been a seamstress for years, and her fine stitches beat all I ever saw.

I anxiously shared my gifts, handing out glass quart jars with bows tied on top. Each held the fixings for hot chocolate. I didn't often share my secret recipes, but the mix included cocoa, sugar, and powdered milk.

"I'm eager to try that hot chocolate as soon as I get home. That is, if I can keep it away from my old man," said Matilda.

"Oh me, I do believe this is the best Christmas I've ever had." Annie clapped her hands together.

"I certainly never had so much delicious food." I patted my belly.

Wheels crunched in Jennie's driveway. A horse neighed. A wagon pulled up outside and stopped.

The boys hollered.

Something was up.

Chapter 9

My sisters and I exchanged glances. I raised my eyebrows and headed for the front door. Who would come calling this late on Christmas Day? Our other relatives lived too far away to be traipsing over at all hours.

I stuck my head out the door, and my sisters poked in around me.

Tillie gasped and covered her mouth with a shaking hand.

Her husband, Frank, obviously drunk, yelled at the top of his lungs, "Woman, get out here this minute!"

Red-faced, Frank jumped from the wagon seat, swaying like a sailor. He caught hold of the buckboard before toppling into the dirt. Matilda and Frank had been spatting off and on for years, their marriage as worrisome as a herd of cranky goats, butting heads, rowdy and unruly. Problems happened mostly when he'd been drinking moonshine. I heard he could be mean as a riled coon and just as nasty.

Matilda bravely pushed us aside and marched down the front porch steps into the dirt-covered yard to face her inebriated husband. "Thought you'd be sober by now. You shouldn't come here when you're sloshed."

"Nice way to treat your man. I come to see the family for Christmas." Frank's sweet tone sounded as fake as his excuse. He took a wobbly step toward Tillie.

My heart raced as he came within arm's length of my sister.

Matilda didn't move.

The menfolk appeared from the side of the wood-frame house, and the boys circled around, fortified by all the grown-ups behind them.

All stood quietly with their arms crossed except Frank Junior, their six years old, who flew to his dad's side and almost knocked him over. A boy might miss his pa no matter how ruthless he's been treated.

Frank used his son to steady himself. "I was in town, and thought I'd stop for a bite of Jennie's famous pies. Came to see you too, if you're hankering to see me as much as I'm hankering to see you."

All eyes flew to Tillie. Couldn't have been quieter if the parson had died. No one wanted to ruin a perfect Christmas by making a scene.

Matilda wiped her forehead with her apron before she spoke. "You're not wanted around here when you're soused, remember? We straightened that out last time you cursed the boys in front of everyone. I'm doing fine and the boys are having a good time. Best you get on home. I'll bring you some pie tonight."

"If I'm going home, I'm taking the boys with me," Frank's words slurred. "They need to milk the cows."

Matilda's boys stepped back.

"We'll do that later, Pa." Howard's squeaky adolescent voice sounded fearful.

"Well, I'm taking Junior."

"When you're drunk, you don't take Frank Junior anywhere." Hands on hips, Matilda took a step toward her husband.

Frank turned to Junior, who stood next to him, and grabbed him by the hair. "Young 'un, we're headed for home. Now climb into the wagon before I beat your behind."

"Ma!" The scrawny boy turned wide eyes toward his mother.

Gasps and growling words came from the gathered family.

Frank Junior thrashed like a trapped deer, fighting for his freedom as his dad thrust him toward the buckboard. The boy fell and landed on the ground at his daddy's feet, his left arm twisted under him.

Matilda ran toward Junior. "See what you've done! You've hurt him! That boy's staying right here with me!"

"Ain't nothing wrong with him. Get up off the ground, you little snit." Frank reached to pick up Junior, but the boy let out another scream that could have woken the whole cavalry.

Thomas dashed forward and pulled a scared Junior into his arms while Howard, who had a more aggressive streak, shoved his dad backward.

"You can't treat our little brother that way. You'll have to fight us first."

Frank stumbled and fell in his drunken state.

Billy, only nine years old himself—certain his uncles stood behind him—raised his fist.

Robert, who stood straight as a sentry throughout the ordeal, suddenly broke loose and ran toward our Tin Lizzie. In two seconds, he rushed back, carrying his new shotgun. He slid to a stop and aimed the gun at Frank. "Time for you to be going," he said Robert with an authoritative voice, mimicking his policeman father.

I couldn't believe my eyes. Robert knew better than to aim a weapon at anyone. At least we hadn't purchased any bullets for the gun. "Put that away," I yelled, and the boy turned the gun toward the ground.

Another boy stepped forward and kicked Frank in the shin. "Yeah. Get gone."

Emboldened, the cousins echoed the words and stepped closer. Fists clenched, they took protective stances as if they were wild Indians battling ten-foot giants. I could imagine war paint on their flushed faces.

Standing side by side, they joined Matilda's boys to protect the family. Even Annie's little tot copied his older cousins.

"Get out of here."

"Leave Junior alone!"

"Come back when you can be nice."

My heart rooted for them, proud as Mama's fat rooster, especially Robert, not for grabbing his shotgun without permission, mind you, but for protecting his family. The boys might have tiffs and scuffles, but they defended one another on the dime. The menfolk appeared just as amazed as we ladies.

Shannon, the police officer of the bunch, stepped up and said, "I'll take care of this, boys." He took the 12-gauge from Robert and scrunched his eyes at him. "Guess we need to start on your gun lessons right soon." He grabbed Frank by the arm and helped him into the old cart. My heart swelled at the way Shannon took charge.

Frank turned from the wagon bed and glared at Howard. "I'll teach you boys a lesson later. You're gonna regret talking back to your pa." We heard him cussing up a blue streak all the way to the cotton mill.

Matilda's face paled as she slumped down on the porch steps with Junior on her lap. He clung to her, sobbing, his face buried in her dress. Jack ran to fetch the doctor while the other boys stood quietly, watching the dust behind the wagon settle into the ground, sobered by the incident.

"Don't need to worry about him anymore," said Thomas, dusting his hands. "At least for now."

"How can I teach them to respect their father when he acts like this?" Matilda's forehead creased in worry, probably as much over their future as for her wounded son. "The boys are brave when they're here with family. At home, they don't talk back to him like that. It'll be bad if Frank remembers any of this."

What would Til's boys face later when they got home?

The doctor came quickly, examined Junior, and announced no broken bones. He put Junior's arm in a sling and sent him to bed for the rest of the day, though I doubted the boy could remain subdued that long.

After being scolded, the boys grinned like mischievous monkeys and returned to their ballgame, arguing about who was the bravest and who was the hero.

***

"Oh dear, Elmer wanted to leave by three," said Susie, as we settled back in the house.

I nodded, knowing she'd follow Elmer's wishes to the grave, sensible or not.

"He wants to get home before dark." Her voice was so low I barely heard her—her way of softening the apology. After all, only spending one night with the family for Christmas was almost offensive. Especially after her long trip and not seeing each other since last summer.

Susie began to pack her dishes, loading leftover desserts into their roadster. Elmer and Susie moved around so much I hardly knew which town they lived in. Born a happy lass, it seemed each year she'd been married to Elmer, her demeanor faded a little more, pushing her down. The girl I remembered had disappeared and I wished to bolster her up. Shaking the tar out of her probably wouldn't help, but that's what I felt like doing.

The family followed Susie to their beat-up sedan. Elmer threw a bag onto the floorboard of the backseat while their two boys refused hugs and lined up to climb in.

I pulled Susie aside and put my arm around her. "I'm here if you need me. Honey, just say the word, and I'll come running your way."

She looked at me with deep, sad eyes. "I'm fine, dear. I've lived with stress for years. Nothing bothers me anymore."

I gave her my I-don't-believe-you look. What was her life really like? Her letters only hinted at discord. I hadn't seen happiness in her family for a long time. No smiles. No joking around. No slap your knee silly. No laughing till the tears rolled. What kind of life was that? It would take something mighty substantial to pull her up by the bootstraps.

The goodbyes were quick and unsettling. We watched the bumper of Elmer's motor car create a dust storm as it sped down the road. My goal to help my sisters seemed beyond reach. I wished for the umpteenth time that I lived closer to them.

Chapter 10

The men wandered down the street to examine a stallion Tommy had recently purchased. Tommy made a living as a barber, but he had an entrepreneur spirit and regularly bartered some deal on a horse or two he kept on the edge of town. Annie, Jennie, and the littlest boys went to take a nap, which left Matilda and me alone in the living room.

I yawned and leaned back in the rocking chair, stretching my arms over my head before I eased down into its comfort. The huge Christmas meal made me want to doze a little myself, but I shook my head awake. I'd missed my chance to talk with Susie and I might not get another chance to talk with Tillie.

Matilda spread out on the sofa facing me and pulled Mama's worn quilt over her knees. Situated, she heaved a loud sigh.

I sought a way to chew over the problems brewing and cheer her up. "Haven't talked to you much since the Shields reunion last summer." Mama, a Shields before she married, had a large family up in north Oklahoma. They gathered once a year from all over the state.

"Been quite a celebration." Matilda's refusal to give me an opening meant she didn't want to discuss her life.

But years of experience had taught me sometimes it took serious talking to pull the prickliness out, and Tillie had lots of prickles.

I dug deeper and went direct. "Darling, how are *you* doing?"

"Been tough." Matilda's voice had a false lilt to it. "But we're making it—even with Frank drinking like booze is as free as water. Jennie thinks I should leave him, but no one understands how hard it is. What would I do if I left him?"

I kept silent, letting her test the walls of her own argument.

Matilda looked at me for a long minute before she rolled onto her back. "All right. All right. Frank's drinking shakes me up, sometimes. But he isn't always violent. Anyway, I can't leave him now."

I pushed my foot against the floor, setting the rocker in motion. "I know you want to stick it out, but there're times to give up on your dreams and start new ones. Maybe what happened today was a sign."

"I can't leave."

"Why not? He's a rotten husband. A rotten man. You got all of us to help you out."

"I haven't told anyone yet—but I'm pregnant."

"Again?" This was her eighth pregnancy. She was almost forty-two years old, and Frank couldn't support the family he had, much less another mouth to feed.

"My boys are all I have left. I'm protecting them. Never expected Frank to hurt Junior, though. That was lousy of him to ruin the boy's Christmas like that."

I waved off that concern. "Oh, Frank Junior's just fine. He's outside playing ball again."

"He is?" Matilda jumped up and headed toward the door. "Why that rascal!"

"Wait, dear." I caught her dress tail. "I checked, and he's back to his normal self."

She plopped back down and heaved like one more worry would break her.

“I understand how much the boys mean to you and about going through hard times.”

“I suppose you do.”

Perhaps if I shared my shameful past about my daughter, Oma Jean, Matilda might open up and release some of her heartache. I could talk about the death and leave out the part that held me hostage with guilt.

I drew a slow breath. “Been nearly eight years since Oma Jean passed on. It might help us both if I told you about that time.”

Tillie nodded and kicked off her shoes. “She died of diphtheria, as I recall. But I never heard you tell of it. Guess I was wrapped up in my own babies.”

She’d lost a baby in the anguishing year after Oma’s death.

I looked at Matilda’s face, white as bleached cotton. “Honey, you were in a hurting mess, too. Sorry I wasn’t much help to you. You of all of us understand how my heart breaks each time I think about my baby girl. Pains me to talk about it, but I’ll share if it’ll help you feel less alone.”

Matilda wrapped the faded quilt around herself as if she wanted to hide beneath it, her pale face peeking over the top. “Go ahead.”

I settled beside her on the sofa and pushed strands of hair out of my face. “Oh, dear. It was the darkest day of my life.”

My thoughts skedaddled back to almost eight years earlier when the undercurrent of tension first surfaced between Shannon and me. The uncomfortable feeling never disappeared, no matter how much laughter we shared.

Tears burned my eyes, and I scolded myself for the bleak feelings. I shivered even though I wasn’t cold. I wished Shannon and I could share stories about Oma Jean and go back to our carefree innocence. Instead, we went on living as if nothing happened. Shannon, a perceptive policeman, looked at the world through keenly trained glasses, analyzing a person's actions with precision. But he never talked about our daughter's death, though he suspected more than the fever took her.

A happy-go-lucky girl by nature, except for this nagging secret that popped up at the oddest times, I tried hard to bury that dreadful ache and pretend it didn't exist.

Oma Jean was a darling, a real blessing, and a sweet little peapod. "It happened on an early June morning."

"A week before Oma Jean's fourth birthday, her fever spiked awfully high, and I couldn't get a giggle out of her. She didn't want to get out of bed." I plastered a pleasant look on my face, as if I could smile through all that grief. No matter how many years passed, pain still lay at the bottom of my thoughts.

Matilda shoved the quilt off and stood. She paced around the room for a minute like she was recalling her own babies, contemplating how much pain she could bear at one sitting. Then she climbed back onto the ancient beige sofa and covered up again. "Go on. I want to hear."

I took a deep breath and began. "Lands above, it looked like Oma Jean had diphtheria, but I couldn't tell for sure until the doctor arrived. She was feverish, but I didn't let her know I was worried. I hugged her and assured her she'd feel better by morning. 'Here, take some aspirin,' I said. 'They're good for you.' She swallowed the pills with a bit of water, and I rocked her in my arms until she fell asleep. By the next morning, my little girl sat up in bed—nearly healed."

"That aspirin sure helped." Matilda glanced over at me.

I smiled. "Darling, I thought that wonder drug could heal anything, from a canker sore to the black plague. Why, I imagined it could even make your hair grow!"

My serious sister Tillie didn't grin. "I'm sure you don't think that now."

How could I respond to that statement? Of course, I didn't believe that now, not after what happened. "I took a washcloth, dipped it in a bowl of cool water and wiped her sweaty little face. I gave Oma Jean the miracle drug again a few hours later, and poured myself two more pills from the bottle, hoping to stave off a headache. Lordy, I didn't need to feel puny with a sick child in the house. I had too much work to do. Shannon might be walking back and forth in the other room, but nursing was my job, not his.

"Later that morning, I made Oma Jean some broth and took it to her. She looked peaked again, her eyes dulled, and she lay there without moving. My gracious, she was a sickly pale. I leaned over and asked her how my best girl was feeling? She didn't answer. My hands shook, and I hoped the diphtheria hadn't taken a turn for the worse. I nursed her for the next hour, catering to her like I knew something serious was happening, pacing the floor and praying for her health to return."

I stopped talking as I remembered. The details were as clear as if the event had happened yesterday, the pain just as intense.

"Before noon, I checked on her again. 'Honey.' I shook her slightly to rouse her. 'Honey.' She groaned and leaned over the side of the bed and vomited. As I cleaned her up, I saw the empty aspirin jar under the bed. 'Sweetie, did you take more aspirin?' She nodded and mumbled, 'Like you said, Mama, they're good for you.'

"I jumped from the side of the bed and screamed for Shannon. My heart beat fast as we rushed her to the doctor in town. I held her to my bosom for the buggy ride and felt her hot forehead, heat rising toward me in waves. She could hardly breathe. I could feel her heart speed up, and for once, I wished we had one of those highfalutin motor cars.

"'Too much aspirin,' the doctor said when I explained what happened. 'An overdose.' My mouth fell open. I didn't want to hear the words, even though I'd feared it all along. I just didn't want to hear it said about my little girl, my Oma Jean.

"The doc gave her charcoal, hoping to counteract the symptoms, but by the time we rushed from the doc's office to the hospital, she was unconscious. Sweet little Oma Jean fell into a coma."

I paused in my story, took a deep breath, and glanced over at Matilda. Scrunched up, she looked as beat down as Jennie's old sofa. She stared at me, her mouth agape. I bared my soul, hoping Matilda would open hers. But was it worth it? It ached as much as when it happened years ago, when I stood in that waiting room looking down at my little darling's flushed cheeks.

"I sat by her bed in the hospital, praying like I never prayed before. In my fair opinion, it's a miracle any baby survives in this world, how tender they are. They pumped her stomach, hoping to revive her." I paused. "She died before midnight—and my heart about died with her."

Neither of us spoke for a few seconds, and then Matilda asked, "How did Shannon take it?"

Matilda always asked the wrong questions at the wrong time. But then, I really didn't know the answer and didn't want to discuss it. Shannon and I had never talked about Oma Jean's death. He'd never brought it up, and neither had I, as if our child was a taboo subject sitting on the park bench between us.

What did Shannon think? He'd been attached to this child as much as I. During those long nights, when I sobbed for hours in self-pity, Shannon held me, a cloud of love surrounding us. He became my constant support, the one who kept me level.

Did he grieve as I did? Or did he blame me for the child's death all these years? Perhaps her demise caused the underlying rift between us. Perhaps we buried the real hurt from each other and carried on like the world was a merry-go-round at the county circus.

I tried to hold back tears, but they came fast. I covered my mouth and kept the deepest shame to myself. I wasn't ready to share that hurtful secret yet.

Guilt gnawed me in two.

We sat in quiet grief for a good long time.

Matilda's face was a picture of heartache. I'd lost my adopted daughter. But my sweet sister Till had lost precious ones, too. I felt helpless, not knowing how to alleviate the personal pain. The only way I knew to comfort was through food.

I couldn't take too much sadness at a time, so I stood, thinking of the desserts in the sunroom. "I'm hankering for some of that fruitcake. How about you?"

Matilda tipped her chin enough for me to assume she agreed. I pulled her up and put my arms around her until her spine found its strength to keep her upright. We had both experienced horrible losses.

She followed me into the sunroom, where I unwrapped that beautiful dark brown concoction and sliced two thick pieces of it.

"I don't need much," Matilda said, looking over my shoulder. "I'm full as a tick from that huge spread."

I gave her the larger piece and looked at mine. My food craving diminished. Wonder of wonders. Maybe I'd fed my shame for too long.

"If Frank were here, I might suspect this fruitcake had a little rum poured on it," I said, trying to lighten the air around us.

Matilda's eyes enlarged like she craved a brandied cake. "Are you saying you didn't pour any on it?"

I snickered. "I'm a strict Baptist and not admitting a thing."

We carried our saucers back to our seats, and I took a bite of the dark, ripe sweetness. Holy Moses, it was delightful. Melt-in-your-mouth good. "Mama's old recipe," I admitted. "Raisins, candied fruit, prunes, and pecans, all steeped in molasses. Worth all the trouble."

We ate in silence, comforting ourselves bite by bite, listening to the sounds of the boys roaring outside. My most damning secret intact.

And Till still hadn't talked.

Chapter 11

The next morning, after breakfast, the holiday spree ended. My sisters donned hairnets, tied on frilly aprons, and got to work. It wouldn't take long to return the house to normal, but it was a much quicker job if we all pitched in and helped with the cleanup.

We ran the menfolk and boys out the front door. They mentioned traveling to see the cows and horses Tommy kept on a leased piece of land south of town, then possibly heading to a horse show at someone's ranch. Annie's husband made a living as a barber, but he had an entrepreneurial spirit and regularly bartered some deal on a horse or two.

After much discussion, my sisters and I decided to take the Christmas tree down first and haul it out. Jennie retrieved the ornament box from the attic, where she stored her decorations.

"Look, here's the Santa Claus I made in the seventh grade!" Annie's voice sounded through the room as she removed an ornament from the tree. She carefully wrapped it in old newspaper and laid it in the Christmas box.

Matilda and I unwound the string of popcorn and cranberries from around the tree, goodies we'd unstring and feed to the chickens. Jennie unclipped the dozen candle clips and placed them in the box. The wax candles she set aside to use through the winter.

The tree was almost bare when Jennie brought over a chair and climbed on it. Tillie and Annie held it as she stretched out, reaching toward the silver star perched on top.

"Be careful, sis. We aren't spring chickens anymore," I reminded her.

"You might not be, but I'm as spry as I ever was." Jennie told the truth. She hadn't lost any of the energy she had since she was a rollicking lass.

"That star's been in the family since Moses left Egypt," Matilda said. "Amazing, it still shines like new."

"Oh pooh, it isn't that old." Annie took it from Jennie's hands so she could climb down. "I remember when we bought it."

Star stored safely, we dragged the bare pine tree out the back door and into the field to be chopped up later, leaving a trail of pine needles.

Back at the house, we found dusting rags and straw brooms and worked for another hour. Jennie handled putting away the Christmas décor and good dishes and festive linens. Matilda finished washing and putting away the dessert dishes and glasses scattered around. Ann dusted and wiped down the living room where most of the revelries had taken place. I swept. I enjoyed sweeping, even if the dirt stirred up my sneezing fits.

We worked for the better part of the morning, bumping into one another, joking at the amount of food consumed, and fussing over who would give out first.

I finished shaking out a rag rug, and heard Jennie hollering, "Time for dessert!"

A break couldn't have come at a better time.

***

My sisters and I congregated in the clean living room and slipped off our shoes. Grabbing pillows to support our aching backs, we heaved a collective sigh. A group of sisters congregating together made any room seem cozy. Tuckered out, Annie huffed and puffed so much I thought she might pass out right there on the living room floor.

She sank into a chair. She'd always been the sickliest among us, tiring out faster with exertion. Looking worse than I felt, despite stepping out to nurse baby Jimmy a time or two during the morning, Annie propped her feet up. The baby slept in the bedroom with the door open so we could hear him when he woke.

Jennie's dress was wrinkled and her hair slipping out of its bun, frizzing around her face. Despite her tiredness, she held out a fancy glass plate filled with assorted leftover cookies and cake—but no fruitcake.

"Saving a piece of that fancy cake for later?" I asked, thinking fruitcake fixed anything, especially tired bones. Thank goodness only a few of us liked it. Then I thought of the little girl in the shack and wished I'd left it on her doorstep.

Jennie gave me a nasty look, then smiled. "Always trying." She set down the tray and disappeared into the kitchen. She returned with a huge slice of fruitcake teetering on a saucer and held it out to me. "I'm sure we'll each gain ten pounds this holiday. Seems to happen when we get together."

"Got to make up for lost time," I said. "Eating soothes my aching bones and untangles my mind. And ten pounds wouldn't hurt you any, as scrawny as you are."

Jennie snatched the fruitcake plate from my hands. "Bless your heart, I changed my mind. I think I'll eat it myself."

"Oh pooh. Since you don't want it, I'll take it." Annie seized it from Jennie.

"You don't even like that cake," I exclaimed.

"How does anyone like this gooey potion? But I'll eat it just to spite you."

I almost grabbed it from Annie, but she spun away and sat out of reach. Balancing the plate on her lap, she took a morsel and grimaced before she spit it into her napkin. "Here, you can have it. Too sweet for me."

Before I could take a taste, Jennie spoke. "I overheard you talking about Oma Jean yesterday." She took an extra big bite of her lemon pie and mumbled, "That was a hard time for you."

"Do you ever get over it? The pain of losing a baby?" Matilda's eyes held sadness deeper than Van Gogh's. I wanted to take a giant paintbrush and paint over her anguish, but even a Renaissance masterpiece couldn't capture the depths. Unfathomable things must be experienced firsthand.

I choked on the cake. How did the conversation turn so serious? I wasn't ready. Avoiding the question, I looked out the window beyond the printed curtains embracing the thin glass. The boys played ball on the dirt road outside. Strong, clever, healthy boys. Good boys. My heart swelled with pride until I saw one on the side, not playing. I wanted to rescue him, but the child would have to face his discouragement on his own. I tossed up a quick prayer.

The wind howled, and the noise pounded through cracks in the old house. I re-entered my heartache.

How could my pain compare to Matilda's? To losing more than one child? To watching your husband mistreat your sons. But pain was pain, no matter how or when it happened.

And guilt was guilt.

"You never get over it. You never get over the loss of a child." My voice broke like glass crackling when it gets too hot. Tears pooled in my eyes. "My sweetie was three years, eleven months and twenty-one days old."

Matilda looked at me and smiled with that fragile smile, so easily broken. She understood my pain like I understood hers. Did she number the days also? Did she cover her pain with sternness instead of food?

"Oh, I went on with life," I said. "You make the beds and cook the bacon, but the ache stays. Don't matter if you gave birth or adopted, still hurts something awful." I didn't tell them I felt chewed up and spit out. Thankfully, the good Lord helped me through that time, or I wouldn't have sat there pushing Jennie's rocking chair like a steam engine.

I paused, unable to share my deepest disgrace. Wasn't sure I ever could. The baby let out a wail and Ann left the room to tend to him.

I hoped Matilda would talk about her life. It was a mystery how talking and sharing details with others released some of the pain. Jennie had been my confidant in the months after Oma Jean died.

"Some days, I don't want to raise my head or get out of bed." Matilda's voice was as empty as a tipped cup. "I feel awful guilty."

"Guilty?" That was the last emotion I thought she'd have.

"Sometimes Frank's as good a dad as any, and I can't dream of leaving him." Matilda's chin fell to her chest. "But other times, he's a downright scalawag, and the boys would be better off if I left. Guess I haven't been a good mother staying with him for so long."

"Darling," I said, "you don't have anything to feel guilty about. You've done nothing wrong by trying to make your marriage work."

Matilda's face drooped toward the floor.

"You're doing the best you can under the circumstances," I continued in my smoothest voice. "You're always taking care of your babies. No sir. A mama duck couldn't do as well. Not a better mother around than Sally Matilda Ready."

Jennie, always the wise one, set her empty plate down and moved to the sofa. She sat beside Matilda and took her hands in hers. "Bless you, dear. You've been through a lot in your life. God knows you're hurting, and I bet he understands that anger jumping to get out. He's helped you this far. Don't give up. He'll not leave you now."

Matilda started bawling.

Her cries punched me in the gut. I hated to see her so dejected about something that was not her fault. But watching her, my guilt gnawed at me and nothing could stop it.

My sin was so much worse than hers.

I gulped, afraid of what my sisters would think of me if I told them the whole truth about Oma Jean. I'd carried around the shame for so long, the bitter tendrils felt almost normal.

In my mind, I thought of Shannon and his righteous stand for good. He'd never do anything wrong, and I was certain he'd disown me if he knew what I'd done.

***

Lunch time brought the menfolk back to the house. They came in slamming doors, roaring with laughter, and claiming their bellies growled with hunger. You'd think the world revolved around them and their needs. Maybe it did.

I rushed to the kitchen to help Jennie set out cold turkey before pulling out every bit of leftover food from the icebox. Enough dessert remained covered on the back enclosure to feed an army of locusts.

Voices clamored over the noise of sandwich making.

"Someone, get out the bread!"

"Are there any pickles left?"

"Here's another jar."

"Hurry, the fellows are waiting."

"Well, they can just wait."

"Shoo, Truman, don't go sneaking in here."

"But I'm hungry."

"Guard that turkey with your life—and don't let Bobbie near it."

I laughed. The banter reminded me of when we used to visit Mama's family during the holidays. Oh, the joy of those gatherings under the shady trees with the kids running loose and the menfolk smoking pipes.

My dear family's chatter surrounded me and I'd carry that picture of togetherness when we returned home to Texas.

***

We washed and put away the never-ending dirty pile of dishes. I looked around and noticed Matilda nibbling on leftovers in the living room. Was it time for me to quit running? If I shared my disgrace, would it encourage my sister to see she'd done nothing as remorseful?

Jennie's old sofa had become our comforting space. Our resting spot. Our chatting pad. In a few days' time, we'd all return to our normal lives, so I had to speak now.

"Tillie, I've had some of that same feeling you have—guilt," I said in my quietest voice once I settled down. "My Oma Jean died of an overdose, remember?" I needed to drag out the worst thing in my life—share my awful deed and admit my sin, even knowing my sisters might never look up to me again—might never talk to me again. But then Matilda would realize she didn't need to feel guilty.

Matilda and Jennie nodded yes.

"Well, I never wanted to say this out loud, but I'll say it anyway. I left that jar of aspirin sitting right next to Oma Jean's bed," I paused to regain control of my shaky voice. "And I'll be doggone. I left it open and uncovered. Right on the end table where she could reach it."

Tears streamed down my cheeks. "I should have moved it."

Tille and Jennie's mouth fell open.

Taking a deep breath, I continued in a hurry. "She was just a wee child, and I should have known better. She saw the open bottle and swallowed those pills, thinking they were good for her. I don't know why I did it, but it's been eating me up. She died because of my carelessness." I stopped talking and swallowed the lump in my throat.

Not even Jesus could forgive a deed as serious as mine. Negligence was downright wicked.

Jennie motioned me to scoot over, and I squeezed in beside her on the sofa. She wiped my wet face with her apron. "Now, Mary Bobbie, you know better than that. Any of us might have done the same thing. You didn't intend to hurt her. And I'm sure if you'd ask, the good Lord will forgive you for being worried that day."

"You don't have anything to be ashamed of," said Matilda.

"God will have to work overtime to cover up my shame."

Oma Jean would have been eleven years old, would have been a teenager in a few years, and graduated high school after that. Now she wouldn't live to have a life because of what I did. I shuddered as grief ate at my soul. How had I lived with myself, knowing what I did? That her death was my fault.

Matilda and I scrunched scrawny Jennie between us in the middle as we hugged each other. Hugs always made a body feel better, even if they didn't solve anything.

It relieved me to know my family's opinion of me hadn't changed. They still loved me. But I wasn't sure about Shannon. My policeman hubby's thoughts might take on hard feelings if he knew my part in Oma Jean's death.

Right was right, and wrong was wrong.

Chapter 12

My sisters knew the rest of my story. After losing Oma Jean, Shannon and I took in other children, fostering when the need arose. I took several little girls to my heart, torn between wanting to find their kin and wishing they'd become adoptable. I yearned for another child to call my own, but I doubted my parenting skills after losing Oma Jean. That pain and guilt had been brain-stabbing.

Fear enveloped me. Fear I couldn't keep a child safe. Holding so many babies and then letting them go made me want to hold tighter on to my Robert. Kodak pictures of the fosters sat on my bedroom dresser, along with Oma Jean's.

I returned to Jennie's rocking chair to bring my thoughts back to reality.

My sister added her wisdom. "Bless me. Sometimes it does a body good to start over. Just pick up and move on. Make a change."

"Like Shannon and I moved to Munday after Oma Jean died?" I rocked like I had a baby in my arms. "Of course, it didn't hurt that he got a better job as Knox County undersheriff or that his family lived near there." I snickered, "Sure thing. Good times happened in Munday."

"Funny how the Lord works that way, bringing joy from heartache." Jennie shook her finger at me.

"What do you mean?" Matilda had sat quietly for several minutes. Tillie, who had gone through so much during her marriage. Giving birth to so many children. Wrangling with Frank, who couldn't hold a job and spent what he made on drinking and carousing. "I can't see much good coming out of Frank being the way he is."

Not saying I could either.

Ann piped up. "You and your boys are safe now, aren't you? Something good to say about that."

Matilda's eyes widened, as if considering the situation. She nodded.

"And you're pregnant—I heard. Maybe you'll have that baby girl we all want." Jennie could find hope in any situation, especially when it concerned Matilda. I'd influenced her well.

Those words of wisdom ruminated in our hearts until Annie and Matilda gathered their young 'uns and left to return to their own homes.

We'd had a wonderful Christmas, after all. Perhaps the right time had come to talk with Shannon and clear up this mess.

***

The next morning after breakfast, I heard Jennie piddling in the kitchen, washing up or whatever she did to keep busy. My energetic sister never tired. Our husbands and boys had left, and the house stood quiet.

I retreated to the bedroom, my fractured mind in turmoil as I sat down on the edge of the bed. The mirror above the wooden dresser reflected my sad countenance. My hair bun slipping down. My eyeglasses askew. My face pale.

I dropped my chin to my chest. Why? Why did I still feel so troubled? I'd confessed to my sisters, confessed the part I played in my daughter's death. That should have made me feel better.

But it didn't. Why? What had I forgotten?

Guilt had niggled me for years, pushed down under the skin, irritating its way to the top. I didn't want to live another eight years with the underlying uneasiness. Or worry that Shannon might find out.

"Dear Lord, please take away this pain. I didn't mean to hurt Oma Jean. You know I didn't. It was all a mistake."

Silence.

No god in heaven heard this prayer, and the pain gnawed at my innards.

I wept. Mostly, I wept for myself—for the awful sorrow inside, for the guilt I heaped upon myself. For missing my girl. Distance stretched between me and the Lord.

As I continued to pray, a nagging thought invaded my mind. Was it from God? I sat up straight and blinked, recalling words hidden so deep they hadn't surfaced in years. A detail I hadn't wanted to remember, buried at the bottom of my mind.

I remembered my last words to Oma Jean.

I had told her, "Take as many pills as you want, dear."

My breath stopped for a long second. Did I truthfully say to my little one, "Take as many pills as you want"? And I didn't return to see how many pills she took?

I pulled Mama's quilt up over my head and sobbed into the soft material. I *was* guilty. How could the Lord forgive a person like me? The more I pretended to be happy and carefree, the more I'd refused to face my sin.

Regret washed over me, and my shame lay bare.

I held my breath. Then I felt the Lord's warmth and understanding surround my heart, his words like soothing rain. *Psalm 147:5 Great is our Lord, and of great power: his understanding is infinite.*

I breathed relief as refreshing air blew into me. The good Lord understood my weakness. He saw my deed and loved me despite my failure.

My loving God forgave me and washed me clean.

But would Shannon?

***

Robert came running in from outside and I heard the screen door slam shut behind him. He ran into my room without knocking.

When he pushed his busboy cap out of his eyes, I saw sweat run down his round, eager face, right over his cute little dimples. "Mama! Mama!"

He stopped by the door when he saw me sprawled out all serious-like on the bed. But he was grinning like a possum sticking his head out of the brambles and couldn't keep quiet if a bobcat were after him.

"What's wrong, sweetie?" I sat up straight.

He stepped toward me, excitement covering his face, red tingeing his cheekbones. "I made a touchdown!"

"Hallelujah! Way to go!"

"The cousins cheered for me and named me the most valuable player of the day! Now everyone wants to play with me!"

"Gracious. Didn't I tell you? You *are* valuable. You're an important part of this big family." He let me tousle his hair in affection before he ran back outside.

Glory be, the good Lord had seen me through another day.

I had no little girl, no Oma Jean. But I had a remarkable son who brought joy to my life. I was so proud of him. Robert was the best gift I'd ever been given. He was going to be just fine.

And so was I. As long as my sweet Shannon didn't eat up all the fruitcake before I got another piece.

Chapter 13

"How about a walk through downtown?" I asked Shannon on our last evening in Hollis. "They still have the Christmas lights up. It should look fabulous." I batted my eyes at him, and he batted his back in jest.

Jones Street, where Jennie's house sat, ran a block parallel north of Broadway. Close enough to buy a bag of sweet potatoes without needing a tractor to haul them home, but far enough away to miss the clamor of Saturday morning chitchat. Friday night mayhem excluded because of the football games at the high school field. But that noise was for another season.

I loved my hometown, a place where everyone knew everyone's business, where a new family would be noticed and welcomed, and where church bells rang on Sunday morning.

I missed this place. Even though downtown was a stone's throw away, I hadn't had time for leisure with Christmas preparations and goings-on. Now, I could relax and enjoy the soothing feel of Hollis.

I washed my face and let my hair down, pulling it to the side with a ribbon. Jennie laughed at me. But even middle-aged ladies liked to look spiffy for their men. I grabbed my new blue shawl and draped it over my shoulders.

Shannon and I held hands as we walked west past the Hollis News and Wilson's Grocery, toward the Empress Theatre. Some stores were familiar, some spanking new. We schemed and rallied, contented like. How could I tell him?

We passed the City Drug Store, where I first saw Shannon.

I looked up at him. “What did you think of me when we first met?” Maybe I was fishing for a compliment or reassurance or something syrupy.

“Besides that sparkle in your eyes?” Shannon’s face glowed as he looked at me. “I thought you were the prettiest girl this side of Alabama.”

I punched him on the shoulder. “You’ve never been to Alabama. Might have been some pretty girls there.”

Shannon reared his head back and chuckled. “You’re something, you know. You always bring a smile to my face.”

Neither of us talked until we ended up on the west of town by the wagon yard. We stopped. No streetlights illuminated that section of Hollis. Only the bright golden moon shone down on us.

A cold front blew in from the north. I shivered. Shannon turned and drew me into his arms for a sweet kiss. He felt inviting and warm, so I nestled close.

We turned around and continued walking back under the storefront eaves until I spied a bench in an inconspicuous place in front of the barbershop. “What say, we sit a spell?”

Shannon nodded, and we sat where we could watch the evening fold up.

“There’s something I’d like to talk to you about.” A cold tingle ran down my spine and I pulled my shawl around my neck, wishing I’d brought a warmer wrap. “I need to confess something.”

Shannon took off his jacket and wrapped it around my shoulders, tucking it under my chin. He looked at me, his sweet eyes tender but inquisitive. “Go ahead. There’s nothing we can’t talk about, and sometimes it does a body good to get things out in the open. What's bothering you?"

I swallowed hard.

The heartache of Oma Jean had dragged my heart down. I didn't realize how fear had captured my heart in a vise. Hadn't I already confessed to my sisters and to the Lord? Wasn't that enough? Shannon's love meant life to me, and I believed he'd never forgive me if I told him the truth about our daughter's death. Should I take the chance?

"Robert asked me about Oma Jean," I said.

Shannon looked surprised. "He did? What did you tell him?"

"Nothing yet, but I reckon we'll have to talk to him soon," I paused. "Do you remember the day Oma Jean died?"

He turned to me. "I'll never forget that day. It's etched in my mind like hardened sap." His eyebrows pulled together. "We don't have to talk about it if you don't want to. Really, I'd rather just leave that day behind us."

I hem-hawed around. "No, it's important. It's been mighty hard to go on without her, even after all these years. I remember her smile and her cute dimples. She looked so much like Robert that every time I look at him, I wonder what she would have looked like today."

"She was a mite pretty little thing. She was." Shannon had been strongly attached, as much as any father, and his face revealed a sweet, tender love. He'd carry her on his shoulders and tickle the daylights out of her in the mornings. Oh, the memories that could go on all night.

"There's something I never told you before." I didn't want to resurrect past hurts if it would cause him to pull away, but I also was tired of pretending. I wanted joy to flow all the way to the bottom of my soul, and the only way I could do that was to clean up the scum at the bottom.

Shannon ran his fingers through the loose curls over my shoulder. "Some things are better left unsaid."

I pulled back, not able to talk with him so close and intimate. "I've never told you all that happened that day. It was so bad I buried it inside."

Shannon took a deep breath. He moved away from me, and I suddenly felt cold again. Either he didn't want to talk about it—or he knew my guilt. Maybe he blamed me for her death. Either way, a load of bricks weighed my heart down. I couldn't go on living with this secret sitting like a death trap between us.

My heart pounded. "I killed her."

He stared at me.

I looked down at my shoes and confessed. "I didn't know how much aspirin to give her, so I gave her too much—more than you or I would take. Not only that, but I left the jar open on the table beside her bed and she…she was able to…to take more. I told her to take more. It was my fault she died."

Silence can be a soothing balm, or it can be electrified tension. This silence felt like a bomb about to blow up. I counted the seconds.

My voice rose as I stood in front of him, waving my arms. "Don't you understand? I killed our baby girl!"

He let his breath out slowly before he hung his head in his hands. Was he angry? Would he forgive me? I wanted to move closer and reassure him I still loved him. I hadn't wanted to hurt our baby. Hadn't wanted her to die. I'd paid a heavy price all these years for holding onto my secret shame.

I'd clearly done wrong.

I could hardly contain my fear. Words came out in another hurried breath. "You must hate me now that I told you. I'll face up to child neglect. I'll go to jail if I need to. You don't have to live with me any longer. I know this is hard on you and I can move out. Live here with my sisters." I touched the top of his head.

Shannon looked up and pulled me to sit beside him. He took my hands in his. "My sweet Mary Bobbie, this is the hardest thing we've ever been through. But you don't hold all the guilt."

"What do you mean?"

He shook his head and paused before he spoke again. "You felt so horrible when she died. It broke my heart to see you cry and suffer. We never talked about it, and I thought it'd be better if you never knew. I was mistaken. We should have shared the pain."

I didn't understand what he was saying. We couldn't share a guilt that was mine alone.

"While you were in the kitchen cooking up some of your famous chicken broth, I went to check on her. That morning. It was that morning. And she looked up at me so miserable like, sweaty and clammy, with pain in her pretty brown eyes. Honey, I wanted to help her, but I didn't know how. So I gave her a sip of water and a handful of those aspirins sitting by the bed. You always said they were like miracle pills. I gave her that medicine. Don't you see? It wasn't you. It was me that caused her death."

Shocked, my body slumped as we fell into each other's arms.

Shannon sobbed. His shoulders shook, and I held onto him and sobbed right along with him. We grieved together for the first time since Oma Jean died. There's something powerful in crying together.

Our tears cried out, I whispered, "guess we both had a part in her death."

"We should have talked about this years ago."

Shannon took my hand. "Lord, we need you. Forgive us for our wrongs and help us get on with our lives the way you want."

Our grief faded as we shared our deep failure. Maybe sharing did that—helped with the pain. I had held onto the secret long enough and needed to let God heal the hurt inside me, and I guessed Shannon felt the same way.

A boulder lifted from my soul. Almost eight years was a long time to keep a secret between us, to keep a heartbreaking guilt at bay. I had planned to encourage my sisters this Christmas, but I had been the one lifted. Aspirin or no aspirin, my sweet daughter's time on earth had ended. Oma Jean, my little girl, had moved to heaven, and I pictured her twirling around in the presence of our Lord, her cute little dimples bringing a smile to his face.

I stood, not wanting the evening to end, but the hour was late. "We'll have to tell Robert about his sister, you know. At least tell him something about her."

"I think he'll want to know about her ticklish spot, and how her dimples looked just like his." Shannon smiled, and like always, a tingle went up my spine.

"This is what Christmas is about." Shannon touched my cheek in a gentle caress.

Confused, I looked up at him. "What do you mean?"

"We've been given a gift. Forgiveness. At least, it feels like a clean slate and all. Like we're starting fresh."

"I like that idea." I put my arm through his. It had taken years for me to have the courage to speak out, but God knew when I'd be ready to open up. "Being forgiven feels like plum jelly in my heart, soft and sweet and squishy." My food thoughts again.

Shannon laughed and stroked my hair. "Isn't it amazing how much God loves us, and how his love can bring two people closer together?"

His smile meant everything. Yes, we had love.

Wheat fields of love.

Shannon wrapped his arms around me, hugging me comfortingly. His large form surrounded me like a big teddy bear who wouldn't let go. "It's been hard keeping this to myself for so long. Let's not keep secrets again."

"I agree." I cozied up to him. My, oh my. My Shannon truly loved me, and I was blessed to have married such a good man.

Sharing secrets might take a lot of courage, but it makes life a heap better.

Hoped my sisters' troubles were as quick to fix.

Author's Notes

Family stories abound about my Great Aunt Bobbie's generous and loving nature.

Mary Bobbie loved to write letters, and the sisters wrote to each other almost every week. From what I understand, no one could read Bob's writing very well except Ann. I found one letter, but it appears the rest have been lost. I interviewed as many family members as I could and spent hours of research online and in Harmon County historical societies and libraries around Oklahoma. I discovered some intriguing facts.

Oma Jean's grave is in Burkburnett, Texas. It is unquestionable whose child she is because the gravestone states: "Oma Jean, daughter of Shannon and Bobbie Layne." The dates are also clear. She was born July 13, 1918 and died July 4, 1922. Some sources suggest the couple adopted two or more baby girls, all of whom died young. I have only confirmed the one baby, Oma Jean, but it's probable that Bob and Shannon fostered several more children. Family memories say Oma Jean died of diphtheria and some say of aspirin overdose. I'm suggesting both were instrumental in her death.

Mary Bobbie and Shannon's adopted son, Robert Layne, joined the Air Force and moved away. Family lore states he was a glider pilot and crashed a couple of gliders. Whatever he did, Aunt Bob was very proud of him. He lived most of his life in Kansas City.

Shannon Layne is said to have been a Texas Ranger in the early 1900s. After he and Bob married, he became the Knox County Sheriff. He got sick and died in March 1941. His gravesite is at Johnson Memorial, Knox County, Texas, where much of his family is buried. His mother, Susan Frances Howard Layne, and a Baby Boy Layne, who died the same day he was born on February 2, 1909, are also buried there. As far as I know, the baby could have been Shannon and Bob's, or one of Shannon's nephews, because other Laynes' tombstones are there.

Bobbie was fifty-three years old when she became a widow. She had a big collie dog with her when she moved back to Hollis a few years later. It was about all she had. Jennie found her a job. Aunt Bob was short and round by then and always had a joke. A happy person, she was always helping other people, especially sick people.

Tom Newberry, Jennie's husband, built a house for Bob on the empty lot next door to their house on Jones Street in Hollis. It had one bedroom, a living room, a kitchen, and a bathroom. She kept an assortment of little girl pictures on her dresser.

She never remarried but became more involved in church and her sisters' lives.

Mary Bobbie Layne passed away on January 5, 1974. She is not buried in Texas with her husband or children but is buried at Eldorado Cemetery in Oklahoma near her parents, James Tolbert and Mary Frances Shields Thomas.

My inspirational historical novels are based on true stories. I welcome feedback because there are always more facets to a story that I may have missed.

Sally Matilda

Thomas Sister #2

Four boys circa 1930s

Sally Matilda

Born January 10, 1888

Chapter 1

July 1930

I stepped out the front door of our ramshackle house where my four boys lounged on the porch steps. In the late afternoon, they looked alike, with their overalls, bare feet, and skin tanned darker than mine. Handsome, like their father. I wished we could provide more for them, but we didn't own much except this shack in the far southwest corner of Oklahoma.

I hoped the '30s would usher in good luck and a better life for my family. At almost forty-two years old, I hankered for some quiet living in our farmhouse just outside my hometown of Hollis. But that was unlikely to happen. Not until the man I'd chosen for a husband came to his senses.

I yelled at my second-born, "Thomas, go fetch me a bucket of water!"

"Ah, Ma." Thomas whined like a champ. "It's Junior's turn."

Frank Junior, my youngest at eight years old, sat on the steps and looked up at me with his sweet, compelling grin. My baby boy hardly ever did anything wrong—if you know what I mean. Fights were his siblings' fault, even though he was prone to pick on his big brothers. His doleful eyes pleaded with me as he stroked our hound dog, even though it probably *was* his turn to fetch the water.

I returned my gaze to Thomas and rubbed my belly. My middle stuck out so far, I couldn't move faster than a snail. I didn't want to fetch the water myself. "Confounded, son. I need water to fix supper. Not to mention your pa'll be home sometime tonight, and I bet he'll want a glass of cool water."

"Bettin' he'll be wantin' whiskey instead of water," Thomas muttered.

I lowered my chin and lifted my eyebrows at him with a you-better-do-as-I-say mother's stare. Thomas ducked and slithered off.

I leaned against the doorframe. After so many pregnancies, I should've been accustomed to feeling huge as a mama bear, but each drew out a little more of my irritation. Irritation aimed at an old man who wouldn't take care of the young 'uns he already had.

Howard, my oldest, inched to the side of the long, wooden porch. I knew what he was doing—sneaking off to see a girl in town. Mattie Neal, I suspected. He'd had his hair cut by my brother-law, Tommy Akin, taken his weekly bath without arguing, and been gone almost every Friday night for the past month.

I stepped to the porch rail. "Howard, you get home before supper, you hear? Don't need you getting in trouble with those drunken hooligans stirring the town."

"Yes, ma'am." He took off toward the road.

"And don't stay out late! That'll get you in more trouble than a can of centipedes."

I'd taught the boys manners somewhere along the way. They knew not to talk back. Even at my age and in my condition, I could out-wrestle any of them, or at least I'd convinced them I could. Fortunately, they hadn't tested me in a while. "And if you see your pa, remind him to get home early for supper," I hollered after him.

Howard ran toward the dirt road, almost bumping into a fence post. That boy was as tenacious and headstrong as me. He'd be who he would be. And I would be, too.

Thomas lugged that big bucket of water through the backdoor and slapped it down on the kitchen counter.

I hugged him right nicely. "You've always been a good son."

He hugged me back. Of all my boys, he had the softest heart. I prayed it continued to grow and bless his future wife.

When I released him, he ran off to join his brothers.

I flattened my apron over my belly. The tiny one kicked, just enough to let me know she'd be a lively one. My sisters claimed it was presumptuous, but I just knew I carried a baby girl.

Boys were prevalent in our family and the only ones who thrived. But I desperately wanted a baby girl. I wanted her more than anything else in the world. More than running water. More than a slice of cold watermelon on a hot summer day. More than candy from the Galbraith Candy Kitchen in town.

I wanted a daughter, and that was just what I was going to have, sure as shootin' and the good Lord willing. And if I had anything to do with it, the good Lord *would* be willing. A baby girl who would share my load and understand my heartaches like no son ever could.

But females never fared well in the Ready household.

Never had.

Chapter 2

Whoever in blazes named me Sally Matilda Thomas had no inkling of my personality. Never had been a Sally nor a Matilda. Mama learned right early how obstinate I was and agreed to shorten my name to Till, though my sisters didn't always go along.

It took years to wake up to the fact that most of my difficulties were by my own doing. Like jumping off the horse before it halted or traipsing out after midnight to meet my honey. After years of trouble, I was dragged into believing in Jesus, of all things. Through trying times, I had blind faith he'd be there when I needed him. I raised my boys the same.

Backing into the house, I watched through the window as Howard disappeared down the dusty road and Thomas sauntered with the boys toward the barn.

The land cottoned to splendor in the evenings when I had time to gaze on it. Beauty momentarily snatched my day. A covey of quail squawked in the distance. The golden sunset lit the wide-open prairie for miles, streaking it with a blaze of orange and purple water paint. My heart thumped at the magnificent sky reminding me of the Creator. The One molding my baby girl.

I pulled in a deep breath and returned my attention to my boys. They were all good-looking and smart. Someday they'd turn girls' heads. Seemed like Howard already had.

Before long, I'd be allowed to trim the younger ones' straggly hair without roping them to a chair with promises of a treat. Nor have to wrestle them into the tin tub or scold them to wash behind their ears. They were all growing up faster than Tommy's new colt.

I rubbed my belly. Caring for the boys was my fate until some sweet girl came along, won their hearts, and took over the job of settling them down. Boys. The male gender who took us girls by surprise.

I'd known who I belonged to before I outgrew my first brassiere—Franklin M. Harris Ready, my high school sweetheart. Frank and I made a handsome couple. Him, the goodlooking, strong football star, and me, the Hollis high school football queen. Puppy love, my sisters insisted, but passion sparked every time we got together. We drank and danced. His kisses were sweeter than moonshine on a Saturday night, and I acted like a fool in love.

I should have guessed our life would end up cock-eyed. The menfolk in his family were known for their drinking and revelry. Not all the Readys were depraved. However, Frank's daddy served as Harmon County Clerk for years. He was also a Mason and a member of the Odd Fellows Lodge. That spoke for something. And Frank's mama, Lizzie, would do anything for me. But they didn't pass on their sense of duty to the community.

Filling a pitcher with fresh water, I set to prepping dinner on my own. I loved my boys, but girls were more useful around the house. They could help me do the laundry and cleaning, tend to the younger children, and stir the pot. Lorene, my first daughter, had brought charm to my life, and I knew the next, little Mary growing in my belly, would be just like her big sister someday. Wished it could have happened. Wished for more kindness in our home, too, but wishing couldn't change the past and who I'd married.

Only girls could change sourdough into sweet rolls.

Chapter 3

Steam stifled the kitchen the next evening, not only from the boiling chicken broth but from the hot steam billowing from my mind. Frank hadn't come home at a decent hour for days, out carousing almost every night.

It took the better part of the afternoon to yank the feathers off, clean, gut, and cut up the chicken. The house smelled like a downtown café, which would have been welcoming if Frank ever ate with us.

I finished rolling out the dumplings and returned the flour jar to its place beside the tin box of coins I'd saved up. I patted my swollen belly, trying to calm my unborn child. If I had more pennies in the can, I'd place a bet on us having a girl over him making it home before supper was ready.

The wind whistled through the tin rooftop and sweat gathered on my forehead. Darn dry summer. Not a raindrop in the sky. I dropped the dumplings into the broth, added a little salt, and waited a few minutes before dishing up chicken and dumplings for my four hungry boys.

After we prayed, they ate like starving urchins. I finished my supper at a more modest pace, then gathered the empty bowls and washed the dishes.

The front door burst open, and tension ran through the air.

"Supper was an hour ago." I spit out the words.

He ignored me and sniffed. "Chicken? We can't afford chicken. What do you think this is? Christmas? Or did somebody die?"

"What do you expect me to feed the boys? Cornbread and buttermilk every day?" I gripped the edge of the drainboard.

"Don't get on your high horse." His voice rose with each syllable. "If not for me, we wouldn't have had that steer we butchered last winter."

"It's all ate up. And if not for you squandering money, we'd own a decent house and be able to milk our own cow." I raised my voice to match his. "You went and lost all that money down at the gambling joint, didn't you?" I put my hands on my hips.

"I'll get that money back and then some. You'll see."

I couldn't hold in my frustration. "You keep losing money, not gaining any. How's that working out?" I'd never been timid, and often spoke before it was wise to do so.

The boys stood silent just beyond the kitchen, looking down at the broken slats on the floor, out the cracked window, anywhere except at Frank and me. They were never quiet when their pa was gone, whooping and carrying on like normal kids, relaxing and laughing at life. But when he entered the room, they clammed up.

Frank plopped down at the dining room table. "You spend every red cent I get." His words grated like sandpaper.

My temper boiled over. It wasn't true. I did my best to make pennies last for weeks, hoarding food and wearing clothes fit for rags. "Hogwash. If you'd lay off drinking and stay home once in a while instead of running around, we might make do."

"What I do ain't none of your business, woman!" He shouted with the same voice I'd heard his father use.

My irritation rose something awful during our fights. It was difficult to control my temper, but better than lying low and taking it. I'd tried hard to stay quiet and be submissive when we first married, but it hadn't lasted long. Not after the misfortunes we'd had. Nope, I'd had enough. "You're a fool," I said sternly.

"Blasted, woman!" Frank jumped up and strode to the kitchen cupboard and yanked it open. He reached for my tin can loaded with the coins I'd stashed.

I'd started taking in sewing to earn funds for clothes and food for the boys who ate like racehorses. They'd nearly outgrown every stitch of clothing in the house. We barely had enough money for grits, much less new shoes. Even Howard, at eighteen, hadn't reached his full height. I passed down the boys' britches, but there was never enough thread left to make it further than the next boy.

"Don't you dare touch that money! We need it." I ran toward Frank, determined to stop him. "We need it for the new baby!"

He caught my arm and shoved me to the floor.

I landed on my rump, grating against the rough wooden slats. I bit my tongue to hold back the tears, refusing to let Frank see me cry.

Howard, my protective boy, jumped to my side, reached down, and pulled me to my feet. Shielding me, he stepped toward his daddy. He was nearly as tall as Frank, but a fair bit slimmer. "What're you doing? You shouldn't be hitting on Ma. She's in the family way."

"Don't you think I know that?"

"She earned that money. You can't take it from her."

Frank took a step toward our eldest son. "Says who?"

Howard stepped backward. His eyes wary. He'd seen his pa's temper before. Many times.

Quick as a rabid dog, Frank reared back his arm.

"No!" I screamed.

Frank punched Howard in the face. "You ain't the boss of this family, rat."

The younger boys melted into the wall, their eyes wide in alarm. Fear sparked the air like dry tinder about to burst into flames. I backed up, too.

I wanted to shout at Frank to act decent and think about what he was doing to his family. But I clamped my mouth shut. Words would do no good when whiskey was talking.

Frank frowned as he poured the coins into his hand, jiggled the money, and shoved Howard out of the way. He clomped out the front door. With all my hard-earned pennies, he might not come home till early morning—if then.

I grabbed a wet rag and wiped the blood off Howard's handsome, baby-smooth face. I met his gaze. The hatred I saw in his eyes turned my blood colder than a winter storm.

"Don't worry, son. You might have a black eye for a few days, but it'll go away."

He pulled away from me. "Why do you let him act like that?"

Wishing to protect the boys from the cold-heartedness of their father, I rattled my brain for an explanation. "He wasn't always like this. Nasty, I mean. He's been on a rampage lately, but he'll get over it once things settle down."

Frank's drinking had gotten worse after some troubling years, but those times were hard to talk about. Many things were hard to talk about, but I had to try.

"He cares, you know, even if he doesn't show it."

Howard's expression told me he didn't believe a word I said. His eyes looked so much like Frank's it nearly took my breath away. *Lord, don't let him turn out mean-spirited like his pa.*

Frank had a habit of coming home drunk and dragging himself through the front door, vicious as a bull. He laid into the boys many a night, which seemed to make them ornerier, more distant and fearful.

When we married, I was unaware Frank was a habitual gambler. Everything was business with him, no bull—or so he said. I should've known something was up since he often traveled around the county and would bring home an old milk cow or sow pig he won somewhere. Dollars came and went with the howling prairie wind.

We never had much money. Frank drank what was in his pocket and gambled away everything else before coming home. I wanted to leave Frank, but he always came back with his sweet-talking words. He fawned over me, gave me puppy dog eyes, and kissed me soundly. Lately, I'd begun to doubt his smooth ways.

I paused to re-wet the rag for Howard and glanced out the kitchen window, staring into the darkness. What did I see in Frank? Had he ever truly loved me?

I wrung the water from the rag.

I held out hope Frank could become a decent husband and father. Even after years of unanswered prayers and begging him to change, I still loved him. I just hated his drinking and hated him losing money at the tables. I hated his rants when he lost. When he'd come home and rouse the kids and me out of bed in the middle of the night. He'd carry on like a madman, as if the law were after him. Some nights, I wished the law *was* after him.

But not until after my baby girl was born.

Chapter 4

Down on my hands and knees, I shoved the patchwork quilts out of the way.

"Thomas? Help me tug this box out from under the bed." I tried to catch the edge, but my belly prevented it.

"Ma, I'll get it." My boy was a lot stronger than he looked. It took no time for him to slide the box out.

I held my breath and opened the trunk, pulling out a small stack of baby boy clothes. Howard laughed at the tiny stitches and the pint-size britches that wouldn't fit on his enormous feet. I passed around a frilly white bonnet and Thomas tried it on. We laughed so much I wished I had a Kodak camera to capture the four boys grinning like happy hound dogs.

As I showed the items to the boys, I recalled something special about each one as a baby.

"Frank Junior, you used to crawl into my bed every night until I scolded you. And Billy, you'd sneak your pet chicken into the house and cuddle with it."

The boys laughed.

"Thomas. you sucked your thumb until you were almost three. And Howard, I remember you walking around wearing your daddy's cowboy hat." I ruffled his hair.

Howard looked pitiful with his shiner turning a deep green.

My, my, how my boys had grown.

At the bottom of the trunk were the baby-girl clothes I'd made with each pregnancy. I clasped a tiny pink pinafore that had lace flowing down the front. I held it up. "Looky here, boys. Do you think we'll have enough pretty clothes for the new baby girl?"

Howard moved to the side of the bed. "I think there's enough to spoil a girl something awful."

I brushed off the sad, sweet memories and looked at my soft-hearted Thomas. Tears slid down his cheeks, and my eyes misted over. "You thinking about your sisters?"

He nodded, his eyes not leaving my face.

"Well, we're going to have another girl soon." I smiled as Billy and Frank Junior gathered closer, staring at the box that held our family's keepsakes. A locket Frank gave me while we were dating. An oval frame that held our black and white wedding picture. A tiny tin cup used by each of my babies.

Billy's eyes narrowed as if he were figuring out a math problem. "What will you do if this baby's a boy?" A clump of hair fell in his eyes, and he tossed it back.

"Shush yourself up. It won't be a boy," I said, even though I'd love the boy if it was. "It'll be a girl, sure as shootin'."

The baby items lay scattered around me. "See this? Isn't it the softest blanket ever made? Needs mending in places." I ran my fingers over the faded pink cotton fabric and held it out. The soft material had touched each of my little lost loved ones.

The boys leaned away, as I knew they would.

Billy laughed and shook his head. "That's girlie stuff. We can't help you with that."

"You're right, son." I held back a snicker. "But in six weeks or so, we're going to have the prettiest girl in the county."

Somehow, looking forward to a new baby in the home helped lighten the mood, even for the male members of the household. My boys would never admit it, but they wanted another little sister as much as I wanted another daughter.

One by one, the boys slipped off to the attic loft and left me alone, knowing I needed time by myself.

I laid out the baby clothes to wash, making several piles. Then I prepared a spot for the infant beside my bed, a mat covered with a sheet and the pink-colored blanket.

I sat down and took a deep breath, all my energy sapped by the little one inside me. I had to be strong.

Tall, stern, and statuesque, I should have been the oldest of my five sisters instead of Mary Bobbie, who was sweet and jovial. I had the air for it. Bob was an easy-going, plump, fun-loving pushover. I missed her something fierce after she married and moved south across the Red River to Texas. She'd always supported me, even when I slipped off on some tomfoolery.

I wasn't like her at all. Stubborn and outspoken, I liked things my way. Maybe that was why Frank and I had so many tussles. However, as I grew older, I caught myself getting more sentimental.

My heart ached as I stared at the pink blanket. I closed my eyes and thought of those two lost girls. Ten years disappeared, and I remembered my eight-year-old Lorene lying on the same sick bed as her three-year-old sister, Mary, who held onto the pink blanket as if it could tether her soul to the earth.

My two little girls caught diphtheria, and I nursed them for days, wiping their pale foreheads with cold washcloths and spoon feeding them chicken broth. The croup caused their throats to swell, so they couldn't eat much. No matter what I did or how hard I prayed or how long I stayed by their sides forcing liquid into their mouths, they only got worse.

Fear like I'd never known before crept into our house and lodged in my heart.

Lorene, my eldest, had the prettiest soft hazel eyes. She loved to help me and could already make a mean pan of buttermilk cornbread. The big sister of the clan, she happily tended to her chores and calmed the younger ones, like when a coon got in the house or thunder made them quiver.

My heart turned somersaults when her breath stopped at just eight years old. A million tears rolled down my face as I cleaned her up, brushed her hair, and slipped on her only dress. Frank, his face stoic, picked up her small, wrapped body and carted her into the undertaker.

The night after Lorene's funeral, Frank stoked the fire. He sat next to it, staring into the flames, not speaking a word. Maybe I should have comforted him, worried about him, but I was too set on saving my other baby girl.

I sat at Mary's bedside and prayed to high heaven for her to get well. Washed her face. Sang her favorite songs. Kissed her forehead. Tucked the pink blanket around her, unable to bear losing a second child.

Mary Alice Ready had been born a spirited tot. She had a smattering of freckles and was as spunky as her mama. I understood why my pa called me hotheaded because here was one who took after me.

It seemed like little Mary couldn't get over the loss of her big sister. She moaned and refused to eat. Three days later, she went to be with Lorene. My heart felt like lead, heavy with grief, and I cried every last tear out of me.

With dust pneumonia, diphtheria, and the Spanish flu hitting hundreds of homes, young ones had a hard time surviving in Oklahoma. For the first time, I understood the pain mothers carried after losing their children. It took a strong woman to survive a birthing, but it required a stronger woman to keep going after losing a child. Only tough women functioned after losing their sweet babies.

I didn't want to be a tough woman anymore.

Mary's funeral at Fairmont brought out dozens of the two thousand people in the small town and the surrounding area. The flowers I'd placed on Lorene's gravesite three days before had dried. The sight of the fresh dirt around both graves was too much for me, too much for my body. My knees gave out. Frank held me up and kept me steady, kept me from keeling right into that hole with my baby girls.

Beside myself with grief, my faith plummeted to the ground. What did I do that was so bad for God to take my daughters? My heart had latched onto them like candy glue. Losing them felt like part of my soul was torn asunder.

I took to my bed afterward, even as Howard, my eldest boy, started coughing in the next room. Unable to handle it, I couldn't watch another part of me die. I guess Frank couldn't handle it either. He disappeared for the next three days. Someone reported seeing him in town hanging onto a bar stool.

My sisters, Jennie and Annie, nursed me like a baby pup. They took care of the kids and tended to Howard. Bless them. I don't know what I would've done without them traipsing in and out of the house. I could barely put my feet to the floor.

They continued to come when they could. Jennie, the only one of my sisters who knew how to operate an automated coach, drove her husband's roadster out to our shack. They came when Frank wasn't around because they didn't care much for my man. The feeling was mutual. He didn't care much for them either.

Jennie brought me a sweet apple pie and her talkative ways lifted me up. Annie, although the whiny sort, was always there if I needed her. She made lemonade, which refreshed me more than iced water would have. I had the best sisters in the world. Susie might have visited from the next county over, but I suspected her situation was worse than mine, if rumors about her hubby were true. And Mary Bobbie lived way down south in Texas.

Howard survived the diphtheria episode with gusto, although he gave us a scare when he fell a few days later and broke his arm diving from the housetop. I declare, sometimes boys don't have the sense God gave a turnip.

Then God gave us our seventh child, another girl, but I couldn't think of her right then. Thinking about the past wouldn't help me.

I rubbed my belly. This was my eighth pregnancy. I grew impatient, gritted my teeth and waited. Pregnancies were no roll in the hay, believe you me. I'd already let Jennie know I'd need her help when the time came. We couldn't afford a doctor by any means, not with Frank snatching up any money I managed to save.

I'd always been a first-rate seamstress, sewing for my four sisters and my nephews. Not a one of them had birthed a girl yet, and I was determined to have the first daughter to survive to adulthood. She'd be the best dressed little gal in the southwest.

After giving birth to so many children, I expected a comfortable confinement with my eighth, but I wasn't graced with it. Only the hope of a daughter sustained me through the hot, sticky summer.

I rolled over and stared at Frank's empty side of the bed. This would be the last child. My last baby.

Chapter 5

Frank got home in the early hours of Saturday morning and slung his arms over me in our old feather bed. I pulled the neck of my worn nightgown tight and pushed him away. Two seconds later, he turned over and began to snore.

He woke up midday, groggy and hungover. Folds and puckers creased his once-handsome face, his graying hair wilder than the boys. He stumbled toward me, and I could feel his whiskers and foul breath on my neck. I pushed him back.

He sat down at the table. “Honey pie, I’m sorry about last night. I get crazy when I drink too much. You know that.” His smooth voice tried to sway me to forgive him. The only good part about his drinking was the fawning the next morning. Usually a sucker for it, my nerves rattled too much to extend much grace.

I kept my mouth closed as I poured a cup of coffee and set a plate of fried eggs along with a slice of bacon in front of him.

The boys had already eaten, done their chores, and come back inside. They watched their pa in silence as he scarfed down the choice slice of meat saved for him.

Frank grabbed another biscuit from the cast-iron skillet and loaded it with homemade plum preserves. “I’m going over to Wellington with some buddies today.”

"Heard about the fair. Half the county will be there." I imagined packing a picnic lunch, loading the wagon, and trailing the fast motor cars out of town as we traveled through the countryside to the outdoor fair. "Maybe me and the boys can go with you."

The boys looked at Frank like baby heifers hoping for a carrot.

"Nah, I'm going to watch the bull riding and cow poking. You ain't interested in those shenanigans. Best you stay here."

Why had I bothered to get my hopes up? Frank hardly ever took us anywhere anymore.

"See ya sometime tomorrow." He pecked my cheek and headed out the door.

Blasted all. Seemed like every weekend Frank and his buddies found something to do. Usually, they went hunting. Our rural area abounded in deer, turkey, and quail. In fact, hunting was so popular in Harmon County, men constantly bragged about their kills.

The boys' faces held the marks of rejection too. When they were little, Howard and Thomas begged to go hunting with Frank. They wanted their pa to take them fishing or wandering through the horse shows, or anywhere, but they'd quit asking years ago.

Frank guarded his gun like gold. Even without one, the boys learned to set traps and occasionally brought home jackrabbits for me to fry up or bake in gravy. They didn't think I knew about all the times they'd snuck into town or run off and gone hunting with their friends. I didn't mind the older boys going as long as they let me know, so I wouldn't stay up all night worrying. But now, they often disappeared without telling. Fear gripped me. I was losing control of my good boys, and Frank didn't see how his absence led to their recklessness. Maybe he didn't care.

When Frank went hunting, he might bring home fresh meat to feed a passel of hungry, growing boys. I didn't complain too much when he showed up dragging a dead deer. But Frank would bring home nothing but empty pockets after gambling on the bull riders at the rodeo.

As I cleaned up breakfast, the boys headed out. My belly bumped the hard edge of the farm sink and the baby pushed back. It wouldn't be long before she'd have her first bath here.

Feeling the baby's movements caused my thoughts to drift back four years to when I gave birth to my seventh child. She was born at home like the rest of them. Since we couldn't afford a doctor, my sister Jennie helped me along. She seemed to know something about everything and made an excellent midwife.

I was delighted to give birth to another girl, even if it couldn't fill the hole Lorene and Mary left.

My third daughter, Annie Sue Ready, was born in 1926, six years after I lost my two girls. She came out a blond-headed kewpie doll, and the boys and I adored her. Such a good little darling, plump as a fat hen, spoiled as a rotten egg. She toted around that worn pink blanket I'd I almost boiled to pieces in case any germs stuck around.

Annie couldn't whimper without a big brother picking her up and rocking her to sleep. Frank Junior, only a tot himself, was utterly smitten with her.

I had high hopes for my little Annie. I dreamed of her helping me with spring cleaning, teaching her how to make beef stew, and watching her reach puberty, then develop into a fine young woman.

My dreams passed away a year later.

She died quick like.

Simply stopped breathing.

No one could tell me why. Probably dust pneumonia, like Doc said had overtaken so many other babies that year. The fine powder filled the little ones' lungs, affecting their breathing. No getting away from it.

Water dripped from the plate I held mid-air. Grief came in waves. One day I could cope, and the next I cried like a newborn.

I drew in a painful breath. Every time I thought about my three daughters, a biting pain jutted into me. My hands shook as I dried the plate. Why did they have to die? Could I have done anything differently?

Their deaths left a hole inside me as big as Kansas. The emptiness threatened to suffocate me.

Frank didn't understand.

No one understood.

I slid the plate atop the others in the cupboard. My belief in Jesus was as chipped as our mismatched dishes. How could he have allowed my girls to be taken from me? I may have had a lousy home life, but until Annie died, I'd always believed he'd see me through.

I'd wondered if it was a punishment for staying with Frank. After Annie's death, I'd gone to stay with Jennie for a few days before I recovered enough to wander back home. Even if it was punishment, my boys needed me.

Chapter 6

Since Annie's death, I hadn't stepped foot in church, not once. No one seemed to notice except my sisters, since I seldom attended anyway.

Yet, deep into this pregnancy, I couldn't help but think about Jesus again. I was tired of being mad at him and wanted his blessing for this new baby. If I got right with him, maybe God would take notice and help me. He could save this latest one if he'd a mind to.

On Sunday morning, I cleaned my good wraparound cotton dress, mended the torn hem, and curled my hair. All four boys came up with quick excuses to not go with me. I didn't have the energy to fuss with them, so I walked the mile into town by myself.

Not intimidated by the three-story brick United Methodist Church, I hauled myself up the tall stairs and slid in beside Jennie on the third row. She leaned over and gave me a big hug. My husband's family were charter members of the church, and Frank didn't mind if I attended as long as I didn't ask him to go. He didn't think church was necessary.

The sanctuary was crowded. Friendly faces turned my way, and folks in crisp dresses and flapper hats, sporting fancy hairdos and red lipstick, smiled at me. I felt shabby in my worn clothes with no makeup. In my younger days, I'd endeavored to look stylish. What had happened to me? How could I have let myself go?

The congregation began to sing the old hymns I remembered from long ago. My eyes burned as I recalled Mama's sweet voice singing *Have Faith in God*. The song reminded me of how she'd always listened to me. Always been there for me.

Fresh sorrow hit me in the gut. Sadness dug so deep I squirmed and clenched my teeth to keep the sniffles at bay. Another song began, and I could no longer hold in my pain. I slipped out of the pew, down the aisle, and out the doors. On the church steps, I leaned against one of the stately columns and let the tears flow.

Living with a man who disregarded me and ignored my needs could be trying. I'd tried my best but the death of my babies about did me in. I missed my mama. She'd know how to help me through. Why did she have to die like my girls?

Someone tapped my shoulder, startling me. I swiped my face and forced a smile before turning to find Harry Payne, an old suitor. Before birthing seven kids and wrestling with a drunkard every night, I'd been a looker. Had lots of beaus even if Frank was the only one I had eyes for. I'd thought our love could move mountains, but I certainly hadn't seen a mountain moved yet. Still, I prayed Frank would come around and start the climb.

"Well, Miss Tillie." Harry squeezed my shoulder. "It's good to see you. Haven't seen you around in a coon's age. A couple years, I reckon."

Harry had done well for himself in Harmon County, his family buying up land east of town while it was still part of Greer County. He'd married an outsider, Linnie, a girl from up north near Mangum.

"Good to see you, too." I wiped my cheeks with the back of my hand and glanced from his horn-buttoned waistcoat up to his kind, blue eyes. Why had I not taken after Harry when we were teens? A subtle spark had always existed between us, even though I tried to ignore it. His strong, tanned face reflected honesty and compassion, traits I seldom saw in Frank.

I asked the first thing that popped into my mind. "Where's your wife?'

He looked away down the road. "She's under the weather today."

"Heard you have a few kids now. What, three or four?" I tucked a stray curl into the bun at the back of my neck.

Harry had always been kind when he saw me. "Four, and they're doing right well." He glanced at my large middle, which couldn't be hidden under my wrap-around dress if I tried. "See you're having another baby. Sorry about the last one. Must be hard to lose young 'uns like that."

Tears blurred my vision. A rejected suitor cared more about me than my own husband. Frank hadn't shed a tear when we'd buried Annie, nor had he mentioned her since. The pain ate at my insides because no one wanted to talk about it. "Losing Annie was like losing my right arm. Got a mite depressed and didn't want to live after that." I don't know what caused me to confess to Harry, of all people, that the baby's death brought such devastating melancholy.

Baring my soul right there on the front steps of the Hollis Methodist Church, I stepped back into the shade of the church columns.

Harry followed, getting closer than I felt comfortable with. I resisted being drawn to him. He seemed concerned more about my well-being than anything untoward. Our conversation rambled on like we were old friends catching up.

The church doors opened, and the preacher's wife exited the building. She glanced our way. Why her? I ducked my head as if I'd done something wrong, thinking of all the people who could see us together.

"I need to go." I turned to leave.

Harry laid his hand on my shoulder. "Let me know if you need anything. Anything."

I held my breath. His kindness seemed like rose petals thrown my way. I didn't want to crush them, but I couldn't accept that kind of caring. "I'm fine, sir, just fine." I shook off his hand and looked around. The preacher's wife and her friends stared at me.

Anxious to get home, I ran down the steps.

How could I have unloaded my sorrows to an upright gentleman like Harry—or to any person, for that matter? In truth, I didn't want anyone to witness tears streaming down my face.

I lifted my chin and walked north down Second Street. I passed the newly built courthouse and the old high school where Frank had played football for the Hollis Tigers. I recalled flirting with him enough to embarrass a hooker. That seemed a lifetime ago.

A motor carriage roared past, and I scurried toward the side. Dirt grew and dissipated as the car disappeared down the road. I looked up and down the street to make sure nothing else was coming, but the shopping district was dead quiet on a Sunday morning.

After I got beyond the small houses at the edge of town, I let my back curl forward and moved my arm to support my belly.

Guilt weighed on my shoulders for talking more to Harry, a married man, than I had to Frank in months. Not that he was around much. Frank didn't like me speaking to men if I could avoid it. But I had to admit, it felt nice to talk with someone who wanted to hear my burdens.

My shoes scuffed against the packed dirt road.

I could leave Frank. My heart hurt deep enough to walk away, but I felt compelled to stick to my commitment. We still had four boys to raise and I couldn't support them on my own. And I wasn't about to let Frank keep them and teach them his ways. They'd be in jail before they turned war age.

I'd never be able to hold my head up in town if I walked out on Frank. I'd be all alone. And what would my family say? No one left their husband. At least no decent, law-abiding pregnant lady.

Chapter 7

The mile-long walk home from church felt like ten, and I still had a half a mile to go, which at this rate might as well have been another ten miles.

Feet aching, I plopped on the ground and leaned against a cottonwood tree sprouting near a fence post. Shade was mighty hard to come by on these lonesome roads. You wouldn't know the Red River was only eight miles south with all this dryness around. Springtime had skipped us this year. The only water nearby was the Richardson's watering hole, and their cows had been wallowing in it. Even the windmills had stopped spinning, the wind rare these days.

Maybe it hadn't been the best idea to walk to town this late in my pregnancy. I closed my eyes and let my body rest, praying the good Lord would send a breeze.

I pushed away thoughts of leaving Frank. Heavens, I still had a baby girl to deliver.

I loved our four boys. But I hankered for a sweet little girl to sit beside me again. It tickled me to think of a new baby to hold and dress up, of fine baby hair I could pull into a ribbon, and the way I could teach her how to cook and embroider handkerchiefs. I hoped the birthing would be soon. The last weeks were the hardest, especially with this hot dust blowing in circles.

My sister Jennie suggested I name the baby Elizabeth, but I determined to name her Bess.

Bess Ready.

***

An engine whined. Dust blossomed on the road coming from town. A roadster zoomed down the packed dirt road. As it neared, it braked hard, stirring up a dust bunny big enough to form a cloud.

I covered my face and didn't move until it settled.

Tom Newberry, Jennie's husband, cut the engine.

As if I'd conjured her, my sister got out, walked over, and sat in the red dirt beside me in her fancy purple-print Sunday dress. She removed her gloves and took off her hat, fanning herself with it. "I thought you'd stay until the church service ended," she said. "They're having a potluck under the awning."

"Didn't mean to worry you none." I looked down at the stack of rocks at my feet and the patch of Indian blanket flowers nearby.. "I got sad thinking about Mama and my baby girls."

She leaned her head near mine. "We can't change the past."

"I know, but not sure I can go on. I'm about ready to lie down and roll over dead, what with Frank acting the way he does, and trying to keep track of four errant boys. Besides, I'm too blasted old to be living through another pregnancy."

Jennie dabbed her sweaty face with her glove. "Moping over loved ones is like standing outside in a dust storm. It'll blow you to pieces if you don't take cover."

"Well, as far as I can see, there's no cover for me. There never has been."

"Don't say that. You can't give up." Jennie put her hand under my chin and turned my face toward her. Maybe she should have been the oldest sister instead of Bobbie, what with the way she took care of the rest of us. "You got a lot to live for, and you can't do it groveling in the dirt like this."

I turned my head away from her. "A woman's got a right to grovel once in a while, doesn't she?"

"Not if she intends to stay there. Bless you, darling, but if you don't like the way things are, then do something about it," Jennie paused. "Want me to send Tom out to talk to Frank again?"

Tom sat in the driver's seat of his fancy motor car with his hat pulled down over his eyes, probably napping.

I shook my head. It would only make things worse. "A woman can only take so much till she can't stand up any longer." I looked over the flat horizon that stretched for miles. Nothing to see. Nothing to feel. Empty like me. "Don't know what to do. Seems like I'm trapped, and making a fuss don't help anyone."

"You're a strong woman, Miss Tillie. You couldn't have made it this far without being strong. I know you don't yearn to talk to Jesus, but he's never left you. If you trust him, he'll help you out."

"I don't see it."

"There's always a way. The good Lord'll see to that, and remember, your sisters are always here when you need us."

I hugged her.

For the next few minutes, we chatted about life and the unexpected places it had taken us. Bobbie adopting babies. Susie moving from town to town around the country. The biggest loss in Ann's life. Even Jennie and I had our share of snags. Jennie, wiser than me, tried to help me see the positive in a bad situation.

"You'll see," she said. "Everything has a silver lining."

Tom stirred. "Hurry up, girls. This ain't no picnic."

Jennie got up and dusted herself off. She turned and offered her hand to help me to my feet. "Let's get you home."

I heaved myself up. Tom started the engine, and Jennie slid into the front seat beside him while I climbed into the back.

"Till, are you doing all right?" Tom yelled over the clamor of the motor. "You can't be wandering around alone in your condition. It isn't safe. I'll give you a ride anytime."

"I'm all right. Appreciate you coming to check on me."

Jennie turned around. "I can cook a roast tomorrow if you want to come by for supper. There'll be plenty for you and the boys."

My stomach growled. "Not that I don't appreciate your offer, but we better stay home. You know Frank doesn't like us going out. Besides, I'm right tired lately. Be glad when this baby makes a showing."

Chapter 8

Late Sunday afternoon, the front door flew open. Frank stormed in, mean as ever. "What's this I hear about you talking to some fancy fellow in town?"

I kept stirring the pot of potato soup. Just my luck, he'd stopped in Hollis on his way home from the Wellington Fair and heard some spiteful gossip. Probably chatted with some buddies at the gristmill or the drugstore or the saloon.

From the corner of my eyes, Howard stood straight and pulled his shoulders back while Thomas shrank against the kitchen wall. The other boys had probably slipped quietly up to the attic where they slept. While it might have gotten them out of Frank's way, they'd still be able to hear.

"Harry Payne, no less!" Frank yelled. "Most high-falutin' guy in town. You talked to Harry!" Frank stomped over to where I stood, and I smelled the stink of liquor.

I refused to look his way, ignoring him as if he were a bag of beans. Using a tea towel, I pulled the bread out of the oven.

"Listen to me when I'm talking." He jerked me around.

The hot metal bread pan banged to the floor, barely missing my stocking feet.

"You want him? Forget it, woman. You're mine, and I won't have you making eyes at some swanky dude, acting like I don't count none."

His breath stunk like sour lemons, and I leaned away. "I didn't flirt with Harry. He just asked how I was doing. Nothing wrong with that."

His eyes narrowed like a starving mountain lion staring me in the face.

My heart raced.

Frank yanked my arm and pulled me toward him. I could see the devil in his eyes.

I pushed him away and felt the heat of the open oven on my hip.

He scowled.

Like two wild animals, we estimated one another.

He pulled, and I pushed. Before I knew what'd happened, I stumbled backward, tripping and landing hard on my rear end.

Frank kicked his booted foot at me several times.

I rolled away from him, but not soon enough. A blow landed on my side. I yelped as I felt the impact all the way through to my insides.

Noise filled the room. Father and son began shouting at one another.

I gasped and squeezed my eyes shut. All I could do was lie there and hold my big belly as they fought.

Heavy boots passed me and tramped out of the house. The door slamming shut.

I looked up.

Howard appeared above me, his left eye shining purple where Frank had hit him a few days before.

The pain inside me became unbearable.

Lord help me, I hoped Frank wouldn't show up again for weeks.

How bad could life get?

***

I lay on the kitchen floor beside the ruined loaf of bread. Unable to move, misery flooded through my body. How could Frank do this to me? He hadn't always been so mean.

Disappointment clouded my vision. Disappointment at Frank, at myself, at the situation, and despair for this new baby.

I could feel the babe coming. Having experienced pregnancy seven times before, I knew the signs. But this time, the baby was weeks early. I didn't want to lose my baby girl. I couldn't lose this baby girl.

I squeezed my eyes shut and tried to draw deep breaths through the pain.

Frank had never been the considerate type, never been kind-hearted, not even when I was in labor over two days with Billy. He disappeared like he couldn't face my pain. The one time I thought he might come around and realize a woman needed a kind word was when I went to the pasture to find our wandering heifer. Never found her, but I traipsed around until after dark. When night fell on those flat plains, it was impossible to tell north from south or up from down.

I realized I was lost. When the coyotes started yelping, I got real scared. I yelled for help until I was hoarse. Frank finally located me and scolded me instead of being glad I was found. I could have used a kind word or two then. His heart never changed, and I stopped expecting to hear nice words from him unless he was trying to coerce me into a good mood.

I opened my eyes. All four boys stood over me like guard dogs, worry on their faces.

Billy and Frank Junior must have come down when their daddy left. Even with the boys worrying over me, I felt alone. I needed help, and they wouldn't know what to do.

"Are you all right?" Thomas asked in a soft voice.

"Help me to the bed," I mumbled. "I think this baby's itching to be born."

The boys' eyes grew as large as round saucers.

I held out my arms, and Thomas and Howard helped me wobble to the bed. I fell into the pillows, yelping with another sharp pain. Frank Junior brought me wet towels and wiped my forehead.

Howard took charge. “Thomas, run to town and get Aunt Jennie and Aunt Ann.”

“I don’t want to leave Ma.” Thomas kneeled beside me, stroking my hand.

“I need to stay here and watch over things,” Howard said. “Now git! Take the horse and hurry!”

Chapter 9

"What's going on here?" Jennie rushed into the room like I was dying. When she and Annie bustled around our small shack, the room filled up pretty quickly.

"Annie, get those boys out of here. We need some space. I believe this baby's coming."

Shooed outside, the lads would sit on the stoop until morning, if need be, waiting for news.

With my sisters, I didn't feel so lonely, bossed around maybe, but not lonely. My sisters were all I had. My daddy, James Tol Thomas, died back in 1910 of a heart attack while returning from a Confederate Soldiers' Convention in Mobile, Alabama. Mama passed on eleven years ago.

Our older brother, Sam, moved to New Mexico before Mama died, and we seldom heard from him, so we were left to fend for ourselves. My sisters and I supported one another like lost orphans with the barest hold on family. I sighed with relief, glad they were there to help.

Between contractions, I rested—but never closed my ears completely. I overheard my sisters whispering in the corner about the baby coming fast. Worry creeped in. Tension filled my body because I knew this birthing wasn't going right.

Jennie leaned over me and dabbed my face with a cloth. "Hey, Tillie. The baby will be here soon. She's early, isn't she? Did something happen? Did you fall? You got a mark the size of Texas on your side."

I shook my head. I didn't want to rat on my husband, my boys' daddy.

Another contraction hit. Jennie let me scream into her shoulder.

The baby came late that night. I heard her weak cry as Annie placed her on my chest.

"It's a girl." Her voice filled with awe and wonder.

"I know it's a girl," I said with a half-smile. "Known it all along."

Jennie cleaned up. "Prettiest baby I ever saw. Perfect as a China doll."

Baby Bess was a puny thing. In the candlelight, she looked to be no bigger than a newborn hound dog. Soft hair covered her translucent skin, and Ann was right—she reminded me of a porcelain doll, pale and perfect.

I stroked her hair and whispered sweet words in her ear. I feared she might not make it, but my heart bonded anyway. The small mite of a girl took my breath away.

The boys came into the room one at a time. Each looked at their tiny sister and backed away, uncertain what to do.

After the boys left, my baby began to gasp, trying to breathe.

I looked up at my sister and saw my fear reflected in her eyes.

Jennie took Bess from me, washed her face, and enveloped her tightly in the pink blanket I'd saved from the other girls. Then she handed Bess back to me as I sat in the rocking chair.

I wrapped both arms around my sweetie, protecting her as if I could keep her safe from all the bad things in this world. She tried to nurse, but had a hard time, seeming to slip farther and farther away. The ache inside my chest grew tighter.

An hour later, Bess closed her eyes and died in my arms. No matter how many babies I lost, each hurt as immensely as the last.

I couldn't even cry. I rocked her all night.

***

We buried Glenna Bess Ready next to Lorene, Mary, and Annie. At least they were together at the Fairmont Cemetery. A hot Oklahoma wind whipped dust through the air. My mouth felt as parched as old bread left out overnight. The burial took the starch right out of me.

I walked over and caressed the carving on Lorene and Mary's gravestones. Identical, the white, granite markers stood taller than either girl ever grew, slender and beautiful, like my sweeties. I wasn't sure who purchased the headstones. We were poor as field mice and couldn't have paid much, especially for ones this ornate. I suspected my sisters had raised the funds.

Annie's grave didn't have a stone yet, only a little flag showing where she was buried. As soon as I could scrimp and save up, I'd buy two flat stones, one for her and one for Bess. That's all I'd be able to afford, but it would be enough.

All four of my sisters attended Bess' funeral. Mary Bobbie and Susie came by train from opposite directions. It comforted me to know they'd taken time to be there. They gathered around me at the graveyard, the hushed flatlands surrounding us.

Bob and Jennie stood on one side of me, Susie and Ann on the other. My five-foot-ten-inch frame was normally half a head taller than theirs, but today, I couldn't stand straight. Dressed in long black dresses, with hats pulled down and netting covering our eyes, we held hands, clinging to each other.

Frank stood to the side and twisted his worn hat in front of him, never looking my way. I wondered if anyone had told Frank that Bess's death was his fault. I hadn't. I refused to speak to him, even when he tried to sweet talk me.

My four boys stood behind him, dressed in their best. Howard with a black eye, Thomas with tears streaming down his face, Billy with a scowl, kicking at the dirt, and Frank Junior with his head hanging to his knees.

The funeral brought back all the memories of my other sweet girls. All the heartaches. All the questions. All the crying.

Once the tears began, I collapsed into Mary Bobbie's arms. Bob, who knew about losing baby girls. The others closed in around me, hugging me in a sisters' embrace.

All their love couldn't fill the void, but then I felt another presence.

I glanced over Ann's shoulder and saw a vision of Jesus holding my baby, Bess. He looked at me gently before wrapping a pink blanket around the tiny infant and cradling her in his arms.

Chapter 10

For the next two days, I slept on the sofa, my face buried in a pillow. I couldn't talk about the baby. Couldn't think about the baby. Couldn't stand to look at a soul. I had put up with Frank's abuse for years, but I could do it no longer.

Our marriage had slipped into madness. Maybe I was to blame. Maybe I shouldn't have followed my passion to marry my sweetheart. I was blind to his faults and had grown used to the violence. Maybe I was too scared to leave him.

I still loved him. Or I loved who he could have been, could still be if he set his mind to it. After I heard him leave, I rolled over, buried my grief, and fell back to sleep.

A loud bang on the door stirred me. "Tillie! Are you up and around yet? Bless your heart, it's almost noon!" Jennie's commanding voice irritated me. Couldn't she just leave me alone?

"Heavens, she's still in her nightgown." Annie's voice might have been softer, but I still hated to hear it.

I didn't want to see anyone. Dern it, didn't they know? I put a throw pillow over my head.

"I declare! That is no way to greet your sister from Texas."

Mary Bobbie? I thought she left town after the funeral. Now I was in hot water.

I peeked out from under the pillow. Four worried mother-hen types stared down on me. Even timid Susie looked at me with as much impatience as the others. I suspected Jennie had something to do with them showing up about the time I needed them.

No one spoke for a few minutes until Mary Bobbie took charge. “Girls, we have our work cut out for us. Time to get our gal up and around.”

Annie and Jennie rolled my legs to the floor, and standing on either side of me, pulled me to my feet. Despondent as an abandoned calf and as annoyed as its mama unable to nurse, I didn’t trust my words, so I stayed silent. Of course, there was no arguing with my sisters. Four to one were not good odds.

Mary Bobbie gave the orders. “Jennie, go put on some water to boil for a bath. She smells like she’s been run over by a skunk.

“Annie, get her a cup of broth. I doubt if she’s had a bite to eat since the funeral.

“Susie, find her some clean clothes. Look in her armoire.”

My shoulders slumped, but an hour later, I felt like I had joined the land of the living again.

My sisters and I sat around the dining room table. They looked relieved, having done their sisterly duty, adding a few more wrinkles since they arrived. I expected them to take their pocketbooks and perky attitudes and traipse on back home. But they wanted to sit and have a lovey-dovey chat.

“What are your plans?” Jennie pushed strands of hair out of her face. Strands laced with silver.

“You’ve got to keep going, even if life doesn’t hand out the best.” Susie knew about living with stress, tied to a man not doing right.

"Your boys need you," said Ann. "They've been out working in your garden, trying to make those corn and tomato plants grow. They're mighty worried."

"I know. I know. I'll get up and cook supper," I said. "I just needed some prodding. Needed someone to get me started. Thanks, girls."

"Jeannie, you brought a pot of stew, didn't you?" Annie asked.

"It's sitting on the stove as we speak." Jennie turned to me, her eyes glittering. "So, you don't have to worry about supper, little lady. It's already made."

"And I brought a chocolate cake," said Ann, looking quite proud of herself.

I groaned. Although I appreciated Ann's efforts, with her cooking abilities, we might have to feed the cake to the hunting dogs.

"We'll be praying for you," said Mary Bobbie. "It might be getting bad around here, but there's nothing so bad the Lord and a little grub can't handle."

Jennie stood to go. "Remember, if you don't feel safe, you can leave. Come on by my house, and we'll talk about it."

I hugged them all. Good sisters were hard to come by.

After they left, I picked up my Bible. I needed Jesus now more than ever. I couldn't change Frank. I couldn't change anything. I needed to step back and trust God had a plan. Step away from the dreams of a happy home with Frank and follow wherever God might lead.

Start over. At my age. Start over.

I'd have to be strong.

That meant Bess would be my last baby.

The last Ready child.

Chapter 11

I made my way into town to Jennie's house on Jones Street, a few blocks north of Main. Frank Junior came with me because the older boys didn't hanker to me traipsing off by myself so soon after losing Bess. That was their excuse, but I knew they didn't cater to watching after their little brother.

Frank Junior and I walked through the screen door, and it banged shut behind us. Hot steam billowed out of the kitchen. Jennie and Ann were canning peaches. The sweet smell wafted through the air, reminding me of when I was a little girl and my mama put up preserves for the winter. Lands, I couldn't imagine how they canned so much in this heat. I had a hard time canning the few vegetables I did.

Jennie's boy, Truman, and Ann's boy, Jerry, were about the same age and fell to chasing each other around in circles, making horse sounds. Ann's younger son, Jimmy, a toddler now, tried to follow them but kept getting knocked down.

"Hush, boys." Annie placed her hands on her hips. "Go on outside and play on the porch." They ran out the door, the screen door banging shut again, with Jimmy barely slipping through.

"Junior, can you keep an eye on the boys for me?" Annie wiped her hands on her apron. She hated canning, hated anything to do with cooking, and usually avoided the kitchen, but she couldn't very well leave all the work to Jennie.

Frank Junior shrugged and walked out. The screen door banged shut one more time. I might have been partial to him, but he was still a good boy.

Jennie eyed me warily. "Have a seat. We're almost finished here."

I plopped into a kitchen chair. Canning supplies were laid out in order on the countertop: glass jars of all sizes, rings with steaming hot seals, ladles, and potholders. "I'm trying to figure out how to leave Frank."

Both of my sisters stopped right in the middle of screwing the lids tightly on the glass jars.

"No need to mince words," Jennie said with a smirk. "Not that you ever have."

"I'm leaving Frank. For good."

"You said the same thing after Annie died. But nothing came of it." Jennie didn't mince words either.

"Not this time. I've had it. I'm trying to work out the details."

"I'm right glad. Don't get me wrong, but that sorry fellow hasn't done you a lick of good. I saw Howard's black eye. He's been hitting on the boys again, hasn't he?" Her eyes flashed toward me with questions and condemnation.

I didn't answer Jennie, but she knew. As the wisest of us, she poked into every detail of our lives.

Annie turned away and began to gather the sealed jars of yellow peaches, placing each on towels spread on the kitchen table in front of me. I admired them. They looked scrumptious and would make tasty peach cobblers during the winter.

Ann said nothing. She would never leave her husband, even if he kept a girlfriend in every city, especially after her first beau's tragedy. She'd follow Tommy Akin down Highway 66 to California in a sandstorm and claim it was the best adventure she ever had. I wasn't sure what she thought of my decision to leave Frank.

"I'm wondering what to do when I leave. I'll have to get a place for me and the boys and find work to support us." My voice gathered speed as the thoughts escaped. "Howard's been working down at the lumberyard lately, helping out. Thomas wants to quit school and get a full-time job, but I won't let him do that. The boys have already picked and sold our measly crop of cotton."

"You could move in with us until you find a place." Jennie, peach fuzz adorning her frizzy hair and stained apron, gathered the dishes to wash. "And I heard of cotton-picking work out on the Newberry Ranch with Tom's brother. Howard should check into that. It'll pay more than what he's getting now."

Ann wiped her hands on her apron, turned to me, and lowered her voice. "Goodness gracious, maybe the trouble will blow over soon." Her eyes pleaded for roses and daffodils, but none existed in my world. Not anymore.

I'd never confided in Annie about Frank's drinking and gambling. She knew we had problems, but not the extent. I'd protected her, the baby of the family. We all protected her, thinking of her as a frail girl. She'd almost died when she was young, and we still treated her like a fragile doll.

Well, now was the time to let her know exactly how I'd been living the last twenty-some years.

By the time I finished telling my tale, the three of us sat in tears.

And we'd made plans, my sisters' full support behind them.

Chapter 12

I didn't say a word to anybody that next week about leaving—except to my boys. I spoke kindly to Frank, who catered to me for a couple of days like he was trying to be kind, but his self-control slipped. Soon enough, he started cursing the boys and kicking the dog. I was not deceived and didn't complain when he left to go hunting for the weekend.

I woke early Saturday morning and packed. Not that we had much to move. Tom Newberry found us a tiny, two-bedroom house near their home in Hollis. Unlike me, Jennie married an honorable man who offered to pay the first month's rent for us.

The boys didn't seem to mind leaving their pap, and we got settled.

None of us were surprised when Frank showed up a few days later, knocking on the front door of our rented house. It isn't easy to hide in a small town.

The sun was setting when I opened the door. Frank's horse and wagon stood in front of the house.

I stepped out onto the front porch, gripping the fabric of my day dress.

Before he'd spoken a word, I picked up the scent of bad beer breath. His wrinkled clothes were as dirty as a boxcar tramp. He'd obviously been on a bender.

"You can't do this to me, Tillie," he said in his sweet, smooth-talking voice. "I need you and the boys to come back home. I promise things'll get better. We just had a rough spot. I'll fix this, and it'll be different from now on, I promise."

Here he was, the man I'd fallen in love with all those years ago. The man who'd stirred my passion like no other. I wanted old Frank Ready back, the one who'd doted on me and made me laugh. I wanted peace with the sweet man I'd married. But buried under that exterior was trash so deep it stunk. He might be salvaged if he'd let the good Lord help—but it might take a million years for him to wake up and realize what family meant. And I didn't have a million years left in me.

So, no sir. I would not go back. I wouldn't even allow myself to consider going back. I'd thought about leaving so many times, my feelings felt caught in a jigsaw. I couldn't trust Frank's sweet whispers anymore.

When I didn't respond to his honeyed words, his eyes narrowed. Knowing his anger was about to burst out, I put my hand on the doorknob. He stepped toward me with his fist raised.

I stepped back over the threshold. "Dagnabbit, Frank. Our marriage is over." I slammed the door in his face, slid the latch, and turned to find the boys right behind me. "Quick, lock everything."

"You won't get away with this!" Frank screamed.

The boys and I rushed around and fastened every door and window while listening to Frank rant like a lunatic. I couldn't let him inside to hurt us or destroy every possession we owned.

A few minutes later, I heard a gunshot.

Billy peeked through the curtains.

I grabbed his arm and pulled. "Get back!"

His face lost its color. "Pa's got his rifle."

"Howard, quick. Run out the back door and get the sheriff." Howard, barefoot and shirtless, bolted out, and I locked the door behind him. Frank saw Howard and shook his weapon in the air, yelling foul language at his firstborn son.

I watched Howard run behind neighboring houses. Thankfully, Frank didn't pursue. Instead, he banged again on our front door, cussing and hollering as if he were being trampled by wild horses.

"Let me in, boys," Frank yelled. "You're my family, and I'll be dogged if you're going to keep me out."

None of us responded as we huddled out of sight. My shoulders tensed, my senses sharp and searing. Minutes went by.

A gunshot blasted a hole in the front window glass.

I jumped and pushed my three boys into the bedroom, closed the door, and put my body in front of it. No telling what would happen if Frank broke in, and I didn't want my boys hurt or in the middle of the chaos. This was my trap, not theirs.

My heart pounded like a locomotive as Frank beat on the front door. The noise shook the foundation of the house. I didn't want him near the kids, not in his condition. My stubborn husband wouldn't leave until I faced him. Maybe if I talked to him, he'd cool down. I reached to unlatch the lock.

My fingers shook. I couldn't. I dropped my hand. There was no reasoning with him when he was drunk.

My anger stirred, I screeched at him. "Go home, Frank. Sleep it off. I won't be changing my mind."

He kicked the front door. The wood splintered, scaring the heebie-jeebies out of me.

My body felt like pins struck each nerve, and my anger changed to fear. I prayed to Jesus so hard I thought my head would explode. But I wasn't about to move aside.

Frank was a mean drunk, especially when riled. None of us were safe, especially with a rifle in his hand. Not even his sons.

A motor car sounded in the distance. Horses neighed, and shouts filled my ears as the clamor got louder and louder.

My heart beat fierce. No one would hurt my boys again. No, sir. I ran to the kitchen and grabbed a knife, prepared to fight for our lives if necessary.

Billy glanced out the bedroom door.

"Take the others and climb out the window!" I yelled before I peeked through the cracked glass of the living room window.

They didn't obey but joined me in the front room.

What I saw took my breath away. There, in the front yard, stood half a dozen men facing the porch. Though I couldn't see him, I imagined Frank was facing them right back.

The sheriff stood beside Tom Newberry, Tommy Akin, Harry Payne, and a few other townspeople. Why, even the preacher of the Methodist church was there.

My boy Howard stood off to the side, wringing his hands. He'd done the right thing getting the sheriff, even if I hated him to see his father act like a fool. I was proud of that boy.

Neighbor folks poked their heads out of their doors to see the commotion, and a crowd began to gather around our house. I could never have imagined such a scene. The whole town took up for us.

Frank stomped off the porch and faced the crowd. "This is my woman, and I'll do what I want with her. Get out of here and let me deal with my family!"

"You're causing a disturbance, Frank," Tom said calmly. "Need to settle down."

Frank stepped toward the men, his rifle facing the sky. "What if I don't want to settle down?"

I saw Howard facing his father, legs spread, arms crossed. Like a guard. My boy's back was straight and strong. "Pa, you're acting crazy. Go on back to the farm." He stepped toward his pa.

"I don't have to listen to you!" said Frank, retreating. "You'll get a tanning for this!"

The fellows surrounded Frank and began to force him toward the wagon. My old man didn't like the shoving and pushing and shot into the air. My heart jumped as if I'd been hit.

"Go on home, Frank," yelled the sheriff. "We've had enough excitement for one day."

I stepped out on the porch, jittery from the ruckus.

Frank turned, his face red, and glared at me and our boys. His eyes scared me. I'd never seen such cold hatred in him, never seen him so livid. Caught.

Frank aimed his rifle at the porch.

I ducked, and Howard leaped in front of me.

Frank, in his drunken stupor, fired, but the bullet zoomed several feet over our heads. Thankfully, he couldn't hit a barndoor.

The sheriff rushed up behind Frank and grabbed his arms. Someone snatched his gun, while others wrestled him toward the ground. He went down kicking and hollering, as I expected. The sheriff clamped handcuffs on him and shoved him down Jones Street. They headed toward the Harmon County Jail, a few blocks west.

While the sheriff and the crowd disappeared down the road, Tom, Tommy, and Harry came and stood in front of me and the boys, hats in their hands. I pulled Frank Junior to me. He was still shaking, but we were safe.

Tom walked up the porch steps. "Nobody's going to hurt you anymore, Till. We're here to see that Frank leaves you alone. If he can't treat you like a lady, he isn't wanted around here. These boys can grow up the way they should."

Harry's eyes bore into me, and I saw kindness and compassion, but he said nothing.

I breathed a huge sigh of relief, and my heart felt like a ton of bricks had been lifted. "You don't know how much this means to me and my boys. We're darn grateful."

The move into town had been the right decision. No matter how hard it might get, I had to be strong for my family's sake. Leaving Frank was the best way to keep my boys safe. My brave boys.

Thank you, Jesus. With his help, I'd broken out of the trap and would never go back.

Chapter 13

With a new home and growing boys, I needed to find work. I couldn't do much, but I could sew.

I walked into the J.C. Penney's store downtown looking for a paying job. "Do you have any work for a seamstress? A good one?"

"Not at the moment." The man behind the counter attended my church. "But if we get extra work, we might be able to use you. Don't get your hopes up, though. Extra work rarely happens—not since this here depression set in."

I must have looked disappointed because he quickly added, "Have you talked to the manager at Gardner's?"

"Not yet."

"There are a few other stores in town. You might chat with J.B. Ellis or the Wilsons."

I checked every department store and clothing shop in the area, and no one needed help.

The next week, I decided my best chance at earning money was to set up my own shop. Ready-made clothes cost more than most people could afford, and having the boys, I'd learned to mend tears and patch britches. I had a useful skill neighbors might need. Many women did their own mending, but some families in town could afford to farm it out.

I sent Howard and Thomas out to the homestead to haul back my old treadle sewing machine.

Within a week, I had a spot to work in. Dear Tom Newberry helped set up my sewing machine in the storage room of his dry goods store. He even brought in a chair and a small table for supplies. Jennie's husband did more than I imagined a brother-in-law felt obligated to do. I'd never be able to pay him back.

My sisters walked through the doorway to my space. They rallied around me more than any person deserved.

"What do you think of Till's new shop?" Jennie asked Annie.

I stood to the side of my new business quarters, pride making my chest feel like it would burst wide open.

"Tom was good enough to let her set up here," Jennie continued chatting. "The space is tiny, but it'll do fine until she builds up clients."

"It's perfect. I love it." Ann glanced around before pulling a small box out of her bag. "Here. Mary Bobbie sent this for you."

"A buttonhole maker? Blazes, I don't know how to use that." I'd always sewn buttonholes by hand.

"Don't worry. I'll show you. Just attach it to the machine, and you can get different sizes in minutes. We'll have your first lesson done in no time."

Susie mailed me a bolt of pale green gingham material, along with a couple of yards of rose-printed cotton. A handwritten note shared her hope I could use it.

I wrote her a long letter, thanking her for the beautiful fabric, insisting she should have made herself a frock from it. But Susie wouldn't sew anything for herself. She wasn't like that. Of all my sisters, she needed to upgrade her wardrobe. I determined to make her a gingham dress out of the fabric and send it to her.

Annie, the stylish one, helped with designs and fashion ideas, carting in used Vogue and McCall's patterns for me to re-use. My button box overflowed after Mary Bobbie and Jennie added their collections to mine.

My sisters were lifesavers, especially during hard times.

***

A few months later, I heard Frank sold the farm and left town after he got out of jail. He moved to Las Vegas as if nothing had ever happened, leaving me and the four boys to fend for ourselves right in the middle of the worst drought I'd ever seen.

Word got around about my proficiency making covered buttons and buckles, not to mention fancy dresses. Business flowed my way. I toiled hard, staying up late most nights to finish the work by the day I promised, which meant a lot to my customers. Their pennies kept me and the boys on our feet.

As I sewed, my fear and anger with Frank began to dissipate. I'd forgive him someday, but it would take a long time for me to trust another man. And if I did, it wouldn't be Frank Ready, no matter how much he begged or sweet-talked.

My hurt had piled up over the years, changing who I was and creating layers of distrust I hadn't had before. The sadness weighed heavy, like I'd buried something precious with my girls.

My sisters never asked why baby Bess came early, and I never told them the whole truth. My boys rallied around me and became my strength. We kept the secret of Bess's death close to our hearts, an event that broke us out of our complacency and gave us a new life.

Even something devastating can bring change.

I kept my religion private and quietly joined the Church of Christ. I still didn't venture into church often, but my faith strengthened. My Bible sat by my bedside, and I almost wore it out, searching for answers about how to forgive, why things happened the way they did, and why love was not always enough.

I never could have walked away from Frank on my own. My courage must have come from the good Lord. He might've hated divorce, but sometimes it had to be done to keep on living.

For the Christmas church potluck, I made myself an elegant outfit from a deep-red rayon crepe.

When I tried it on, I promised myself to never dress in rags again. I combed my long hair and set it in rolls, washed my face, and dabbed on some of Jennie's blush. Looking at myself in the mirror, I smiled. I didn't look so bad. In fact, I could hold my own with any woman my age and felt quite the lady.

I held my head high as I attended church with my boys and enjoyed the potluck after. The good Lord had seen us through our bleak, dark days, and I trusted him to take care of me and the boys through the years ahead.

No matter what difficulties came, we'd face them together.

Author's Notes

My family shared whispers and secrets while I was growing up, and I loved to eavesdrop and jot down notes. The grownups seemed unaware of my interest. As I've created stories from the information and research I gathered, I've stuck to the facts as much as possible, adding dialogue and assumptions as needed.

I based this story on my Great Aunt Till. Sallie Matilda Thomas was one of my Grandma's older siblings, one of the five sisters. I remember her as a tall, stylish lady, sometimes brash, but intelligent and understanding.

Family lore indicates Frank's abuse and neglect were well known in the family, as were his excessive drinking and gambling.

Till and Franklin Harris Ready separated right after their fourth baby girl died in 1930. No record exists explaining how or why the baby did not survive; just that she passed away the same year she was born. I surmised the circumstances because Till could have left Frank after her previous daughters died, but she didn't. She stayed with him. Therefore, I assumed some crisis must have happened for her to finally decide to leave him.

Frank moved to Las Vegas after the divorce and died at a gambling table of a heart attack in 1952. It appears he never changed. He was buried at Fairmont Cemetery in Hollis along with their son, Thomas, who died in 1945.

Till raised her boys as a single mom. Sometime late in the 1930s or '40s, she and her boys moved to Yuba City, California, where she worked as a seamstress. She was living there when she married again. This time to Harry Payne.

Harry W. Payne, another real person, homesteaded in Magnum, Oklahoma, in 1901. He owned the Payne Home Place southeast of Gould. He and Till married in 1951 after his first wife, Linnie Richardson, died in 1949. Harry and Till lived in Yuba City, California, where they retired.

My family moved to Roseville, California, in the late 50s and frequently visited Aunt Till. She did a lot of canning and had many walnut trees. While there, we sent a hundred pounds of walnuts back to our family in Oklahoma. Harry had a saddle that belonged to Roy Rogers, a neighbor's friend, which seemed important at the time.

In 1961, while living in California, Sally Matilda fell and broke her hip. She died April the first. Her body was brought back to Hollis, Oklahoma, to be buried in the Fairmont Cemetery beside her four little daughters and one of her sons.

About 2010, my father and I drove from Shawnee to Hollis for his high school class reunion. We visited several cemeteries, including Fairmont, where much of his family is buried.

We found Till's gravestone next to her four girls. The stones marking Lorene's and Mary's graves were tall, narrow, identical monuments, probably supplied by Till's family since she was destitute at that time. Annie's and Bess's small stones are in the same family plot.

Aunt Till's grown sons had alcohol-related issues, or so family stories go. I've only been able to contact one of Till's great-grandsons who resides in Oklahoma. An upstanding young man.

I think of Aunt Till as a survivor and a strong woman. But I have many questions I'd love to ask any surviving members of her family.

Susie May

Thomas Sister #3

Marvin & Jack Lindsey

Susie May

Born November 15, 1889

Chapter 1

My heart spun like a ball of yarn as I ran from room to room, helping my sisters put my newly rented house in order. Sporting faded aprons and scarves to hold our hair in place, we scrubbed the cabinets, hung pictures, and shuffled items from place to place. My sisters took charge as if the four walls belonged to them and not my little family.

"Susie May!" My sister Jennie Rue's voice rang through the open kitchen door. "Where're the rest of the dishes? I'm tryin' to wash them all up."

Before I could answer, Sally Matilda yelled, "I'll take charge of the bathroom!"

I pointed out the remaining boxes of dishes to Jennie before following Till as she slipped into the tiny lavatory.

I bit my lip as I leaned against the doorframe. "Oh, dearie. I use baking soda on the sink instead of bleach. I don't mean to offend. If you think bleach is better, go ahead. I just prefer the powder." I hoped my words weren't too harsh. I didn't want to upset my outspoken sisters, but I liked things done a certain way.

She shrugged and stooped to search the crate of supplies on the floor. My siblings were definitely take-charge girls. Their over-the-top energy exhausted me.

"Where does this trunk go?" Anna Lee, pregnant with her third child, called from the living room. "By the window or in the corner?"

Matilda popped her head out from the privy. "Annie, don't you dare move anything heavier than a breadbox!" The second of us five sisters, Till was tall, stern, and regal, and had more gumption than the rest of us put together. "You don't want to lose that baby girl you're carrying."

I hurried to the front room only to find Annie shoving my steamer trunk all by herself. "Lordy, Ann! Wait! I'll help you."

Together, we edged the trunk toward the corner.

As I straightened up, Ann picked up my husband's saxophone.

I cringed. "Please, please, don't touch Elmer's instruments. He'll take care of those himself." As a band teacher, my husband's music possessions were the most valuable pieces we owned.

"If you say so." Ann laid the saxophone down beside an open box of books. "We can leave the books for Mary Bobbie to arrange when she gets here. She'll need something to do."

Our oldest sister, Bobbie, planned to arrive from Texas the coming weekend. Her lightheartedness would be welcome. She'd also bring a ton of sweet creations—enough for the whole clan.

I sighed and pushed my wire-trimmed eyeglasses up on my nose. Dusting my hands on my apron, I hurried into the kitchen just in time to see Jennie place a fork in the wrong slot of the silverware drawer.

"Honey, that's fine. But I usually do it like this." I smiled and took the next dried utensil from her. "The forks go on the left, the spoons in the middle, and the knives on the right."

That was Jennie, always helpful, even if she tended to put items in the wrong place.

It tickled me to be living near my sisters for the first time in years. I didn't want to hurt their feelings or push them away, but I'd moved so many times I could set up housekeeping in my sleep. Still, they insisted on helping, so I gently corrected them.

An hour later, Jennie whipped up bacon and tomato sandwiches on homemade bread, along with peach cobbler and sweet iced tea for lunch. While gobbling down the delicious food, we discussed our sons' outgrown overalls and reminisced about the times we snuck out the shared bedroom window after dark without our mother noticing.

"So happy you moved back to Hollis, Susie May." Till's words echoed sweet music to my ears. "You make this small town almost bearable again." We all laughed, but, for me, the move brought hope. Hope for a better future.

***

The answer to my prayer of living closer to my sisters happened suddenly. Just a few months earlier, on the last day of school, my husband, Elmer Lindsey, came home, his refined features downcast.

"We're moving. Pack up everything. I found a band director job at another school." His tall, thin body leaned against the door frame.

"Where?" I asked, my stomach knotting against the uncertainty. We'd moved around the country for almost twenty years and had only lived in Corbett nine months. I hated the thought of moving again. Hated it with a dread that grew with each move.

"Hollis. I'll be teaching band at Hollis."

Tingles ran down my spine. My eyes widened in delight. For the first time, I'd looked forward to relocating.

Hollis, Oklahoma, was my home, and the town where my sisters lived, all except Bobbie who moved to Munday, Texas. Nearing our prime, though none of us wanted to admit it, we loved getting together.

As I packed, I'd looked forward to being right down the street from Jennie, Ann, and Matilda.

Being the quiet, sensitive sister had its advantages. No one expected me to make tough decisions or solve problems. But it had been so long since I'd lived near them, I worried. Would they meddle in my family's affairs? Of course they would. Sisters did that. Although we shared personal problems in our weekly letters to each other, I'd kept most of my troubling family life to myself.

Many folks considered me as pliant as a tadpole—naïve and innocent. Truth was, I was born right in the middle of five daughters and simply overlooked. It seemed my lot in life. In a houseful of talkative females, I had to work hard to be noticed amidst the constant chatter.

Papa was the only family member who didn't ignore me, a surprising approach, since he was surrounded by a passel of adoring daughters. Papa was my hero, the one I loved beyond measure, the one I revered. I'd pull off his work boots, bring him a glass of cool water, and rub his aching back when he got home from plowing the field. I sat at his feet, idolizing like a faithful dog, as he told stories. He loved me with a warm and kind understanding that I felt nowhere else.

After my sister's intrusion today, it'd be hard to keep my worries hidden because secrets tended to leak out in daily goings on.

As we returned to washing the thin-paned windows, scrubbing the linoleum floors, and wiping down the wallpaper, Jennie sang. Annie rested often, and Matilda muttered under her breath, especially when we took almost an hour to put the beds together. My mind wavered between gratefulness and exhaustion, landing on relief.

They cared.

A few hours later, I approached my sister who perched on a chair reaching toward the top kitchen shelf. "Jennie Rue?"

She jumped down, dust blowing around her dungarees. “What do you need?”

How was she so limber after the day’s work? Only three years younger than me, she made me feel old and stodgy. I took a deep breath, exhausted from the move before we ever arrived in Hollis. “We’ve worked up another dust storm. The boys’ll be home soon, and I’m tired. Why don’t we start again in the morning?”

Jennie turned to me. “Oh, bless your little heart, don’t fret so. It won’t take long to finish.”

I pushed fly-away hair out of my face and wiped sweat from my forehead. “I’m plum tuckered out.”

“You *have* had a long day. We can call it quits—but we’ll be back first thing in the morning.” She hollered at the other sisters. “Come on girls, time to go home to our own!”

Ann took off her frilly apron, folded it, and set it on the table.

“Let me hang these boys’ britches first. Then I’ll be done.” Matilda called from down the hall.

I could insist on finishing by myself, but my sisters’ efforts meant a lot to me. I felt a sudden burst of joy. “Thank you for your help today, but you didn’t have to do so much!” Warmed by their concern, I uncharacteristically reached out and hugged each one.

“Don’t lift a finger until we return tomorrow, Susie. You’ve done enough.” Jennie shook her finger at me as she headed for the door. “I’ll hang those new kitchen curtains before you can blink an eye. And I’ll get Tom to replace those light bulbs for you. Then you won’t have to ask Elmer to do it.”

I stepped back. How had she known Elmer didn’t like to change light bulbs? Or that he was too busy to help around the house? Maybe she’d guessed since he’d been gone all day running errands. Did she discern more than that?

Jennie turned to Ann, who looked as exhausted as I did. “If you’re tired, Tillie and I can finish up here tomorrow. You should stay home and rest.”

“Thanks, sis, I might just do that. I’m worn to a frazzle.” Ann heaved loudly and patted her pregnant belly. “Tommy won’t want to watch the boys another day, anyway.”

I glanced around at my sisters’ smiling faces. I loved my sisters, even if they tended to take charge. They were dearer to me than butterscotch fudge. This move, the best move of my life, tasted sweeter than a dozen of those delicacies. The autumn ahead looked promising. Living so close, we’d spend hours together, mending heartaches, and bringing joy back into our lives.

After my sisters left, I walked from room to room, assessing the unpacking still to be done. I considered how I could fix some of their attempts to help without them noticing.

I couldn’t.

I could never intentionally hurt them. Not after praying so hard to move back to Hollis. And here I was, right down the street. Thank the Lord, he’d brought me home. I knelt right there on the cold floor and prayed that my husband and boys would adjust and love the town as much as I did.

However, if I wasn’t careful, our family dysfunctions would be on display in front of everyone in Hollis. I prayed even harder that the nasty rumors about Elmer wouldn’t follow us to town.

Chapter 2

Evening shadows caused our house to look dingy and creepy, but new homes were like that. They looked foreign until we'd lived in them a month or two.

I scurried to prepare a light supper, opening every cabinet door, searching for a jar of green beans and a bag of flour to make biscuits. Jennie may have been organized, but I couldn't find a bowl to save my life. Tiredness made me cranky. Why hadn't I told my sisters I could move in by myself? It's hard having someone else put away your dishes. Hadn't I always done it without help? All the forty-eleven times we'd moved?

The moment I got the news, I'd begun packing for our relocation to Hollis. I'd boxed up the glassware and later dug through the crates to find a cup when I needed it. I'd folded the towels and stuffed them in pillowcases, only to have to pull them out again. I removed all the pictures on the walls, not that we had many. At fifteen and nineteen years old, the boys were too old for train sets, so I gave away their remaining toys.

"Are you all right, Ma?" Marvin, our oldest, slid in through the door. He could always tell my slightest mood change.

"Where've you been, dearie? Your Aunt Till asked about you. She hasn't seen you since we arrived."

"I hid out at Aunt Jennie's house. She has a mile-high stack of magazines in her attic."

Marvin rarely read magazines, but I understood. He didn't want to get entangled in the move or listen to the women yakking in the house. I had halfway hoped he was out looking for a job. Elmer mentioned that Tom Newberry might have work at his dry goods store, the Newberry Mercantile.

I swiped sweat from my forehead with the back of my arm before flouring the counter and plopping the dough from the bowl. "Supper's almost ready. I need to roll out the biscuits. Could you open the window for me?"

The sunbaked ground radiated heat, but with the windows propped open, an evening breeze might blow through.

Marvin shoved open the sash and turned to me. He took the rolling pin from my hands. "Let me roll the biscuits for you, Mother."

Marvin, my boy. He used to help around the house like he was my own personal maid. It didn't happen often now.

I stepped aside and watched him work with pride. When Marvin was born, I enjoyed staying home with him—my first baby. I felt isolated, far away from family, and it helped that Marvin was such a caring, delicate child. He was sweet—like his father—and helped to stave off the mountain of loneliness that threatened to consume me. I coddled him too much, I suppose, bonding so closely that a hairpin couldn't get between us. Marvin made few friends as we moved from town to town. He became more isolated and reclusive, staying inside the house instead of going out to play with other children.

"Mom!" Jack, our younger boy, stomped through the front door and looked around, leaving dusty tracks on the floor. "Gee whillikers, this place is a mess. What's for supper?"

I stirred flour into the pan grease. "I'm finishing the gravy. We'll eat after your dad gets home."

"Ah, Ma. I'm starving. Not sure I can wait that long."

I couldn't help but smile at my lively boy. Jack, a bright child at the top of his class at school—until recently—got bored easily. Going through a rebellious stage, he skipped school, smoked cigarettes, and sassed his teachers. I prayed he'd outgrow it soon.

My boys appeared opposites. Both were intelligent, but one soft and subtle, the other loud and aggressive. Hopefully, they would find friends in Hollis. Living near family might not only be good for me but for my boys having all their cousins around. It might take a while because they were a bit difficult, living by their own rules.

As supper cooked, I pushed aside boxes and found a place on the table to put four place settings, enough for our small family to eat like we always did. Forks on the left, knives and spoons on the right, half an inch from the plate. The meager food would fill us, even if it wasn't as fancy as a Sunday pot roast. I had a mincemeat pie Annie brought over that morning, but with her talent as a cook, I put little hope in it. The poor girl was hardly an accomplished chef.

Half an hour later, Elmer walked in the front door. Always an impressive dresser, he wore a pair of high-waisted, baggy-legged trousers held up by suspenders. His button-down dress shirt was tucked neatly at the waist. With his hair slicked to one side, he pulled off the image of a well-to-do man.

I'd fallen hard for him right here in Hollis the autumn after I finished high school. The football team played Looney High, a one-horse town just to the south. I'd attended the game with a couple of girlfriends, football being the main activity on a Friday night unless a new show played at the opera house. All the girls swooned over the refined young Looney High band director's long eyelashes and pin-striped trousers. But he flirted with me at the hot dog stand and asked for my address. A few weeks later, to my surprise, he called on me.

Elmer interrupted my thoughts as he hung his fedora on the coat rack. "I can't believe this town. The band room doesn't have instruments, and it's so musty, I'll have to air it out."

"Oh, my." I continued to set the table, hoping Elmer would like what I'd fixed for supper. "I'm glad the school's only a few blocks away. That's a short walk for Jack. Maybe you can walk together,"

Elmer's words flew over mine. "I went down to the Motley Hotel to see Tommy. He's an expert at haircuts and gives splendid shaves. I plan to see him on a regular basis."

"I'm enrolling Jack on Tuesday."

Elmer straightened his shoulders and pulled himself up to his full height. "Got to look nice for my students." He ran his hand across his cheek. His smooth skin made him look younger than me. At least I thought so.

"I don't need to be babied," said Jack. "I can go by myself."

I glanced down and noticed Elmer's brogue shoes had been spit-shined. Probably down at the hotel, too. "Did Tommy mention how Ann is doing?" I asked. "She's having another baby, you know."

"Isn't dinner ready yet?" Elmer ignored my comment as if he didn't hear me.

I hurried to put the meat platter on the table, and, as usual, the conversation died—except Jack chattering on about the ballgame he'd played with the Ready boys. He seemed glad to be living in Hollis. Then he, too, grew quiet.

"Do the green beans need more bacon grease? Do you think the meat is tough?" I tried hard to please Elmer and worried nonstop if he enjoyed my cooking.

Elmer's placid face showed no emotion. What went on in that prodigy mind of his? Blasted, a girl could tire of being ignored. It was hard to believe he'd once swept me off my feet, petting my hand and calling me "honey bun." He promised me free music lessons and to make me a great musician. Told me I had the most beautiful dimples he'd ever seen. A childlike and innocent face, he said.

I never understood what he saw in me. Not that it mattered now. We barely spoke to one another beyond daily mundane requirements.

Why was it so difficult for our family to communicate? Were we too preoccupied to listen to each other? Or did our world center around our own needs, unable to be heard?

My frustration had grown through the years until it took on a life of its own. Living near my candid sisters, perhaps I could get advice and gain confidence to speak up for myself. Maybe they could offer spiritual advice—words to help Elmer see how much the Lord loved him.

Who was I kidding? I'd been away from my sisters most of the past twenty years. Talking about the boys' and our common marital angst would be easy enough, but some issues would be hard to bring up, much less discuss.

***

My papa, the only one who loved me enough to listen to me, used to say, "God has a special task for you, Susie May." He liked Elmer and encouraged the relationship. "Love him like you love me," Papa told me, but I thought I could never love anyone as much as I loved my papa.

The following May, Papa died suddenly. His death left an emptiness so shattering, I thought I couldn't survive. Elmer stepped in and comforted my broken heart.

My sisters pushed for a quick wedding.

Perhaps they were afraid I might lose a choice catch like Elmer, or that I'd never find another man so handsome and accomplished. Maybe they felt he'd take care of me, a girl who needed taken care of. Then perhaps they saw how I transferred my love for Papa to Elmer, focusing my attention on a man I thought deserved my adoration.

My sisters chose the wedding date, a month after Papa's death. They chose the summer decorations and the fancy chocolate wedding cake as if they were planning their own weddings. A twenty-year-old sheltered girl, I wore Till's wedding dress, which she'd tailored since I was the shortest of the bunch. I walked down the aisle, scared, nervous, and as innocent as a child. I committed my life to him and set my devotion in stone.

After we married, Elmer and I moved into a run-down house in Looney where we stayed for the rest of the school year. That summer, when ugly rumors surrounded us, Elmer claimed we needed to move. He found a band director job in Arkansas. A different school in a different town.

I hated Arkansas. For the first time, I knew loneliness—but it wouldn't be the last.

Chapter 3

After supper, Elmer examined his instruments, first looking over the clarinet case to make sure it survived the move. He unlatched the box, took out the sleek black instrument, and assembled the pieces. He took the reed and tightened it onto the mouthpiece, his long, thin fingers gracefully caressing the metal curves. Then, holding the clarinet to his mouth, he played several hollow notes. He was a gentle man, the most sensitive and talented person I'd ever known. Brilliant to a fault.

Most evenings at home, Elmer would sit and practice his music, seemingly mesmerized by the sounds floating in the air. Instead of words, musical notes filled our home with passionate melodies, sometimes soft, sometimes overwhelming.

Gently removing the clarinet from his mouth, he licked his lips as if contemplating whether the notes had been perfect or whether he liked the feel of the reed on his tongue. After cleaning the instrument and putting it back into its case, he moved on to the trumpet and inspected it. Then he tested the tenor saxophone in the same way. He played that sax as well as any member of the Benny Goodman Band.

I watched in awe and dismay. Elmer was the center of my world, except for my sweet Jesus, and I craved my husband's attention more than breath. Did Elmer care more for his musical apparatuses than he did for me?

Elmer leaned back in his favorite wingback chair and picked up a pile of sheet music. As he flipped through the pages, he glanced at Jack. "I enrolled you in band. You need to take it this year."

My problem-solver, Jack, sat in the corner, bent over a puzzle. His head popped up, hair falling into his eyes. "I don't want to join the band."

"You have potential," said Elmer without looking up. "There's no sense wasting it. I need a solid musician for the band to be successful this year."

"I'm not taking band." Jack set down the puzzle pieces and glared at his dad. "I won't! If you make me, I'll skip the class."

My shoulders knotted. I hated when Jack spoke to his dad in that tone. I sent up a quick prayer that the discord would dissolve.

"You're disregarding your talent." Elmer's smooth voice made it clear he expected to get what he wanted. "I'll let you choose which instrument to play. Whatever you want."

"Marvin didn't take band. You didn't make him." Jack's defiance rang through the room as he stood.

I gripped my knitting needles. I should have moved in front of Jack and begged him to comply, but I couldn't. Lord living. Neither could I escape the turmoil in my heart. My thoughts stayed hidden, waiting for a better time to discuss our son's rebellious nature, waiting for a moment alone where I could beg God for wisdom.

"Leave your brother out of this." Elmer's words bit the air like cymbals. "Your brother doesn't have your talent."

My heart quickened. Elmer had never raised a hand against any of us, but his words could be as sharp as the straight edge Tommy Akin used in his barber shop.

Beside me on the sofa, Marvin snickered. I ignored him, hoping not to draw attention to him. I'd lost influence on my boys years ago. Elmer had never shown much interest in them. Too busy with his job, he never disciplined them.

Jack looked at his brother knitting with me and shook his head. His eyes narrowed. "I hate you, Marvin. You're ruining my life."

"Now, Jack," I cautioned.

He turned to me. "You like him better. Admit it!" Jack moved closer. "You baby him. He's your favorite."

"What do you mean, dear?" I leaned forward and stammered. "He's not a baby. He's practically a grown man. He doesn't need me to discipline him." We weren't partial to Marvin, but Jack was the one always throwing a hissy fit. He demanded our full attention. I swear he'd argue with Al Capone in the flesh.

"Well, if he's so grown, why isn't he working? You probably won't even make him get a job. He'll live with you until he's a hundred! And don't blame it on the move. He hasn't kept a job since high school."

"Jack, that's enough." Elmer's soft hand swirled midair, like he could cut off his son like his band students. "No one wants to hear your complaining. The other boys your age have real problems. They're running off to California to find food. As usual, you're being thoughtless and inconsiderate."

"Don't you understand?" Jack glared at his father. "I can't have friends over because of Marvin and his weirdness. There's not a normal person in this house. I hate this family. I hate everyone!"

Shocked, I covered my mouth. My family had never functioned well. But even with these problems, Jack couldn't *hate* us.

Elmer ignored Jack's outburst and returned to his sheet music. Once again, he allowed the boys to argue and be disrespectful, with no correction.

Jack's face turned an angry red. He swiped his arms across the table, scattering the puzzle he'd been working on.

I jumped from the sofa, but before I could stop him, he stomped off to his room and slammed the door.

My heart sank as low as a bass fiddle. Lordy above, that boy was as resentful as a caught coon. I should've been accustomed to Jack's outbursts. He was often angry. But they always took me by surprise. Did he realize how well we had it? So many local families had lost jobs and homes when the fields dried up. The prairie wind that once cooled the farmers as they worked bountiful crops in the summer heat now blew the barren topsoil to the heavens. Each day, someone moved away from all they'd ever known, hoping to find farm work west of the Rockies. The irony of coming home when everyone else was moving away was not lost on me.

I retreated to the sofa. I'd become a recluse when Jack was born. A fussy baby was a good excuse not to show my face in town when Elmer and I were going through a bumpy time in our marriage. But the fussing turned to tantrums as Jack grew older. A rough-and-tumble young boy, he didn't fit into our quiet family well. His delicate father didn't know how to respond to him, and by the time Jack started school, his temper had grown uncontrollable and intense.

Marvin knit with fury beside me, withdrawn to his hidden world. Vexation seemed just below the surface. Marvin was a funny child, fragile like his daddy. From the time he was a tot, he'd follow me around. I didn't mind, seeing as how I didn't have a daughter like I wanted. Sometimes, I wished he'd been born a girl. A girl would have made my life complete. But like my sisters, I never got a daughter who'd love me. The only love I felt was from the Lord, and I cherished the time I prayed and read my Bible.

Perhaps the support of my tenacious sisters would bring strength to my prayers.

***

The next morning, Jennie showed up before my second cup of coffee. How she managed to look so put-together so early, I'd never comprehend. My prairie dress was ragged around the edges. My hair hung loose, not yet pulled into its normal tight bun. I felt frumpy beside her.

"I thought about it last night," Jennie said. "I think you should put your plates in the cabinet near the stove."

I held my tongue. I liked where my plates sat.

Before I could find a kind way to say it, Matilda walked in the front door, wearing trousers and an oversized shirt and carrying a dutch pot. "I brought lunch. Leftover chicken and dumplings from last night."

"Aren't you all a blessing," I took the heavy dish from her and carried it to the stove. "I planned to run to Wilson's Grocery, but I'm waiting for the ice truck to arrive. Can't keep much food on hand without ice."

The back screen door slammed behind me. My boys ran across the backyard, escaping without a word to me or their aunts. Elmer had left hours earlier in less hurry, but equal silence.

I sighed, seeing the boys didn't connect with family, except maybe to Jennie for her mouth-watering cookies, or when Jack played ball with his cousins. I'd excused it because we only saw them a few times a year, but I doubted time would improve their relationships. Still, perhaps my stronger-willed sisters could help my boys develop into presentable young men like theirs. I could hope.

Matilda headed for the boys' room to unpack and hang the rest of their clothes.

I followed Jennie as she walked through the house, surveying the work left to do. She stopped in the corner of my bedroom beside a cardboard box that had seen better days. A tattered string tying it together had come unfastened.

"It's the only box left. Do you want me to unpack it?"

Actually, I didn't want her help, but then I did want her help. Life was confusing.

I shooed her away. "We move so often those aren't worth unpacking."

Jennie ignored me and opened the box. She pulled a delicate plate from the newspaper wrapping. "Aren't these the China dishes you got at your wedding?"

A wistful ache built in my chest. "I'm saving it for when we have a home of our own." Years ago, Elmer had promised we'd purchase a house. I'd wrapped the dishes to save for that memorable day.

"And when would that be?"

I shrugged. Would it ever happen?

Lord knows, I'd lost count of the number of places we'd lived. Mangum, Gould, Wellington, Vinson, Willow, and a few other towns around western Oklahoma and Arkansas. We even lived once in Texas where Elmer tried to teach in a one-room country schoolhouse. He had twenty children of all ages. He hated it.

Moving every school year or two had become routine. Jennie couldn't understand because she'd never moved away from Harmon County, never lived anywhere else. She'd remained in the same house for over twenty years.

Usually, our moves were due to accusations of misconduct, an unfair way to get Elmer to leave if the school board didn't like him. But Elmer never seemed concerned because he always managed to secure another job in a different town.

It never made sense to me, though. Elmer was an excellent musician and a talented teacher. Other educators spent years at the same school, but he never could. Why did people circulate spiteful stories? Had he done something wrong? Made people upset? My chest tightened to think about it.

I pushed my suspicions aside, determined to trust his side of the story over rumors. As a wife, what else could I do? I'd prayed for years, hoping God would answer and see fit to give Elmer a new heart. Anyway, now that we lived in my hometown, I was certain nothing wayward would happen. Nope. Not in Hollis, Oklahoma.

Chapter 4

The next day, my sister, Mary Bobbie, arrived from Texas earlier than expected. “Lands ‘o living, that was the longest trip I ever made,” she said, walking up our porch steps. “I should’ve taken the rail, the way that ferry struggled to get across the river. Heavens, that river’s nearly as dry as Grandma’s biscuits. A mule could have made better time.”

I laughed. I hadn’t seen her since last Christmas, and I’d missed her sense of humor. “Glad you made it. Not much rain this year. Even the cotton farmers are complaining.”

Bobbie handed me a round tin. “Honey, there may not be many cookies left because I snuck a few myself. You know how traveling makes a body hungry. I’ll bake another batch before I leave.” Even though she looked frazzled and came to help with preparations for Annie’s coming baby, she’d still bake up a storm.

“Wish you could stay more than a few weeks.”

“I wish that too, but we’ll see. I prayed this awful heat would lift, but it’s as hot as last summer when the hogs fainted dead away.” She raised her eyebrows higher than her grin.

Mary Bobbie had rounded out more since I last saw her, but that was expected since she loved sweets more than anything except her husband Shannon and her son. Even after being married for a quarter of a century, anyone could see how much they enjoyed each other's company. I wished Elmer and I had such a sweet relationship.

Sadness fell on me, but I pushed it away. "My word, dearie, I was hoping Robert would come with you." Her son, near in age to Jack, had a level head. He'd be a good influence on my boy.

"School has already started, and honey, I couldn't take him out. Not that he wouldn't have loved missing class. The boy's sense of adventure has never included textbooks."

Bobbie inspected each room of our small house, admiring the layout, her dress swirling about her, and her full body overwhelming the small space. She did most of the talking, always had, ever since I could remember.

The late summer heat baked the wood structure. We moved to the living room and took turns standing in front of the round electric fan. I picked up two magazines, handing one to Bobbie. We fanned ourselves with *Good Housekeeping*. Even then, nothing could keep the sweat from running down my spine.

My sister reorganized the books on the bookshelf. I sat in the rocking chair and watched, wishing she'd leave them as they were. I'd shelved them in alphabetical order and liked them that way. We had a dozen or so music books and a few children's books, like *Dr. Dolittle* and *The Wizard of Oz*. She stacked up the magazines I thumbed through daily.

Then she held up the novel, *The Age of Innocence*. She looked at me askance, as if it reminded her of the days before our troubles began. "Darling, are you as well as can be expected? Elmer behaving himself lately? You've been on my mind, and I've been worried about you all."

Something about the way Mary Bobbie asked about Elmer, and the look in her eyes, made me wonder. Did she suspect something?

***

A few days later, all four of my sisters meandered to my front porch for iced tea and dessert. We looked similar enough that outsiders could tell we were kin. Pale skin, fine noses, brown hair with Jennie's a shade darker, and active dispositions. Nevertheless, we each had our own distinctive personalities. We presented a diversified bunch, with Mary Bobbie leaning toward the fun, outgoing type while I teetered on the other end as a recluse.

If any family liked to share sweets, it was mine. Jennie and Matilda had loaded me down with enough cherry pie and apple cobbler to last a month. It was their way of showing hospitality—a welcoming committee of sisters.

We gathered, pie in hand. Jennie and Till settled on the swing, and the rest of us on chairs from the dining room. Several of us took off our shoes.

"How're you doing, Annie dear?" asked Bobbie, patting Ann on the leg. "You weren't feeling well the last time I heard from you." Letters regularly flowed among us sisters, and Ann must have written about her poor health and difficult pregnancy.

"Oh, me-oh-my. Some days are better than others," she groaned. "Some days I can't get out of bed. It's those times I fret about my boys. Those two are a rowdy lot, and I just don't know how I can manage them and this new baby, too."

My other sisters nodded in understanding. Forks clanged against my wedding China that Jennie had convinced me to unpack. I diverted my attention to my cherry pie, slicing bites from alternating sides to keep it even. I liked things in order and talk of the boys was a messy subject.

"Mm … mm. I do believe this is the best cherry pie I've ever eaten." Ann rubbed her swollen belly. "I wish I could bake like that. Tommy has to eat my poor cooking every day."

"You'll get the hang of it. Just keep practicing," Jennie insisted.

Ann smiled. “That’s the problem. I’ve been practicing since we got married, and it hasn’t improved yet.”

We all laughed. It was true. Cooking was not among her greatest skills.

“You could help Tillie with her sewing business instead of cooking,” bossy Mary Bobbie added.

“You do like dressing up in the latest fashions,” said Jennie. “And you’re better at sewing than cooking. Your boys can attest to that.”

I nodded in agreement with my sisters’ assessment of Annie’s talent but said nothing. I didn’t know if silk scarves and circular skirts were in style, or the difference between a sailor collar and Peter Pan collar. But Ann, the best dresser of the bunch, did.

“Good idea. What about it, Tillie?” asked Jennie. “Could you use Annie here with your new sewing business? You have a lot more customers since you’ve moved into your own place.” Jennie had a knack for directness, and when an idea got started, she was the one to finish it.

“I spend more time mending tears than creating new fashions,” Matilda said. “But it seems to pile up. Come on by the house, Ann, and we’ll talk about it.” Till had softened since she left that Frank rascal. Kindness peeked through where there’d been toughness before.

“Heavens, sister. Let’s wait until after this baby’s born.” Ann’s eyes widened. Then she perked up and lifted her chin in confidence. “My baby girl, that is!”

Everyone snickered because all of us hoped along with her. Our family sorely needed lace-covered, pink pinafores on a child.

“You may not have much time to sew after the baby’s born.” Jennie filled her mouth with the last bite of her cobbler.

Annie grinned. The ability to make her own clothing suited her well, but having a third child would put a damper on her style. “I’m sure I can find the time if the kids stay quiet long enough.”

A dog barked next door. Some of our boys started a stickball game in the street, stirring up the dust. The littlest ones swung on a rope hanging from a catalpa tree at the edge of the property. Marvin pulled a chair under another shade tree to protect his pale skin and watched the boys play. He was a good cousin, making sure no one got hurt. But maybe I thought that because he was my boy.

Mary Bobbie turned her gaze from Ann to me. "Honey, Marvin needs something to do. He's good with children. Perhaps he can help Ann out."

The cherry pie in my stomach churned. "Oh, Marvin finds plenty to do." Unfortunately, Tom didn't have work for him down at his store. While Marvin needed a job, I wasn't about to volunteer him for work without speaking to him first.

I tried to shift the conversation. "He's learning to crochet with the items he got for Christmas. You wouldn't believe how quickly he's picked it up. He already knows how to knit. He said working with his hands helps him relax."

My sisters didn't meet my eyes, and an awkward silence fell. Had I said something wrong?

"Do you think that's healthy?" Matilda, who had four rowdy boys of her own, leaned forward. "I mean, most boys don't like to sit around and do girl stuff."

Jennie nodded. "The other boys might make fun of him. I heard one call him a ninny."

Marvin was not a girlie boy. Brilliant, yes. A little eccentric, maybe. None of my sisters understood him. No one understood him but me, and sometimes even I didn't. Elmer had never taken the time to appreciate Marvin, which made me sad. How could a boy grow up to be confident with a preoccupied father who focused more on his students than his sons?

"Susie May, I made you a loaf of homemade zucchini bread." Mary Bobbie changed the subject. "Let me get us a slice—just a taste since we've already filled up on pie!"

As she disappeared into the house with our empty plates, Matilda and Jennie pulled out funeral fans and wafted the surrounding air. The shade under the porch helped break the heat, but a breeze would have been more effective.

"Don't you worry, honey. Someday Marvin will find his way." Jennie knew me better than the others because we were so close in age. Her insight always felt comforting, up until she pried into my personal life with Elmer. "I like your new curtains. Are they the ones Tillie made for you?"

"The curtains are nice," I said, thinking I could tolerate them. "Till's a wonderful seamstress."

Sally Matilda seemed embarrassed by the compliment. Fluffy words weren't in her vocabulary. In fact, they weren't often said while we were growing up. Still all my sisters' faces were full of smiles, leaving my heart warm and full.

I felt content living close to them, even if they intruded into my life. I'd have to become accustomed to nosy and pushy again, but I would. I was ready to grow some roots. I never wanted to leave Hollis, change schools, find another house, pack up belongings, and set up housekeeping in a new space. I certainly didn't want to leave my family now that I'd finally come home to them.

The sadness I'd felt for years seemed to have been wiped away—or at least lessened. I prayed Elmer could keep this job.

Chapter 5

"How was your day?" I asked Elmer a few weeks into the new school year.

"I can't believe they expect me to teach three hours of history while teaching band." Elmer set his saxophone case on the floor near me. "I won't have time to tutor but a few kids who need it."

I sat on the rug sorting out *Life* magazines by date, the newest ones on top. "But you must enjoy history more than the English class you taught last year. Did Jack show up for band?"

"I'm teaching junior high *and* high school band this year, which is a time-consuming headache."

"What about Jack?"

Elmer dropped onto the sofa and looked out the front window. "I've always preferred the younger students."

I looked at him, surprised. Had I known that? Was I not paying attention to my husband? Thoughts of Jack disappeared. "Why do you like teaching the younger ones?"

"Easy. The kids are more trusting and adaptable. They don't complain as much as the older students when I call them to task. You wouldn't believe the excuses I get for not practicing at home like they should."

I nodded. That made sense. Of course, Elmer could make anything sound reasonable.

"And the younger ones look up to me more. They seem to respond better. Naturally, I enjoy being treated as a famous maestro." Elmer tossed his head, and I could see his glee. I was glad someone besides me appreciated his outstanding gift, even if it was only the young students.

"They're also more willing to be tutored after class, which reminds me, I'm going to stay late after school three days a week. I don't want to, you know, but some of these students have promising talent. They need someone to take them under their wing. A few students are interested. A girl named Lulu, especially, has great musical ability. I've already made arrangements with her."

I gritted my teeth. Who was Lulu?

When we first married, I suspected flirting when he tutored his high school students. I swore I smelled perfume on his clothes. And girls giggled when we passed them on the street. But he was a handsome man, and I remembered the innocence of high school crushes on teachers.

But I grew to hate when Elmer stayed after school.

I stopped my negative thoughts and tried to replace them with good ones, just like Jesus would have me do. After all, this was Elmer, my husband. And he came home to me every night.

***

A windstorm blew in the next week. Another of the many dust storms we'd lived through, but the first in this house. The strong wind howled and squealed as it passed through every loose board and window jam. Somehow, it found the narrowest places to whistle and blow in layers of dust. This house had a thousand gaps where powder filtered in. I sprinted around stuffing paper and rags into the cracks.

Marvin sat in the corner of the living room where his hands worked full-speed crocheting. His thin hair fell over his pale face, and his eyes focused downward as he worked.

Grime attached to the sweat beading on my brow. The late summer heat could make anyone grouchy, especially me. My mousy colored hair lay flat around my face, waiting for hair-washing day on Saturday. A secluded feeling clung to me like those bits of sticky dirt. My emotions wailed in and out with the wind, collecting in my heart's crevices. I felt isolated, even if my sisters lived only minutes away.

"Ma, it's terrible out there!" Jack yelled as he bolted through the front door, letting in more swirling dirt. He forced the door shut against the wind. "Every store in town closed up early. Already knocked our fence post down." He dusted himself off and removed the cloth from around his face. Without washing his hands, he grabbed an apple from the counter and ran to his bedroom to hunker down.

I shook my head. He'd hide under a blanket with a book the way he liked to do when a crisis occurred.

Marvin stopped his work and grabbed a snack before disappearing to his room as well. I expected half as much. The school, just a few blocks away, meant Elmer would be shortly behind Jack after all the students were sent home.

The clock ticked away the time while I heated dinner in lidded pots. When the food was past ready, I worried something might have happened to him. He wasn't as familiar with the town as I was. What if he didn't make it home safely in the raging dust storm? I challenged the thought. More likely, he was staying with his students who didn't want to walk home in the storm. The thought of Elmer calming down some young missy made my chest ache.

An electric charge sparked through the dry air. Incensed, like me.

I called the boys to wash up and fed them. I joined them at the table but didn't eat. Instead, I stewed. My papa used to listen to me as if my thoughts mattered, but he left way too early. I missed him and ached for someone who understood my needs. Since Papa died, nobody had taken the time to hear me. My sisters cared, of course, but they weren't usually quiet long enough to hear my soft-spoken voice. I was the listener of the family.

My own table was silent. They scarfed down their food and returned to their rooms. The swirling wind continued.

Elmer sauntered through the door as if no storm raged outside. He took off his shiny, pointed shoes and dusted the silt off before placing them near the door.

I wiped the silt off the table, turned his plate right side up and served him boiled potatoes, green peas, and canned meat. I tried to start a conversation with Elmer about his delay, but he shrugged, not interested in my feelings. He didn't seem to notice when I withdrew in silence to wash the dishes. Did he even sense the anger sitting on my shoulders when I served him a second helping of peas, cleaned his dishes, or scoured the kitchen table until it shined?

It's difficult to be angry with someone who ignores you. My fury and love intermingled, tearing at my essence like the windstorm did to everything it touched. I wondered how I could stay married to a man like him for so many years. Maybe I'd buried my feelings under layers of fine silt like the storms did.

Elmer removed his clarinet from its case and sat in his usual chair as if nothing was wrong. Musical notes filled the surrounding air, his talent and professionalism evident. Even I could appreciate that. Why was I unhappy? Elmer provided for me. He treated me well. I loved him. What more did I want?

Uncomfortable thoughts jabbed at me.

Several days after the dust storm, I visited my brother-in-law's dry goods store. Inside Newberry's, I collected the lard, sugar, bacon, greens, and salt that I needed, and placed them on the counter so they'd be ready when I left.

I wandered to a table loaded with bolts of material in the back of the store. We didn't have money for the pretty printed cotton, but nearby in a cubbyhole, lay a pile of scrap material for sale. I crouched to rummage through the pieces, hoping to find enough to start a sunshine quilt.

The front door opened, and the bell jingled. Knowing Tom would be busy with another customer, I took my time picking through the colorful scraps.

Low voices passed through the open areas between the bolts of fabric. "Did you hear about the new band teacher?" A husky woman's voice sounded conspiratorial.

I perked up but didn't recognize the person.

"I heard he scared a girl in Madill. Do you know any details?" A second woman with a nasally voice asked.

"Well, I heard it like this. . ." The first women whispered.

I overheard the word pregnant, which scared me something awful. I moved closer to the bolts of fabric.

"The girl told her mama what happened, and her mama went to the sheriff. They didn't file charges because they couldn't prove anything. The girls' word against his. And he's a grown man, and a well-respected teacher at that. *Humph*. Men in our town aren't likely to believe a female, either."

I gripped the scraps and stayed as quietly as I could—not that I was ever very loud. I'd learned to keep my mouth closed and tiptoe around gossipers. But also, I felt the shame of being discovered eavesdropping.

The second woman hissed, "Well, you heard about that other girl, right? He hoodwinked her into . . ."

"You can't go on what you hear," the first scolded. "They're not through checking into it yet."

"My husband said if it happens in Hollis, Mr. Lindsey will be run out of town so fast the hound dogs couldn't catch him."

"If the girl's telling the truth, he may be run out sooner than that."

Both women laughed, not a funny laugh, though, but a nasty laugh like only gossipers share.

I was shocked by their hateful words—wounded—and I didn't want to believe any of it. None of this gossip was true, was it? Their words were simply spiteful, wrong conclusions based on hearsay. They had to be. My husband was a hard worker and a talented musician. Why did people find fault in him? Didn't they realize that musicians tended to be eccentric?

Just like Papa instructed me to do, I loved my husband with all that was in me, like I'd loved and served my dear papa. My whole heart, my whole life, was woven into Elmer's. But could the rumors be true? Could Elmer have faults I didn't want to acknowledge?

We'd moved to so many different towns, and I'd been in so many stores like this one, heard so much prattle like this, that it all started to look and sound the same. But this was my hometown. Could the gossip have followed us here?

I waited for the women to make their purchases and leave the store before I dropped the materials scraps I'd chosen and ran out. As I hurried home, tears stung my face. I forgot about my groceries, feeling like that old fence post in our front yard.

Everyone liked Elmer when they first met him. He could smooth-talk a Brahma bull into licking your hand—a nice-talking, sophisticated gentleman.

But were these women right about him?

Chapter 6

Through the years, you get to know your sisters pretty well. Everyone knew Mary Bobbie liked two things—besides her family, that is. Eating and having fun. No one around her could claim boredom. And if life got the least bit slow, she'd find an event, create a riot, or drag us all the way to happiness, screaming and kicking.

Irked because there was little to do in Hollis with the Depression closing so many businesses, Bobbie stopped peeling potatoes and said, "What say we take a spin over to Altus tomorrow? We can spend the day shopping and get back before supper."

"And whose jalopy do you suggest we take?" Jennie, the practical sister, enjoyed life, too, but realism ruled most of her decisions. "And if we found a ride, we'd have to leave early, and I need to finish two pies before supper. I promised Mrs. Bateman."

"Ah, you're no fun. Then let's go to a picture show. There's a good flick showing in town, and honey, I do like a good laugh." Bobbie was not one to give up.

"Don't suggest that Frankenstein horror movie I heard the boys talk about. Sounds like a nightmare. Angry townspeople attacking a scorned and lonely creature."

That sounded like an event Elmer and I might have lived through. "I've never been to a picture show," I said. Elmer didn't see fit to waste time watching make-believe stories or listening to a half-talented spinster playing the piano in the background, although my boys had probably snuck off to watch a film or two.

"You've never been to the cinema?" Both Mary Bobbie and Jennie turned and looked at me like I was a stranger.

"In that case, it's as good as done. I'll even fund the whole thing," said Mary Bobbie. "We'll get the girls together and go to the matinee tomorrow afternoon. The new Charlie Chaplin movie is showing. Jennie, tell Tillie to be ready at one-thirty with her high-heeled boots on. She needs a break from work, anyway. And I'll coerce Annie into coming."

I sighed in resignation a lot, but this time, the sigh thoroughly filled with excitement. I'd secretly always wanted to go to the theater.

***

The five of us agreed to meet at Jennie's at precisely one-thirty.

On my way, I stopped by Anna Lee's to borrow a sash to match my dress, and she opened the door in a frump. "Oh, pooh, I look plain dowdy in this maternity dress, Susie. But nothing I can do about it." Her top had gathers flowing down over the front, stopping just past her baby belly. The two-piece dress looked pressed and starched, and the collar matched her low-heeled, lace-up shoes.

"You look great," I said. "You look perky even if you waddle." Poor girl. A walk in this heat might be trying.

There was no way to hurry Ann, but we still arrived at Jennie's before Matilda did.

"Who's watching the boys?" Jennie asked Ann as we entered the living room.

"Mrs. Weston. She'll put them down for a nap."

Jennie walked in all gussied up. The print fabric of her waisted dress was bias cut, had scallops, and flattered her figure. The hemline was shorter than mine, suggestive of new styles.

Matilda arrived five minutes later. I hadn't seen her look so spiffy since Easter potluck. She must have been making herself new clothes in the evenings after sewing for everybody in town.

Mary Bobbie entered the room with a flourish. The draped bodice of her attire had voluminous dramatic sleeves which matched her bobbing hat. The style flattered her small waist and rounded figure. She looked grand.

"Where did you get that gorgeous dress? Is that what they're wearing down in Texas?" Sally Matilda, the town seamstress, awed over the creation. "I'd love to get the pattern from you."

"Done, my dear. I'll send it with my next letter." Bobbie pranced around the room like royalty before she stopped to ask Annie to fasten her necklace. Dressed to the hilt for an afternoon at the theater, I wished we could have taken a photograph.

After the admiration show, Jennie offered, "We'll have tea after the flick, and Bobbie baked us up a chocolate pie."

I smiled. Mary Bobbie would have thought of food. To her, a get-together wasn't proper without sweets.

We grabbed our pocketbooks stuffed with red lipstick, spectacles, and handkerchiefs, and prepared to go, more excited than on Christmas morning. We pulled on our gloves and scooted out the door.

"What's the name of the show?" asked Matilda, as we crossed a street, careful of an oncoming motorcar. "I haven't been to the cinema since last spring."

"*City Lights*," said Bobbie, "and you're going to love it."

We bustled down the street in our finery like we owned the town. Tom Newberry even waved at us from the front of his store. I could see the picture show's shiny marquee a block away and couldn't help but grin.

Each of us insisted on paying our quarter. One by one, a young whippersnapper ushered us down the aisle. My high heels were uncomfortable on the steep decline, but I made it to my seat.

We spoke in hushed tones as we smoothed our dresses. Something about the heavy, red velvet curtain covering the screen gave off an aura of majesty. A lady played soft piano music in the background before the lights dimmed and the curtains parted. We fell silent in anticipation. A cartoon played a Looney Tunes show called *Basko, the Talk-Ink Kid*. I would remember every detail once I figured out what talk-ink meant.

Then the black and white silent movie started. Charlie Chaplain played a character named the Little Tramp. He fell in love with a blind flower girl and developed a friendship with a drunken, crazy millionaire.

No one spoke for a few minutes after the delightful film ended. We twittered as we filed out the front door. Walking toward Jennie's, we laughed and giggled like schoolgirls. I halfway expected us to join arms, do the can-can, and start singing, *Ain't Misbehavin*. I hadn't experienced so much merriment in my life. At least not in years.

"Thank you for putting this together," I said. "I didn't know how much fun the theater could be." Living close to my sisters was already enriching my life. I enjoyed being around them, enjoyed the interaction, the playfulness, and the love we shared. God had blessed me immensely by bringing me back to Hollis.

Chapter 7

Saturday morning, I woke up early and walked over to Annie's house to collect a few eggs for breakfast. Her husband, Tommy, kept hens in a backyard chicken coop, so they had a consistent supply of fresh eggs.

As I started to open the door, I heard a man's voice coming from inside. "So far, it's only a rumor."

Something about the man's conspiratory tone made me pause.

Through the open kitchen window, I saw my two brothers-in-law, Tom Newberry and Tommy Akin, drinking coffee at the kitchen table. The rich smell drifted out the window.

"Oscar came to get his hair cut yesterday like he does once a month," said Tommy. "He's angry at Elmer enough to run him out of town."

"Why? What does he have against Elmer?"

"He says his daughter's self-respect is on the line."

Oh no. It was happening again. Elmer's reputation was being questioned. Now I knew why people turned away when I went out or didn't speak when I approached.

"Is Oscar the guy who owns that service station on the edge of town?" asked Tom.

"That's the one. He stays awful dirty, but can't help it, working on people's old jalopies." Tommy knew most everyone in town. He probably knew most everyone from Altus to Kansas City, considering the many fellows who drove through town and stopped at his barbershop or looked over a heifer or steer he had for sale.

"From what I hear, Oscar's an honest fellow," said Tom. "Heard his daughter, Lulu, hasn't been to school all week."

My stomach turned over as I realized who they meant. Oscar's thirteen-year-old daughter, Lulu, was in Elmer's band class. He had mentioned her. Tutored her.

"It's hard to know what's true and what isn't," Tommy said.

"I can believe this. Elmer's had trouble before, and we don't need a scandal." Tom's words as a town leader were full of concern and also, I thought, a bit of judgment.

I didn't want to get my sisters' families involved, and I especially didn't want anyone to feel sorry for us. Having heard enough, I put my hand on the doorknob and opened the door. I didn't want to hear any more rumors, but I could read between the lines. Rumors had started. People would believe what they wanted to believe.

The men jerked their faces toward me and stared.

I averted my eyes so they couldn't see my tears and walked with my face straight ahead. "Hey, Tommy. Annie said I could grab a few eggs."

He nodded.

I grabbed three and slipped out the door.

One thought lifted me from total despair. The townspeople would see things differently after the Christmas concert. They'd hear the glorious thrill of a big band performance in the middle of the dusty Oklahoma plains. They'd see Elmer's talent and ability to get the best from his pupils. That would change their minds, and the townspeople would want him to stay.

That hadn't happened at previous schools, but I didn't want to think about that. This was my hometown. Surely, we were wanted here.

I recalled an incident in Hobart, or whatever town it was, when the school board flat out accused Elmer of misconduct. Misconduct? More like perversion. Shameful. Accusing an upstanding man like Elmer of fondling a little girl? How could they? Not that I hadn't had doubts at times, usually when he talked about the pretty young students. I subdued my suspicions and tried to remember all the ways Elmer provided for me and the boys.

Rumors. Just rumors.

Ignore the rumors.

But I couldn't.

These rumors were started by a well-established man named Oscar Benton who claimed Elmer messed with his daughter.

Oscar wanted Elmer Lindsey to leave town.

I hurried home and went straight to bed.

Chapter 8

I didn't leave my house for three days after overhearing the men talk about Oscar's claim. Depression settled around me. I couldn't even read my Bible and make any sense of it. Couldn't pray a tadpole to a frog if my life depended on it. I could barely cook a meal for my family, much less keep the kitchen as organized and spotless as I liked. The more disorganized and dirtier it became, the more I sank into despair. What if the rumors were true?

My front door opened, and someone entered without knocking.

I grabbed the edges of my robe and squealed as I jumped from my chair.

Sally Matilda studied me.

I'd forgotten how family just showed up at your house and walked in. We never had company when we lived in other towns. "Good gracious, you scared me."

"Go on and get dressed, Susie May, we're going out." Till, in her straightforward way, looked as serious as a mile-high squall. Had she heard about the rumors? I hoped not.

"I don't want to go. You go ahead." Midmorning, and I was still in my nightclothes while, in contrast, Till's little pillbox hat matched her calf-length dress perfectly.

Sally Matilda pursed her lips. She didn't know how to give up. "No excuses. Now go on."

I didn't have the strength to resist her pleading. I dragged my feet to my room and took my time to don a simple dress and arrange my old-fashioned bonnet over a tight bun.

Stepping out, I found she'd cleaned my neglected, sand-encrusted kitchen. She wiped her hands on a towel, grabbed her purse and my arm, and ushered me out the door.

Hollis was a typical, small Midwestern town. A tiny settlement compared to a metropolis like Fort Worth. We sauntered down Broadway Street on the boardwalk, looking into the store windows. Ellis Department Store was having a sale, and the Piggy Wiggly looked empty. Not a soul out shopping. Dirt swirled around the main street, and tumbleweeds stacked against many of the buildings. Color dotted the dingy town, like the red and white striped barber pole, the hotel billboard, and several brightly painted storefronts. Normally a busy place, like time stood still, waiting for the next drastic event to happen, but maybe that was just in my mind.

Matilda and I discussed the changes that had happened in town since we were kids. How motor cars were the new fad, scaring horses and citizens alike. How telephones changed the way we communicated. How electric lights made the town safer.

For some reason, it was easier to talk with my sisters one-on-one than in a group. "Does your tailoring business keep you and the boys fed?" I noticed my worn, cotton shirtwaist fell too close to my ankles to be stylish. While Sally Matilda was stepping into the future, I was stuck in the past.

"As good as can be expected."

We stopped in front of Gardner's, and she led me inside. I took a deep breath. Memories came flooding through me. Pushing aside the lady gossipers' words, I recalled our younger days when we'd buy penny candy displayed on this same glass countertop. I thought of the red metal top I wanted when I was ten years old and how Mary Bobbie bought it for me with money she'd saved.

"Back here," shouted Matilda.

I followed her to the bolts of material.

"Pick out something you like, and I'll make you a new dress. You'll be prancing around like a peacock."

"I can't do that. We don't have extra funds." I yearned for something new and showy to feel better about myself, but I didn't feel like I deserved it. Or that Elmer would approve.

"Oh, it's from Jennie and me. We're buying you an early birthday present." Till held up some pretty crimson material. "Perfect for a new dress."

Elmer would be shocked if I stepped out sporting fancy new attire. He spent money on his outfits but said I didn't need much since I stayed home all the time.

Why, my boys wouldn't recognize their own mother!

The crimson color caught my eye, and I rubbed the soft fabric between my fingers. It'd been years since I had a new dress. I sniffed the lovely, pressed material and smiled. It would make an adorable frock, especially with a pleated skirt and white lace collar.

I exhaled and shoved the material aside. "I don't need it. Maybe I'll ask Elmer when he gets his next paycheck."

Matilda's eyes held an understanding I didn't want to see. I hated for her to guess my despondency. My distressing marriage. My doubts. Maybe she recognized my despair from her own time when she had nothing.

Till shook her head and frowned.

We left the store and continued our walk under the downtown awning. Whiffs of heavenly bread came from Wards Bakery, and we gawked at the new fashions in the display window of J. C. Penney's. Rose pink, sea green, and soft yellow dominated the new dresses in the window. We wondered when the next talkie film would come to the Empress Theatre and stopped to examine a poster for the upcoming movie.

At the end of the five blocks of Broadway, Till stopped and looked at me. "Now tell me. What's going on with you, sis?"

My tongue stuck to the roof of my mouth. I couldn't tell her I feared Elmer had a problem. She would dismiss my thoughts as nonsense and not understand the big, aching hole in my heart.

"I don't think Elmer loves me." The words flew out of my mouth before I had a chance to stop them. Did I believe that? It took very little thought before I knew it was true. I'd never been able to satisfy Elmer. Maybe that was why he seldom stayed home. Why he spent so many evenings tutoring young students. He didn't like my company. It was my fault. "I can't keep him happy. I try, but I can't love him enough."

I started walking again. Matilda followed, and we turned around at the corner of Hudson and strode down the south side of Broadway. Storefronts dimmed as my eyes watered, and I blinked back tears.

Finally, my sister reached out and turned me toward her. "Now, Susie May, I'm sure Elmer cares for you. You've been together for a long time. Love doesn't always solve all our problems."

"I shouldn't have said that. Elmer takes good care of me and the boys. We never lack for anything." We started walking again.

"You think your job as Elmer's wife is to keep your mouth shut and grit your teeth?" Till's stern voice scolded me. "Hold in the pain. Is that it?"

"Isn't that what a good Christian wife is supposed to do?"

Till's mouth flattened like she was deciding which words to let loose. I hoped they weren't bad ones.

"Well, isn't that what Jesus did?" I said quietly. "He didn't complain, did he? He didn't run away from his problems. He just stood there and took it."

Matilda halted again. She hesitated like she didn't want to hurt me, but her loud voice echoed through my mind. "I don't think Jesus was a pushover, if that's what you mean." She paused, and I could see concern filter through her anger. "And he'd never condone perversion." Her voice sounded quieter than usual.

I stared at her. Realization came slowly. It could be true. All the accusations. All the rumors through the years. And my sisters, everybody, knew it. The pain hit hard, like when I fell from a bucking horse, and it kicked me in the stomach. I didn't want to hear the truth I'd avoided for years.

I covered my ears like a child, desperate to keep the truth from penetrating. My sister stared at me. Probably everybody in town was staring at me. I wanted to run away, to hide in my house and never leave again.

Matilda rested her hand on my arm, and I lowered my hands from my ears. Her expression became kind and understanding. And Sally Matilda probably thought she understood because her husband often beat her and the boys and made himself into the town drunk and a losing gambler. Of course, she *had* to leave Frank.

But Elmer wasn't like that. He didn't drink, didn't make a spectacle of himself. He'd never raised a hand to us. He was a good man.

A good man.

Except he wasn't a good man. If the accusations were true, then Elmer was the worst kind of man.

"Have you thought of leaving him? The Lord would understand." Till looked away. "I had to leave Frank even when I didn't want to."

"The rumors can't be true. They can't. God can still fix this."

I held onto the little thread of hope that Jesus cared. He understood how my marriage worked and would help me through. Maybe Elmer had an explanation.

My sister frowned but took my arm and started us back toward home. She would never understand how my heart sped up every time I thought of leaving Elmer. My throat tightened. No, I couldn't allow those thoughts to wiggle into my mind. But what could I do if the rumors were true?

I couldn't leave.

But I couldn't stay with a man like that.

I hated myself.

I hated my life.

I hated Elmer.

Without speaking again, Matilda and I arrived at my front porch. She gave me a long hug and said, "I love you, sis. I'm down the road if you need to talk."

***

Without rain in months, the leaves shriveled into a dull brown—duller than the reddish-brown sky. Duller than my daily life.

Marvin became more introverted than ever, keeping to himself. Meanwhile, Jack spent most of his time running with Matilda's boys. I hoped they could lead him in the right direction, but I wasn't too sure. Jack had never walked into Elmer's band room, not even once.

Going through the motions, I woke late and rushed to start cooking bacon, scrambled eggs, and homemade biscuits. Still in my nightgown and robe, a scarf wrapped turban-style around my head, I hurried to get breakfast on the table before school. I stayed awake much of the night, quietly crying, praying, and worrying.

I grumbled to myself, turning the fire up higher under the bacon while I rolled out biscuit dough.

Elmer sauntered in, dressed for the day, immaculate as always. He sat down in his regular chair and casually opened the newspaper I'd placed on the table for him. He didn't notice my gloominess.

A burning smell hit my nostrils. I jumped and yanked the skillet off the flames.

"Something smells awful. What's wrong?"

"I burned the bacon." I dished out the bacon still eatable and carried the skillet outside and set it in the grass. I'd deal with that later. Rushing through to the kitchen, I pulled out another pan, added bacon grease, and poured in the egg mixture.

"At this rate, I'm going to be late for work. This isn't the day to decide to burn something." He stood. "I'll skip breakfast."

I continued cooking, ignoring his comment. "What time will you be home tonight? I'm baking a chicken pot pie and need to know when to have it ready."

"Don't worry about dinner. Just feed the boys. I won't be home until late."

"Late? How late?"

"I have a meeting with the school board."

Why did Elmer have a school meeting on a Friday night? I must have made a face, because he made eye contact.

"Don't worry your head about it." He grabbed his hat from the rack and walked confidently out the door like a prima donna strutting across a hick town stage.

***

That afternoon, Jennie walked into our house without knocking, as usual. "Susie, I brought sugar cookies."

My sisters were checking on me. Till had dropped by a few days before. And Mary Bobbie had popped in before her return to Texas. "Let me know if you need me to traipse back up here," she told me. I believed her. She'd travel from Argentina if I needed her help.

Only Annie, who was laid up ready to have a baby, hadn't appeared, though I didn't expect her. I felt guilty not helping her during her confinement, but I didn't want my depression to sour her mood.

I sat up from where I'd been lounging on the sofa, ran my fingers through my long hair, and tied the unruly mess in a knot at my neck. "You shouldn't have brought sweets, sis."

Jennie dropped them on the table and sat at the other end of the sofa. "I heard you were depressed. I've been there," she said. "Ann's having a bad day, too."

Anna Lee, the baby in the family, could not be depressed. She'd always been protected, looked after, pampered. "What does she know about heartache?"

Jennie regarded me through narrowed eyes. "Did you forget what Annie went through? Before she married Tom, she was engaged to Adelai, the love of her life."

Oh my. I felt lower than an earthworm. How could I have forgotten that horrible time in Ann's life? Her loss had thrown her into a hole wider than the west coast. I didn't know if she'd ever recover, and frankly, I'd been too deep in my own sorrow to find out. Now poor Annie was fighting the baby blues.

"I'm sorry. When I'm melancholy, I forget others have been hurt, too."

"Bless your pea-picking heart. You worry too much." Jennie patted my shoulder. "You're in a slump right now."

"I'll survive, sis. The rumors make me panic. That's all. It'll pass."

"I'm with you this time." Jennie leaned forward and grabbed the plate of cookies, holding it in front of me. "Here, have one. It's a special recipe."

I picked up a sugar cookie and took a bite. Delicious. Comforting. Warming.

"Did you know there's a school board meeting tonight?" Jennie asked.

Dread filled me and I washed the cookie down with bitter coffee. We'd experienced school board meetings before. "I heard about it." My voice squeaked. "Elmer said I didn't need to worry about it." Over the years, Elmer kept me away from school difficulties. I attended the winter and spring band concerts, but that was all. I'd never set foot in his classroom, hiding like an ostrich puts her head in the sand.

"Some people are bringing accusations against Elmer. I think you should go."

I shook my head. "Oh, no. He said he can take care of it himself." My thoughts scattered as I considered the packing I would need to do if he was asked to leave the school.

"You won't be alone. I'll go with you." Jennie could never take no for an answer.

Dare I go? Elmer wouldn't want me there, but perhaps I needed to see it—to hear it—before word filtered out to the rest of my family. With Jennie beside me, I could muster the backbone to attend.

"Okay. I'll go."

Chapter 9

The school board meeting was set to begin at six-thirty at the Hollis school gymnasium. I made an early dinner for the boys, then walked to Jennie's. She linked arms with me as we walked into the gym. My shoulders tensed. Even though I didn't want to go, I resolved to face their accusations. Something inside me ached to hear the evidence presented against Elmer. What were lies and what were rumors?

He'd be angry if he saw me, but it didn't matter. Didn't I have the right to know the truth?

Only a scattering of people sat in the bleachers, for which I was grateful. Soon more entered. A group of five men sat in the middle of the court behind a table, the school board members, I assumed. Tom Newberry sat among them. My brother-in-law, a good man, would get to the bottom of this and dispel the speculations. I hoped that was possible.

Jennie and I sat near the side door, and I tilted my worn felt hat to the side to get a better look. Jennie removed her gloves and folded them neatly in her lap.

"There's Elmer." Jennie pointed to the front row.

He looked calm, as I would expect. Nothing seemed to rile him.

One of the board members called the special meeting to order and announced that the purpose was to hear complaints about the band teacher. My eyes bulged in surprise. This was the only reason for the meeting—to discuss Elmer's indiscretions?

They called a man named Oscar to the floor. He shifted from foot to foot, his hands in his pockets. Obviously, a country mechanic, his face and arms were darkened by sun exposure and his clothes stained with grease.

"What's your complaint, sir?"

"Well, it's like this. My little girl…Well, she's not such a little girl anymore, going on thirteen years old. Well, she was crying in her room one night, and if you know my little Lulu, you know she hardly ever gets sad. I've only seen her cry once, and that was when her little brother died last year with the dust pneumonia. Anyhow, here she is a-crying, and I don't like to see her cry, so I sent her mama into her room to find out what's wrong. She's in Lulu's room for so long I get worried about them. I hear both of them a-crying now. Seems like an hour goes by but might have been longer than that 'cause the sun was starting to set early like it does these days. Been setting earlier and earlier, as you know. That's why I been closing the shop around six o'clock."

"Sir, we'd appreciate you getting to the point. We don't need to know how long she cried."

Oscar's fingers, etched with black grease, twirled his hat in nervous circles.

"Well, Lulu's crying finally slowed down, so I knock on the door, and she says to come on in and I see Lulu and her mama with red faces from crying so much."

Jennie groaned beside me. At this rate, Oscar might talk all night, never get to the facts of the incident.

"I sit down in the chair beside them and ask what's the matter. That starts Lulu crying again, but it doesn't last too long this time. She tells me that this here trickster, the band teacher, has done something terribly bad." Oscar pointed his finger toward Elmer, but Elmer sat still, glaring at the floor.

"He manhandled her in the classroom after school. She's been taking tutoring from him to help her get better on the saxophone. Of course, that scoundrel promised the moon. Said she might be a great musician if he taught her.

"Well, sirs, it's looking like that conman had ulterior motives in his noggin. He kissed her and put his hands all over her in ways that made her most uncomfortable. Molested her. That's what he did. I ain't going for it." He gestured wildly, flapping his hat in the air, unable to control his emotions. His voice grew. "I want that man run out of town so fast a galloping hyena couldn't catch him. You should arrest him! Throw him in jail! He ain't fit to teach our children."

Oscar took a deep breath and plopped down into his chair.

I thought I might faint. He accused my husband of being a pervert. An abuser? My chest rose up and down as I tried to breathe. My racing heartbeat finally slowed as the board members whispered among themselves. This might not have been a court of law, but they could decide my family's fate. They could decide if this young girl's accusations would make a difference in this school, in this town.

"We'd like to hear Lulu's testimony, if you don't mind. She's a bit young to be standing up here, but she can speak with your permission." Tom's voice sounded official.

Oscar jumped to his feet. "She didn't want anyone to know about this, but I convinced her to come today. She'll talk." He motioned to a girl who sat behind him with an older woman. Her mother?

Lulu walked to the front and stood in front of the group of men. A pretty girl with blond hair falling down around her shoulders. She looked so young and naïve that my heart broke. Had Elmer seduced this child?

Tom began. “Now, Lulu, this is really important. I want you to tell us the truth, and don’t leave anything out. You don’t have to be embarrassed by any of this. It isn’t your fault. We’re here to help you.”

Lulu, small-statured and beginning to blossom, glanced at her father, who sat in a chair behind her. I could see fear poking through her round face. I stared at this innocent, wide-eyed child, and my heart fell to the floor. I would never be able to pick it up again.

“I didn’t mean to get Mr. Lindsey in trouble. He’s a g…good teacher.”

She stammered something pitiful. I probably would, too, talking in front of these high-standing men of the town.

“We know he’s a good teacher,” Tom said. “Just tell us what happened.”

“From the first day of class, I thought Mr. Lindsey was mighty h … handsome. All the girls thought so.” She spoke slowly with a mousy voice. “I shouldn’t have flirted with him. H … he started talking to me like I was special. I thought it right nice. Umm. I liked it a lot.”

Lulu blushed and ducked her head, her hair falling over her face.

“Go on,” Tom said, pushing his spectacles up on his nose.

“I stayed after school for l . . . lessons. He began to sit closer and closer. Then he held my hand and said n . . . nice words. When he put his arm around me, I liked it.” She paused again. “Then the first time he kissed me, I thought I’d c … choke.”

One of the men laughed.

My heart turned a somersault. Her description reminded me of Elmer offering to teach me when we first met. Years ago, he’d approached me the same way, telling my parents he could teach me to play a clarinet. I was eighteen, older than this girl, but still as innocent and inexperienced.

I heard Lulu crying, saying she didn’t want to say any more. I understood how she felt. I didn’t want to hear anymore.

I covered my ears and let out a whimper. Jennie put her arm around me and drew me close. I shook her off, stood, and stumbled toward the door. These words left little doubt about Elmer's behavior.

Snickers came from the far corner. I turned and saw a few teenage boys. Jack, my boy, sat among them. He turned to me, but instead of ridicule on his face, I saw anger. Icy fear ran through me, and I shivered. Was this why he hated his father so much? Did he know the girls his father tutored? How would my boy ever recover from the shame his father had brought to our family?

Jennie followed me out the door. We were the only ones in the dark, cold hallway. She touched my arm. "Don't you want to hear Elmer's side?"

Ambushed, I turned to her so fast my hat slid off the side of my head. I stuffed it back on. When I looked into Jennie's eyes, I saw the sad reflection of my own pain, a reflection of my husband's behavior. "I don't think I can sit through this."

Jennie nodded. "I'll stay and let you know how it turns out." She disappeared inside.

***

In the empty hallway, I stopped short. My heart raced, and rage seethed through me. I clenched my fists and felt my shoulders go stiff.

I wanted to run away, run home to bed where I didn't have to confront the truth. But I couldn't. I needed to hear it all. Here I was, a coward, and it would take all my courage to turn around and go back into that meeting.

I breathed deeply and paced up and down the hallway, gathering myself together. Then I opened that heavy wooden door and entered the room where my husband was being accused of so much awfulness, I couldn't comprehend it.

I scooted back in beside Jennie. The board had gathered away from the rest of the people.

I wanted to know, but I didn't want to hear the details. "How is it going?"

"It's worse than we thought. Lulu accused him of pushing her past touching. Then Elmer denied any wrongdoing. He claimed Lulu was the one flirting with him. Claimed it was all her fault—or her imagination." Jennie's smirk and rolled eyes showed what she thought about that. "According to Elmer, Lulu just wanted attention."

I swallowed and closed my eyes. "And what did the school board decide?" What about our future? What about the girl's? I was torn, wanting the girl vindicated, but also wanting the incident swept away.

"We don't know yet."

One of the board members motioned Elmer and Oscar over to the closed group. They went to opposite sides of the circle, adopting a boxing match stance. I watched closely as they glared at one another. I tried to interpret the anxious hand gestures, red faces, and adamant voices. Then Oscar held up a threatening fist toward Elmer, grimaced and walked away.

"It looks rather heated," Jennie spoke nervously as Elmer returned to his seat.

Another ten minutes of quiet deliberation passed.

"Look," said Jennie as the board filed back to their chairs and sat down. "Here they come. There's Tom. Maybe he'll make an announcement."

What would they decide to do? Would they arrest him? Send him to jail? Would they make us leave Hollis?

Tom stood in front of the table facing the audience, his tall, wiry body exuding authority. The minutes seemed like hours. He cleared his throat, pushed his thick glasses up, and everyone in the courtroom quieted.

"This is an unfortunate incident. Elmer Lindsey is a good teacher, conscientious and concerned about his pupils. Lulu is awfully young and probably was flirting. Sometimes situations can be misinterpreted. We do have to protect our young ones, but we also have to understand that teenage girls tend to swoon over any show of attention. I'm not saying that is the case here, but we do have to consider it."

Jennie turned toward me and whispered angrily. "Unfortunate incident! They believe Elmer more than Lulu?" She gritted her teeth.

Tom continued. "And what with the Christmas concert practice going on, and the lack of anyone to take his place as a music teacher, we've decided to keep him for the rest of the school year. We're asking Elmer to apologize to Lulu, which he said he would be glad to do. And to refrain from tutoring young girls alone after school. That would not be wise under the circumstances."

Even so, Elmer was not declared innocent. Was he, in fact, guilty?

Elmer got up, walked to the front of the group, and turned to face the audience. "I'm sorry if there was a misunderstanding. I was only trying to help Lulu. Sometimes, girls fall in love with their teachers, but that doesn't make it the teacher's fault, does it? I meant no harm." He never looked directly at anyone, but spoke over everyone's head, examining the ceiling. He knew how to talk his way out of trouble.

I glanced at Oscar. His face had turned a deep red, and rage emanated from him. He opened and closed his fists before punching the seat. He looked like he wanted to punch Elmer too, and probably would if given the chance.

Lulu had her head down in her hands.

Shame threatened to choke me. Shame at what my husband had done. Shame at how I'd handled it. Shame that I'd stayed married to him all this time. That I'd allowed his behavior, and that my boys had been raised by this man.

Even the board's decision made me feel ashamed. I couldn't face the girl, Lulu, and her family. I couldn't hold my head up in town. I gulped down the bile in my throat before I grabbed Jennie's hand and held it tight.

Disgust filtered through my mind, and I took a deep breath. The crisis was over, at least for now, but something needed to be addressed. I would have to summon all my nerves to confront my husband. Let him know my abhorrence at his behavior. Let him know I considered leaving him. Could I do that? Leave my husband?

The gathering dispersed quickly, and we were left alone. Elmer, I noticed, had snuck out the side door. I hoped he hadn't seen me.

"I don't know about next year. He probably won't be asked to come back." Jennie pulled her gloves on, gathered her shawl, and stood to leave.

"What should I do?" I asked, not expecting an answer. Part of me knew that no good could come from staying with Elmer. My boys couldn't respect a father like him, but then part of me remembered my commitment—for better or for worse. Would this behavior justify me leaving him? Maybe that was the right thing to do. The right thing for us.

"Only you can make that decision, dear," said Jennie.

I closed my eyes for a few seconds and nodded. "Thank you for being here with me. I couldn't have sat through this alone."

Jennie put her arms around me, swallowing me in a big hug. "That's what sisters are for. Helpers through life, through the good times and the not-so-good times." She smiled, looking directly in my eyes. "Remember, we're here for you."

As I walked home, alarm clutched me tightly. My thoughts jumbled inside my head as I reviewed the details of the last few weeks. The last months. The last years.

Was my husband seducing young girls?

I covered my face and cried.

The truth seemed clear. Now I had to decide what to do with this information. I'd ignored it long enough.

Chapter 10

Saturday morning, I heard the door slam shut. I'd heard Elmer and the boys leave before breakfast.

"Susie May, where are you?" Matilda had a voice louder than a tuba.

I didn't answer.

When Til appeared at the entry of my bedroom, I covered my head with the patchwork quilt, not wanting to talk to her. Not wanting to talk to anyone. When Elmer asked me what was wrong last night, I pretended to be sick. Indeed, I was sick. I tossed and turned in bed for hours—the allegations running through my mind. I wanted to be left alone. I had a lot of thinking to do, and I did it best wrapped in my cocoon.

Matilda stepped toward the footboard and lowered her voice to a stern command, "Susie May. You get out of that bed right now. We need to talk."

"You heard about Elmer?"

"Well, of course, I did. Sisters don't keep secrets. And it'll be all over town soon."

I pushed myself up, swung my legs over the side, and pulled my bed jacket around me. "I don't know what to do. Are you disappointed?"

"Disappointed in you? No, of course not. Now Elmer is a different matter."

I followed Till into the kitchen where she scooped coffee grounds into a saucepan, added water, and set it on the stovetop to boil.

Running my fingers through my hair, I spewed anxious thoughts toward my sister. “What should I do? I promised to be his wife—for better or worse. And this is the worst. Should I leave him?”

“No one knows, except you. I can’t tell you what to do—though I’d like to.”

Torn asunder like a worn-out bedsheet, I vacillated, pacing the kitchen in a circle from the icebox to the window to the cookstove where the coffee was brewing. Then I turned around and began again.

“What *is* the right answer?” I asked.

Matilda, naturally, had an opinion about every situation and couldn’t hold it in. “You could leave him, of course. You don’t have to stay in a marriage with a rascal like that, and I think under the circumstances, God wouldn’t condemn you.”

“Is that true? The Lord would understand if I walked away?”

Till didn’t speak. She had walked away.

The coffee grounds had settled to the bottom of the pot. She poured off the top liquid into two cups. She set them on the dining room table before taking a seat.

I continued pacing, ignoring the coffee. My thoughts went around in circles as I considered the consequences, weighing each option. Leaving Elmer would be difficult. “I can’t support myself. I’ve never had a job because he’s always taken care of us.” I went on with my rampage, my soft voice growing louder. “And where would I live? And what about the boys?”

“You’ve been through a lot. If you want my real thoughts, they should string him up. Make you a proper widow.” Till paused. “But I can’t live your life.”

I was on my own. Family, good as they were, couldn't decide my future for me.

"You have mountains of faith." Matilda calmly sipped her coffee. "More conviction than the rest of us put together, so I'm sure God will help you through."

I gestured wildly with my hands. "Will He? No doubt, a boulder would be lifted from my shoulders if I leave Elmer. But *should* I? What about my commitment to God to love him until 'death do us part'? But can I stay in the same bed with a man like him? If I stay, will God give me the strength to love him? To live with this broken person?" I never had so many words before.

"It's your choice, sis. You can stay, or you can go."

Till's eyes held mine, and I knew she'd never tell me what to do. The questions still lingered, but it helped to vocalize them. I felt shattered and sunk into a chair. "Staying will take more pluck than I've ever had."

Matilda rinsed out her coffee mug, then she took mine from the table and poured it out. It had grown cold anyway. "Yep, sis, either way, it'll take more stamina and patience than riding a bucking horse. But the girls and I will support you—whatever you decide." Till's last words before she left.

I bowed my head and prayed for Elmer and my boys. And for me.

***

My heart felt dead, shriveled up and buried, cold as a winter wind piercing through my body.

Bits and pieces of our life came to my mind. Life had not been all bad. In his own way, Elmer cared. He'd sat beside me when I had pneumonia and almost died. Nursed me until I could get out of bed. And he never forgot to buy me flowers on our anniversary. In some ways, he'd been a decent, considerate husband.

But there were other times. Like when he stayed late after school. And the time he didn't come home until past midnight. And the week after I gave birth when he disappeared for two days, saying he got caught in a dust storm and couldn't make it. Maybe he did. Maybe he didn't.

I had to know. I had to talk to him.

We sat alone by the fireplace that evening. My hands shook as I tried to knit a scarf while he shuffled through sheet music. I finally blurted out, "Was it true? Did you touch the girl?

He looked confused. Shrugged like it didn't matter. "What are you talking about? What girl?"

He assumed I knew nothing about it. He never saw me at the school board meeting.

"I was there last night and heard what the girl said."

His eyes glared at me above his glasses, his frown revealing displeasure. "I told you it was none of your business. You needn't get involved in things like this."

"But it does matter. It matters a lot."

"In that case. No. The girl overreacted when I was nice to her. I can't dictate how a student behaves."

I looked down at the yarn stitches missed. I'd ruined several rows and would need to start over. Could I start over on a marriage that was years in the making, falling apart around me?

What was God asking me to do? Stay?

No, God. I can't! The shrill scream in my mind didn't come out of my mouth, even though it felt louder than crashing cymbals. The atmosphere felt heavy. Creepy, as if a monster sat in the room with us. I didn't look at Elmer.

Finally, he spoke again, his voice sweet and silky like when he wanted to smooth over life's ruffles. "Now, Susie May, I hope you aren't concerned about this. You know, it's just part of my job. I hate rumors as much as you do."

I unraveled every stitch of knitting I had done the last few days and wadded the yarn into a ball.

"I'll make it up to you. We'll take a trip to Altus, and I'll take you out to a nice, quiet restaurant. Won't you like that?" He hated conflict and would do anything to avoid confrontation. Even pretend. Or lie.

A nice meal could never repair my damaged heart. Hot tears streamed down my face. Had God given me more than I could handle?

Elmer laid his music on the floor. He stood, walked over to me, and placed his hand on top of my head, stroking my hair. "Now. Now, dear. Don't get so upset. These things pass. But we're still fine, aren't we?"

I moved away from his caress and slipped into the kitchen. Elmer might be fine, but I wasn't.

He didn't follow. Just gave me space and returned to his work.

***

Sunday morning, I decided to attend church for the first time since we'd moved to Hollis. I'd felt ostracized at the church we attended in our last town. Oh, at first, everyone welcomed Elmer and me with open arms, but that changed after the rumors started. The shunning cut deep.

My sisters pulled me toward their respective denominations. Although Elmer didn't go to church, his family belonged to the Church of Christ. He never made a fuss over me attending, so that's where I decided to go. It helped that fewer people attended there than in the Baptist and Methodist churches.

I put on my old cloak and walked down the dirt road.

Part of me didn't want to go out in public, but I certainly didn't want to go back home, either, where I felt trapped, wanting to run away and sneak into Annie's house. Or Jennie's or Matilda's. Anywhere to hide.

No. Anger wouldn't let me hide.

Driven by an internal force, I stomped toward the church, a place of refuge.

Arriving a few minutes late, I tiptoed through the door and slid onto an empty wooden pew. I didn't want to see anyone. Not even family. I didn't want to talk to people about the horrible affair, certain I couldn't answer questions they posed. Hopefully, most didn't know my circumstances.

A good long talk with the Lord was in order. I needed a heavy dose of wise guidance. It had taken a lot of knee bending to keep myself sane, the good Lord and I discussing Elmer so many times I had callouses.

Sitting on that cold pew for an hour made me think about life. The beast in my chest felt heavy, heavier since the school board meeting because I now knew my marriage was doomed to be a disappointment. It would never be fulfilling. Elmer's problems were my problems. Hope left and a sinking feeling overcame me. Neither leaving nor staying brought peace.

My spirit struggled, and I never wanted to see Elmer again.

Never cook for him.

Never sleep with him.

Never think about him. I clenched my mouth closed. Anger ate at my mind, and my heart grew hard.

Torn asunder, I fell into a deep dungeon rankled by fear and clasped my hands together in a tight knot. What was the right thing to do?

The preacher droned on and on. "God is always with us. His love never fails. Though life gets difficult, he will see us through." A monotonous liturgy I'd heard many times.

Aching inside, I thought of Papa and how he would line us up and lead us to church. How did Papa acquire so much faith? How did he know I needed extra attention? To be loved in a definite way? He had always been there when I needed him, and I missed him more than I missed anyone in the world. I shivered as I thought of the love I could no longer touch. Did anyone around me care?

Where was God? Did he care?

Voices lifted in song. I'd missed attending church, especially hearing hymns sung, bringing a bit of heaven down to earth. It was as if Jesus sat beside me, and it felt good to be there.

As I prayed, a warmth spread over me. God's spirit loved me the way Papa used to love me. My heart opened and a wave of peace moved within me. God's love became more encompassing than Papa's love, filling my lonely spirit with a divine peace. Right there in the midst of the church building, tears ran down my cheeks.

I *was* loved. And with God by my side and his strength to help me, I could withstand any hardship brought my way.

Calmness surrounded me like a warm, hand-woven feedsack quilt.

It didn't matter if I stayed with Elmer or left him. Whatever happened, the Lord would be with me.

Chapter 11

After church, I walked toward my house, weeping the whole way. Oh, I wasn't sad for myself. I'd been lifted up. But I was sad for Elmer. I didn't hate him. I loved him. But I did hate what he had become.

A block before I arrived, I heard the sound of the saxophone. The wind carried the pitiful whine as the tune echoed with deep, low notes. Sad and despondent. Wayward and moving. Haunting. Signals of a man in distress, caught in a hole as deep as Daddy's well.

I stopped to listen, standing still as chills ran up my arms.

Elmer's music sounded melancholy when he was downhearted. A maestro at music, he could pull passion from any instrument. Emotion drifted out of our house like crystals turned into drops of gold and I sensed feelings of loneliness. Despair. Guilt.

I couldn't move. His music was his voice crying out to me. Begging me to stay.

Then I recalled how much I had needed God through the past years. How much God had helped me. How my papa had loved me.

Elmer needed me now—more than I needed him. Lost in a quagmire of sin and lies, his sad soul required a touch from above.

That was the hardest decision I ever made in my life. As a wife, I'd be the closest to a prayer warrior my husband would ever have. Truthfully, I was probably the only person in the world praying for him—

and he certainly needed a lot of prayers. I made a commitment when we married, a promise to God that I would stay with Elmer for better or for worse.

That's when I knew my answer. I would stay.

I might not approve of what Elmer did, but I'd live with him and show him love the way Papa showed me love. I couldn't leave my spouse.

My loyalty wouldn't allow it.

My allegiance to Papa wouldn't allow it.

My commitment to God wouldn't allow it.

No matter his weaknesses—or his problems—I would not turn away from the man God placed in my life. The one God gave me for a husband.

It only took a few minutes to walk the rest of the way home.

I sat on the side of my bed and picked up the Bible I kept on the nightstand and clutched it to my heart. I prayed for Lulu and her family, who I heard were moving to California with two other couples. I prayed like the dickens that Jack would grow up and become an honest, hardworking man. That Marvin would find a job and get interested in a nice young lady. That Elmer would become a God-fearing man. It didn't look like any of this would happen anytime soon, so I'd have to wait and be patient. Keep on pleading.

I also prayed I'd learn to love Elmer in a better way. And whatever happened, I'd be faithful to him.

Even if he wasn't faithful to me.

Remaining with Elmer meant I'd need a lot of faith. To never give up. It would take courage to stay. God hadn't given me an easy life, but then, as my wise papa told me, life was not a bed of roses. Thorns protected the beauty underneath.

It didn't matter how I'd ended up married to a man like Elmer. My journey was set, and now that I knew the kind of man I'd married, I wouldn't live in fear.

Facing the truth brought its own kind of freedom.

***

I walked into the kitchen, pulled five pennies out of my pocketbook, and dropped them into a tin can. Someday I'd purchase that crimson material down at Tom's store and pay Matilda to sew me a spanking new dress. And I'd proudly wear a flouncy hat to match my jacket and bright red lipstick. I looked in the mirror and loosened my hair into a softer bun. Changes were not always bad. Maybe I'd cut my hair, visit the band room, take cookies to the students, and introduce myself as Elmer's wife.

I'd stand up for myself and learn to love Elmer without being his doormat. I'd try to discuss these terrible issues, even if he never listened. Find a way to help our family and be a better wife. A sharp blade of sadness struck me. Was God the only one who truly cared about me? I felt alone, as alone as I'd been for twenty years.

I rearranged the silverware. The forks on the left, the spoons in the middle, and the knives on the right. Then I mixed them up, scattering them around the drawer in disarray.

This was *my* house

This was *my* life.

I would live the way God wanted me to live—no matter what gossipers said.

Chapter 12

My muscles ached when I woke Monday morning as if I'd been wrung through a wringer wearing dirty clothes. Not clean. Nothing would be clean again.

Elmer and the boys left early. I wasn't sure where they'd gone, but the quiet house calmed me. I pulled on a robe, stumbled into the kitchen, and made myself a cup of coffee. No one in the family drank as much coffee as I did. I'd need more than three cups to get through the day.

I slumped into a kitchen chair.

Now that this terrible information was out in the open, my family would be hurt. My sisters would think I was nutty for staying with Elmer. That I should leave him. The whole town would reject us.

My resolve remained as a steady reassurance in my mind. However, going through daily life knowing what I knew, would take all my strength. And I'd never been the strong one in our family.

"Hello," Jennie's voice came through the screen door. "Are you awake? Thought I'd bring you some biscuits for breakfast. We had some left over." She didn't wait for me to answer but walked into the house and set a pan of hot, fluffy biscuits on the kitchen counter. "I also brought a pint of that sand plum jelly you like so well." Jennie put two biscuits on a plate and opened the jar of jelly. She put her hands on the table and looked me up and down. "Well, bless your heart. Look at you."

"Go ahead and have a seat," I grumbled.

My talkative sister always showed up when I felt at my worst. She arrived on mornings when words couldn't form in my mind, much less my mouth.

"Don't mind if I do." Jennie sat across from me and cut a biscuit in two, spread it with jelly, and pushed the plate toward me. "It's a beautiful morning. Clear, bright sunshine means life must go on, no matter what yesterday brought."

I hung my head, leaned over my coffee, and sniffed the pick-me-up aroma, hoping for magic.

Jennie continued her chatter, and in a way, I didn't mind. Her words kept me from dwelling on my husband's infidelity. Her busyness would get me through the day, cover the sadness.

"You look like a drowned rat. Life could be worse, dearie. Think of those families living up the panhandle with no means of growing a crop. Now that's a dire situation if I ever heard one." Jennie picked up the second biscuit and took a bite. "I can see why you like this jelly so much. It has a sweet, tangy flavor, and this batch is the best I've ever made."

I didn't respond but sipped my coffee.

"Have you decided what you're going to do? You don't have to stay with Elmer, you know. The sisters and I are ready and waiting to help if you leave him."

I stared at Jennie. Even with her thick hair pulled into a bun and her few wrinkles, she looked amazingly healthy and happy with the work she managed to do. Where did she find the energy? What would she think about my decision? "I'm staying with Elmer. The good Lord doesn't want me to leave, so I'm keeping my vows."

The front door slammed.

"I heard that." Matilda walked into the room and pulled out a chair.

"Don't try to talk me out of it. I've already decided."

"Of course, we understand. Blazes, you have two young boys who need you."

As Till sat down at the metal table, Jennie jumped up to get another biscuit. She slid the plate across the table, and it stopped in front of Matilda.

Till slathered jelly on her bread and took a huge bite. "Mm. You make the best sourdough biscuits in the world. But, of course, you already know that."

"I made extra this morning, thinking we might need a bit of nourishment today."

"You're getting to be more like Mary Bobbie every day, bless her heart, what with all the baking you do. Trying to fatten us up, are you?"

I wasn't sure what my sisters needed this morning, or why they were here, or what I should share with them. Every bit of news or gossip would have already floated around our small town, so I had no doubt my sisters had heard all about my husband's shenanigans. Hopefully, they wouldn't want to discuss it.

The door slammed again. What now?

Annie walked in, and I declare, her belly must have grown overnight. She waddled toward the kitchen without speaking, her two small, tow-headed boys following her. "Boys, go on into the sitting room and draw on that paper I gave you. Try sketching a horse or cow—like we talked about. Now that's good boys." She shewed them away. When they disappeared into the other room, Annie turned to us. "Well, that'll keep 'em busy for five minutes."

What was it about mornings and coffee? My sisters showing up was getting to be a habit. A good habit.

"What brings you out so early, dear," Jennie asked, slicing another biscuit in half, and handing it to Annie.

"Same thing as you, I imagine. Checking on our sister here and making sure she's surviving okay."

"The woman's staying with the man. That is, wherever he goes, she goes." Till's attempt at humor fell flat.

Annie glanced at me, her face a picture of sympathy. "Susie, whatever you decide is okay with us. It isn't a good situation, but it's your choice. And if you stick by Elmer, we're behind you."

I declare, my sisters fretted more than the preacher's wife down at the church. My tired mind sat in limbo, snatches of strength jutting through at intervals. "I'm fine, girls. Really, I am."

"Whatever you want to do, we'll be here." Till nodded her head. "No matter what problems come our way, we're sisters. Aren't we, gals? And we love each other."

"We do love you, Susie May. Nothing's going to run us off." Jennie put her hand on mine and looked at me with sincerity shining through those big brown eyes. "You don't have to go through hard times by yourself."

My sisters loved me and supported me. The thought rose like sweet cream in my soul.

I was wrong. I wasn't alone. I'd never be alone. Love felt like a snippet of heaven surrounding my kitchen table. I smiled. Those lovely, meddlesome sisters fretted over me something fierce.

Annie's five minutes passed quickly, and her boys came rooting for Jennie's cold biscuits. We stood, and each of my sisters hugged me, Jennie holding on for an extra amount of time, warmth flowing from her.

After she let go, I pulled my shoulders back and air filled my lungs.

I could make it. No, I *would* make it.

Author's Notes

Fascinating stories have abounded in my family throughout the years. Some verifiable. Some hearsay. Some discouraging. Some enlightening.

I have a copy of the marriage license of Susie M. Thomas and Elmer Lindsey. He was two years older than her. They married June 2, 1910, in Harmon County, Oklahoma.

Susie's father died exactly one month earlier on May 2, 1910.

The 1930 U.S. census showed Susie and Elmer lived in Eastland County, Texas, and by the 1940 census, they were in Garvin County with Marvin, at age 28, still living with them.

It was no secret in the family that Uncle Elmer messed with young girls. Parents ran him off twice from Hollis. He moved from town to town every few years, working as a teacher and band director.

Susie's son, Tom Marvin Lindsey, was born in 1911 and died in 1971. Although he was born Marvin, he changed his name to Marvaine somewhere along the way. That's the spelling on his gravestone in Fairmont Cemetery in Hollis. He was not buried beside his parents. What else can I say about him? His preference for young boys was known, and other stories told about him were even less flattering. He never married. A brilliant man, he worked as a translator for the government and could speak four or five different languages.

Jack didn't get along with his mom and dad. They fought mostly over Marvin, or so I was told. None of the family was surprised when Jack ran off before his eighteenth birthday. No one heard from him for years. He moved to San Francisco, California, when he got back from the war and only contacted his family once or twice.

My family visited Jack and his wife and children in California when we lived there in the '50s. Susie and Elmer came to visit Jack in California, and we visited them. But it didn't take Jack long to ask his parents to leave. I have no idea why, but Susie and Elmer quickly drove back to Hollis.

For years, Susie grieved for her son, Jack, or John Charles, desperate to hear more from him. Another family member (Fred) sent Susie flowers with Jack's name on it. She was ecstatic. When Jack found out, he was furious. I can only surmise that Jack never understood why his mother ignored the dysfunction in their home and stayed with Elmer and babied Marvin. Maybe there's more to the story that we don't know.

Ann and Tommy Akin took care of Susie and Elmer when they were older, in the late 1960s. Tommy rented a large house next door to them in Shawnee, Oklahoma. Marvin moved in with them for a short while after he retired. Tommy had a garden and gave them food and supplies. Eventually, Susie and Elmer went into a nursing home in Hollis, where they spent their last days.

Susie died in July, 1972, a servant all her life. Elmer died almost four years later. I don't know if Elmer ever quit messing with young girls. I like to think he did, since their marriage lasted for sixty-two years. His wife's love and devotion must have affected him.

Jennie Rue

Thomas Sister #4

Truman Newberry

Jennie Rue

Born March 12, 1892

Chapter 1

October 1931

Everyone said I was an energetic and natural-born caretaker. That's like saying the grass was green, or the sky was blue. It's simply who I was.

I first learned to serve others by helping with my baby sister, Annie. My other sister, Till, didn't like me calling her Annie because it reminded her of her own baby Annie who died. But I'd used that name for my little sister since she was born.

When we were children, a serious outbreak of diphtheria hit the United States. Even children who took the miracle serum perished. Any time a child got sick, fear gripped the family like the earth was about to split open. I remember my mother's frantic tears when Annie's fever soared. She was four years old. I, Jennifer Rue Thomas, was seven.

Annie almost died. She lost some of her hair and her hearing in one ear.

But she didn't leave this earth.

I liked to think she survived because I stood by her bed, wiping her forehead with a wet washcloth and feeding her chicken broth. My poor mother couldn't drag me away. I nursed Annie as if my own baby doll had fallen ill, talking to her like I knew all about the moon and the stars and the way people ought to be nice to one another. Mama told me to hush and let her rest. I rambled on more than anyone else in my family, and she didn't want to hear me every minute of every day.

From the time I saved my sister, I aspired to be a nurse and help people when I grew up.

Growing up, Annie was always sickly, but I never minded caring for her. Sometimes I think she pretended to be sick just so I could show off my skills. Taking care of people came easily. If only I'd known how my natural abilities would be tested before the autumn of 1931 was behind us.

***

Every family needs at least one woman who likes to sew, mend, and darn. Matilda and Annie, my two sisters and family seamstresses, also liked to hook rugs, darn socks, and patch overalls, something I'd never had a hankering to do. I preferred shucking corn, canning tomatoes, and snapping green beans to needlework any day.

Saturday afternoon, my sisters dropped by for a chat.

Bobbie, the eldest sister who was visiting from Texas, had planned to stick around until Annie gave birth to her baby—a girl, we all hoped. But days passed with no stitch of warning and Bobbie needed to get back to her family.

With her soon to leave, we took advantage of the menfolk agreeing to keep an eye on the boys. With eleven sons between us, it was no small feat. While they were occupied, we gathered on the circle of stuffed sofas and worn chairs in my living room, cozy enough for each of us to find a comfortable spot and relax.

Till plopped into the fancy Cogswell chair and set her sewing kit on the floor beside the claw foot. "I brought my needlework. Got so many clients, I can't let a minute go by." She took out a pile of handiwork and began to organize it. Her new sewing business kept her busier than the new filling station down the street.

"I brought my work, too." After arranging a pillow behind her, Annie retrieved a sewing box stuffed with scissors, thimbles, different colors of thread and buttons, and probably a used metal zipper or two. She spread the goods around her large baby belly.

Susie landed on the sofa while Bobbie sat in the rickety old rocking chair. It creaked as she pressed her foot against the floor. I scrambled around and passed out sweet, iced tea and warm butter cookies.

Bobbie grabbed a handful of cookies and laughed. "Don't tell anyone about my sweet tooth now."

"As if everyone doesn't know." I set her glass on the coffee table.

We giggled. Although in our late thirties and early forties, we still acted like five silly girls when we got together. We chattered like magpies about non-important issues, skirting around the hard ones.

"I can't get started." Annie squinted as she held the needle and thread up to her face. "Jennie, would you thread this needle for me?"

I put on my spectacles and took the needle from her. I slid the pink thread through the eye and pulled out a long length. The thread spun off the wooden spool onto the floor. Bobbie grabbed it and handed it back. "Here you go. A runaway pink rose. Sure do like that color." The pale pink matched the dress Ann was making for the baby girl who would soon join us.

I handed the needle and thread to Annie and looked over the top of my glasses at my sister Susie. "I'm glad you've moved back to Hollis."

After years of moving from town to town, she'd settled back here in Hollis. She seemed surer of herself since accepting the truth about her husband's reputation. She even held her head higher in public.

"You seem more content. How are Elmer and the boys?"

She didn't answer. While I talked the most, Susie was the quietest. Maybe she wasn't ready to talk about the fallout at home after the fiasco at the recent school board meeting.

The silence was uncomfortable, but I continued, "You got your house set up, I understand. I can bring you some homemade dinner rolls, if you want. Did Bob get your books organized?"

Susie nodded and took a sip of her iced tea. "She did."

"Susie insisted the books wait for you, Bobbie." Till pulled out a pin cushion. "She likes everything in place, you know. She was eager for you to come and put the finishing touches on her house. Ouch!" Till put her finger in her mouth. "Stuck myself." She shuffled around in her sewing box, then held up a thimble.

"I didn't have much to do." Bobbie wiped the cookie crumbs from her mouth. "Susie's house looks rather nicely put together." She crossed her arms over her large bosom. "Honey, a designer couldn't have done it better. Wasn't much to do except rake up the dust."

Susie beamed, as if she seldom received compliments.

"I've been dusting up a storm this week." Annie moved her needle in and out of the fabric. "That last sandstorm must have blown a hundred miles an hour. I had dirt an inch thick in every crevice of the house."

"I've run out of sheets and towels to stuff around the windows." Till pulled out another boy's shirt to mend. With so many male offspring among us, the chore was never ending.

"Did you see the dry goods store is selling dishtowels by the dozen? That is, if anyone needs them." I'd collected a dozen myself from my husband's store.

"Darling, we should've torn the boys' worn-out long johns into strips to use as towels. Now that's an idea. Who would have thought we'd be hanging onto our boys' old dirty britches and stuffing them into cracks?" Mary Bobbie paused. "But at least they're clean…I hope so anyway."

Till spit out her tea.

Bobbie's boisterous laugh filled my living room. When she got tickled, we all got tickled. As soon as one sister pulled herself together, another would hiccup and laugh and the madhouse would start again. I wiped away tears.

Only when Annie, ripe with pregnancy, ran to the toilet did we collect ourselves.

I loved our sister times together, so different than when we were growing up, bickering and playing jokes on one another. Well, maybe not so different, but I loved it.

***

Our conversation in the living room jumped from topic to topic like hot potatoes. The sisters covered everything from the upcoming church bazaar to the sale at J. C. Penney's until we were parched.

The fall weather was far warmer than usual. I fetched another round of iced tea for everyone. "I heard September was the hottest on record. We averaged over eighty degrees every day."

Bobbie swiped her brow. "Not possible. The news people are flat-out wrong. Feels like a hundred and twenty." She fanned herself with a magazine.

Till took a glass from the tray. "Eighty degrees isn't nearly cool enough. I'm ready for relief after the summer. Can't live with this swirling dirt and sweat and tumbleweeds."

The conversation lulled as everyone enjoyed the freshly iced drinks.

"I saw Mrs. Tillman yesterday," Annie finally commented. "Not quite seventy years old and she just married Widower Jones. He must be almost ninety."

Everyone mulled over the news. My thoughts sat unsure, like a swig of cold coffee in my mouth.

"Good for her!" Bobbie said. Her comment didn't surprise me. Of all of us, she was the most happily married.

"Nothing wrong with marrying an older man." I thought of my marriage to Tom Newberry, my senior by fifteen years. He was already an accomplished, experienced gentleman when we married, and I was a young, innocent lass.

Susie turned to me. "Jennie, do you ever regret it? Marrying a fellow so much older than yourself?"

Till stopped stitching and looked at me like an inquisitor. "You're a lucky girl, married to a respected town leader. Do you ever feel intimidated?"

My warm, comfortable living room began to feel like an interrogation room. I thought for a moment. I'd never used the word 'intimidated' before. It'd be something to mull over later.

At times, I wondered if marrying Tom was the smartest decision I'd ever made. But mostly, I felt inferior to him. He had fought in the Spanish-American War, was a Grand Master at the Masonic Lodge, plus he'd been married before and fathered two children with his first wife.

Why had he chosen me? My cute little face could never compare to a homecoming beauty queen like Matilda. How had I attracted the most outstanding gentleman in the country? Did he truly love me?

I ignored Till's question, pushed the troubling thought aside, and leaned toward Annie. "Those are the smallest, straightest stitches I've ever seen."

An hour later, Till and Annie folded their hand stitching, packed their material and needlework, and prepared to leave.

"Does anyone want to take home butter cookies?" I always baked enough for the cavalry.

"Sure."

"Of course."

"Not a bad idea."

As I packed up enough for each to take to their menfolk, we agreed to meet after church the next day, unless the baby decided to come.

However, as they walked away, my thoughts dwelt on that one question. Did I regret marrying an older man?

Chapter 2

Cleaning the kitchen after my sisters left was a breeze for an energetic girl like me. Scrubbing pans gave my thoughts time to travel back to when I first met Tom, the man of my dreams, fifteen years ago.

As a naïve, sheltered girl of twenty-two, I left home to work. My brother Sam set up the job for me. I'd work during the week at the store and go home on Sundays. Every weekend, someone from my family drive the buggy eight miles to pick me up, and every Monday, drive me back.

My sister Till carried me out to Shrewder in her wagon the first time. I'd never lived away before, and my nerves tingled at the thought of leaving the security of home. On the edge of Harmon County, and originally called the Blue Goose Community, the small town of Shrewder lay in the flat plains of southwest Oklahoma about eight miles north of Gould where we lived.

As we arrived, we passed the sawmill, a blacksmith shop, a laundry, a post office, and two or three small houses. Above a wooden structure, a sign read *The Shrewder Store*—the dry goods mercantile where I'd be employed.

Till didn't even get out of the buggy, saying she had a meeting in Hollis to attend. She left me standing there in my best floor-length dress with my bag of necessities. I worked up the courage to go inside. A bell clanged when I pushed open the front door, and a tall, lanky man walked in from the back.

"You must be Sam's sister. So glad you agreed to come help me out." Taller than anyone I knew, Tom Newberry looked down at me.

I'd admired Mr. Newberry before I ever met him. The *Hollis Post Herald* ran articles about good folks in the area, and I'd read all about him. He was well-known in Harmon County as the owner of the Shrewder General Store. It sat on the corner of the Newberry Ranch, which was owned by Tom's cousin, Henry. They had come together from Tennessee in 1900.

I patted my dress smooth after the wagon ride and straightened my hat. A simple country girl, I never thought I'd get a chance to work in a real store. "You must be Mr. Newberry. My brother said you'd be my boss."

The man nodded.

"Thank you for hiring me, sir."

He wore thick glasses and had a calm air about him. "Come on back and I'll introduce you to my wife and the little ones."

We moved toward the living quarters in the rear.

I took in all the goods the store kept in stock. "I've always wanted to help people choose material and canned goods and such. I know more than you think. I'm sure I'll enjoy it, especially the chance to talk to folks as they browse through the merchandise. Not that I know everything, that is. But I'm a quick learner."

"I'm sure you can learn fast, but I don't want you to get the wrong impression." Tom stopped at the door and turned to me. "I need a nursemaid for my wife and a nanny for the children."

"Oh." I stopped and looked around at the glass countertops full of items to sell and barrels of supplies. I wouldn't be working in the store. Confused, I stared up at the tall merchant.

"My wife, Jenny Mae…" He paused. "Ah. Yes. Same first name as you. She recently had a baby. She hasn't recovered, and the doctor says she shouldn't get out of bed. I can't take care of the store and my family at the same time, you understand."

Not sure exactly what my duties would be, I followed him through their living area and entered a small bedroom.

He pointed to the bed. "This is Jenny Mae."

The frail woman was at least a dozen years older than me. She lay on the four-poster bed, ashen white and listless, but regal. Large brown eyes. A beautiful woman.

I nodded to her.

A faint smile flittered across Jenny Mae's pale face. "Thank you for coming to help." Sadness lingered in her eyes and my heart went out to her. It would be disheartening to be too weak to care for your own children.

"I'm happy to be here. I always wanted to teach, and now I have the chance to be with children. I can wake up early and cook breakfast. And after you get well, I can help in the store. You'll get better. You'll see." I might've been petite and wiry, but with my strong arms and tough constitution, I figured I could make the lady of the house comfortable enough to recover before the week ended. I had plenty of experience nursing my sisters.

"And this is Virginia and Thomas." Tom motioned to a girl holding a baby in a nearby chair. Virginia, about five or six years old, didn't look up as she chewed on her bottom lip and focused on the bottle in the baby's mouth. A picture wrapped itself in my mind of a girl who had to grow up too quickly in order to care for her baby brother.

Instead of being disappointed I wouldn't be working in the store, I jumped at this new task. Nursing and caring for people came easily to me. I'd manage the housework and watch the children while Mr. Newberry tended the store.

I stepped toward the pretty little girl who clung to baby Thomas. Squatting in front of her, I asked, "So, your name is Virginia?"

She nodded without looking up at me.

"You're doing right fine with your brother. Would you be willing to let me hold him?"

Virginia looked at me, surprised, as if a stranger dared intrude in her family life. She hesitated, her eyes full of sorrow and stubbornness. I recognized her I-can-take-care-of-myself attitude. She needed me as much as Jenny Mae's baby did.

Setting aside my wandering thoughts, I shook out the tea towel and stored the remaining dishes. How had the years passed so quickly? Although Tom and I had been married a year later in 1917, I still wondered what he saw in me, a bumbling nobody.

Would that insecure feeling ever change?

***

The next day, after church going and a home cooked meal for our families, my sisters came traipsing over for our last visit together. Most of our men folk busied themselves with naps while the younger boys played stick ball.

Till, Bobbie, Susie, and I all attended different denominations, but we agreed to disagree on the minor points as long as Jesus was the center of everything. We never let our denominational preferences stop us from showing up at each other's social functions and welfare endeavors.

We gathered on the front porch, one of our favorite places to congregate. The awning drooped and the faded brown wood shingles looked sun kissed. We moved like a herd of turtles nestling down after a big home-cooked meal, but we all agreed that naptime hit hard on most Sunday afternoons.

My husband, Tom, and I had lived in Hollis, Oklahoma, the county seat of Harmon, for nearly ten years. The close-knit community had one stoplight at the corner of Highway 62 and Highway 30, the two main roads that passed through town. Some folks didn't like our spread-out part of the country, surrounded as we were by miles and miles of treeless cotton and wheat fields. Maybe because I grew up in the area, I loved the plains, tumbleweeds and all. I remembered visiting the Wichita Mountains near Lawton and feeling claustrophobic and penned in. I'd been glad to get home to the wide-open plains.

Midafternoon, Bobbie slipped out my front door carrying a tray full of glasses of sweet, iced tea. "At your service, ladies. Tea for the taking."

No one turned it down.

I took a big sip, hoping to ease my aching head. Leaning back, I closed my eyes and listened to my sisters' conversation wander from the new etched-pink milky glassware to what they'd take to the next church potluck. I lost track as they skipped around topics, popping like jumping beans in a tin can. I rubbed my forehead, patting my dark, thick hair. The mass had given me headaches since I was a child with thick tresses flowing past my waist.

"Sis, are you doing all right? You look a little peaked." Bobbie's lighter colored thin hair tickled her temples, and the dull, mousey color now streaked with gray.

"I have this awful headache today, girls," I admitted. "Feels like my head's going to fall off. I need to go inside and rest a bit. You go on and visit though. Don't mind about me." I pushed myself to get out of the chair.

"Now, honey, don't you go sneaking out of here. It's probably your heavy hair. I'll be glad to cut it. Won't take but a second." Till had always styled my hair. She'd gotten better since the first time she cut it when I was a teenager. I had looked like a wild woman, a disaster even if it had given me relief.

"I'm sure Tommy can cut it when he gets off work down at the barbershop," Annie offered. Her husband cut men's hair for a living, not women's, and I didn't trust him with mine. But I didn't want to tell her that.

"No thanks, sis. Till always does a great job," I said. "My hair grows so fast, I don't notice 'til I start getting these headaches." Hollis had few places a woman could get a decent haircut for a decent price, except maybe at Lottie's house down the road or in Ethel's tiny kitchen.

"Susie, hand me that tea towel." Till unpacked her sewing box, pulled out a pair of scissors, and stood up. She motioned me to sit on a chair in front of her near the edge of the porch and draped the towel around my shoulders.

I couldn't have said no if I'd wanted to, because Till usually got her way. She stood behind me, loosened my braided bun, and ran her fingers through my soft hair.

My favorite smell, rainwater, floated around me, reminding me I'd rinsed my hair the day before. I liked to keep it past my shoulders, short enough to reduce the weight, but long enough to pull back into a decent bun.

I sighed, not worried. The best seamstress in the family could at least cut a straight line. Till began snipping.

The conversation resumed, jumping from the scorching dirt storms that appeared out of nowhere to which boys needed their britches let down to the awful cotton crop failures. It got heated when we discussed the best solution for dry, wrinkling skin, which was pertinent since we were aging quicker now. Till favored a honey-milk solution. Susie claimed that adding an egg white produced the best concoction. Bobbie claimed no amount of face cream could fix the wrinkles taking root around her eyes, but that a slab of butter might be beneficial. We all laughed.

I suggested Pond's cold cream, a product Tom stocked at his store, but was voted down because of the cost. Would it embarrass my sisters if I bought them jars of cold cream as gifts? Maybe. But I might do it anyway.

Till hacked away at my hair so long I thought I'd end up bald. When she finished, I shook my head vigorously. My headache disappeared immediately. Sweet relief. Cut locks produced a liberated feeling that matched my freestyle character.

Till moved to the side of the porch and shook my brunette hair out of the towel. Wisps of gray mingled with my dark hair, but she ignored it. I suspected she wanted to comment but refrained.

"What do you think?" I asked Susie, who'd been rather quiet through the haircut.

She bit her lip.

Chatterbox me couldn't stop talking if I'd wanted to. "Till always does a nice job, doesn't she?" I asked. "Did she miss a spot? Do you think it's too short in the back?"

"I like it, Jennie, but there's a long strand on that side." She pointed to the right, and Till immediately began to chop again.

When she didn't stop, I stood and dusted myself off. I didn't need my hair shorter than my laugh lines.

Annie shifted in her seat.

I hurried over. "Are you all right? Do you need to go inside and rest? I can get a pillow to prop your feet up."

Annie handed me her empty glass. "You can take this. Getting up and down wears my body out." Her hand touched mine. I looked at her long, dainty fingers and well-groomed nails. My hands looked like a cowpoke's next to hers. Rough and calloused since most weeks, I washed her clothes along with mine.

My little sister looked uncomfortable in the small dining room chair, her pregnant belly wider than a red barn. That infant she carried should make an appearance any day now. About to give birth to her third baby, she needed me. She didn't look as healthy as the last two times. Her cheeks sunk in and her eyes had lost their luster. And to be frank, even though she was the youngest of us five sisters, at thirty-six she was too spanking old to be having a baby.

"Jennie, set yourself down a spell." Bobbie took the glass and refilled it. "No use rushing things. She's all right."

"Honey, you worry too much," said Till. "Don't baby her. Let her alone."

"A watched pot never boils," added Susie.

I held back a grin and tried to ignore my sisters' comments. Annie's well-being fell on my shoulders, as it always had. No one else understood her like I did.

I returned to my chair, cherishing the last evening with my sisters. Our time together ran as smooth as chess pie, the connection feeling as tight as ever.

Chapter 3

For the first few weeks after I began working at the Shrewder Ranch as a young girl, Tom and I expected Jenny Mae to get up out of bed and be on her feet again. His strong faith nearly matched mine. I had faith, but I also believed the chicken broth and herbs I fed Jenny Mae would restore her strength.

Working hard, I set up a schedule to clean every room in the house, cook wholesome meals, and change dirtied bed linens. I checked on Jenny Mae frequently. While she rested, I spent hours with the children walking down the dusty road to the corner, picking wildflowers from the field, and making sugar cookies with Virginia while Thomas sat in his highchair giggling at us.

Usually, after the midday meal and before naptime, I took the children to visit their mama. That is, when she could sit up without getting too tired. “Here you go.” I sat Thomas in the crook of Jenny Mae’s arm. “He’s been a bit cranky today, but he probably needs sleep. He stayed awake last night with the hoot owls. I’ll be glad when he sleeps through.”

“I don’t know what I’d do without you. You’re so good with them.”

“Oh, nonsense. I’m just doing my job. They still need their mother, and you’ll get up and around before you know it.”

Virginia climbed onto the other side of the bed and laid her head on her mama’s shoulder.

"You'll make an excellent mother someday." Jenny Mae's shallow breathing scared me. "I'm happy these two have taken to you like sweet cakes."

I stilled, uncomfortable with the wistful tone of her voice. A child's mother could never be replaced.

Her eyes began to drift closed.

"Time for a nap." I herded Thomas and Virginia to the other room. After tucking them in, I returned to spend time with Jenny Mae and encourage her to drink another cup of broth.

But as I approached her room, I heard voices. I stood outside the ajar door, listening to Tom coax his wife like a mama bear nudging her cub, sweet suffering like. "I love you, dearest. I know you're feeling poorly, but it's time to get well. The children and I need you."

I should have left, but I couldn't tear myself away. I peeked in.

Tom sat beside her bed, holding her hand like he often did. After she had a difficult day, he'd come in from the store and sit in the hardback chair, caressing her hand and wiping away her tears. Tom's love for Jenny Mae warmed my insides.

The lilt in his voice sounded like a lullaby as he stroked her cheek. "I know you're doing the best you can, and I don't want to push you, but watching you suffer like this is breaking my heart."

"Jennie Rue's doing great with the children. Don't you think?" Jenny Mae's voice was just above a whisper. "They love her already."

"Don't you worry about the kids, dear. We all want you to get better soon."

Jenny Mae nodded off to sleep. Tom got down on his knees beside the bed and prayed over her, like a preacher focused on saving that one precious soul. Seemed like she was the only person who existed in his world.

I swiped the tears from my cheeks and slipped into the kitchen.

In the coming days, Tom stayed right by her side every moment he could spare. She grew frailer but managed to smile when he entered the room. Her face lit up like a lantern at his tenderness. They'd been married for six years, not long compared to my parents, but long enough to grow so attached that a breeze couldn't come between them.

A desire grew in me to someday find a man to love me the same way Tom loved Jenny Mae. A strong man, godly and gentle.

***

The morning after our sister's chat, Bobbie prepared to catch the train back to Munday, Texas. "Sure dread leaving, but Shannon can't survive without me." She primped her hair into place, smoothed her dress, and did a little jig. That was Bobbie.

"Wish you could stay longer." I turned her around and tied the bonnet strings beneath her double chin. Even though it was so early in the morning, the rooster hadn't crowed yet, Tillie, Annie, and Susie gathered to give hugs and see her off. Bobbie needed to get to Altus to catch another train south to Texas in order to arrive home before dark.

She hefted the bags I'd helped her finish packing.

I smiled, knowing she'd find a tin of cookies I tucked into the smaller of her two bags. "I loved having you. Remember, you're welcome any time you can get back up this way. We're always excited to see you."

Bobbie looked at each of us. "I've stayed in Hollis as long as I could, dearies. Unfortunately, I can't wait any longer for Ann to give birth to that new baby."

Till patted Annie's belly. "We're anxious as a cat with her first litter. This might be the last baby among us Thomas sisters."

"Unless the Lord has something outrageous in mind." Bobbie waggled her eyebrow.

We all chuckled at the thought of any of us having another. We were all hopefully past pregnancy age.

"Shannon will be glad to see you for sure." Till handed her a fresh-baked loaf of pumpkin bread. "He's lucky you married him."

Annie offered Bobbie a small sack. I assumed it was some of the taffy we'd pulled a few days earlier. Bob should have enough gifts for her menfolk and treats for herself for the next two weeks. But perhaps not with the way she liked to eat.

"I'll be glad to see him, too." Bobie pulled a worn wrap around her shoulders. "That man brings me more giggles than a puppy dog licking my face." Her contagious smile made us shake our heads and grin.

"Tell Robert and Shannon we missed them," said Susie, suppressing a yawn.

"Wish you could stay, sis," I whispered when we hugged goodbye. "Annie ain't young anymore, and the baby's getting mighty cozy. Could be a difficult delivery."

"Darlin', don't fret so much. Babies are born every day."

I tried to keep Bobbie's words in my mind, but Annie's age and pale complexion worried me just the same. We didn't need to lose another baby girl.

Chapter 4

Instead of napping the next Sunday afternoon like most folks in Hollis, I took a walk. I'd been so busy with Mary Bobbie's visit and taking care of family that I'd had no time to myself. Jones Street, a packed dirt road, led from the east side of town to the west, ten blocks or so, a good mile. I walked it often.

I passed the tall Methodist Church, and my thoughts jumbled about the coming fall bazaar. Planning had fallen into my lap again. I'd been in charge for the past three years and no one else spoke up to take my place. I'd already enlisted volunteers, arranged for booths, and asked women to decorate. But a mountain of work was still left to do.

I'd thought Annie would have had her baby by now, but it hadn't happened. Hopefully, she won't have it during the bazaar next weekend.

Heavens to Betsy, my life was busier than a beaver chewing logs for his den. And there was no one to ask for help. No one that understood and had the time, that is. Tillie had her sewing work to tend to. No doubt, Susie needed to focus on her marriage. And Tom stayed busy with his store. I couldn't add to his work. Not that I hadn't gone out of my way to always be there for him.

I quickened my pace.

Why did frustration with my marriage pop up now? I had too much work to be reminiscing. Did I keep busy to avoid worries about Tom? Wondering if he really loved me. Why he married me.

"Mind if I walk with you?" Tillie appeared beside me. "We're going the same way."

I took her offered arm. "Of course not. I'm just stretching my legs, is all."

We walked half a block before she spoke again. "You're walking faster than a freight train. What's got you so anxious?"

That question broke me open. I spilled my heart. "Tom and I've been married fourteen years. We've journeyed together through having a baby and building our house. Not to mention all the drama brought by the dust storms and the family chaos that surrounds us. Crazy to think about, but at times, I still wonder if Tom really loves me or if he only married me because I was there when he needed someone. You know, someone to go through Jenny Mae's clothes and toiletries, and clean out closets and counters, all the while darning his socks and making oatmeal mush for his kids."

Till didn't comment. We walked on in silence. A whirlwind picked up dust, blowing it around us. We shielded our faces, almost missing the colorful clouds spread out in the west as the sun hung low.

Our walk took us down the wooden sidewalk in front of my husband's store. Till stopped and looked at the sign above the entrance. The name was whitewashed over the bricks above the awning. *T. A. Newberry*. A second line added *Dry Goods-Clothing*.

She leaned close. "I'm still surprised Tom named the store after himself."

"I know. I laughed when he named it," I said. "That man doesn't have a proud bone in his body. So naming a store after himself was a surprise, to say the least." Throughout our move to town, I'd stayed busier than a bee making honey, following him around and keeping him together as he moved his children and business.

"This is where I was headed." Till pulled my arm. "Come in with me. At least we'll be out of the wind." Naturally, as a seamstress, she loved to sift through new bolts of printed cotton or corded dimity at Tom's store.

The heavy glass door echoed shut behind us. Several customers milled around, and I recognized the clerk standing behind the counter.

"Are you here to see Mr. Newberry?" the young man asked politely.

I nodded. While there, I should say hello to Tom, who spent most of his days in a small office behind the store.

"I'm going to look for some soft gingham." Till disappeared toward the back, where tables held piles of material.

I looked around. How Tom managed to keep the store so neat with nothing out of place and not a speck of dust anywhere was a mystery. I couldn't even do that at home in this dusty land, though I worked hard at it.

Tom appeared, pushing his glasses up on his nose, muttering to himself as if preoccupied with numbers or inventory or Lord knows what. He met me at the glass counter. "Are you all right? Is something wrong?"

True, I didn't visit him often in the store, especially at the end of the day, but I hoped he'd be happy to see me. Reassure me of his undying love. Instead, I felt in his way, a burden. "Thought you'd be glad to see me."

"I am. Of course, I am. But I'm working on the month's reports. Got lots of paperwork to finish up."

I felt lower than a tadpole in a big pond, bothering my hard-working husband during his busiest time. I wished he would take a day off work and spend it with me, now and then. Wouldn't that prove how much he loved me?

Tillie stepped over before I could think of an encouraging word. Carrying a bolt of pale print cotton, she held up a McCall's flared-skirt dress pattern, which cost a quarter. "Do you like it? I can use it to make you a house dress, too. A few tucks here and there. We both need new ones."

She stopped talking and looked up at Tom. "Oh, hello. I didn't see you there. How's the store? I'm going to help out by buying this material and pattern. Looks like a great deal to me." She held up the material. "Do you think this color looks good on Jennie?"

Tom nodded slowly.

I rushed to explain that Till asked to join me in a walk. "Nothing important. We'll talk when you get home—when you aren't so busy." I hated to get in Tom's way, hated to bother him, hated that we seldom talked any more. I unloaded Till's bundle and handed it to the clerk.

The clerk rang up the item. "The material isn't on sale. Do you still want it?"

Tillie hesitated while digging through her overlarge pocketbook. The pattern cost a quarter and I wasn't sure how much the material cost, but it appeared to be more than she could afford.

"Let's go," I said. "We can come back later. We both need to get back home."

She looked up. "Oh, that's all right. I've found enough change."

"Wait." Tom stepped in front of her. "You don't need to pay for it. It's on me."

I looked at Tom. He meant it. He was offering Till, who had very little money, the material for free. My husband may not have catered to my every whim, but he took care of me and my extended family. Always had. My heart warmed like a kerosene lantern on a frosty night.

As we walked out, Tillie gratefully claimed the material would have been a bargain anyway, cheaper than any place else in town. But now she had enough material to make us both dresses. She hummed, carrying the package under her arm.

My thoughts centered on Tom as we strode under the downtown awning toward home. Unable to refrain from saying what was on my mind, I confided in my sister. "I don't understand what he sees in me. A lowly housewife, a nanny, a cook—a nobody. He wears a Freemason ring. A loyal Mason since way back in 1910. He's a Grand Master at that, living an upstanding and moral life. How can I feel important compared to him?"

We reached the edge of town before Tillie spoke. "Hasn't Tom provided you with a good life?"

"Yes. He *is* a consistent, steady man—if not the most romantic." I laughed at the thought of him bringing me cut flowers or eating by candlelight. That had never happened.

"You mean like Tommy brings Ann baked goods home from the hotel café where he works? He thinks about her. Doesn't want her long, dainty fingers to get callouses."

Tillie and I giggled. Our youngest sister hated housework. Her husband treated her like a queen, unlike Till's husband, who'd been a mean alcoholic and gambler.

"I can't complain," I said. "A few years after our wedding, Tom sold his homestead in Shrewder to a short man named Little John, because he knew how lonely I was in the country. He claimed the move was to improve us financially, but I knew it was as much for me. He's wise like that. We moved into this booming metropolis. Hollis may not look like much now, but I felt like we'd moved to New York."

My admiration for Tom had climbed higher as each year passed.

His son Thomas, nearly grown, would leave home soon. We'd sent Virginia off to college at Texas Tech after spending most of her growing up years with her real mama's folks. Self-motivated, she insisted on an education and was willing to borrow or beg for tuition. It'd been harder to be a stepmother than I'd expected, and Virginia and I were not always close. Thirteen, when our son Truman was born, she'd been through so much in her life. Maybe jealousy surfaced when she saw her father rock his newborn Truman, or perhaps she thought her papa was too old for babies. After all, he was close to fifty by then.

Why did I crave the reassurance of this honorable man's love?

Till and I parted ways at the corner of Main and Sixth Street, hugging goodbye.

As she walked off, Till turned and yelled, "Let me know if you need more help with the bazaar!"

I smiled and waved in acknowledgment of her offer. Then I took a long way home, thinking about the deep hole left by Tom's first wife.

Several months after I started working at the Shrewder Store, Jenny Mae had taken a turn for the worse. The doctor rushed in from Hollis and examined her. He came out of the room shaking his head, whispering to Tom in the hall.

I tucked the blanket around Jenny Mae, her eyes closed peacefully. Then I snuck out to put the children down to sleep. They were restless and wanted me to read a book. By the time I finished reading and returned, Tom lay on the bed beside Jennie Mae, his arms wrapped around her frail body, holding her like a fragile doll. Her hair fell over his shoulder. I turned around and softly closed the door behind me.

Jenny Mae died later that night, and Tom grieved something fierce, walking around for days in a trance. I felt like I'd failed him. I worried that my nursing skills were lacking, but my sisters tried to reassure me her death was not my fault.

Still, I questioned myself. Had I helped her enough? Had I asked the Lord to intervene enough?

I shook my head to clear the cobwebs and entered the back door of our Hollis house. The kitchen shined—my zeal for cleanliness evident. If only my mind had been so spotless. Doubts of Tom's love invaded more now than when we first married.

Chapter 5

The day of the church bazaar snuck up on me before I could tie my shoes. Our annual tradition brought volunteers from all over the county, church members or not. This year's bazaar, we raised money for new choir robes.

I woke up bright and early Saturday morning with plans to arrive at church and make sure everything was ready. Tom fired up his roadster, loaded it down with pies for my booth, and drove us over to the church.

I'd been preparing non-stop for the past week, baking more than two dozen pies. Pecan, apple, and mincemeat pies lasted forever, and I made a half dozen of my famous sweet potato pies. Lemon and chocolate chess pies were baked the day before, and I added fluffy meringue on top late last night.

I spotted my sister as we pulled alongside the building. "Susie, so glad you're here." I rushed up to her, carrying a pie in each hand.

Susie grabbed a mincemeat pie from me and carried it down to the basement, setting it down on a table. "Our booth isn't set up yet, so we'll put the pies here." She'd volunteered to help with my pie booth—pie-baking my specialty, not hers. She'd made a couple of blackberry cobblers to help out.

Annie and Tillie, along with a few other volunteers, bustled around setting up booths. The menfolk brought in tables, chairs and pre-made posters. Tom joined them for a few minutes, slapping the town's banker on the back, shaking hands with the minister, nodding to a newcomer. He'd have to leave soon to open his dry goods store for the day.

I circled the church basement, checking with every booth leader to make sure they didn't need anything. I tried to be clear and specific, reminding each volunteer what to do.

All was ready.

People waited at the door when we opened.

Women, dressed to the hilt, came from around the county, eager for a fun afternoon. Men congregated around the side of the building or left to do business. Young daughters followed the women, carrying little ones or giggling with their friends.

Sales were brisk. Excitement contagious.

My sweet potato pies sold out first, and the others were disappearing fast. Susie and I spun around, trying to speak to each customer.

Old Mrs. Tennyson dropped by our booth and asked why I didn't have a vinegar pie. She inquired at least once a year. I'd never made a vinegar pie because I didn't know how, but she swore it was better than chocolate candy.

After a couple hours, sales slowed. "Can you man the booth while I walk around?" I asked Susie, who, normally shy, had enjoyed chatting with the ladies.

"Go on. I can handle this," she said.

I wanted to purchase several items I'd seen earlier. Our neighbor had set up a table of canned goods, with shelves chockful of jams, jellies, relishes, and preserves. For a dime, I purchased a quart of plum preserves, Tom's favorite.

Homemade items were abundant. Potholders, tea towels, embroidery work, and a few rag rugs. I knew how much effort had been put into them. The preacher's wife displayed baby and doll clothes she'd made from scraps. Her adorable work was selling well.

I stopped at an old high school friend's booth. "All my jars of pickle relish sold out within an hour. I don't have a pint left." She grinned.

I walked leisurely, surveying the goods. Another church lady filled a large box with baked goods, staples for any get-together. The yummy smell of cakes, cookies, and bread wafted through the air.

I passed my sisters' booth and stopped to admire their wares. "How're sales?"

"Doing better than expected. Harmon County ladies sure like their aprons." Till and Annie had combined their handiwork, hanging up an assortment of colorful aprons, trimmed with rickrack and embroidered with flowers. Several had pockets along the front. Till waited on customers while Annie shifted awkwardly in a chair where she took coins as the merchandise sold. Her little boys played on the floor nearby.

I spotted my husband near the next booth. Why was Tom talking with Mrs. Abernathy? Her large family had been in the county for a hundred years. My thoughts broke into a cacophony of accusations. He shouldn't even be here. He should be down at his store working.

Was I jealous of a woman years older than me?

I walked over, and their conversation stopped. "Oh, hi," I said, as if I hadn't seen them. "Did I interrupt something?"

"No. We've just finished." Tom walked away without an explanation.

I stared at his tall, statuesque back and turned back to Mrs. Abernathy. "I'd like to purchase three of those fried pies." If there was one thing I didn't need, it was another pie.

"Your sweet husband was giving me advice on how to sell my old carriage. I don't need it any more since my man bought a motor car. Scares me to smithereens, but I guess I'll adjust."

Embarrassed, but relieved, I wondered why I'd been jealous of a middle-aged, church-going farmer's wife.

As I left Mrs. Abernathy's booth, I couldn't help but notice a boisterous community atmosphere pervaded the basement. We featured a lunch for a nominal fee, chicken soup with cornbread or homemade biscuits slathered in butter. A large bowl of soup and a beverage cost only pennies. Our minister for the last six years took time out to sit at a table, eat lunch, and talk. Most of the children gathered in the corner where a raffle was set up for them. Attic and sale items filled a table at the opposite end of the circle from my own.

When we closed hours later, I compiled a list of items sold and tallied our sales. We did well. Very well.

With the way our boys ate, the two leftover pies and the fried pies wouldn't last long.

***

After Jenny Mae passed away, Tom convinced me to continue helping with the children. Unable to focus on their care, he begged me to stay on. At first, Tom sat at the dining room table and nibbled at his food without speaking. But as the days passed, he started to talk and hug the children again. We began to have long discussions about the care of Virginia and little Thomas, and the future of the store.

I looked forward to evenings after I'd washed the supper dishes and the children played with wooden blocks. Tom and I sat by the fireplace and discussed President Roosevelt's attempt to help the economy and the latest flick showing at the La Vista Theatre in Hollis.

He worked hard all day, came in at night, and rocked the baby and read stories to his daughter. I watched him care for the two young children and marveled at his concern for them.

After the children slept, he'd pull out his worn Bible and read a short passage out loud, commenting on the passage. We worked together. We grieved together. We gradually became comfortable with each other, and I forgot he was my boss.

I had goals, and he listened as I shared them. All of us sisters had graduated from high school. An achievement, at the time. Even though I grew up on a farm, I wanted to teach children in a classroom someday, since nursing school was too costly. Instead, I stayed on with Tom as a nanny to help with his little ones.

The Shrewder Store, the only retail establishment within five miles, was the center of community affairs. I enjoyed the customers who came in, helped them find what they needed, and chatted about local news from the surrounding towns. But drop-ins were getting farther and farther apart. The new-fangled automobiles made it easy to drive into larger towns like Hollis or Altus for supplies. It got lonely staying in the increasingly desolate area with no one to talk to most of the day.

With fewer customers and fewer orders for goods, Tom had less work to do. He'd stand near me while I cooked or washed dishes. He'd brush my shoulder, making my heart pound louder than a bullhorn. He stared at me with those big, sad eyes, revealing how much he enjoyed having me around. I began to wonder if he wanted to be near me as much as I wanted to be near him. I wanted him to pull me into his arms and grieve together, but fear ate at me. How could he ever care for someone like me? Especially after his overwhelming love for Jenny Mae?

Tom Newberry was thirty-nine and an upstanding citizen. He'd fought in the Spanish-American War with Teddy Roosevelt and worked as a cowboy on the Goodnight Ranch. He was on the Harmon County

Election Board and was a well-respected charter member of the Gould Masonic Lodge. He made a good living, was a church-going man, and well-respected around the area.

But he was fifteen years older than me!

My papa was sixteen years older than my mother. Mama would have understood my care for this man had she been alive to ask for advice, but sadly, most of my questions remained unanswered. Was I transferring love for my dear papa to this man—Tom Newberry?

Tom's age mattered little to me, the more I considered it. What mattered were the differences in our status. As a farmer's daughter, I would never be good enough for him. Compared to him, I had done nothing outstanding. I could never measure up to an icon of a man like Tom Newberry. I felt like a commoner among royalty.

Soon after, I realized I wanted to marry Tom. Who wouldn't have? My heart sped up every time he got near. Heat rose in my face, and I stumbled over my words. But I wondered — would I be replacing Jenny Mae? My brain rattled. Did he still love his first wife? Could he love me as much as he loved her? I had seen the way he catered to her. I'd watched as he'd nursed her, massaged her back, and brushed her long hair.

One night, Tom sat down beside me on the front porch swing. He took my hand and looked deep into my eyes. I was tense and being near him caused my heart to race like a wildcat. I waited for him to speak first.

"Jennie Rue, you know we get along well. You're a good, kind lady and the kids have grown to love you." Tom licked his lips. "I think a lot of you and wondered if you feel the same about me."

Words would not come. All I could do was nod.

He leaned over and gave me the sweetest kiss in the world, sweeter than sugar plum candy. I kissed him back and let him know how much I'd also grown to care for him. I'll never forget the magical feeling of that first kiss, like little angels lighting up around us.

We married the next year in March 1917.

Nine months after his wife died.

But I always carried the question in my mind. Did he love me as much as he had loved Jenny Mae? Or was the marriage based on convenience?

Chapter 6

Exhausted the day after the bazaar, my sisters and I lounged on the porch and chatted like magpies. Several boys streaked from the side of the house through the dry yard as if a bobcat were chasing them. They pulled up and stopped in front of us. We mothers looked up in sync. The boys hushed, their eyes wide.

“Mama, can I go hunting with the fellows?” Truman, my seven-year-old son, spoke first. He bounced from one foot to the other, always excited around his cousins. But then, seven was an excitable age.

I’d always wanted to give birth to a child, like any woman, I guess. But it didn’t happen until years after Tom and I married. When I gave birth to Truman, I doted on him.

“Where’re you boys going?” I took in the handful of eager faces. “You can’t be gallivanting around without letting your mamas know your whereabouts. Don’t want us sending out a search party, do you?” Most of the boys did pretty much what they wanted, but we moms liked to pretend to be involved in their world.

“We’re going down to the river to hunt,” said Frank Junior.

The Red River, about six miles due south, bordered Texas and was a favorite with the menfolk. I rattled on to Truman like I was thinking out loud. “You’d have to spend the nights without your papa there, and it’s dark and scary. I know your cousins will take care of you, but that’s awfully far away. Who'll do the cooking, and what if it gets cold? If anyone gets hurt, you'd be miles away from home and a doctor." I looked Truman in the eyes and shook my finger at him. "And I really don't want you to go that far away without me or your dad with you."

My husband let my stepson Thomas do whatever he wanted, claiming that at fifteen, he could gallivant around the county as he pleased, going hunting, riding horses across the plains, or traipsing over to the next town. I'm sure Thomas did more than that, but never told us. That boy and I butted heads so often I felt like I was in a boxing ring with Joe Louis.

"Ah, Mom," said Truman. "We'll be fine. Howard's going. And Frank Junior's going, and he's only eight. He has his own shotgun and all, too."

Frank Junior nodded in agreement.

I raised my eyebrows. A mother could worry about her son.

"Aunt Jennie," Howard said, "I'd never let anything happen to the boys. We'll be safe. I promise. And we'll be back in a day or two." Howard, who was Till's boy and the oldest cousin at twenty, was normally dependable, but not always. I heard he took a chug or two occasionally. I hoped he didn't take after his father, Frank Ready, who was known for his drinking and gambling.

I looked over the row of good-looking boys standing in the front yard before tried and tested mothers. Annie's boy Jimmy was the youngest at two years old, while Till had the oldest boys. Lands, there was a slew of male offspring, and they weren't even all there.

Till spoke up. "My four boys are going, and they plan on taking Jack and Thomas with them. Marvin might go. And Frank Junior would love to have Truman to play with."

"I doubt if Marvin will go." Susie's voice was defensive. "He doesn't enjoy camping or hunting, or any outdoor activities, for that matter."

Thomas would go, but would I let Truman leave town with a bunch of older boys, even if they were his family? Of course not. The menfolk thought I was overprotective of Truman, and maybe I was. But I'd heard of boys getting in over their head in the deep water or shot accidentally. I'd never rest with Truman running around with his cousins holding rifles in their hands and shooting ducks and turkeys. "I'm sorry, Truman. Not this time. You can go hunting with them after you turn eight. Your daddy can take you."

"Ah, Ma." Truman's shoulders slumped. It hurt his pride to stay home with Annie's knee babies.

Till stepped off the porch and headed to her house. "I'll go pack some fixings. Those boys could eat an alligator while it's gnawing off their leg. Especially my hooligans."

The number of boys my sisters and I had produced over the last two decades could have supplied a battalion. Eleven boys in the family, and no girls around anywhere. Annie could change the situation with this next baby, but prayers for a girl hadn't helped so far.

***

Sunday evening, I carried my rain bucket to the east side of the house and set it down. Little rain had fallen all year, but I hoped those clouds in the sky predicted a half inch or so. I loved to wash my hair and rinse it in fresh water. Nothing like the smell and softness it brought.

The kitchen had cooled from the midday cooking, but heat poured through the rest of the house and out the windows. The sun created a shadow beside the east side of the house, so that's where my sisters and I gathered, right in sight of the water well and my rain bucket.

"Hope our boys are behaving themselves." Till pulled strands of her damp hair back with a bobby pin. "I scolded them enough before they left, so I won't have to scold them after they get back."

"I'll round us up some more iced tea. I think there's enough left for each of us to have a sip." I left the girls yakking about the new preacher and went through the back door to the kitchen to gather glasses for our treat.

Tom and the fellows were talking politics in the living room. He'd turned on the blessed water cooler inside our living room. The new machine ran during the heat of the afternoon and brought joy and moisture to this dry, hot air.

I overheard my name and stopped in my tracks in order to eavesdrop. In a democratic county, my views differed somewhat from the norm and I was curious about what the menfolk thought. Discussion about the bridge war. A few months before, Governor Murray argued with Texas about the free bridge over the Red River. He even declared martial law at the site, bringing in the Oklahoma National Guard. Could you imagine the fiasco when Texas sent in the Texas Rangers? I personally thought the only good our governor had done was establishing programs to feed the poor.

Tom's voice held laughter. "Jennie and I don't always agree on these issues."

That statement was true. Tom and I might view most things the same, but not when it came to politics.

Another man spoke up. "Women can think the darndest things. I bet your first wife was never disagreeable, was she? Heard she was an angel to everyone who knew her." The voice belonged to Ann's husband, Tommy Akin.

I leaned forward to hear more. I might have expected conversation about Governor Murray closing oil wells to help the economy or the famous Oklahoman, Wiley Post, completing an around-the-world flight. But talk about wives? Did my husband complain to the fellows about me being sullen? I stiffened.

"That Jenny Mae of mine *was* a sweetheart." Tom's voice got all soft and dreamy. "Yep. She was a darling. Wouldn't hurt a fly. Some things in life are awful hard to get over. I still miss her sometimes."

"Wives can be a blessing or a curse. That's what I say."

"A pretty girl is worth it, as long as she's pretty on the inside too," Tom spoke softly, but I could hear him plain as daylight. "I loved her something fierce."

My heart shuddered. After all this time, my husband still loved his first wife? Still loved Jenny Mae? Did he think of her at times? My heart bottomed out. I could never compare favorably to an angel.

I heard the men's footsteps as they headed out the front door. It slammed shut and their voices faded. I folded my arms around myself and felt cold, shivering in the heat. Why did I have to hear that? Why did I doubt his love for me?

I shook off the cold. I would not let my feelings dampen the evening.

Chapter 7

Papa was the hero in our family as we grew up.

James Tolbert Thomas married Mama in 1883. Mary Frances Shields, or Molly, originally came from Tennessee, whereas he came from Kentucky. After their youngest child, my sister Annie, was born in Saint Jo, Texas, he and Mama homesteaded in Harmon County, which was then in Texas, not in Oklahoma. I guess the government couldn't make up its mind who should rule that part of the plains. Some folks still claimed we were Texans, but I'd put up a fight over that one.

Homesteading was a magic word back then because it meant free land and all.

The first thing James Tol did after claiming his 160-acre homestead south of Gould was to build a dugout. He dug five feet under the ground and put in timber walls to hold up the structure. The bunker had a wooden roof and, being underground, was warm in the winter and cool in the summer. Later, Mama and Papa built a T-shaped frame house in front of the bunker, but the old dugout was always there when I was a kid. I played in it during the summer.

Papa was bigger than life to us. He was a Mason and served with the Sixth Texas Rangers. That held some respect with the townsfolk. He'd been married before he moved out west and had a boy named Hugh Thomas. But something must have happened to his first wife because he didn't bring her with him, nor the boy. When I questioned him, a sad look crossed his face, and he didn't want to talk about it.

The last time I saw my papa, all us girls were hanging onto him, begging him not to get on the train and travel back east. In April 1910, Papa left to attend a Confederate War reunion. On the way back, he got off the train in Madill, Oklahoma, and went to a hotel room. He never did anything like that, so he must have fallen ill.

The sheriff found him on May 2nd, 1910, in bed, dead from an apparent heart attack. We buried our daddy at the El Dorado Cemetery. Seventy-one years old, he was a fifty-year Mason and a strong Christian. In my mind, no man had ever lived up to my papa's hero status, although my Tom got awful close.

I was fifteen when Papa died. Mama passed away a few years later, leaving us homeless.

***

At sunrise, my husband kissed me goodbye and walked to the store, as was his usual practice. We had a stable, predictable marriage. Nothing exciting, but then I wasn't sure I wanted exciting.

The quietness in the house felt eerie with half the extended family gone, the older cousins out hunting, and the menfolk working. Truman was mad and avoided me for not letting him go. Usually, he and the other boys were in and out of the house when they weren't in school.

Annie and her young ones rested at home with her baby due any day. Susie, Till, and I took turns going to her house to watch her boys and cook lunch. This was my day off.

I took the rare quiet day to bake homemade bread for the family. Lord knows, when Annie's baby came, I wouldn't have much time for baking.

Marvin sauntered into my kitchen as he occasionally did. Evidently, he didn't go camping with the boys. "I can help if you want." He ran his hand over his smooth hair.

"No thanks, but I appreciate the offer." I felt uncomfortable with Marvin helping in my kitchen. Not that he wasn't capable, but I enjoyed the time to myself. "Why don't you go in and check on Truman? He's feeling left out today, pouting a bit. Maybe you can pull out the checker game and play with him. You're mighty good at checkers. Give him some hints about how to win."

Marvin was brilliant in his own odd way, the only one of us able to speak Spanish to the folks on the other side of town. The only boy who wasn't rough and tough and getting into fights. The one who'd rather scribble on his notepad, prop his feet up, or piddle around the house dusting knick-knacks. Odd. Just odd. But then, his musician father was a softhearted one, odd himself. Who could be normal with a father like Elmer?

Marvin disappeared to the back of the house.

I sifted the flour and salt and added the yeast, which I'd dissolved in warm water, then mixed it up. I kneaded the dough, pounding it, folding it, and pounding it down again and again. While the bread dough rose, I cleaned up the kitchen.

After I put the loaves of bread in the oven, enough for Annie and me, I went to Truman's room to check on the boys. They'd been quiet, for which I was grateful. I opened the door without knocking, glancing at a stack of dirty clothes near the window before I turned to them. "How's the checker lesson? You didn't let Truman beat you, did you? He's mighty smart, but I don't want him to win every time."

The checkers were scattered over the rug. Marvin and Truman sat on the floor, leaning up against the bed, their laps covered with a blanket. Marvin had a book in front of him, but his hands were underneath the blanket. Underneath. The blanket. Moving on Truman's lap. Marvin pulled his hands out quickly, and Truman's eyes widened.

My dander rose as quickly as the bread rising in the oven. I clenched my mouth closed.

Lord, help us.

Marvin, at nineteen years old, knew better. His face turned a deep shade of red, knowing he'd been caught. Both boys jumped up, Truman pulling up his pants.

"Go home, Marvin," I said sternly, my head down in a bullish stance. "You're not welcome here anymore."

Lands 'o Goshen, Marvin ran from the room.

I sat down with Truman to explain a few things, my hands shaking. Anger coursed through me, but I wanted to remain calm for my boy. I determined to never let Marvin around Truman again. Not alone. I would keep this incident between me and the boys and not start rumors in our family.

But Truman, my baby, needed to be protected.

Even from his cousins.

Chapter 8

I arrived early the next day to deliver Annie's laundry. Susie sat on the edge of the rocking chair. She, Till, and Annie were discussing babies, birthing, and who knows what.

Annie and I had an agreement. She sewed for me and I washed for her. The arrangement kept us both happy. Annie didn't have an automatic washer, and Tom had recently bought me the ringer type. I would fill the tub with hot water and soap, and the machine did all the work. I just had to keep my hands and arms out of the way while feeding the clothes through the wringer after they washed. I also had a long clothesline, so I hung her clothes along with mine.

"Here you go. All cleaned and ironed." I laid the folded clothes on a chair. The habit of helping Annie started after our parents died. I felt more responsible, always worrying about her well-being. Catering to her needy ways.

"Thank you, sis. I don't know what I'd do without you." Annie rose to help me put the laundry away. "I can hardly lift a finger some days."

"I'm glad you have family nearby," said Susie. "I didn't have anyone either time I gave birth. It makes a difference."

"You showed how strong you are, Susie Q. If you could make it through that, you can make it through anything, can't you?" Till, blunter than the rest of us, was learning to be kind after going through so many trials.

Susie smiled, but I knew she'd be glad to get away from the spotlight. I sat beside Annie and leaned close. "Your middle has stretched so much I think you might have more than one baby. Like the famous Key quadruplets. Do you remember them? Born right here in Hollis?"

"Close that mouth of yours! One girl will be plenty of baby for me." Annie sat in the middle of the sofa, looking like she held a barrel on her lap. "My sides *are* spread wider than a giant mule."

"There could be twins in the family. We don't know," said Susie.

"Or you could have miscalculated the date." Hopefully, I was correct. "There's always the possibility you might not have a girl as you want."

"Don't you dare say that, Jennie Rue!" Annie jumped up, stomped her foot and put her hands on her thickened waist. Here she was in the family way for the third time with two little boys hanging onto her shirt tails, and she acted like that.

I might have laughed at my sister, but this baby was the last chance one of us birthing another girl. My four sisters and I produced sons, not that our husbands minded, of course. The daughters we'd had hadn't survived in the plains of southwest Oklahoma, but Annie was certain this pregnancy would be different. So sure that she'd connived us sisters into collecting and sewing up girl clothes. That baby would be in fine form the day she arrived.

Annie looked flat worn out, so I brought her a pillow to put behind her head. She fell back onto the sofa again. "Oh, dearie, I'm so tired I can hardly move. And this hair of mine is so frizzy I can't do anything with it." Annie patted down her fly-away hair. She'd had thin hair since her childhood sickness. "This baby should have been here a week ago."

"You whine more than a sick mule," said Tillie, who'd given birth to eight healthy children, even if they had not all survived. Till went on as if nothing was risky about giving birth, as if her marriage hadn't ended badly. I couldn't believe she rambled around town, dragging all those boys around with her, more persistent than a wild horse heading toward the free range in Montana.

"Morning sickness is dreadful this go around," said Annie, leaning back. "That's another difference between carrying a boy and carrying a girl. This confinement is not the same, I tell you. I'm as miserable as an old goose."

"Mind you, honey, girls are like diamonds in our family," said Till. "Just need one to shine." Till's diamonds referred to her four little daughters who hadn't reached adulthood. Sisters can read each other like that.

"Bless your heart, this could be the one. The girl we've been waiting for."

"Do you have everything ready for a baby?" asked Tillie.

I held out my hand to help Annie off the couch as she heaved her way up. "We'd like to see this place you prepared for the next baby in the family. Heard you've been working on the room for weeks now. Let's have a look see."

Tillie, Susie, and I followed Annie into the bedroom to examine what she had set up for the newborn. On top of a dresser sat a pile of cloth diapers and safety pins, along with a supply of Johnson & Johnson baby products in cute little metal cans. Next on the stack sat more talcum powder than one baby could ever use. Nearby lay neatly pressed short, loose, off-white dresses made of cotton or muslin, and a light cardigan to wear with them. Baby girl clothes. Crocheted blankets, bonnets, and a teething ring with a soft rubber nipple topped the pile.

Each sister had contributed to the adorable, dainty display. Since none of us expected to have any more babies—the Lord be praised—we added our baby items to her arrangement.

"Ah, that's precious."

"Kiss my grits!" exclaimed Tillie, pointing to a baby carriage, a pram to be exact, sitting in the corner. "I've never seen one like that except in a Sears & Roebuck catalog."

Even the carriage had a pink ribbon tied around the handle.

Annie's pale cheeks blushed.

"Everyone out now," I said, after all the gawking. I felt like I was shooing chickens out of a coop. "We've worn out Annie enough for one day. Time for her to rest if she's going to insist on carrying this baby any longer. Go on. Get gone. All of you."

It didn't take long for Till and Susie to skedaddle out the door. They knew when I meant business. Annie was my charge. My responsibility. And I was going to make sure this baby would be birthed with care.

Chapter 9

Tuesday, I wanted to make lye soap because I hated using the fancy, smelly soaps Tom sold in his dry goods store. Those soaps didn't clean as well as the good, old-fashioned kind. Till promised she'd show me how, since she had made it frequently while living on the farm with Frank. Actually, I'd watched Mama make it when we were children, but I'd never tried it myself.

"Come on in. I'm in the back!" I heard the front door slam shut early in the morning. I stood over my big cast-iron pot outside, stoking up the fire beneath it. Aluminum pots would never do, Till had told me.

Till popped through the kitchen door dressed in an old shift dress, her hair pulled back with a scarf. "Are you ready for a long day?"

"Ready as I'll ever be." I pointed to two large gallons of lard drippings saved from cooking bacon and meat scraps. I'd been adding to the pail since spring. "Do you think this is enough grease for a decent batch?"

"I usually make soap in the fall when a pig is slaughtered and lard's plentiful, but this looks like enough for the both of us."

"Here're the pot ashes." I pointed to a bucket full of white residue. "Tom has been saving it up for me."

"From a hardwood tree? From those scrub oaks out back?"

I nodded.

"They make good ashes. Soft woods don't work." I must have looked puzzled, because Till explained. "Softwood has too much resin to mix with the fat."

"Oh." I had a lot to learn.

"Where's your rainwater?" Till walked around to the other side of the black pot.

Rainwater. I knew about that. I'd collected runoff in the outside barrel for years, in addition to the bucket full I used to rinse my tangled mane of hair.

"We'll boil the ashes in rainwater first. Maybe half an hour or so," said Till. "When the ashes cool and settle to the bottom of the pan, we'll skim the liquid lye off the top."

I was glad my sister was there to help. Making lye soap was one of the most difficult tasks for a homemaker and hard to make alone. Difficult to get the measuring right, it could be disastrous if done incorrectly.

"Now let's get started. You pour the water into the ashes. Slowly. If we do it the other way, it might blow up."

Hence, the danger.

We combined the two together and boiled the liquid down until it would float a fresh egg. The lye stunk worse than a dead dog. I wrinkled my nose, glad we'd made the soap outdoors.

We let the mixture settle before Tillie put an old piece of cloth over the bucket and strained the lye water into it, careful not to get any on herself. That left a clear liquid lye concoction.

"We'll let it cool and start making soap this afternoon."

***

Tillie and I made fresh tomato and bologna sandwiches with sliced, vinegared cucumbers for lunch and sat down to eat and rest.

“Whitens better than anything in the store,” Till said with her mouth full. “Cleans anything from stained clothes to dirty dishes to muddy floors.” She finished her bite of sandwich. “But oh, that awful smell, the heat, and the continuous stirring.”

“The worst part is my hands.” I held them up and examined the callouses, torn cuticles, and broken nails. I turned my paws over and saw the lye burns, then rubbed my hands together in dismay. “Mine look awful.”

“Ah, Jennie. Don’t complain. We need some of that lotion your husband sells for a pretty penny.” Till’s fingers were smoother than mine. Of course, I did much of the family’s laundry and cleaning while Tillie sewed. Darning and mending were not nearly as rough on a woman’s hands.

“Can’t imagine a dignified man like Tom having a backwoods wife like me. I like gardening and canning peaches more than I enjoy sitting at a women’s club meeting. Dressing up fancy for an afternoon to gossip doesn’t suit me at all. I wasn’t cut out to be a hoity-toity lady. Can’t do it.” A sinking feeling ran through me. Did Tom look down on me because I was a down-to-earth, hard-working housewife?

After we finished lunch, Till and I started our chore once again. We wanted to finish before the boys got home.

“Put the lard in the kettle.” Till held up her hands. “Wait! Not so much! Not over half full. That’s about right. Now heat it until it turns into a liquid. We’ll strain out the scraps.”

When the temperature of the lye and the lard were about the same, both strained, warm but not bubbling, we added the lye mix to the hot grease.

“How much lye water do we put in the lard?” I asked.

"I eyeball it." Our exacting sister Susie would not have liked that answer, but Tillie had done this many times. "Not quite half as much as you have lard."

After fifteen minutes of constant stirring, my arm got tired, and Tillie and I switched places. We stirred until the mixture reached the consistency of thick cornmeal mush. It felt like two hours.

"Don't want it to get too hot or too cold. Stir until little dots come to the top and it gets thick." Till added her secret ingredient—a dash of salt to help the soap harden.

"With four rollicking boys dirtying up their clothes, I can put this soap to work. I brought a few wooden box molds. We'll cover the bottoms with grease to keep the soap from sticking."

We wrapped a towel around the boxes and set them aside for a day or two to cool and harden. "After it sets up, we'll cut the hardened soap into bars."

Making backwoods soft soap took patience. It might be four or five weeks before it was ready to use, long after Annie had her baby.

Maybe my charred hands would heal by then.

Chapter 10

Annie lived a few blocks from our house, while Till rented a house near her. Susie lived all the way across town, not that the town was that big. Their houses, like ours and most others in town, were three-bedroom, wood-frame buildings. Ours had a large attic room, and Tom had built a closed-in sunroom off the kitchen, which gave us more space.

Although I hated sewing, I loved quilting.

Several ladies from church, and sometimes my sisters, met in our upstairs attic space to quilt when the weather permitted. We'd talk and talk. Usually, along with the quilting, we'd have Bible studies or pray for the salvation of the wayward. I loved talking about the good Lord and sharing what I'd learned.

When it was cold outside, the upstairs became too chilly. But if there was a little sunshine, we'd gather to work. With the weather warm and the boys safely back in town from their camping trip, we planned a quilting day for Friday afternoon.

Tillie and our friends Florence, Nettie, and Opal came, each bringing sweets to share. Opal set her famous dried apricot fried pies in the middle of the kitchen table. I eyed the heavenly-looking platter while preparing a pitcher of tea for when we needed a break.

We gabbed while we waited for Annie to show up. She wasn't usually this late.

Jerry, Annie's boy, came running through the propped open door. "Aunt Jennie! Aunt Jennie! Momma needs you. The baby's coming!"

"Go ahead without me!" I hollered to the ladies, knowing they wouldn't sit quietly and quilt while a baby was on its way. I ran down the street to check on my sister.

I banged open the screen door. "Annie! Are you all right?"

At first, I heard nothing. Then a groan came from the bedroom. Her husband Tommy Akin must have been barbering down at the Motley Hotel. He worked as many hours as he could because they needed the money.

The quilting ladies arrived at Annie's house soon after. When I told them all to go home, they encouraged me to keep the loads of desserts for Annie's family.

Till stayed to help with household chores and anything I needed. Impatient, I looked back at her. "Don't just sit there, run get Tommy. And holler at Susie along the way."

She turned and skedaddled. Sisters are angels on earth, and I was grateful for Tillie, especially since she normally avoided birthings.

I'd attended to many ladies giving birth, but I wished the doctor was there. Something seemed wrong.

Annie's face dripped with perspiration. "I don't want to do this, Jennie. I don't. Help me. It hurts so much."

When I wiped Annie's face, she looked at me with those pretty brown eyes, trusting and sad. Her hair had fallen down around her shoulders, and I pulled it back into a ribbon. She didn't need her hair tickling her while she focused on breathing and pushing. I'd helped her with her other two births, and I knew she'd be sensitive to any touch. My heart sputtered as I remembered Jenny Mae's pale complexion and exhaustion.

I couldn't lose my sister like Tom lost his first wife. I just couldn't.

Annie cried out, the sound like a trapped hyena. Well, maybe not exactly that bad. But then, I'd never actually heard a trapped hyena. I was in my element, knowing I was needed even as my hands trembled. I stayed beside her for the next hour while Till and Susie took care of her two little boys.

When I left the room to scrub again with our lye soap and get more warm water, Tommy, Annie's husband, stood right outside the bedroom doorway. "Go get the doctor," I said. "I think it's time."

He didn't move.

I took him by the arm and pushed him toward the front door. "Hurry! This could be a huge baby. She may be struggling. Go on now." I shoved him out onto the porch.

Tommy came back alone thirty minutes later, explaining that the doctor was over by Vinson, helping a man who had fallen from his horse. Three cotton gins in town, but only one doctor. How could we have gotten so out of balance? Where were the midwives?

The contractions lasted until dark. I kept up a steady stream of prayers, and as the evening wore on, I prayed harder than when Truman broke his arm. Tillie brought me a bowl of chicken soup, but I couldn't eat. The baby's head began to show.

Just before nine o'clock, the doctor arrived. I was never so glad to see a man in my life. He took over and ordered me around as if he were running a bakery and I was the lackey. Tired as a fat mule, I took a minute to rest my feet before I ran to bring the doctor what he needed. Tommy had fallen asleep on the floor. Susie was tucking the boys into bed. And Tillie was sprawled out on the sofa with her shoes off, a pillow behind her head, snoring loudly. I couldn't believe they hadn't heard the doctor come in.

I nudged Tillie's shoulder. "Doc's here. It's almost time."

She jumped to her feet, glancing around. "The baby's here?"

I shook my head. Till's uselessness at birthing should have been a record. Most women would have been more helpful. Even after all the births she'd had, she acted like babies eased their way into life like soft little butterflies landing on a pedestal. At least she was here, which meant a lot.

I stepped back into the bedroom carrying a load of clean towels. Till followed, but stood in a corner. It was standard practice to give laboring mothers morphine, but our doc didn't have any available. He couldn't help with her pain. Reminded me of a Bible verse, *In sorrow, thou shalt bring forth children*. Why, Lord, why?

"Hold on, dearie. She's almost here." I rushed to Annie's side and grabbed her hand.

Her eyes were wild.

"Just a few more minutes."

Then I heard a baby cry, and I took in a deep breath and held it. Nothing was sweeter than the first sound of a newborn.

Annie smiled, reaching toward the baby. "May I see her?"

"You can," said Doctor Wilson, "but you don't have a girl. You have a fine boy here, even if he's a tiny, little thing."

Annie's smile faded, and she shrunk back. "A boy?"

"And it appears you're not finished. There's another baby coming."

Till gasped. "Well, I'll be a monkey's uncle!"

My head snapped over toward the doc. He was serious.

Annie looked up at me in a panic. The pain wasn't over yet. However, the chances of having a girl were still open.

"Twins." I grabbed Annie's hand. "You're having twins." Now I understood why her belly had grown so large. Why something had seemed wrong.

Till took the first scrawny baby, washed him, and wrapped him in a baby blanket. It took another half an hour for the second baby's head to appear. I could tell Annie's strength was draining.

Finally, a second baby slipped into the doctor's hands. I didn't assume it was a girl this time. Not with the luck of the Thomas sisters.

Annie didn't ask, so worn that she probably didn't care, the poor thing. Her eyes closed and her arms fell limp.

I patted her hand. "You did it, sister. You gave birth to two babies today. That's quite an endeavor." I bowed my head. "Thank you, Lord, for these two healthy little ones."

"Amen." The doctor handed the baby to me. Another boy. My heart sank to the ground, knowing how dispirited Annie would be. Actually, we all would be.

I held out the baby boy to her. She looked at him, then looked at me with empty eyes and shook her head. She didn't want to hold the baby. I gave the bundle to Susie, who stood nearby.

What was God thinking? Twin boys would have been a handful for anyone, but for my little sister? How would she hold up and manage four small boys? And she'd been so sure she'd have a girl.

After the doctor left, Tommy entered the room. I've never seen a man be unhappy with a son, and I was right. However, Tommy looked overwhelmed as he took in the sight of those two baby boys.

I tried to place the babies beside Annie in the bed, but she whispered, "Take them away, Jennie. I don't want them."

She refused to hold either one. Tears streaming down her cheeks, she turned away and faced the wall.

Chapter 11

I knew Annie would change her mind and accept what God had given, but I didn't know how long it would take. Perhaps tired from the long, drawn-out affair, she instantly fell asleep. I tiptoed out of the room.

A few minutes later, I felt a cold draft as the front door opened. My Tom walked in carrying a load of firewood. "Thought they might need this," he said. "Noticed they were getting low." He nodded to Tommy as he set the firewood down inside the wood bin.

My dear sweet husband always thought of other's needs. My needs. Even my smallest need. Even when I didn't ask.

We had to put the babies somewhere since Annie didn't want them near her in the bed. "Would you fellows go out and bring in that baby bed sitting in the barn? The babies need a place to sleep, and she can't have both in bed with her. I'll stay up tonight and watch Annie to make sure she's all right."

Annie's Tommy and my Tom trudged outside and were gone an extra amount of time. Finally, they carried the baby bed inside and set it up in Annie's room. She didn't budge while I washed it down, lined it with cloth, and laid the snugly wrapped babies in it.

Tommy sat down beside his wife while I walked my husband to the front door.

Tom didn't seem to know what to do. "Best be getting back home," he said as we stepped out onto the porch. He stopped and turned toward me. "I missed you tonight, but I'm proud of the way you're always helping others. The way you're helping Annie. You're a good woman, you are, Jennie Rue."

Jennie Rue. I liked when he called me Jennie Rue. He was not thinking of his first wife, Jenny Mae, but of me.

He pulled me close, and I laid my tired head on his chest. Exhausted almost as much as my sister, I felt warm comfort being near him.

He stroked my hair without speaking. "I love you, darling. And I'm glad to be married to you. I don't say it too often, but I notice all the work you do caring for people. Yes, sir, you're a right impressive lady."

My heart swelled like a balloon and fluttered as if it might burst. Over the years, Tom had become my hero, my comfort, and my love. A warm feeling spread through me as all the times of caring flooded my mind.

"I love you, too, Mr. Tom Newberry. And I'm very glad you asked me to marry you."

Tom bent over and gave me the deepest kiss an old girl like me could want. I felt loved to the moon and back, wondering why I ever doubted him. No one could take his first wife's place, but we certainly had something special.

He left to go home to watch over Truman. With a father like Tom, I didn't need to worry about protecting my son. His father would be there for him. Heavens, it would take both of us to raise that son of ours right.

Annie slept for several hours while Tillie and I rested. Finally, toward the next morning, she rolled over and opened her eyes. I sat on the side of her bed. "Annie, you've had a difficult time delivering two babies, and two baby boys at that. You're discouraged now, but you have to get up and take care of them.

They won't thrive otherwise. If you don't sit up here and nurse these babies, I'll have to look for a wet nurse."

She rolled away. "Go ahead."

My heart broke.

No wet nurses were available that I knew about, so I sterilized two glass bottles and warmed goat's milk to feed the precious little ones. Tillie and Susie each fed a baby, admiring them. Small, but perfectly formed and adorable, if you asked me. God's perfect creation.

Two more boys for the cousins' club.

***

The next Sunday morning, I walked with my family down Jones Street in Hollis toward the Methodist Church, Tom and my boy Truman on either side. I clutched my handbag and tucked my worn Bible under my arm. With the clear, chilly weather and no dust storms on the horizon, people appeared from all over town. I looked over my shoulder and saw our adolescent Thomas straggling behind. At least, he agreed to attend.

The church was a beautiful, massive, three-story brick building on Second Street. The corner tower could be seen for miles around. I clung to the railing as we walked up the steps. I felt comfortable there. Tom had attended the Methodist Church with his first wife before she died and wanted to continue, so I went with him. The church people were good to us. I didn't care which denomination we attended. I could joyfully praise God anywhere. And I loved helping with the choir and the children's classes.

Tom had to stop and shake every man's hand and tip his trilby hat to every lady. He wore a sleek double-breasted jacket, which accentuated his handsome features. He carried himself like a warrior chief.

Proud of my man, I sucked in a deep breath and pulled my shoulders back. I was blessed to have him as a husband. I straightened my bobbin lace collar and stopped beside him at the back of the auditorium, aware that my pointed, high-heeled shoes and silk stockings showed off shapely ankles. Even Truman, near us, had his hair slicked down.

"How are you doing, Mrs. Newberry?" asked the minister when he shook my hand. His wife nudged me, her feathered hat waving as she spoke. "How about giving me the recipe for that lemon pie you made last potluck? I need something special for the next deacon's meeting. When can I get it?"

I smiled, refraining from chatting too much with the minister's wife, or any of the ladies, for that matter. A difficult feat, given my propensity to say whatever was on my mind. I wanted to act dignified, a woman Tom would be proud of.

During the church service, I prayed for Governor Alfalfa Bill Murray and all the folks who had a hard time making ends meet during this desperate time. I prayed for Annie. I prayed for all of us, especially for the boys we were raising. Every last one of them needed God. A shoeshine boy at the barbershop where Tommy worked had finally named the twins. Maybe we'd used up all the boy's names we could think of, focusing on girls so much. The twins were named Ted Gene and Fred Jack. Good names.

Lastly, I prayed for myself. I looked back at how foolish I'd been. How could I have doubted Tom's love or felt inferior to him? He always held me in the highest regard, as I did him, and, grateful for such a husband, my heart sang.

I squeezed Tom's hand. I respected the man more every day. I admired the way he got involved in the community, and provided for the family. He encouraged me to be the best I could be. What more could a woman ask for?

There were a few drawbacks to marrying someone as old as Tom. He needed reading glasses years before I did. And he couldn't keep up with me. But when I thought about it, most people had trouble keeping up with me since I fluttered around like a hummingbird.

There were many advantages to his age. Already a Mason, he encouraged me to join the Eastern Stars and other ladies' organizations in town. He was well-off financially, which made it easy for me to be generous and feed the whole population of Harmon County if I wanted. This compassionate man understood my heartaches and needs. He might grow old before me, but I'd have the strength to care for him.

When Annie awoke from her delirious state and began to nurse her baby boys, I'd be there to help her. With my husband's blessings.

Maybe that's the way God planned it.

I had married a good man.

One who loved me, no end.

Author's Notes

I always loved my Uncle Tom and Aunt Jennie's story. Their solid love for each other and godly lives encouraged everyone around them. Jennifer Rue Thomas was born in Saint Jo, Texas, on March 22, 1892. Her story is basically true, including nursing Tom Newberry's first wife while she was ill. Her heavy hair and penchant for rainwater were well known to the family, even up to the day she died in the middle of the night after setting out her rain bucket.

Thomas Andrew Newberry (Tom) was born August 30th, 1877, in Green County, Tennessee. He traveled by train to Harmon County, Oklahoma, with his cousin, Henry Newberry, about 1900 or 1901. They'd both previously fought in the Spanish-American War, enlisting in the U.S. Army on May 15th, 1896. Henry homesteaded the Newberry Ranch, which was later declared an Oklahoma Centennial Ranch by the Oklahoma Historical Society and the Oklahoma Department of Agriculture. A sign commemorating this ghost town can be seen at the old Shrewder Store on the corner of N1800 and E1550 Roads.

Tom homesteaded next to Henry, where he built the Shrewder Store. His first wife was also named Jennie. I found her grave at the Gould Cemetery. She was born on June 14, 1886, and died on June 28, 1916, the same year her son Thomas was born.

Tom's daughter, Virginia, is said to have attained four degrees. She married Roy Nichols, and they had four children. Their daughter Patricia Ann was named after Ann Akin, or so I was told. Virginia and Roy both taught at Texas Tech. Virginia taught music. They moved to Lubbock, Texas. I haven't verified this information and would love to talk with some of the family members.

All I could substantiate for Tom's son, Thomas Newberry, was that he married Hattie and moved to Oklahoma City, where he owned a produce company. She had two children from a previous marriage, but they had no children together. He died around 1976, and his wife died earlier from cancer.

Jennie Rue's son, Truman, joined the U.S. Army Corps in 1943 and stayed until 1947. He married Maybelle Chapman and moved to Montgomery, Alabama. They had twin daughters in 1952, Debra and Donna, and then a son, Dana in 1956. Two other sons died in infancy: Mark Dale in 1958 and Daryl Alan in 1960.

Tom and Jennie Newberry were charter members of the Hollis Eastern Star Chapter, where Tom was past grand master, per a newspaper article I found honoring their golden wedding anniversary. He was also a member of the Gould Masonic Lodge. Documents support the many accomplishments listed for Tom. I also have a photo of the front of Tom's store, T. A. Newberry Dry Goods—Clothing.

Jennie's grandson, Dana Newberry, helped fill in blanks of this story, and more information about the Newberry history can be found at a website about the children of Stephen and Sarah Chambers Newberry.

Tom Newberry contracted emphysema from smoking all his life and carried an oxygen tank around with him during his last years. He died in January 1968, and the funeral service was held at the First Methodist Church in Hollis, Oklahoma.

Jennie passed away June 22, 1975, seven and a half years after Tom.

The story of Ann's rejection of her twin boys is true. My grandmother, Ann, admitted it with a laugh. Their birthday was on July 23 of that year, but I moved it back a few months for the story to work better with Susie's.

The short man who purchased the Shrewder Store was really called Little John. And I found a list of Hollis businesses in the 1930s at the Hollis Historical Museum, which helped with details of the town's settings. The "Historical Sketch of the First Baptist Church in Hollis" gave pertinent details from 1898 to 1983.

Aunt Jennie's love shone to anyone who met her.

Annie Crump

Thomas Sister #5

Jerry, Jimmy, Ted, and Fred Akin

Annie Crump

Born January 22, 1895

Chapter 1

July 1935

Five years later.

"What's all the ruckus?" My older sister, Sally Matilda, burst through the front door as one of my twin boys yanked a toy truck away from the other.

I threw my hands up in despair. "Siblings. Why can't my boys get along?" Sometimes their devotion to one another seemed as deep as a clear water well. Other times, jealousy struck kindness a blow that could make a grown woman scream.

With four boys under nine years old, chaos ruled our home. I cooked oatmeal for one and toast for another. Scrubbed red dirt out of britches and washed mud off scrunched-up faces.

My sister Susie, hidden by Tillie who was taller than the rest of us, poked her head in. "What's the problem?"

"This day-to-day fuss keeps me frazzled." I pushed loose hair out of my face. "I can't wait 'til the boys are grown enough to take care of themselves." What kind of mother was I, not wanting to pamper my babies?

"Annie, you don't mean it." Tillie knew more about boys than I did. Her four were older than my four. "Blazes, you should know by now that little boys have the energy of longhorn bulls and the common sense of a barrel of monkeys. Here, I baked bread for you." She stomped into the kitchen, the fresh yeast aroma following her.

"And here's a pat of butter I churned, Anna Lee," said Susie, the only one who called me that. When I came into the world in 1895, I was named after the doctor who delivered me, of all monikers, Dr. John Crump. Who wants to go through life answering to Ann Crump? Nobody. My sisters changed their names, so I changed mine, insisting on being called Anna Lee, but Mama never took me seriously.

"One of your young un's came by my house this morning. Said your meal last night had shortcomings." Till's lighthearted voice meant she didn't intend to be mean. She was right, though—my cooking abilities were nonexistent. Thankfully, Till and Susie lived with a few blocks of me in our small town of Hollis, Oklahoma.

I laughed with her, ashamed of my inadequacy. "Burned cornbread and flavorless beans just about goosed their gander. No one ate much of anything."

Disappointment bound me with goat rope when my third pregnancy resulted in sons. Twin sons, no less, when I'd wanted a daughter so badly. I cried for hours. Looking back, I'm ashamed of how I acted—refusing to nurse the boys for three days. I couldn't believe I rejected them. After their birth, due to female problems which ended in an operation, I lay in bed for two months, weaker than I've ever been. I never quite recovered. Never birthed another.

My four sisters and I had thirteen boys between us—a baker's dozen—but no girls. Not one who survived anyway. Our mama, explaining after she had five girls in a row, informed us that daughters were more precious than sons and would stick with you through thick and thin. Made us thirst for our own.

My sisters and I gave up on having a little girl in the family when the twin boys came along—the last of the Thomas sister babies. Sometimes even family dreams must fade away.

I flopped into a chair, feeling incapacitated, helpless, and plum worn out. And I wasn't even forty yet. At least, not for another few weeks.

What was I doing, pretending to be a good mother?

***

My older sisters took care of me, and I rested for the next hour.

As the youngest of five girls, Mama used to say I grew up spoiled as a barrel of rotten taters. My parents died when I was young, and as the only child left at home, I felt abandoned with no permanent place to call my own. Unfortunate luck for a growing girl.

My sisters took care of me for years, babied me no end. I spent time at each one's house, moving from around as convenient. Sometimes I enjoyed being the youngest and not having many chores to do, and other times I didn't like it, especially when everyone fussed over me so much I could hardly breathe. I depended upon them for everything. Couldn't cross my eyes without worry lines creasing my sisters' faces. I never learned to cook before getting married and had learned little since.

Learned little about a lot of things, I discovered. Rather disheartening to wonder if your husband still held secrets after you've been married for years.

My siblings were by my side most of my life, and I needed them more than a Sunday dinner served on a silver platter. One helping of my sisters' yummy yeast bread and fresh butter could soothe anyone's discontent.

How was I going to survive raising four rambunctious boys? Honestly, I loved them to high heaven, and tried to be a devoted mother, but I felt helpless. How could I get them fed, clothed, and taught to act like decent human beings? Impossible in my state of mind.

Chapter 2

At breakfast the next morning, my husband, Tommy Akin, brought in the Hollis Post-Herald newspaper. He'd only gone to the third grade in school but liked to say he got an education by reading the newspaper. He was wrong. I claimed the honor of having taught him, since I patiently explained each word he spelled out loud to me.

"Are you finished with the paper?" I put a plate of scrambled eggs and ham in front of him. Our two oldest boys had eaten and run off to play, and the twins still slept. Hopefully, they'd stay quiet for another half hour while I attempted to bake a chocolate cake. I wasn't ready for another round of battling naughtiness.

"There isn't much news, unless you count the grime that covers the whole state." Tommy tossed me the folded pages. "No one has to read a piece of paper to know another dust storm hit us."

"True. We've had so many storms, none seem spectacular anymore."

"Except the one last spring."

I agreed. According to the Post-Herald, Black Sunday, which they'd taken to calling it, had been worse in the panhandle, but plenty of stinging grains of sand blew around Hollis. It gusted eighteen days straight, brining dust so severe that day turned into night. No rain had come since, and pastures remained as dry as cow bones.

I drank down the memory with a sip of coffee. "How're we going to survive if the town disappears? We can't sit here and shrivel up with it."

"You worry too much." Tommy never acknowledged anything bothered him. With a slightly receding hairline and sparkling eyes, he always seemed to have a smirk on his face. A sense of security I seldom felt.

"I wish Tom and Jennie hadn't moved away." My sister Jennie's husband, Tom Newberry, had a difficult time making a living from the dry goods store he owned in Hollis, the T.A. Newberry Mercantile. His older two children had taken off on their own several years ago. He'd drawn his store back to the bare minimum, found a fellow to run it, and invested his life savings in an onion farm down in El Paso, Texas. Tom, Jennie, and their son, Truman, moved away. Just packed up and left town. For an onion farm!

How could Jennie have left me, knowing I needed help with my four boys? She used to bring me hot broth when I was sick and helped with the spring cleaning. She also kept my boys fed and rounded up. By my side all my life, I missed her more than honeysuckle. Her sweet presence could soothe over a beehive of anxieties.

I stood and gathered dirty plates from the table, dropping them into the sink to wash later. Then I mixed sugar, eggs, cocoa, and butter for a chocolate cake. "I hate her living in Texas," I mumbled under my breath. "I hope onion prices drop to nothing."

According to letters I received from Jennie, the dratted onion sales couldn't be better. Tom irrigated their Texas farm, and onions grew well enough to ship fifty-pound bags north by train to sell in different cities.

"Not likely they'll move back with the entire country going bust," Tommy grunted and walked out the door.

Even after eleven years of marriage and having all these boys together, I couldn't understand my husband. Some days, he acted like I was a nuisance, and other days, he treated me like a homecoming queen. Did he care about my needs or not? I didn't always know.

On the other hand, it'd always been clear what my four older sisters thought about me. I was their baby, treated like a fragile porcelain doll, unable to do wrong in their sight. Unfortunately, two of my sisters, Mary Bobbie and Jennie Rue, had moved to Texas. But fortunately, Susie and her husband had moved back to Hollis for a second try.

I added the dry ingredients to the chocolate cake, finished beating it, and turned on the oven. Someone banged on the front door, and I ran to see who it was. The mailman handed me a letter from Bobbie and chatted with me for a while.

Ten minutes later, I walked back into the kitchen. "My cake! Where's my cake bowl?"

Stomping through the house, I heard my daring twins snickering under the bed. "Come out of there, you two! I hear you." I leaned down and dragged out two lads along with my almost empty bowl of cake batter. Spoons in their hands and faces smeared with chocolate, their dancing eyes betrayed two unrepentant spirits.

How in heavens? This day was going to be as chaotic as the last. I couldn't even manage to make a cake. Not that it would've been edible.

For years, Jennie and I had traded jobs. She cooked for my family while I sewed for hers. Since she moved away, my meals were not up to par, to say the least. When my boys experienced the results of my sad-looking sourdough bread, they begged Aunt Jennie to come home. I agreed with them. We needed her.

How could I manage? I was on the verge of a nervous breakdown already.

Chapter 3

I was twenty-three years old when I fell in love for the first time. Adelai Mathews, a handsome gentleman, adored me. A small tassel of his brown, curly hair lay across his forehead, and his eyes were the color of honey.

Self-conscious of my thin hair, I wore it in a bun. I had diphtheria as a young child, which weakened me forever. I remember little of it, but I lost most of my hair. What was left of my thin strands looked as scraggly as the stray dog who slept under our front porch. My sweet Adelai didn't mind. Told me I was beautiful.

Every time I thought of our time together, my heart fluttered like water shimmering on the pond. The sweetest courtship a girl could ask for. He brought me candies from the drugstore, walked me to church, and picked red roses from the Horton's yard. Being a private person, I couldn't confide in my sisters about our times together, but it was all proper, you might say. After he asked me to marry him, we made plans for a fancy wedding that would take half a year to orchestrate.

My fiancé was the most wonderful man, and not much older than me at twenty-five. He'd followed his father's footsteps and became a banker, interested in political advancements. Our love was sweeter than sugarcane, and we could hardly wait to get married. He promised to always take care of me.

Preparations for the wedding consumed my time. I wanted the candles, the indigo and milkweed flowers, and the wedding cake to be perfect. My older sisters were already married and in the midst of having babies, so they looked forward to me joining the group.

A week before our June wedding, I sat down next to Jennie to hem her bridesmaid dress, a measuring tape hanging around my neck. "I hope you like this pattern, Jennie Rue." I'd chosen pastel green satin for long silky dresses.

Indulged when young, I had access to the beautiful satins and ginghams sold in her husband's dry goods store, and she encouraged me to choose anything I wanted. She pampered me something awful. Perhaps that was why I loved living with her.

Getting Jennie to sit still long enough to put the wedding attire together was like bridling old Nellie. I'd lived with my sister long enough to know her habits. Tiny, energetic Jennie would do whatever she needed to do. She could do anything, except sit still.

"Bless you, child. It's lovely, but I'm glad you didn't choose one of those new-fangled beaded fashions. They're too short for my tastes."

"Ouch." I stuck my finger with a needle and put it into my mouth to ease the pain. I handed the dress to Jennie. "Here, it's almost finished."

Jennie hated hand stitching, but I hoped she could complete the dress with little effort.

I stepped over to the black Singer sewing machine. "I've almost finished Till's dress. She's been too busy to sew for herself." Designing the latest fashions was my favorite pastime. And although Till worked as a professional seamstress, she seldom made herself anything new to wear.

I pressed my foot down on the iron treadle and rocked it in a steady rhythm, completing the sleeves and the neckline. I laid the dress across my lap and ran my hand over the fabric, relishing the smooth feel that reminded me of a soft newborn calf.

I couldn't wait to see my sisters in their bride's maid dresses.

While I dreamed of my coming wedding, Till came running through the front door, out of breath, her hair flying around her face. The door banged shut behind her. "Adelai. Have you heard about Adelai?"

I jumped to my feet, the material falling about me. "Why? What's wrong?"

"He passed out and they rushed him to the hospital. I think it's the flu." The Spanish flu pandemic had exploded across the world and thousands had died from it. My insides turned cold at the thought.

Adelai had not been feeling well the day before, complaining of a bellyache. But I had no idea he was seriously ill. I rushed to the Harmon County Hospital where I found him lying on a white sheet, his face pale and unmoving. My heart did somersaults, not knowing the extent of his illness.

"What happened? How is he?" I looked over at the nurse beside him, dreading the answer. "Does he have the flu?"

"No. He has appendicitis. It burst inside him."

I kneeled by his bed and buried my face in my hands. Someone drew up a chair and for the next few days, I sat by my fiancé's side, holding his hands and staring at his handsome, smooth cheeks, his tassel of brown hair, and his closed eyes.

He grew weaker and weaker.

Terrified, I reminded him in whispers about our wedding plans. How he promised to take care of me. I told him how much I loved him and tried to understand how life wasn't going my way anymore. How life could change so swiftly.

Adelai never recovered enough to talk to me.

He died on June 1st, 1918, three days before our wedding was scheduled to take place. His body was taken to Mound City, Kansas, where his family lived.

My heart was crushed.

How could losing a loved one hurt so much your insides quake? How could God do this? I cried. I raged. I spit nails at the dogs. My spirit sank deeper than grandpa's well.

I would never get over it. Never.

My sisters surrounded me, consoling me the best they could. I'll never forget the hugs and the gallons of sweet tea. The shared tears. The late night talks.

I boxed up a few of Adelai's things: papers, several letters, a dried rose, and added them to my keepsakes. Adelai's mother mailed me a copy of his funeral memorial service and I tucked it inside my Bible and cried each time I looked at it.

When I lost my first love, I declared no man would ever steal my heart again. It hurt too bad.

Chapter 4

After my Adelai died, despondency sent me into a cave for months. My sisters intervened and pulled me back to life. Grief flows over a person and landslides to the bottom, covering all the beauty and pain with a fresh layer of living. Though I didn't want to, I had to go on.

Sometimes crisis changes you on the inside. Although I wished for an angel to watch over me, I had to start looking out for myself. A deep sadness settled in. Adelai wasn't there to care for me.

Several years after I lost my love, I moved to Cushing, Oklahoma, to live with my sister, Susie. Cushing, nearly the same size as Hollis in 1923, lay miles away from all the heartaches I'd encountered in my hometown. I hoped to find a job and forget about the loss of my fiancé. Forget and start over with my life.

Susie's husband, Elmer Lindsey, was a school band director, and they moved around every year or two due to nasty rumors about him and young girls. I never knew whether the gossip carried any truth because my days were too full to question him.

I helped with their boys, Marvin and Jack, to offset any costs for taking me in. Those two rascals never got along. Jack was so angry at Marvin that steam rolled from his head, while Marvin tried to act innocent and denied any wrongdoing. I grew fond of them, but I was never good with children.

I began working in a mercantile store in downtown Cushing. Even only a few years after the oil boom, the town's women still loved to buy fancy clothes. I sold dresses like hot cakes.

The latest outfits were easy for me to replicate. I could study designs in a magazine and sew most clothes so well they looked better than the ready-made ones. I purchased pocketbooks and two-toned heels to match my new dresses. And I dreamed. I dreamed that someday I'd have a daughter to love, to dress in fancy frills and lace and linen. Not to mention embroidered collars, hair ribbons, and those cute little Shirley Temple dresses.

Those dreams never came true. Instead, I had sons. I was not prepared to raise four rambunctious boys.

***

I remember the day I met Tommy Akin. How could I forget?

I left Cushing to travel home to Hollis for a long-awaited vacation. As I stumbled near my seat on the train, my arms were full and I dropped a book, *The Great Gatsby,* which I'd planned to read on the ride. I reached down to grab it, trying to balance my packages, my pocketbook, and an umbrella.

A nice-looking gentleman sitting across from my seat picked up the book. When he handed it to me, I noticed his smooth hands, then his shiny brogue shoes and starched wide-legged trousers. I looked up and saw his sharp brown eyes staring at me from under a straw hat.

I arranged myself by the window as the train bellowed and lurched forward. "Thank you for helping, sir."

He tipped his hat in return. "My pleasure."

Turning my head to watch the rolling hills of Oklahoma country, I heard someone slide into the seat next to mine. I looked over, startled. The nice-looking fellow had moved to sit beside me. He smiled, almost in apology.

I smoothed down my chiffon dress and wiggled my cloche hat into place.

He nodded. “My name’s Thomas Elisha Akin, but you can call me Tommy. I know you don’t know me, and you probably wonder why I’m being so bold. But this might be a long, lonely trip. I figure we may as well get to know one another. I work in Oilton as a barber.”

I gave him a half-smile, which encouraged him to keep talking.

“My family’s from around Konawa. They originally moved to Oklahoma from Beebe, Arkansas, but that was years ago. Mind if I ask your name?”

I’d never met a man so talkative, and I was flattered that this handsome man took an interest in me.

Tommy, two years older than me, had been in the military during the Great War with the 57th Infantry Company D. He was six feet tall, even though he looked taller when he stood to close the window. I loved the way he dressed, fancy and all. I learned he had six sisters and two brothers. His grandfather, Jesse Levi Akin, was the first person buried at the Floyd Cemetery in Arkansas. Evidently, he was out hunting hogs when killed by bushwhackers during the end of the Civil War.

Funny how you can learn so much about a man when he’s talking about his family. Funny some of the things you don’t learn.

I shared little about my past except to say I’d been engaged and my fiancé had died. I never told him it’d be hard to give my heart away to someone else, even someone as attractive and courtly as Tommy Akin. That no one could compare to my Adelai.

Dashing and debonair, Tommy impressed me. Before he stepped off the train in Oklahoma City, he tipped his hat. "I promise. I'll travel to Cushing to see you in a few weeks."

I waved goodbye from the train window and thought I'd seen the last of the compelling man, but he did as he'd promised. Three weeks later, he looked me up at the mercantile and invited me to the opera.

Since Tommy was a friendly, verbose fellow, the courtship didn't last long before my sisters decided it was time for me to marry. My age made a difference. I was twenty-nine, and old maid status was coming upon me faster than ruffians made moonshine.

Then he said the magic words, "I promise I'll always take care of you."

And although no one could touch my heart like Adelai, Tommy lifted my spirits enough I'd try to put the past behind me.

I had a few reservations. He'd avoided answering when I asked what he'd been doing the last few years, and I wondered if there was something he didn't want to share. Pushing for answers didn't seem right, because he hadn't pushed me to share about Adelai.

I agreed to marry.

But what was I getting into? I hardly knew this man. I had four brothers-in-law, all different as sour grapes and honey. Would he drink too much like Till's husband? Or be distant like Susie's? Surely not. I prayed my new husband would either be fun like Bob's or kind-hearted like Jennie's. Whatever he was like, this marriage would be for life.

I wish I'd known what kind of life. I wish I'd known more about Tommy.

Chapter 5

For the next few months after Tommy and I married, I'm embarrassed to say I pouted like a baby wanting a sucker. I pouted about living in a rented two-room place. I pouted about living away from my sisters. Truthfully, it felt like the heartache had begun all over again. I pouted so much that Tommy found a job in Hollis and moved us back to my hometown.

We bought a wood-frame house on Jones Street and began to fix it up. Cheesecloth came in rolls of forty-eight inches wide, and I helped Tommy put it on the walls over the wood to contain the warmth. We glued wallpaper on top of the cheesecloth, papering up to the ceiling. Every lumber yard had several wallpaper designs, and I chose a pale blue with dainty flowers dotted over it. We had no real insulation in the walls because we couldn't afford it. Gas cost around a dollar and a quarter a month, but it cost nothing if you didn't use it, so we kept the house pretty cold.

I spent days fixing up our little home, making curtains, scrubbing the floors and windows, rearranging the dishes in the cupboard. Delighted to finally have a place to call my own, I thrived.

Tommy catered to me and treated me well. We had the sweet kind of love that makes flowers bloom and fills the air with incense.

We soon had two boys and after they were old enough to climb the ladder to the attic, that's where they slept. Then, when the twins were old enough to maneuver the steps, the four boys slept together up there.

The attic floor was terribly cold in the winter, and they shared a feather bed, which they fought over incessantly. It had an iron bed frame, and from experience, I knew why they liked it. That old feather bed would curl up around you and make you feel like you were sleeping in the clouds. Half a dozen big, heavy quilts lay on top. My mischievous little boys would hide from me under the covers, giggling and thinking I couldn't hear them.

I insisted on a regular toilet, and Tommy did his best to appease me. The only place the city sewer system could hook up to our pipes was inside the barn. So that's where Tommy installed a commode. He set the toilet stool on a platform in the middle of the barn but failed to put walls around it.

One day, I walked to the barn privy, stepped up onto the stage, and sat down without looking inside. Suddenly, something flapped onto my backside. I jumped like a spider crawled up my skirt. I went screaming out of that barn, yelling like a banshee. I don't think I even pulled my drawers up properly.

"What's wrong?" Tommy came running. "Is the barn on fire?"

I pointed. "Something's in there!"

Tommy went inside and came out carrying a banty hen, which had apparently fallen into the stool. That bird scared the living daylights out of me, and I probably scared her too. He and the boys never let me live that one down, telling the story at the next family gathering until we all laughed. I'd be mortified for the rest of my life.

After all our work, I was proud of our new house—even the barn toilet. Maybe I shouldn't have gotten so attached. Disasters could always happen.

***

I questioned Tommy about the failing economy, fearful for our future. What would happen to us if this depression didn't lift?

"Nothing to worry about. Men need haircuts and shaves even in the worst of times. Makes 'em feel better about themselves," Tommy claimed.

He loved his work at the barbershop. Men, young and old, bragged about his shave.

Occasionally, I watched him work. Early in the morning, Tommy lit the hot water heater in his shop. Each evening, he turned it off. He used the best shaving cream he could buy, usually Colgate or Barbasol. He'd whip up the cream in a white glass cup, use a soft brush to lather it onto a fellow's face, and then place hot towels on the man from the forehead to his neck. After he took off the towel, he put on more soap and shaved the fellow with a straight-edge razor which had been sharpened on a leather strap the night before. Then he rubbed cream on the man's face and added another hot towel.

He'd go over the person's face again and again until the man had the smoothest skin in the country.

"He uses so much cream and hot towels, you don't need to shave for a month," a customer claimed.

"Makes your face feel as smooth as a baby's bottom. I spent a whole buck on it."

"I'd spend a million, I tell you—if I had it."

Tommy worked hard and steadily. His hands betrayed his vocation. They weren't calloused, rough like my papa's farming hands, but soft like silk. We weren't wealthy, but we always had enough to survive.

Tommy, an outgoing, occasionally uncouth man, had been taught few formal manners. A country-style man and more handsome than anyone I ever saw, even compared to Adelai. He could talk to a fence post, and I would get jealous when he talked to every woman he saw.

But with all his chattering, I felt like secrets lay between us.

And I was right.

Chapter 6

"Got some bad news." Tommy hung his hat on the wall peg and washed his hands in the water bucket sitting by the back door. He stalled, sat down on the rocking chair, slowly untied his shoes, and slipped them off.

"Well, what is it?" I asked. No one likes a hard conversation, especially when the carrier dallies around like a tree might grow up in the front yard before he says anything.

He rolled the tops of his brown socks down to his ankles and pulled each off, gingerly, like needles were stuck in them. "My first wife wants money. She claims I haven't supported her since the divorce."

I gasped, not sure I heard right, but then my left ear had been damaged in the diphtheria episode when I was young. All I heard was, "My first wife wants money."

Tommy had a *first* wife? He was divorced? And he'd never told me?

"She filed a lien against me for the house." Tommy's face looked drawn, frown lines showing on the edge of his mouth as he held up an envelope and took out legal papers.

"I don't understand. You were married before?" Feeling deceived, I leaned away from him. Betrayed.

"We had a son. I never thought I'd hear from them again, so I never said anything."

A son? How could he keep this from me? I took a deep breath to calm myself and perched on the edge of a chair across from him, stress holding me in place. "I don't understand. How can someone waltz into our lives and make these demands? Who is this woman, anyway?" My voice sounded whiny. Tense.

Tommy scrunched his lips together before he spoke. "I got out of the army early, like I told you. Got an honorable discharge due to family distress, my brother getting mustard gassed in the war and all. After I got out, I began barbering. I met Ruth in Guthrie, and she and I got close, and things happened that shouldn't have happened."

I felt my jaw drop, and then snapped it shut. Tommy, my Tommy. What had he done?

"No matter now," he said. "She got pregnant and threw a conniption fit for me to marry her. She didn't want to be embarrassed and have a baby out of wedlock. I did the right thing, and we married in '21 and named the boy Thomas, after me." He paused, waiting for my response, but I remained quiet. "The marriage didn't set well for either of us."

I shook my head. What kind of woman was this Ruth? Had he loved her? Did he still love her? My heart sank with a heavy thud. "Surely that part of your life is over."

"She'll do whatever she wants. I never saw a woman so difficult. Maybe it was more her parents' fault because they butted-in a lot." Tommy, clearly distressed, swayed hard in my rocking chair.

I wanted reassurance that he'd never leave me and would always take care of me, but instead of voicing my concerns, I asked, "Are you sure the child is yours?"

"That's what she said." He claimed the woman manipulated him. He'd only married her because of the baby, and her parents' insistence.

I wanted to believe him. But fear for our future made me tremble. "She can't take away our house, can she? We bought this house. We fixed it up." This was the first place I'd felt content since moving from home to home during childhood.

Tommy looked down at the floor. "She threatened to suspend my barber's license if I don't give up the house." His voice lowered to a base level, gravely like a man stuck in a dugout.

My voice, conversely, rose to a squeak. "What? She can't do that. You're a barber. That's your livelihood." Tommy received a license from the State of Colorado when he was seventeen years old. He was proud of being a barber, our only means of support.

"Not much I can do about it," he said. "Maybe it was only a threat."

Congress had recently enacted the Social Security Act to provide welfare when a parent couldn't. It was intended to assist families during this depressed time, those with a deceased or disabled parent. But if a living parent refused to support his children, then those kids also met the criteria. The government sought the absent father for support. Apparently, according to his ex-wife, Tommy fit that last category.

I wrung my hands, discussed it with my sisters, and soaked my pillow with tears. How had life brought us to this point of confusion? Would we lose everything? And in this disastrous economy?

What would happen to our family? I didn't want to revert to the helplessness I felt when depending upon my sisters for everything. But my emotions fluttered. My childhood need to be taken care of surfaced and fear crept in. Fear and despair.

How would we cope?

Chapter 7

Tommy didn't contest his ex-wife's claim against our property. Perhaps he felt guilty for not supporting his firstborn through the years. With little recourse, he was found in contempt of court for not paying back child support. I suppose his ex-wife, Ruth, needed money to support herself and her son, but no one, not even Tommy and I, were in good financial shape. A battered society saw to that.

The dire situation alarmed me. Between the dust storms and the dragging national crisis, almost every family suffered losses. Houses sat empty after the occupants loaded up and moved west. Fields lay unplowed, unplanted, and bare. Shelves at the local dry goods store emptied. Water ran low, and people bickered about the price of a loaf of bread.

Now, our home was in jeopardy. "Lord," I prayed. "What are we to do?"

"We have to move by the end of the month." Tom's voice dropped as he grumbled under his breath. All day, he'd acted like a different man, dragging his usual buoyant self around the house in despair. "Two weeks. We have to move in two weeks."

How could I respond? Was this his fault? Well, yes. But we could do nothing about it now. We'd been married for years and had four boys together. I was not about to walk away and leave him. He'd always supported me. Was it time for me to stand by him?

Others had taken care of me all my life, and I didn't want to be a shrew about this. Scared maybe, but I couldn't hide under the covers, worried.

"We'll make do," I tussled his hair as he slumped into a stuffed chair.

"We're barely getting by. How are we going to…?"

"Don't worry. We'll get through." Where had those thoughts come from? Daddy always said that difficult times make you stronger. I didn't feel stronger. But just saying those words gave me more confidence.

***

A week later, after breakfast, Tommy, as usual, left to walk to the barbershop. I coerced the boys into the kitchen to help pack pots and pans for our move, even though we hadn't found a place yet.

We heard a noise and ran to the front window. A tow truck was backing up to our car.

We scrambled out to the front porch and stood speechless as a fellow hooked onto our vehicle. By the time I yelled, "No. You can't do that!" our automobile was being hauled off.

"Why are they taking it?" Jimmy looked up at me with his big brown eyes. "Why are they taking our lizzie?"

"Your daddy will figure it out. He always does." I clenched my jaw as I said it. Anger rose in my chest as I thought of this heartless woman I'd never met.

All the money in our bank account was withdrawn, leaving almost nothing. Fifty cents remained in our savings account and Tommy closed it. He would have gone to jail if he'd attempted to keep anything. After losing our house and car, worrying about this horrible drought throughout the country, and dozens of banks closing, now Tommy's ex-wife is taking our last dime.

I had to get down on my knees and pray a lot to forgive this woman for the distress she caused my family.

My husband didn't trust the banking industry any longer. He took a tin can and buried most of his next week's earnings in the backyard of Jennie's empty house. He didn't offer to show me where he buried the money, but I suspected from then on, we'd have enough to make ends meet.

I clenched my jaw and determined to not let this woman ruin my family. Tommy, me, and the boys would start over.

We would.

Chapter 8

We had no place to live.

I wrote Jennie, and she and Tom let us move into their empty house, since their onion farm in Texas was still supporting itself. Their house was larger than we needed, and comfortable. Don't know as I'd ever told her how much I appreciated her. I needed to do that.

Money was tight, especially with folks hanging on to their last dollar or moving out of town. Tommy kept his barbering job at the hotel but found additional ways to earn money to keep us going. Being a big talker, he was good at bartering. He proved excellent at it, in fact, a natural born trader, and people tended to trust him.

One man said he'd gathered all he wanted from an eighty-acre patch of sweet potatoes, and Tommy could gather what was left. The boys and I climbed into the beat-up Ford jalopy Tommy purchased for twenty-five dollars. Probably traded something for it.

We went with him to dig potatoes. An afternoon of dirty work, I'll say, and all I did was dust off the potatoes before loading them into the car. Potato digging was downright hard, grimy, and miserable. I was as tired as a hound dog.

When we drove home in the old flivver, the trunk and most of the backseat were full of sweet potatoes. I put a fair share away for the winter, enough for me and my sisters, but it didn't make a dent in the pile left in the Chevy.

Tommy wasn't about to toss out perfectly good food, so the next day he drove around town selling taters for fifty cents a bucket. He came home with half the potatoes gone and enough money to get us through the next few weeks. Still, too many remained.

"Get in the car," said Tommy, so the boys and I piled onto those torn leather seats. He drove us down to the colored section of town, a two-block stretch of houses. The poorer part of town.

"Don't worry, honey," Tommy said, "I know most of these folks. I've sold them goods before."

Tommy parked on a dirt road near the corner, got out and opened his trunk load of sweet potatoes. I rolled down my window and stayed in the car. The boys jumped out to help, excited about the adventure.

Sure enough, Mexicans and black folks recognized Tommy and came running over to see what he brought. Women came to dicker for food, fellows came to chat, and kids came out of curiosity. Some nice ladies came to the window and thanked me for the food, even if it was Tommy that had the good sense to share it. When it came to haggling, he could finagle like the best, but he never liked to let anything go to waste.

Good potatoes that Tommy didn't sell cheap, I helped him give away to widows rocking on their front porches. How he knew who needed food, I'll never know, but I was proud of him for it.

A week later, Tommy purchased a trailer load of corn for next to nothing and went around town selling ears, two for a nickel. I'll be. He might never admit his generous heart, but I could see right through him clear as day.

Tommy also traded animals. He'd buy horses and turn around and sell them for a profit so often, I never knew what livestock we owned. Not that I cared one whit about it—I was too busy keeping track of four strong-willed boys. We had a cow for milk, even though when I met him, Tommy didn't know how to milk a cow.

Our chickens laid so many eggs, I sold a few dozen every week and gave the rest away. And as for tomatoes and corn, I can't recall how many jars I put up with my sisters' help, storing them in the cellar where it stayed cool, but it'd be enough to last all winter. He showed me how to put a rabbit in gravy and bake it, making the meat tender enough to eat.

I shook my head in wonder. We were surviving.

Tommy might have lacked in the romance department, but he could be depended upon to supply our physical needs. We'd gone through the worst times together and endured. I felt safe with him around, safe and protected. Taken care of.

Our family never had to live on handouts. We ate—even through the hard times—we just didn't know how long the hard times would last. Or what hardships would come next.

Chapter 9

School started within a month. Jerry, my oldest, walked to the elementary school building down the street to attend the fourth grade. When he got home from class, I'd go over his schooling. Sensitive and brilliant, the child loved books and was serious and thoughtful and easy to teach. But then, all my boys were sharp as nails.

After graduating from high school, I earned a certificate for teaching, so lessons were no problem for me, even if I hadn't enjoyed teaching.

Jimmy started first grade. My second-born was growing up.

The first week, after a hard day playing outside, Jimmy came into the house, dropped onto the floor, and laid his head down.

"What's wrong?" I asked, panicking. Several little ones in the community had succumbed to dust pneumonia or scarlet fever in the last few months.

He didn't answer.

I knelt beside him and felt his forehead. His head was scorching hot to the touch. As I carried him to bed, his breathing grew labored, and I heard a rattle in his chest.

"Jerry, run get Aunt Till!" I hollered.

Till rushed over and suggested I keep him warm. I held a rag covered with red mustard salve to the fire until it grew hot. Then I spread it over Jimmy's body before pulling the wool wrap tight around his chest. I put long handles on over that. Hopefully, the salve would break up anything keeping him from breathing right.

Nothing helped. I stayed awake with him through the night, fretting. Crying. Beside myself with worry.

Tommy came into the room the next morning and looked at Jimmy lying in bed. "How is he?"

"He can't breathe very well, and I'm worried. The Wilson boy died with this last week. I know we don't have extra money sitting around, but we need to call the doctor. This is an emergency."

"I'll go get Doctor Husband." The doctor was one of Tommy's regular customers at the barbershop. The same doctor had removed all four boys' tonsils on the same day in '33. Tommy had made a deal and given the doc a cow in exchange for the operations, but why he had to do it all at once, I'll never know. He didn't have to nursemaid four whiny boys at the same time.

I trusted Tommy bargained again.

The doctor took his time examining Jimmy. "He has dust pneumonia, all right. Might last three to four months."

"Months!" I couldn't believe it. My energetic boy, the one full of confidence, would have to stay home? How would I manage?

"Many children are coming down with it. Keep him inside, keep him cool, and call me if he gets worse."

Jimmy, still sick two days later, lay listless, crying, and not like himself at all. The other boys sensed the gravity of Jimmy's illness and were troopers as they tiptoed through the house. I regretted all those times I'd wished for quiet children, because now the silence seemed unbearable.

As Jimmy flailed in bed, miserable and feverish, my fear of losing him felt like ropes tied around my heart. My anxiety didn't lessen until a few days later when his fever went down, and I saw he was going to make it. By then, I wanted to climb into bed with him and sleep off my weariness. My health didn't take to this mothering as it should have.

That night, we moved Jimmy's bed into the living room. By the looks of it, he'd survive this illness.

Unfortunately, he'd miss most of the first grade.

***

Cotton-picking season started, and most everyone in Hollis looked forward to the pulling. Children as young as four pulled cotton bolls, even though they weren't as fast as adults. Tommy told the boys they could start at school age.

Jerry came running through the house yelling, "They're here! They're here!"

I spun in a circle, trying to get him to slow down. "Who's here?"

"The trucks. The cotton picker trucks! And I'm going to make me a fortune. Buy that baseball glove I saw."

Migrant workers, croppers, and locals came as fast as they could to sign up.

Jimmy looked up from his daybed. "Can I go?" He'd looked forward to working with Jerry and his cousins for the first time.

"No, son. Doc said you're too sick to go outside."

"Ah, Mama. Please."

I understood. I'd love to see my boy jump out of bed and go pick cotton.

Midmorning, I carried jugs of water out to the workers. Working at top speed, the group looked hot in their long-sleeve shirts, gloves, and straw hats.

I saw Till, dubbed a slave driver, in the far field. I heard she set the rhythm for pulling boles. That amazing woman could fill a fifty-pound sack as fast as anyone.

One fellow filled his bag and dragged it over to the trailer and the cotton scales. Paid by the pound, after taking off three pounds—the weight of the bag—he'd pulled almost three hundred pounds. I couldn't believe it.

At noon, the dinner bell rang, and the workers came traipsing over to eat under a shade tree. The children's laughter cheered everyone, the way they kept going—hot, tired or what not.

Jerry arrived, his fingers cut and sore and his face red from the sun. But he was proud, boasting about keeping up with his older cousins. "Daddy let me keep all the money I earned." The boy got paid a nickel a pound and made about a half dollar a day.

The week's cotton bolls were loaded onto wagons and sent to the cotton gin. Life looked hopeful, and the town threw a celebration. Nothing like cotton-pulling to pull a settlement together.

Or wear a woman out.

Living in a small town like Hollis had its blessings, along with its hardships.

Chapter10

With Jerry in school, the younger three and I walked to Sally Matilda's for lunch. As we entered the front door, the aroma of chicken and dumplings filled the whole place. She must have added secret ingredients unknown to the rest of us. I'll say, my house never smelled that delicious.

My Jerry, along with Till's youngest boy, Frank Junior, rushed in the door, their faces flushed from running home from school for lunch.

I set bowls on the table, poured lemonade for everyone, and attempted to get the boys calmed down and situated. Frank Junior, although a little ornery, would do nothing untoward in front of his mother. Jerry sat down quietly, but then he usually did. Jimmy took a little longer, a boy with a mind of his own. The twins, however, couldn't have been rowdier. If I hadn't set small bowls of soup in front of them, they never would have made it to the table.

The boys' eyes grew big with anticipation. Food was never this good at our house. I said a blessing and looked up. The boys were already spooning fluffy dumplings into their mouths. Boys are so easy to please. They gobbled their meal and Jerry and Frank Junior left to return to school. While Jimmy rested on the sofa recovering from his illness, the other two took off somewhere.

"Tillie, go sit down. You cooked this mouth-watering lunch, so the least I can do is clean up for you."

"You know better than that." Till poured water into a pot and set it on the stove to heat. "I can't rest while you're cleaning."

Although usually catered to, I helped scrape leftovers into a pan for the neighbor's hogs and set the remaining food aside for an evening meal. After the table was clean and the dishes washed and put away, Till and I sat down to chat, our usual routine.

We laughed about my toilet experience, discussed a new dress she designed for a church lady, and exclaimed quite rightly that the weather was the worst either of us had ever seen.

I heard a scuffle in the other room. The twins. I'd assumed they were playing quietly in the bedroom. But I should have known better.

Jumping to my feet, I yelled. "Boys! You get in here right now!"

More scuffling and scrapping.

"Now—or I'm coming to get you!" My voice boomed through the house.

Matilda stood close enough behind me I could feel her breath. "Now Annie, they're just boys. You can't expect them to behave all the time. Set your foot down and they'll come around." Till might have been a heavy-duty mama, but she obviously didn't know my boys. They could get into mischief that would never enter the mind of other children.

I stomped into Till's bedroom and yelled loud enough to frighten a scarecrow. No child was in sight. Beside a small bed, the room held an old armoire with knickknacks stacked on top, so full of mending it wouldn't close. Her winter clothing hung on one side, boots in a corner, a box of McCall's patterns from the '20s, and an assortment of material stacked against one wall. A person could get lost in there.

Someone coughed. I followed the sound and threw back a starburst quilt slung over a faded Victorian armchair. Twin boys scuttled out.

Puffs of beige stuffing covered the area around the chair like dirty snowflakes. The old cushions must have had a tear, and the boys pulled out the wadding. They ran down the hallway before I could compose myself.

I closed my eyes and breathed deeply

Boys. Boys. What would I do with my boys?

***

On Saturday, Billy came running through our front door, letting it slam behind him. "Aunt Ann! Come quick! Susie needs you!" His voice, louder than most ten-year-old boys, pierced all the way back to the kitchen where I peeled onions. "Jack's disappeared! He's missing, and no one knows where he is!"

Susie's boy was missing? Not possible. One of our thirteen boys couldn't just up and disappear. Billy must have misunderstood. We might have had the rowdiest kids this side of the Red River, but they clung together through thick and thin.

I swiped my hands on my apron, picked up my skirts, and ran out the door behind him.

By the time I arrived at Elmer and Susie's house, most of the family had gathered, clucking about like chickens. "What happened?" I asked when Till rushed over to me.

"No one knows for sure, but he hasn't been seen in three days."

"Three days!" The older boy cousins often went off camping or traveled to the next biggest town, but never without another lad along with them. How could Jack be missing for three days?

"Howard and Thomas went to Altus to look for him, and word's been sent out around the countryside. No one's located him anywhere."

The sheriff stood nearby talking with Elmer, and I turned to listen. "Nothing we can do since he's eighteen." The booming voice sounding impatient. “Boys get a hankering to run. Can’t do much about it except wait for him to contact you. Best if you don’t worry none.”

Many young boys left home in search of jobs, taking the train to California, and Jack, an adventurous kid, may have done that. He may have been kidnapped, but not likely, with his stubborn ways. I wasn’t sure, but maybe he ran away from his family. I recalled a recent argument between Jack and Marvin. No idea what about, but heard it was a doozy.

“Where’s Susie?” I worried about my tender-hearted sister.

“She’s inside the house, crying like a hurt puppy.”

Susie knew about trouble, but to have a boy missing? That would only deepen her normally sad demeanor. My sister needed us. Till and I rushed into the room to comfort her.

How long before they found Jack?

I’d be frantic if one of my boys disappeared.

Chapter 11

Tom Newberry sent seven boxcars of onions up north to sell. Prices dropped out of sight and, due to the depressed economy, no one could afford to buy onions, not even store owners. Every last buyer reneged on their contract. Tom's last order couldn't be distributed because people had no money. He sold at less than cost and didn't earn enough to recoup his transportation expenses.

When Tom took the big loss, he decided to quit the onion business, and Jennie wrote they were moving back to Hollis. We still didn't have a place to live, so when Tom and Jennie returned, we crowded together in their house. Tom took over his store and picked up where he'd left off the year before.

I was right happy to be living with family, glad to have someone to help with my boys and do some of the cooking and cleaning. My body had ached for so long, I forgot how much tiredness could get me down. I'd never been so grateful. I told Jennie how much I appreciated her, how I'd never known how much she'd done for me. Living without her support had been brutal.

Jimmy was ready to attend school again. After being sick for so long, I worried about his weakness and entry back into a rough school life. Thankfully, he only went for a few hours each morning, coming home at lunch to rest for the afternoon.

"I'll help. I'll put Jimmy on my shoulders and carry him to class," Truman, Jennie's boy, told me. "No one will bother him that way." A year older than my Jerry and big for his age, Truman was a sixth grader. He carried lightweight, frail Jimmy for the first week and then walked beside him to school after that. "I'll walk with him 'til he's better. Don't want anyone making fun of him."

Truman took after his mother, a committed caregiver. I felt relief.

Cousins were good like that. They would watch out for my boys.

***

I could have lived with Jennie's sweet family forever, but Tommy bought us an old house down the street. He paid four hundred dollars for a mighty fine half-acre lot and a semi-dilapidated building. We planned to move at the beginning of next month and started designs to renovate the house.

Tommy and I sat in our bedroom at Jennie's and discussed the new house, when we would move, and who could help us. "The icebox is a goner," said Tommy. "But I'll try to buy one of those electric gadgets after we move in."

"Tom said we could use his old pickup to haul everything," I said. "And Jennie and Till offered to help clean as much as possible."

The move was easier than I expected. While the womenfolk pitched in to pack kitchen pots and pans, boxes of clothes, and linens, the menfolk hauled the heavier items. Family certainly made a difference.

I couldn't imagine how Susie moved so often without family around to help. Family meant everything.

***

The first sunrise in our new house, I made biscuits for breakfast. Tommy liked them with apple butter, and the boys liked them with sorghum molasses. Cold leftover biscuits would be gone by noon, disappearing into little hands that snuck into the kitchen for a snack. They didn't realize I made extra biscuits for that purpose.

When Tommy and I first got married, I didn't know how to make biscuits. They always burned on the bottom, so I turned the oven higher so the biscuits would get done before they burned. I kept turning the oven higher and higher until finally Till explained that a lower temperature would brown them before burning.

How was I supposed to know?

I finally learned to make flaky buttermilk biscuits, but I still created a disaster while doing it. I cut the lard into the flour and, with flour all over my hands, opened the cabinet door to get the salt and baking powder. Then I pushed my cat eyeglasses up on my nose and groaned. I couldn't see through the glasses because they were smudged with flour. I dusted my hands on my apron, poured in the buttermilk, and kneaded the dough before rolling it out with a rolling pin. By the time I put the biscuits into the hot cast-iron skillet, white powder covered everything in the kitchen from the floor to ceiling, including all over me. It looked like a winter wonderland.

I had to laugh at myself, because it happened every day.

Housework seemed twice as difficult for me as it was for my sisters. I didn't know what I did wrong, but often dropped in exhaustion halfway through a task. I sat several times a day to rest and asked why the Lord gave me such a weak body.

After one long day, I finished washing supper dishes, without help from the boys, I might add. I plopped into a chair and put my feet up to rest. I'd never felt so flat worn out, like bricks hung from my arms and legs. Four boys traipsing in and out of the house could make a person lose ground faster than a three-legged horse. And I still hadn't recovered from the move.

Tommy had been gone all evening. I assumed swapping tales at the barbershop or talking horses at the barn down the street. Left alone to care for the four rambunctious rascals, it felt like wrestling with bears.

More tired and frustrated than usual, my nerves couldn't take anymore bickering. Tears threatened, ones that came when I couldn't hold out any longer.

Mothering didn't come easy for me.

Chapter 12

Spring came early. Trying to decide how to make potato soup from the pile of potatoes, I looked out the kitchen window toward the yard next door. Smoke rose from the ground in the far corner.

"Boys!" I yelled as I ran outside, the twins on my heels.

My oldest boy, Jerry, a sly nine-year-old, pushed a wooden cover off a hole in the ground and popped his head out. Jimmy's head appeared next, and the two boys scrambled out of that dugout faster than a spooked turkey. Both coughed, bent over, and vomited over the dry ground.

After I pounded each boy on the back, wiped their faces, and made sure they were breathing all right, I asked, "What happened?"

Neither boy would look at me.

I investigated the dirt-packed hole, which was at least three feet deep, to see if a fire smoldered. I nearly choked on the smoke. Based on the scent, it was not from a wood fire. I'd seen the rascals digging but paid no mind. After all, boys will be boys. I didn't realize they'd made a cave, put old boards over the top, and crawled in.

I fanned the haze away from me. "Were you smoking cigarettes down in that hole?"

"Wasn't me," Jerry said, his face smeared with grit.

"We found a cigar." Jimmy had the same black smudges on his face.

"Don't tell." Jerry frowned at his brother.

"But it was nasty."

My errant boys smelled of cigar smoke and vomit.

I was at my wit's end. "You best have that dugout filled before your daddy comes home."

I returned to the house to figure out dinner. I needed help. I couldn't manage my troop by myself.

The next day, I saw Jerry jump from the neighbor's tree, the highest in town. Not that it was very tall in a flat plains-area like Hollis, but it looked dangerous.

Fred, the younger one of my twins, broke his arm when he was less than a year old. I'd placed him on a feed sack at the general store and he fell off. I didn't want another broken arm in the family. So I told their dad, and he lectured Jerry good.

How did my mother manage with six children? Of course, five of them were girls. That had to be much easier.

My boys were dragging me to the grave. I could barely take care of myself, and now I was a failure at caring for my sons. At this rate, I'd be surprised if they survived intact to adulthood.

***

The next day, I heard boys screaming outside, making a racket louder than July firecrackers. I opened the front door and stomped out onto the porch where my oldest boys, Jerry and Jimmy, and some of their cousins were shooting slingshots. They'd made rubber bands out of old tires and whittled sticks into a 'y' shape.

I yelled at the rascals. "Boys, put those weapons away! You're going to hurt someone."

The noise abated, at least for a brief span, so I scurried to go back inside.

The door didn't close well, and Ted scrambled past me and poked his head out, curious to see what was going on. He made a dash for his freedom from naptime.

Before I could grab him, he screamed and fell backward.

For some ungodly reason only little boys could understand, Jimmy slung his rock toward the house. The stone flew toward Ted and landed in the middle of his forehead.

I don't know who felt worse, Jimmy or Ted. Both cried hard and needed settling down. I calmed them to find out if permanent damage had been done. Ted had a large knot on his forehead but seemed fine. Jimmy, rascal that he was, lost his slingshot privileges.

I was exasperated with my boys. I couldn't keep up with them. They seemed to know how much orneriness I could take and push me past that. I never had the energy my sisters had.

I'd have given a gold mine for some help.

Chapter 13

August brought weather hot enough to scorch my sundress. To keep the urchins busy for a few more minutes, I encouraged them to play outside until bedtime. But bedtime came quicker than I liked.

Marvin, Susie's boy, or more correctly, young man, swaggered in through the front door.

I looked up at him.

"I'm free tonight," said Marvin. "Need help with the boys?" My good nephew came around often to assist me.

Perhaps he missed his brother, Jack. We'd been relieved when Jack sent his mother a note stating he'd joined the U.S. Army, but nothing more. Susie reconciled to losing her boy, prayed for another letter, and moaned with pain when we talked about it.

We all felt the loss.

"Sure," I told Marvin. "I'll do some mending." Getting the children ready for bed every night was a chore I hated. Calming four rowdy boys could make a grown man yank his hair out. Grateful for the extra help, I sighed in relief. With Marvin's assistance, I might get through the next few years.

"Tonight's bath night, isn't it? I'll run the bathwater and help them undress," said Marvin. "I don't mind."

"Thanks. I appreciate you rounding them up."

"It's no trouble. You go ahead and get some sewing done. Rest if you need to."

I wanted to keep my feet elevated a smidgeon longer. Not that the older boys needed much help, but they hated bath time, and I hated struggling with them.

Weekly bath time was a curse, and I didn't want to face it. Relieved for any bit of help, I suspected nothing. Marvin seemed like a godsend.

***

One evening a few days later, Marvin arrived again and helped the boys to bed while Tommy stretched his legs, cleaned his barbering tools at the kitchen table, and sharpened his razor with a leather strap. I finished the dishes and sat down with a needle and thread to work on a new blouse for Jennie.

Marvin approached Tommy and me. "I've been doing some thinking lately." He smoothed his thin hair out of his face. "I got a good job out in New Mexico working for the federal government. I'll be translating for them."

"We heard about that. Congratulations," I said. Marvin was a brilliant boy, able to speak several languages.

"I'll be leaving soon and, well, I'll be making a lot of money. They offered a salary I can't refuse."

Tommy didn't look up but nodded his head, while Marvin plopped into a chair before speaking again. "The Ellis' left town and since they have only one kid, they took a nephew with them. The family has six kids and couldn't take care of them all. Seems like a smart plan. I'm willing to take Jerry with me out to New Mexico and raise him as my own."

My hands stilled in the middle of mending, and I looked up. He wanted to take our son?

"It'll be easy to fill out paperwork to give me custody. He's a smart kid, and I promise a good life for him. I'll pay for his college. He deserves a chance." Marvin rubbed his hands together and looked at me. "Ya'll are good parents, but you're down on your luck. Aunt Ann, you can hardly keep up with four growing rascals. This'll benefit everyone."

College *was* a temptation since we could never afford to send him. Times were so tough I worried about making it through the next week, much less anything down the road. My bones ached from exhaustion. I wavered before taking a deep breath and tilting my head. "I know you like the boys, but Jerry's only nine. He needs his mama."

Marvin claimed he understood it'd require sacrifices to see that Jerry was well cared for. Jerry, a brilliant lad, would have a finer life.

"We'll think about it," said Tommy.

After Marvin left, Tommy and I discussed the possibility of him taking Jerry away. On the surface, it seemed like a wonderful opportunity. Our bright boy would have better opportunities than we could offer. He could get an education. My nephew would do what was best for our son. Wouldn't he?

We talked about it until late into the night.

Part of me thought it was a great idea. Taking care of four boys caused my nerves to be on edge. I hadn't been a great mom and maybe the child needed more than I could give. I doubted my abilities. Another part of me couldn't bear to lose my little boy. It was a heart-pulling anguish a mother should never have to consider.

Marvin came by several times over the next few weeks. "I'm leaving next month and want to get it settled before I go. You need to let me know soon."

He made me feel selfish for not wanting Jerry to go. I considered discussing the situation with my sisters, but Tommy, in all his independence, thought we should decide ourselves. I agreed. It was time for me to stand on my own two feet and make my own way.

I'd been thinking of myself and my needs long enough. About time I gave up my desires for the sake of my son.

Chapter 14

When I was a little girl, I sometimes slept with my mama's mother, Grandma Mary Molly Shields. There weren't enough beds to go around and when we visited, I slept with her. We giggled and whispered until late into the night. Once she told me how she came over on a boat. I thought about that a lot, wondering exactly when and where she crossed over to America. It must have been as far back as the 1830s.

That was in the good old days before the dust tornadoes, the plunging price of goods, and the evil of the Ku Klux Klan, which caused trouble all over the state with scant signs of letting up. The KKK kept us on edge.

Tommy and I and the boys traveled to Altus for an outing. Deep dark surrounded us as we drove home on a backwoods dusty road. The boys slept in the rear seat so we couldn't discuss Marvin taking Jerry and how it might be for his own good.

Suddenly, three men in white robes and pointed hats stepped in front of us. Tommy slammed on the brakes, stopping so quickly I jerked forward.

I screeched and grabbed the dashboard. The boys lurched awake, screaming like the boogeyman got them. Fear shook me worse than when Adelai died. I'd heard the KKK killed white people along with blacks, tortured men like Tommy who befriended colored folks. Aggressive and mean was how they were described in nervous whispers. A lot of good people wouldn't join them, and I was proud of my husband for standing against their reign of terror. He thought their behavior senseless.

Looking behind me, I saw four sets of wide eyes staring wildly.

"Stay quiet, lads," said Tommy.

"Anyone hurt? You fellows okay?" I didn't hear a peep, but they all seemed unharmed. I didn't want to appear afraid, scaring my boys, so I held my tears in check, trying to look strong and unconcerned. Calmness wasn't easy with my heart beating like thunder.

Little Fred reached his hand toward the front seat and clutched my shoulder. I patted his paw and motioned for him to sit back.

Tommy got out of the motor car and the white sheets surrounded him. Someone pushed him and he stumbled. I heard him say, "Don't want any of your scare tactics alarming the family and all."

I almost fainted.

Normally, Tommy's talking could calm a wild horse. However, as he chatted, his knack for talk seemed more of a curse than an asset. I wished he'd keep quiet. I cringed as he argued with them, defending his right to be on the road.

The enemies grew impatient, and I whispered to myself, "Don't rile the fanatics."

One man grabbed Tommy and hit him about the shoulders with a stick. I heard yelling before they dragged him behind a nearby tree.

A half hour passed, or it seemed like it, as I tried to keep the boys calm. Naturally, they wanted to get out and run to their daddy, believing they could protect him. Tension mounted. What would they do to Tommy? What would they do to us?

Finally, two white-clothed men appeared from the shadows, and I could hear their low conspiring voices. Snatches of the conversation implied they weren't sure what to do with us.

A sheeted man went up to Tommy and spoke. "I know who you are. You're Tom Newberry's brother-in-law." The man growled in a low voice. "Heard you been feeding them black folk. You're lucky this time. We'll let you go, but don't come this way again. You don't have any business here."

"Go on and get out of here," someone yelled. "You aren't the fellow we're looking for."

Tommy scrambled back into the old Ford quicker than a scared rabbit. He and I looked at each other and relief flooded the car. They wouldn't harm us, at least not tonight.

For reasons unknown, I thought of Adelai and wondered if he would have stood against the KKK like Tommy. Would my Adelai, a dedicated Mason and politically ambitious gent, have opposed them, or would he have become a fellow member? My gut told me he might have worn a white pointed sheet over his head to impress town leaders, but I let go of that thought.

So many years had passed since Adelai died, and maybe I'd put him on a throne. Maybe he wasn't the perfect man I remembered. I might not have understood why Adelai died, but God saw fit to give me a husband who would stand up for me and the boys. Indeed, the Lord gave me a good, committed man, one who would take care of me through the ups and downs. One who always tried to do right. I was mighty proud of him.

Tom turned on the engine and left dust flying as we sped away. We were back on the edge of Hollis before my heart slowed down.

It took fear to get me thinking about God again. I thanked Him all the way home. For the husband he gave me. For the boys who'd fallen back asleep. For keeping us safe that night.

Somersaults still threatened my insides, especially when I thought this might be the last family trip together. Marvin would be leaving next week, taking Jerry with him. I hadn't the heart to tell the boy yet.

Maybe I should thank God for Jerry's good luck. I cringed.

Something didn't feel right about that.

Chapter 15

My religious upbringing had limits. My sisters attended different Christian denominations and agreed not to push me into any of them.

Jennie was a Methodist. Mary Bobbie, a Baptist. Susie went to the Church of Christ, and Sally Matilda seldom attended any church, although she read her Bible regularly. I was downright confused.

After having my twins, I decided to choose a church, as Tommy didn't care where I went. My sisters willingly supplied information from their respective denominations, bringing me books and pamphlets and discussing the pros and cons. I even talked to their pastors.

Folks encouraged me to keep searching until I was satisfied with my decision. They didn't pressure me but let me make up my own mind. Gallant of them, especially considering how long it took me to decide.

For several months, I'd dressed in the latest fashions and visited different churches in town. I eyed the way they conducted services, what they taught, and how they cared for one another.

After much consideration, I joined the Hollis Baptist Church, and by the following year, they invited me to teach a Sunday School class. My Bible became my most prized possession. I tucked treasures inside—baby announcements, wedding invitations, and Adelai's funeral memorandum.

***

After the incident on our way home, I was grateful to sit in church with all four of my boys. As we walked home afterward, my swanky dress flittered around my calves. I balanced myself on proper heels and held onto my large-brimmed hat. The delicious smell of a meal cooking wafted from the house before we opened the front door.

Tommy had cooked a juicy steak and boiled some potatoes. He rarely went to church with me, except maybe Easter or Christmas, but sometimes his thoughtfulness warmed me inside. He would surprise me occasionally and bring home extra carrots from a friends' garden or make sure his dirty boots didn't scruff my clean floor.

I helped finish the meal, and after dinner, we sent the boys to the yard, cautioning them to stay out of trouble—an unlikely request. I began to remove dishes from the table.

"Sit down a minute, Ann."

My chest tightened. It must have been important, because Tommy never asked me to sit and chat. I dropped into a chair.

"I found another bed for the boys," he said. "I'll pick it up tomorrow from the Nelsons'."

Why would he ask me to sit down to discuss a bed for the boys? I scrunched my brow in confusion. "Since Jerry's leaving with Marvin, we don't need another bed. And it's about time to tell him that he's going away. He might not like the idea at first."

Marvin was departing in two days. We'd signed a consent form and had it ready.

Tommy's mouth hardened into a straight line. "That's it. That's the problem. We can't let Marvin take Jerry away."

I squinted my eyes, unable to understand his attitude change. "I'm torn about it, too. But I want a better life for him. He's our son. If letting him go is best, we have to do it—even if it's hard. It's probably the best chance he'll ever have."

Had I come to the wrong conclusion? Was I right to send my son away? Guilt swam around my thoughts. Did I want this for myself, being worn out from caring for the boys, or was it the best choice for Jerry? I began to doubt my decision. Was it too late to change my mind?

Tommy hesitated, looked at the floor, and then spoke without turning to me. "People down at the Motley Hotel where I work told me tales about Marvin I don't like."

"That's gossip. You know people in this town like to talk."

What people thought didn't seem important enough to have any bearing. I hadn't even told my sisters yet, wanting them to think I was wise enough to make decisions without them.

"I agree, except Newberry told me the same thing when I talked with him. It seems everyone in town knows but us. Marvin's motives are not pure. They're not what we think they are."

Confusion clouded my mind. What was Tommy saying?

"He's been accused of handling little boys."

I gasped. "What? Marvin?"

"Yes. Several older boys confirmed it." Tommy shook his head and took my hand in his. "Can't take no chances."

My thoughts went back to the evenings Marvin spent with my boys. Time spent bathing them, tucking them into bed, and talking to them late at night. My stomach twisted into knots, and I felt sick. I clutched my stomach. How many times had I left them alone with Marvin? I gagged, held my breath, and wanted to die.

How could I have been so blind? How could I not see what was going on? Maybe with all our sons? Was that why Jack ran away from his family? Did my sisters know about this and not mention it?

Jerry would *not* be going to live with Marvin. Not as long as I had breath in me. I might not be perfect, but I'd stand up for my boys.

I stomped to the bedroom and tore the custody papers into tiny shreds. As I threw dirty shirts in a pile to wash, angry tears streamed down my face.

My time of laying back was over. I'd be the strongest mama in all of Garvin County.

I'd protect those young 'uns til my dying day.

Chapter 16

"Bring out those stools from the kitchen!" Jennie shouted. "Till, don't you have extra chairs at your house? Susie, would you check on the little boys? I think they're playing in the front yard."

My sister Jennie was organizing our family picnic. Since she moved back from Texas, life had been smoother, almost returning to normal—not that normal was saying much around our family. We had our differences.

For the first time in several years, all five sisters would gather in one place. We hadn't been together in so long cobwebs could have taken over the attic. Mary Bobbie and her family traveled up from Texas for a visit. Their son, Robert, had grown nearly a foot and was almost as tall as his daddy, Police Chief Shannon Layne, no less.

Elmer got a new job as band director in Chandler, and he and Susie would move on again soon. They couldn't seem to stay in one place long. Marvin had left by himself for his new job in New Mexico, and no one had heard from Jack again, leaving Susie with an empty household.

"Tommy!" I yelled from Jennie's yard, stretching his name over a long minute. "Bring those boards from the shed and put them on sawhorses. We're going to need extra tables with this much food."

Jennie and Till made enough fried chicken to feed the Confederate Army. Susie brought fresh green beans seasoned to perfection. We had plates of potato salad, baked beans topped with bacon, bread and butter pickles, sliced tomatoes, deviled eggs, and creamed corn cut off the cob.

"Time to eat!" Jennie's voice was loud enough for the neighbors across town to hear. "Can't be waiting on you slow-pokes."

I noticed Bob scooting toward the food table and eyeing that spread like a hawk ready to swoop. She hollered at the menfolk. "Don't eat up everything before it's our turn."

"There's plenty of food for the whole Harmon County all the way to Greer," I hollered back.

"Keep room for dessert!" Till yelled.

The table with desserts may have been bigger than the one with food. Delicious-looking egg custards, chocolate cakes, and cookies galore. Tommy had requested my cherry pies, so I'd proudly made two of them, hoping they turned out all right. Sometimes they did and sometimes they didn't. I always left the cherry pits in the pies, but Tommy never complained.

Before grace was said, a car drove up. Our brother Sam stuck his head out the window. He and his youngest boy, Jay Tol, had driven in from New Mexico to visit. We hadn't seen them in a coon's age.

What a delight. What a way to celebrate!

After the meal, the older folks sat on chairs under the elm tree in the backyard. A watermelon sat cooling in the tin barrel, and the boys begged to cut it open. They sliced that red juicy melon with a knife, and shortly afterward lined up for a watermelon seed spitting contest. Such entertainment! Even my little ones tried to spit, laughing so much they could hardly compete.

I never saw such a row of good-looking fellows. Knowing this would be a picture-taking day, they'd dressed up with suspenders, vests, and newsboy caps. Half the boys were grown, even if we didn't want to admit it. Developed into fine young men. The other half were still growing, and it wouldn't take long before they all left home.

My heart stilled. Handsome young men, all of them.

Mama was wrong.

Boys were as precious as girls.

***

The food was put away, dishes cleaned up, and tables dismantled. It'd been a successful picnic and a memorable family reunion.

The fellows wandered down to see a colored man who was breaking one of Tommy's new horses. Most of the boys followed along to watch the fellow hang on for dear life, clinging to the bareback of a bucking horse. I'd had my share of watching him, too.

We ladies sat outside in a semi-circle, cooling from the day's excitement and hoping the evening breeze would come along soon.

"Well, well. Our youngest sister has finally reached forty years old." Mary Bobbie always made me feel like a kid. "Join the club. It isn't so bad." She reached down, untied her shoes, and took them off.

I knew my sisters wouldn't let my birthday slip by quietly, but age stole up on all of us, what with traces of gray hair, spectacles, and wrinkles here and there. Even Susie's pretty face showed signs of aging.

"Got some news for you," said Till, a hint of mischief in her voice.

I hoped she was making new aprons again. My old one had more gravy stains than a printer's palate.

"I'm moving to California."

"What?" Jennie jumped and shrieked like a banshee chased her.

"You're leaving?" I couldn't have been more shocked. My sister would be one of the Okies who left their homeland to travel west? Well, I'll be.

I didn't like it. Not one bit.

"Been wanting to tell you, but I didn't have the guts. Had to tell you gals before we told everyone else."

"Maybe you should consider Oklahoma City or Tulsa, someplace closer," Jennie suggested.

Our fear of California may have been unfounded, but hundreds of folks had left. Folks we never heard from again. Ambiguous news came from those who wrote home. Some friends spouted about first-class jobs and numerous opportunities, while others' announced California farms were inundated with Okies who weren't treated well or paid fair wages.

"Not much to keep us around here." Till's excitement showed in every word she spoke. Divorced and caring for four boys, she'd kept up her sewing business in Hollis, but with the dry weather and hundreds leaving town, her shop wasn't doing well. "We're leaving Saturday morning and should make it to Amarillo by nightfall."

Susie, who'd been inside the house, stepped in late to the conversation. "Amarillo? Who's going to Amarillo?"

"I am," Till said. "We're driving to California. I've already started packing."

"Oh, my." Susie looked like she was going to swoon right there. "Are the boys going with you?"

"The boys are why I'm risking the move in the first place. They can't find decent jobs here in Hollis, and they'll have a better chance out west. They're as eager to get going as I am." Till's voice almost danced. "I'm looking forward to getting there. First thing I'll do is set up a sewing shop."

"How can you be excited about moving to California when all your sisters live here?" I was almost angry, not that us sisters ever lost our tempers with each other. At least not since we were kids.

"Oklahoma's your home." Susie's voice broke as she said it.

"Don't worry about me." Till pulled her chin up, turned, and patted Susie's shoulder. "Oklahoma will always be my home. I'll come back and visit. And I'll write."

Would we ever see her again? Many people migrated westward, but that didn't make it easier. Letters were not the same as sitting across the table and eating cherry pie together.

Till's news sank deep into the bones of my tired body. I looked around at the faces of my precious sisters.

Susie was moving away again. Mary Bobbie was living far down in Texas. And now Till was leaving for California. I could hardly stand it. Why, even Tommy talked about moving in a few years up to where his folks lived—to the Konawa or Shawnee area. Our family was being torn apart like taffy, stretching across the countryside in all directions. We'd never be able to pull it back together.

Tears sprang to my eyes, and I noticed my sisters pulling out their hankies and wiping their faces. Life would have to go on, but, oh, the pain it yanked out of you.

***

The men began sauntering in from the barn. We saw them down the road, straggling in a few at a time, the boys running in and out among them, which meant our sisters' talking time was over.

Till's youngest son, Frank Junior, a big boy of twelve, ran up to the porch ahead of the menfolk. "Mama, Mama! Can we tell them now?"

"Soon as everyone's here, we'll announce it. How's that?" Till tried to slick down Frank Junior's wild hair, but he'd have none of it.

"What's going on here?" Tommy asked, our boys right beside him as if they knew something was up. The yard was soon full of our menfolk, from the little boys on up to Tom Newberry, the family patriarch who was getting on up close to sixty.

The chattering noise rose, and I looked around. None of the sisters paid any mind. We didn't have all day for this. I stood on the porch in front of the group and yelled. "Folks, listen up! Matilda, here, has some news to share!"

Everyone got quiet.

When I stepped back, my heart soared. Me, the youngest sister, could guide the family if the need arose.

"Howard, go ahead and tell them," Till instructed her eldest son, who already looked like a tall beach bum with blond hair and tanned skin.

He walked up the porch steps, turned and put his hands on his suspenders, announcing matter-of-factly like he was the man of the house, "I got a letter from a friend in Yuba City. He says there's a job waiting for me. So, a few days ago, the family talked, and me and the boys and Ma are going to pack up and move out to California."

Questions flew from the men and boys.

"You really going?"

"When?"

"What about your dog?"

"Do you need help packing?"

"When will you come back?"

"Can I go with you?" That last question came from my Jerry, and I was glad we never told him about Marvin's offer.

Till butted into the stream of questions, holding up both hands. "Hold on, fellows. We'll set off in a week. I figure what we can't sell, we'll store in Tommy's barn. If jobs work out in California, we'll be staying there for a while. We may not come home for a year or so, depending on how things are looking."

"I'll check your jalopy," Shannon offered. "I'll make sure it can get that far. We don't want you stranded by the side of the road."

"Thanks," said Till. "I've been worried about that."

"We're going back to Texas in two days, so I'll look at it in the morning."

"I'll give the boys a free haircut," Tommy said. "Don't want them looking like bums when you get there." He rarely gave away free haircuts. Discounted maybe, but he'd offered what he could.

"Come by the store," Tom Newberry added.

And if I knew my sisters, they'd be baking up a storm the next few days, packing every crack of Till's jalopy with food to take along with them.

The afternoon was passing, and the sun lowered in the sky. I didn't want this day to end. I hugged my dear sister, holding on tightly. I whispered how much I'd miss her because I sure didn't want her to leave. It might be the last time my siblings and I got together for years. I slipped her a ten-dollar bill and tears came.

"Let's start mixing that homemade ice cream." Jennie said when the talk died down.

I shook off my melancholy thoughts. "Tommy," I yelled across the yard. "Go haul over that block of ice from Till's house. We need it chopped for the ice cream maker."

Jennie and I whipped up eggs, cream, and sugar, then beat the mixture until it was fluffy before pouring it into the hand-cranked freezer.

Now, if this season of our lives had to end, this was the best way. Homemade vanilla ice cream with cherries on top could make anyone feel better.

Sally Matilda looked at me and nodded her head, smiling bigger than Kansas. I smiled back. No matter where life took us, we'd always be family.

Always be sisters.

Epilogue

The Fifth Bible

Anna Lee Akin

June 25, 1975

Forty years later.

My thin hand trembled as I opened the drawer handle beside my sister's bed. Jennie, at seventy-nine-years old, had lived alone for the past several years in her large house. Food was brought in, and nurses stopped by occasionally to check her heart rate and blood pressure.

Jennie's husband, Tom Newberry, had passed away a few years before from emphysema.

Last Sunday, she didn't show up for Sunday School, as was her usual habit, and church members went to check on her. They traced her last steps. It'd rained the prior evening, and she'd evidently taken her rain bucket outside to collect rainwater for her hair—she claimed rinsing her heavy hair in rainwater made it soft. Her bed was not turned down, but she lay peacefully on top of the covers. It didn't look like she suffered.

I traveled the day before from Shawnee, Oklahoma, back home to Hollis, a six-hour road trip. Jennie's funeral would be the next day, after the rest of the family arrived. Her stepson and stepdaughter would come along with some of their children and grandchildren. Truman, her son, and his twin girls and a boy would bring a trailer to haul some of Jennie's things to Alabama.

My four boys and most of their families would attend the funeral, along with other relatives and most everyone in the small town of Hollis since Jennie had lived there all her life.

The drawer squeaked from its worn-out runners as I pulled it open. I found the old, faded photos I knew would be there. They belonged to Jennie's children, of course, like everything else, but I wanted one last look at the family we had. My mama and papa, my brother, and my four sisters, Sally Matilda, Mary Bobbie, Susie May, and Jennie Rue.

Papa died sixty-five years ago when I was ten. He was older than anyone else I knew and had deep wrinkles over his face and hands. When I was small, I'd sit on his lap and plait his long white beard. He was patient with me and, since I was his youngest, he more-or-less let me do whatever I pleased.

They'd all passed away. I, the youngest, was the only one left, which nobody predicted since I'd always been the sickly one. I should have been the first to die.

I stared at my vanished family and raised the photo to my lips. Kissing the timeworn, colorless snapshot, my heart ached with a stark loneliness that wouldn't disappear in a hundred full moons.

I rifled through the drawer, moved the hairbrush and lotion, and stopped. Underneath another sepia-colored picture lay a frayed black Bible. Jennie's Bible. I picked it up and leafed through it. Sporadic writing angled along the edges of a few passages. On the front page was

Jennie's name, Jennifer Luella Thomas, born December 10th, 1888, baptized June 13th, 1917.

Yes, I remembered Jennie's baptism and our scattered talks through the years about God and providence, church and mission work. Jennie had been faithful even after she married a man years older than herself with two children. Would Truman, Jennie's only birth son, appreciate the Bible's significance? I set it aside and shuffled through the papers.

I could hardly believe what I saw. Deeper in Jennie's bedroom drawer, lay another precious Bible—my sister Mary Bobbie's. She passed away in 1974, fourteen months ago. She and Jennie had been so close.

I ran my hand over the worn, bumpy cover, and remembered her carrying this same Bible to women's meetings. She'd been a teen when our parents gave it to her. I flipped through the pages and saw where she'd underlined the word 'faith' in a dozens places.

The Bible fell open to Romans One and a verse that held the word faith. *That you and I may be mutually encouraged by each other's faith.* Oh, how she encouraged me through the years to hold on to my faith. Bob had adopted two children, a son and a daughter. The tiny girl died before she reached school age. A family tragedy.

Bob became a middle-aged widow when her husband got ill and passed away while performing his duties as a police officer. She dedicated the rest of her life to church and family. Bob and I could have shared so much if only we'd lived closer to each other.

Opening the second drawer, I found a book bound in brown paper. After carefully unwrapping it, I gasped. A third worn-out Bible lay in front of me, its front cover missing, and the spine threadbare. I thumbed through it, and a funeral notice fell out. Susie May Lindsey's obituary dated three years ago, July 19th, 1972.

Tears came to my eyes as I touched the precious announcement. Had Jennie put it there?

Susie had always been the quiet one, even when her husband and sons disgraced her. Her husband had been kicked out of many small towns for molesting little girls, resulting in two wayward sons. I always wondered how my sister managed to stay in that unhappy marriage. Had God been her helper?

I stared out the window, and memories flooded me. Laughter among sisters, listening to soap operas around the radio, strolling arm in arm down Broadway to see a flick. Afternoons on the front porch sipping sweet, iced tea. An ache filled me and sank deep. We shared much love and held one another up through the good times and the bad. What would I have done without them? My heart raced. Could it be possible?

I dug around the layer of cards and letters in the bottom drawer and pulled out the fourth Bible. A smaller book than the other two, the edges had come undone, the binding loosed. It was tied together with a brown cord across and over. Sally Matilda, the first to leave this earth back in April of '61.

I clutched the Holy Book to my heart. Dear sister Till, nine years older than me, gave birth to eight children before leaving her abusive husband. She lost all four of her baby girls, one of the most heartbreaking events in our family, and then moved away to California to start over with her four sons. Till kept in touch with me, married a good man, and her sons … Well, her sons never admitted their need for God.

Where had the sisters gone wrong? Had Mama's unwavering faith disappeared through the years? None of us had daughters who lived to adulthood, and none of our sons followed wholeheartedly after God. With the stack of four Bibles on my lap, I reflected.

What would happen to my sisters' precious Bibles and, for that matter, what about mine, Annie Crump? I had an obituary tucked in mine—Adelai's, my first love. Also, an assortment of wedding and birth announcements. Bible lessons that guided me through life's struggles.

What trace of my faith would be left after I died? I'd almost given up on God working in my family. How many hours had I prayed for them? None of my sons attended church, at least not regularly, nor seemed to care about spiritual matters. Even the youngest twin, who'd once seemed interested, had weakened.

God, I prayed, *please don't let our faith die. Don't give up on our family yet. Let me pass on this devotion.*

"I'm taking the Bibles," I said out loud to no one.

Jennie's children would not want them.

***

Months later, I sat down at my dresser, the place where I brushed my hair, penned letters, and read my daily devotionals. My husband Tommy had just passed away, leaving me alone, the last of my generation. My sisters' Bibles sat where I'd stared at them every day since bringing them home.

My own Bible lay nearby, protectively holding the precious, torn remnants of the lives of my loved ones, including Tommy's recent obituary. Within the pages also lay smeared notes, lessons where I'd studied to teach a ladies Sunday School class. The book included family records of births, marriages, and deaths.

Who would treasure these as much as I? These five sisters' Bibles?

I smiled as an idea came to me.

I knew who'd receive these treasures. My granddaughter. My first grandchild, a girl like I'd always wanted, and the first living female born in my family in decades. Yes, though still young, she'd understand the significance of these five Bibles.

She'd remember the sisters. She'd recall the trials.

And she'd share our faith.

Author's Notes

Ann and Tommy Akin were my dad's parents. I used the name "Tommy" to designate him from Tom Newberry. But also because Ann always called him with a high-pitched, drawn-out voice, "Tommy," always accentuating the last syllable with a screech.

Adelai Mathews' story is true. He was buried in Linn County, Kansas. He died at the height of the Spanish flu pandemic. Jimmy, my dad, had diphtheria in the first grade and stayed home from school until after Christmas, missing most of the semester. Ann held him back, and he went through the first grade again.

My grandfather, Thomas Elisha Akin, received a certificate from the Colorado State Board of Barbers at the age of seventeen. I have a copy. That seems awfully young. Then, in 1918, during WWI, he was inducted into the U.S. Army. A Private Thomas Elisha Akin from Maud, Oklahoma, is listed in the 1918 History and Photographic Record of the 57th U.S. Infantry, Colonel D.J. Baker commanding. Tom Akin's picture is included.

On January 11th, 1919, Tommy purchased a five-year, war-risk insurance policy at six and a half dollars per month. He was discharged from the Army on January 13th, 1919. His honorable discharge papers state the reason for his dismissal as "Dependents and Distress in Family."

I haven't been able to confirm the reason for his discharge, but one of his older brothers did die of exposure to mustard gas. Or maybe Tommy needed to go home for other reasons. The discharge papers also stated that he had brown eyes, dark hair, a ruddy complexion, and was six feet tall.

Tommy's father, Elisha Levi Akin, purchased land on the southwestern edge of Shawnee in 1920, borrowed money to plant cotton, owned two horses, a milk cow, and a wagon and harness, according to the Assessment List of 1921. He was seventy years old at the time. According to records, he was 5' 8" and weighed 160 pounds. In 1928, E. L. Akin purchased a different five acres on Union Street in Shawnee, Oklahoma, for $3,795.

One week, while researching Tommy Akin's first marriage, I couldn't find any names, dates, or information about the first wife or his first son. It was frustrating.

A week later, I received a phone message from Ana Akin in California. When we connected, we discovered her husband was the son of my grandfather Tom's first son. Her husband was my first cousin!

That was an amazing discovery.

They had been looking for information about us for forty years and supplied some details I'd been looking for.

According to their family, Tommy Akin married Ruth Reed in 1921 and had a son, Thomas Russell Akin or "Rusty" in 1922. Ruth and her son, Rusty Akin, registered as living with her parents in the 1940 census. In 1976, Rusty from California attended Tommy Akin's funeral, his father in Oklahoma, but it appears that Ann was concerned he would take her goods like his mother did and didn't welcome him.

Jerry Akin is listed in the 1943 Tiger High School Annual with the words "Lover of Books: Good Clerk" beside his picture. He entered the Navy in 1944 during WWII, the day after Christmas, and received his boot training at the Great Lakes. From there, he was sent to the Pacific front—the Philippines, to be exact. Jerry's Form 2025 Notice of Separation from the U.S. Naval Service states he received many medals. He has a tragic story of his own, which I may write someday. He was almost six feet, a tall man like all the Akin boys.

One of the twins, Ted, was in the Korean Conflict with the U.S. Air Force. He became a Staff Sergeant, serving most of his time in London. Neither Jerry nor Ted ever married. Ted's twin, Fred, remained in Shawnee, Oklahoma, married and had two children.

Ann and Tommy Akin moved to Shawnee in about 1949. Ann didn't raise much of a raucous because she believed the boys could get better jobs in Shawnee. That's where Jimmy met my mother, Margaret Pope, which begins another story.

I remember a cherry tree beside my Grandma Ann's house and how she loved to make cherry pies. She always left the pits in the pie though, and as children, we would count to see how many pits we had. Always competing. Always with family love.

Thomas Elisha Akin died March 9th, 1976 and Anna Lee Akin died November 7th, 1985. They are buried together at Tecumseh Cemetery in Oklahoma.

***

When I received Ann Akin's Bible, a paper fluttered out of it. My grandmother must have gazed frequently on the worn and tattered announcement of her first fiancé's funeral, as it was barely legible from wear. Inscribed on the announcement was:

"In Loving Remembrance of our Beloved: The Golden Gates were opened wide. A Gentle Voice said, 'Come!' And Angels from the other Side, welcomed our loved one home."

Below that was written these words:

Adlai E. Mathews, Born February 25th, 1893, Died June 1st, 1918. Age 25 years, 3 months, 3 days. Also inscribed on that memorial is a poem:

> A precious one from us has gone,
> A voice we loved is stilled;
> A place is vacant in our home,
> Which never can be filled,
> God in His wisdom has recalled,
> The boon his love had given,
> And though the body slumbers here,
> The soul is safe in Heaven.

I miss all these great aunts and uncles and other family members who have gone on before. I keep them near my heart along with the Bibles in a box in my closet.

Kathryn Ann Akin Spurgeon

Annie Crump, Jennie Rue, Susie May,
Mary Bobbie, and Sally Matilda, circa 1950

Acknowledgments

So many people have encouraged me with this book series. I am blessed beyond my wildest imagination.

Wonderful editors are essential. Thank you, Robyn Patchen, even though I probably undid every correction you made as I expanded the short stories. And thank you Staci Mauney for your work. Jessica White has poured over these words to make them better. She is amazing.

The ladies at the Harmon County Historical Museum have been most helpful, and Heather Leach, you are more than creative. I simply love the covers from Seedlings, Inc.

The writers in my writing groups have been by my side for years. Friends first, writers second. The HHBC writers group are precious to me, Alesia Campbell, Mary Comm, Janie Contway, Connie Hallam, Pam Humphreys, Louise Tucker Jones, Bonnie Lanthripe, Diane Stout, and Dotti Young. They've all touched me in some way. Love these ladies. Thank you so much!

ACFW Writers moved me along. They prodded where I needed it. Gave lessons that pushed me along. Thanks to fellow travelers along this writing road: Ruth Collins, Darlene Franklin, J.J. Johnson, Kat Lewis, Vickie McDonough, Shannon Pearson, Alanna Radle Rodriquez, T.J. Radle, Chris Tarpley, Laurel Thomas, and Kristi Woods. They, and many others have encouraged me to keep writing.

And zoom groups? What would I do without their consistent help? Fellow writers like Kristen Kaldahl are my steadfast friends. Thank you all.

Everyone needs at least one committed, unmovable fan. A person who loves everything you write no matter. Mothers fit that role. LaVerle Spurgeon, my mother-in-law, has sold more books than any individual. And I could not have written this without my mama's memories. Margaret Akin is an amazing historian. The best in the world, at least my world, and I love her dearly. Thank you, Mom, for your many hours of input.

Thank you, READER for reading this novel. If you liked it, would you be willing to leave a review on your favorite retailer? Also, please tell a friend about my books. I would greatly appreciate it.

If you'd like to get my emails with news and information about my book, you can sign up for my newsletter. I won't share your information with anyone or send you frequent messages. I'd love to hear from you. Keep in touch to hear what's going on with me and to share what's going on with you.

And check out www.KathrynSpurgeon.com to find out about my other books in progress.

Thank you. I love sharing stories that show what God can do in people's lives. He is amazing.

You are loved,

Kathryn Spurgeon

The Thomas Sisters Series

Five sister stories. Their strong dedication and understanding helps each deal with tragedies and heartaches in their lives, during a disastrous time in Oklahoma.

Mary Bobbie, *Thomas Sister #1,* the oldest and most jovial of the sisters, marries a happy-go-lucky but strict policemen. However, for ten years, she's kept a terrible secret.. Will her husband and family be disappointed if they find out what she has done? Will they still look up to her?

Sally Matilda *Thomas Sister* #2, Once a high school football queen, she marries the school's most handsome running back. Her perfect life shatters when the man she loves falls into abusiveness and addictions. How many times must she be devastated and still bounce back? How will she respond when a final, life-changing crisis comes?

Susie May *Thomas Sister #3*, The petite, shy, middle daughter, marries the most attractive band director in the country. He's suave and debonair, but he's suspected of leading a double life. After many moves around the country, and too many disappointments, is Susie willing to face his tragic lifestyle, especially when it becomes known in her hometown?

Jennie Rue *Thomas Sister #4*, Stable and God-fearing, Jennie agrees to nurse the sickly wife of an older man with two children. When he becomes a widow and wants to marry her, is it for love or convenience?

Annie Crump Thomas Sister #5, The youngest sister grieves the loss of her fiancé, but a a few years later, tall, good-looking barber comes along to melt her heart. However, he never speaks about his former life. How will she manage when an ex-wife appears and files a lawsuit to take everything they own?

The Promise Series

by Kathryn Spurgeon

Christian historical fiction based on a true story in Oklahoma during the 1930s and the Great Depression. A heart-warming family saga.

A Promise to Break, *Love, Faith, and Politics in the 1930s.* Sibyl Trimble, a banker's daughter, meets a destitute hobo returning from California. What will her father say when they fall in love?

A Promise Child, *Faith, Loss, and Hope in the 1930s.* The topsoil blows away and the economy falls apart. Even Fremont, her strong, stable husband, considers leaving as they struggle to put food on the table. What will happen to her children?

Fremont's Promise, *Faith, Prospects, and Dreams of the 1940s*. Fremont Pope promises to move his wife, Sibyl, and family away from their difficulties and start over. Will God allow them to move or will they stay in their hometown of Shawnee, Oklahoma?

A Promise of Home, *A WW2 Family Saga.* Fremont finds work at an ammunitions plant in Colorado where he and wife Sibyl, leaving their cantankerous family behind. Then their family follows them to Colorado. They yearn to go home, but where is home? Will it take another tragedy for them to find their way?

Published as Short Story Fiction

Mary Bobbie, Kathryn Spurgeon, 116pp.
Memory House Publishing, 2019

Sally Matilda, Kathryn Spurgeon,103 pp.
Memory House Publishing, 2019

Susie May, Kathryn Spurgeon, 120 pp.
Memory House Publishing, 2019

Jennie Rue, Kathryn Spurgeon 110 pp.
Memory House Publishing, 2019

Annie Crump, Kathryn Spurgeon 106 pp.,
Memory House Publishing, 2020

Made in the USA
Columbia, SC
04 January 2025